One Hundred Names

By the same author

PS, I Love You
Where Rainbows End
If You Could See Me Now
A Place Called Here
Thanks for the Memories
The Gift
The Book of Tomorrow
The Time of My Life

Short stories
Girl in the Mirror

CECELIA AHERN

One Hundred Names

HarperCollins*Publishers*

HarperCollins*Publishers*
77–85 Fulham Palace Road,
Hammersmith, London W6 8JB

www.harpercollins.co.uk

Published by HarperCollinsPublishers
1

A catalogue record for this book
is available from the British Library

ISBN: 978–0–00–735046–9

Set in Sabon LT Std by Palimpsest Book Production Limited, Falkirk, Stirlingshire

Printed and bound in Great Britain by
Clays Ltd, St Ives plc

MIX
Paper from
responsible sources
FSC™ C007454

FSC™ is a non-profit international organisation established to promote
the responsible management of the world's forests. Products carrying the
FSC label are independently certified to assure consumers that they come
from forests that are managed to meet the social, economic and
ecological needs of present and future generations,
and other controlled sources.

Find out more about HarperCollins and the environment at
www.harpercollins.co.uk/green

Dedicated to my uncle Robert (Hoppy) Ellis.
We love you, and miss you, and thank you for all the memories.

CHAPTER ONE

She was nicknamed The Graveyard. Any secret, any piece of confidential information, personal or otherwise, that went in never, ever came back out. You knew you were safe; you knew you would never be judged or, if you were it would be silently, so you'd never know. She was perfectly named with a birth name that meant consistency and fortitude, and she was appropriately nicknamed; she was solid, permanent and steady, stoic but oddly comforting. Which is why visiting her in this place was all the more agonising. And it *was* agonising, not just mentally challenging; Kitty felt a physical pain in her chest, more specifically in her heart, that began with the thought of having to go, grew with the reality of actually being there, and then worsened with the knowledge that it wasn't a dream, it wasn't a false alarm, this was life in its rawest form. A life that had been challenged, and would subsequently be lost, to death.

Kitty made her way through the private hospital, taking the stairs when she could take elevators, making deliberate wrong turns, graciously allowing others to walk before her at every opportunity, particularly if they were patients moving at a snail's pace with walking frames or wheeling intravenous lines on poles. She was aware of the stares, which were a result of the current crisis she was in, and the fact she had at times walked in circles around the ward. She was attentive to any bit of conversation that any random

1

person wished to have with her, anything and everything that she could do to postpone arriving at Constance's room. Eventually her delaying tactics could continue no longer as she reached a dead end: a semicircle with four doors. Three doors were open, the occupants of the rooms and their visitors visible from where Kitty stood, though she didn't need to look inside. Without even seeing the numbers, she knew which room contained her friend and mentor. She was grateful to the closed door for the final delay she had been granted.

She knocked lightly, not fully committing to it, wanting to make the effort to visit but truly hoping she wouldn't be heard, so she could walk away, so she could always say she'd tried, so she could rest easily, guilt free. The tiny part of her that still clung to rationality knew that this wasn't realistic, that it wasn't right. Her heart was pounding, her shoes were squeaking on the floor as she moved from foot to foot, and she felt weak from the smell. She hated that hospital smell. A wave of nausea rushed through her and she breathed deeply and prayed for composure, for the supposed benefits of adulthood to finally kick in so she could get through this moment.

While Kitty was in the process of looking at her feet and taking deep breaths, the door opened and she was faced, unprepared, with a nurse and a shockingly deteriorated Constance. She blinked once, twice, and knew on the third time that she ought to be pretending, that it would not help Constance to see her visitor's true reaction to her appearance. So she tried to think of something to say and words failed her. There was nothing funny, nothing mundane, nothing even nothing, that she could think of to say to the friend she'd known for ten years.

'I've never seen her before in my life,' Constance said, her French accent audible despite her living in Ireland for over thirty years. Surprisingly, her voice was still strong and solid, assured and unwavering, as she had always been. 'Call security and have her removed from the premises immediately.'

The nurse smiled, opened the door wider and then returned to Constance's side.

'I can come back,' Kitty finally said. She turned away but found herself faced with more hospital paraphernalia and so turned again, searching for something normal, something ordinary and everyday that she could focus on that would fool her mind into thinking she wasn't there in a hospital, with that smell, with her terminally ill friend.

'I'm almost finished there. I'll just take your temperature,' the nurse said, placing a thermometer in Constance's ear.

'Come. Sit.' Constance motioned to the chair beside her bed.

Kitty couldn't look her in the eye. She knew it was rude, but her eyes kept moving away as though pulled by magnetic force to things that weren't sick and didn't remind her of people that were sick, so she busied herself with the gifts in her arms.

'I brought you flowers.' She looked around for somewhere to put them.

Constance hated flowers. She always left them to die in their vase whenever anybody attempted to bribe her, apologise to her or simply brighten her office. Despite knowing that, buying them had been a part of Kitty's procrastination, particularly as there had been an enticing queue before her.

'Oh dear,' the nurse said. 'Security should have told you that flowers aren't allowed in the ward.'

'Oh. Well, that's not a problem, I'll get rid of them.' Kitty tried to hide her relief as she stood up to make her escape.

'I'll take them,' the nurse said. 'I'll leave them at reception for you so you can take them home. No point in a beautiful bouquet like that going to waste.'

'At least I brought cupcakes.' Kitty took a box from her bag.

The nurse and Constance looked at one another again.

'You're joking. No cupcakes either?'

'The chef prefers patients to eat food which has come only from his kitchen.'

3

Kitty handed the contraband to the nurse.

'You can take them home too,' she laughed, studying the thermometer. 'You're fine,' she smiled at Constance. They shared a knowing look before she left, as if those two words meant something entirely different – they must have done – because she wasn't fine. She was eaten away by cancer. Her hair had begun to grow back, but sprouted in uneven patterns around her head, her protruding chest bones were visible above the shapeless hospital gown and she had wires and tubes connected to both arms, which were thin and bruised from injections and tube insertions.

'I'm glad I didn't tell her about the cocaine in my bag,' Kitty said just as the door closed behind the nurse, and they heard her laugh heartily from the corridor. 'I know you hate flowers but I panicked. I was going to bring you gold nail varnish, incense and a mirror, because I thought it would be funny.'

'Why didn't you?' Constance's eyes were still a sparkling blue and if Kitty could concentrate on just them, so full of life, she could almost forget the emaciated frame. Almost, but not quite.

'Because then I realised it wasn't funny.'

'I would have laughed.'

'I'll bring them next time.'

'It won't be so funny then. I've already heard the joke. My dear . . .' She reached for Kitty and they clasped hands tightly on the bed. Kitty couldn't look at Constance's hands, they were so sore and thin. 'It is so good to see you.'

'I'm sorry I'm late.'

'It took you a while.'

'The traffic . . .' Kitty began and then gave up joking. She was over a month late.

There was a silence and Kitty realised it was a pause for her to explain why she hadn't visited.

'I hate hospitals.'

'I know you do. Noscomephobia,' said Constance.

'What's that?'

4

'Fear of hospitals.'

'I didn't know there was a word for it.'

'There's a word for everything. I haven't been able to poop for two weeks; they call it anismus.'

'I should do a story on that,' Kitty said, her mind drifting.

'You will not. My rectal inertia is between you, me, Bob and the nice woman I allow to look at my bottom.'

'I meant a piece on phobia of hospitals. That would make a good story.'

'Tell me why.'

'Imagine I found somebody who is really sick and they can't get treatment.'

'So they medicate at home. Big deal.'

'Or what about a woman in labour? She's pacing up and down on the street outside but she just can't bring herself to go through the doors of the hospital.'

'So she has the baby in an ambulance or at home or on the street.' Constance shrugged. 'I once did a story on a woman who gave birth whilst in hiding in Kosovo. She was all by herself and it was her first child. They weren't found until two weeks after, perfectly healthy and happy together. Women in Africa have their babies while working the fields, then they go straight back to work. Tribal women dance their babies out. The Western world goes about childbirth the wrong way around,' she said, waving her hand dismissively in the air, despite having no children herself. 'I wrote an article on that before.'

'A doctor who can't go to work . . .' Kitty continued to push her idea.

'That's ridiculous. He should lose his licence.'

Kitty laughed. 'Thanks for your honesty, as usual.' Then her smile faded and she concentrated on Constance's hand wrapped around hers. 'Or how about a selfish woman whose best friend is sick and she wouldn't visit her?'

'But you're here now and I'm happy to see you.'

Kitty swallowed. 'You haven't mentioned anything about it.'

'About what?'

'You know what.'

'I didn't know if you wanted to talk about it.'

'I don't really.'

'Well, then.'

They sat in silence.

'I'm being torn apart in the newspapers, the radio, everywhere,' Kitty said, bringing it up anyway.

'I haven't seen any papers.'

Kitty ignored the pile of papers on the windowsill. 'Everywhere I go, all week, everyone is looking at me, pointing, whispering as if I'm the scarlet woman.'

'That is the price of being in the limelight. You are a TV star now.'

'I'm not a TV star, I'm an idiot who made a fool of herself on TV. There's a distinct difference.'

Constance shrugged again as if it wasn't a big deal.

'You never wanted me to work on the show in the first place. Why don't you just say "I told you so" and get it over with?'

'They are not words that I use. They do nothing productive.'

Kitty removed her hand from Constance's and asked quietly, 'Do I still have a job?'

'Haven't you spoken to Pete?' She looked angry with her duty editor.

'I have. But I need to hear it from you. It's more important that I hear it from you.'

'*Etcetera*'s stance on hiring you as a reporter has not changed,' Constance said firmly.

'Thank you,' Kitty whispered.

'I supported you doing *Thirty Minutes* because I know that you're a good reporter and you have it in you to be a great reporter. We all make mistakes, some bigger than others, but none of us is perfect. We use these times to become better reporters and, more importantly, better people. When you came to be interviewed by me ten years ago do you remember the story you tried to sell to me?'

Kitty laughed and cringed. 'No,' she lied.

'Of course you do. Well, if you won't say it, I will. I asked you if you were to write a story for me then and there about absolutely anything, what would it be?'

'We really don't have to go through this again. I was there, remember?' Kitty blushed.

'And you said,' Constance continued as though Kitty had never spoken, 'that you had heard of a caterpillar that could not turn into a butterfly . . .'

'Yes, yes, I know.'

'And you would like to examine how it would feel to be denied such a beautiful thing. You would like to know how it feels for the caterpillar to watch other caterpillars transform while all the time knowing he would never have that opportunity. Our interview was on the day of a US presidential election, and on the day a cruise liner sank with four thousand five hundred people aboard. Of the twelve interviewees I saw that day, you were the only person who did not mention anything about politics, about the ship, or about wanting to spend a day with Nelson Mandela, for that matter. What concerned you most was this poor little caterpillar.'

Kitty smiled. 'Yeah, well, I was just out of college. I think I still had too much weed in my system.'

'No,' Constance whispered, reaching out for Kitty's hand again. 'You were the only person who truly told me in that interview that you weren't afraid to fly, that in fact you were afraid that you wouldn't.'

Kitty swallowed hard, close to tears. She certainly hadn't flown yet and was, she felt, further from it than ever.

'Some people say that you shouldn't operate from a place of fear,' Constance went on, 'but if there is no fear, how is there a challenge? Often that is when I've done my best work, because I have embraced the fear and challenged myself. I saw this young girl who was afraid she wouldn't fly and I thought – a-ha – she is the girl for us. And that is what *Etcetera* is about. Sure, we cover politics but we cover the people behind the politics. We want them for their emotional journeys, not just so we can hear their policies but so we can hear the reason for their policies. What happened to make them believe in this, what happened to make them feel this way? Yes, we sometimes talk about diets, but not organic this and wholewheat that, but of *why* and *who*. We are all about people, about feeling, about emotions. We may sell fewer but we mean more, though that is merely my opinion, of course. *Etcetera* will continue to publish your stories, Kitty, as long as you are writing what is true to you and definitely *not* what somebody else is telling you will make a good story. Nobody can pretend to know what people want to read or hear or see. People rarely know it themselves; they only know it after the fact. That is what creating something original is all about. Finding the new, not rehashing the old and feeding a market.' She raised her eyebrows.

'It was my story,' Kitty said quietly. 'I can't blame anyone else.'

'There are more people involved in telling a story than the writer, and you know that. If you had come to me with this story, well, I would not have covered it, but hypothetically, if I had, I would have pulled it before it was too late. There were signs and someone above you should have been able to see them, but if you want to take the entire blame, well then, you ask yourself why you wanted to tell that story so badly.'

Kitty wasn't sure if she was meant to answer then and there but Constance gathered her energy and continued: 'I once interviewed a man who seemed increasingly amused by my questions. When I asked him what he found so entertaining, he told me that he found the questions an interviewer asked revealed much more about the interviewer than any of his answers revealed about himself. During our interview he learned far more about me than I about him. I found that interesting and he was right, on that occasion at least. I think that the story one covers often reveals more about the person writing it than perhaps the story is revealing itself. Journalism classes teach us that one must extract oneself from the story in order to report without bias, but often we need to be in the story in order to understand, to connect, to help the audience identify or else it has no heart; it could be a robot telling the story, for all anyone cares. And that does not mean injecting *opinion* into the pieces, Kitty, for that bothers me too. I don't like it when reporters use a story to tell us how they feel. Who cares what one person thinks? A nation? A genre? A sex? That interests me more. I mean inject understanding in all aspects of the story, show the audience that there is feeling behind the words.'

Kitty didn't want to have to think about what covering that story said about her – she never wanted to have to think or talk about it again – but that was impossible because her network was being sued and she was a day away from going into a libel court. Her head was pounding, she was tired of thinking about it, tired of analysing what on earth had happened, but she suddenly felt the need to repent, to apologise for everything she had ever done wrong just to feel worthy again.

'I have a confession.'

'I love confessions.'

'You know, when you gave me the job, I was so excited, the first story I wanted to write for you was the caterpillar story.'

'Really?'

'Of course I couldn't interview a caterpillar, but I wanted it to form the basis of a story about people who couldn't fly when they really wanted to, what it meant to be held back, to have your wings clipped.' Kitty looked at her friend fading away in the bed, big eyes staring up at her, and she fought the urge to cry. She was sure Constance understood exactly what she meant. 'I started researching the story . . . I'm sorry . . .' She held her hand to her mouth and tried to compose herself but she couldn't, and the tears fell. 'It turned out I was wrong. The caterpillar I told you about, the Oleander, it turns out it does fly after all. It just turns into a moth.' Kitty felt ridiculous for crying at that point but she couldn't help it. It wasn't the caterpillar's predicament that made her sad but the fact her research then as now had been appalling, something that had got her into serious trouble this time. 'The network have suspended me.'

'They've done you a favour. Wait for it to settle and you can resume telling your stories.'

'I don't know what stories to tell any more. I'm afraid I'll get it wrong again.'

'You won't get it wrong, Kitty. You know, telling a story – or, as I like to say, seeking the truth – is not necessarily to go on a mission all guns blazing in order to reveal a lie. Neither is it to be particularly groundbreaking. It is simply to get to the heart of what is real.'

Kitty nodded and sniffed. 'I'm sorry, this visit wasn't supposed to be about me. I'm so sorry.' She bent over in her chair and placed her head on the bed, embarrassed that Constance was seeing her like this, embarrassed to be behaving this way when her friend was so sick and had more important things to worry about.

'Shush now,' Constance said soothingly, running her hand gently through Kitty's hair. 'That is an even better ending than I originally wished for. Our poor caterpillar got to fly after all.'

When Kitty lifted her head, Constance suddenly appeared exhausted.

'Are you okay? Should I call a nurse?'

'No . . . no. It comes on suddenly,' she said, her eyelids heavy and fluttering. 'I'll have a short nap and I'll be all right again. I don't want you to go. There is so much for us to talk about. Such as Glen,' she smiled weakly.

Kitty faked a smile in return. 'Yes. You sleep,' she whispered. 'I'll be right here.'

Constance could always read her expressions, could dismantle her lies in seconds. 'I didn't like him much anyway.'

Within seconds Constance's eyes fluttered closed.

Kitty sat on the windowsill in Constance's hospital room, looking down at the people passing below, trying to figure out the route home where the fewest people would see her. A flow of French snapped her out of her trance and she turned to Constance in surprise. Apart from when Constance swore, in all the ten years she had known her, Kitty had never heard her speak French.

'What did you say?'

Constance seemed momentarily confused. She cleared her throat and gathered herself. 'You look far away.'

'I was thinking.'

'I shall alert the authorities at once.'

'I have a question I've always wanted to ask you.' Kitty moved to the chair beside Constance's bed.

'Oh, yes? Why didn't Bob and I have children?' She sat up in the bed and reached for her water. She sucked the tiniest amount from a straw.

'No, know-it-all. You've killed every plant you've ever owned, I can't imagine what you'd have been like with a child. No, I wanted to ask you, is there any story you wish you'd written but for whatever reason never wrote?'

Constance lit up at the question. 'Oh, that *is* a good question. A story in itself perhaps.' She raised her eyebrows at Kitty. 'A piece where you interview retired writers about the story that got away, ha? What do you think? I should talk to Pete about that. Or perhaps we should contact retired writers and ask them to write the story that they never wrote, especially for the magazine. People like Oisín O'Ceallaigh and Olivia Wallace. Give them their opportunity to tell it. It could be a special edition.'

Kitty laughed. 'Do you ever stop?'

There was a light knock on the door and Constance's husband,

Bob, entered. He looked tired but as soon as he laid eyes on Constance, he softened.

'Hello, darling. Ah, hello, Kitty. Nice of you to join us.'

'Traffic,' Kitty said, awkwardly.

'I know the feeling,' he smiled, coming around and kissing her on the head. 'It often slows me down too, but better late than never, eh?' He looked at Constance, her face all twisted up in concentration. 'Are you trying to poo, my love?'

Kitty laughed.

'Kitty asked me what story have I always wanted to write but never have.'

'Ah. You're not supposed to make her think, the doctors said so,' he joked. 'But that's a good question. Let me guess. Is it that time during the oil spillage when you had the exclusive interview with the penguin who saw everything?'

'I did not have an exclusive with the penguin,' Constance laughed, then winced with pain.

Kitty became nervous but Bob, used to it, continued.

'Oh, it was the whale then. The whale who saw everything. Told everyone who so much as inched near him about what he saw.'

'It was the captain of the ship,' she threw at Bob, but lovingly.

'Why didn't you interview him?' Kitty asked, arrested by their love for one another.

'My flight got delayed,' she said, fixing her bedcovers.

'She couldn't find her passport,' Bob outed her. 'You know what the flat is like, the Dead Sea Scrolls could be in there, for all we know. The passports have since found their home in the toaster, lest we forget again. Anyway, so she missed her flight and instead of Constance's great exclusive, the captain spoke to someone else who we shall not name.' He turned to Kitty and whispered, 'Dan Cummings.'

'Oh, you've done it, you've killed me now,' Constance said dramatically, pretending to die.

Kitty covered her face in her hands, feeling it wrong to laugh.

'Ah, finally we are rid of her,' Bob teased gently. 'So what is the answer, my love? I'm intrigued.'

'Do you really not know this?' Kitty asked Bob. He shook his head and they watched Constance thinking, which really was an amusing sight.

'Ah,' she said suddenly, eyes lighting up, 'I've got it. It's rather a recent idea, actually, something I thought of last year before . . . well, it was somewhat of an experiment but it has occupied my mind since I've been here.'

Kitty moved in closer to listen.

Constance enjoyed making Bob and Kitty wait.

'Possibly one of my greatest.'

Kitty groaned impatiently.

'I'll tell you what, the file is at home. In my office. Teresa will let you in if she's not too busy watching Jeremy Kyle. It's filed under N. Titled "Names". You get it for me and bring it back and I'll tell you about it.'

'No!' Kitty laughed. 'You know how impatient I am. Please don't make me wait.'

'If I tell you now, you might never come back.'

'I promise I will.'

Constance smiled. 'Okay, you get the file, and I'll tell you the story.'

'It's a deal.'

They shook on it.

CHAPTER TWO

Choosing the quieter back roads, and feeling like a rat scuttling along in the gutter, Kitty cycled home feeling exhausted. Initially on a high after spending time with a friend, she was back to feeling hopeless again now the reality of what lay ahead for both of them had sunk in.

Thirty Minutes, the television show Kitty had started working on the previous year, the show with which she had received her big break and which had then ironically broken her, had viewing figures of half a million, which was impressive for a country with a population of five million, but not enough for Kitty to become the next Katie Couric. Now, thanks to her disastrous story, she found herself suspended from reporting on the network and in court to face a charge of libel. The story had aired four months previously, in January, but it was the impending court case, merely a day away now, that had made headlines. Her face, her mistake, and her name were now known to many more than half a million people.

She knew she would be quickly forgotten in the minds of the public, but that her professional name would suffer in the long run; it had already been destroyed. She knew she was lucky that *Etcetera*, the magazine Constance had founded and edited, was continuing to employ her, though the only reason she had a job was because Constance was her biggest supporter. She didn't have many of those right now, and though Bob was deputy editor and a good friend she wasn't sure how much longer she'd keep her job without Constance there to throw her weight around. Kitty dreaded the day that her mentor wouldn't be in her life, never mind her professional life. Constance had been there for her since the beginning, had guided her, had advised her and had also given her the freedom to find her own voice and make her own decisions, which meant that Kitty owned her successes, but also meant her name was stamped all over every single one of her mistakes, a fact that was glaringly evident now.

Her phone vibrated again in her pocket and she ignored it as she had been doing all week. Journalists had been calling her since news of the case going to trial had broken, people she had considered friends were close to harassing her just to get a quote. They'd all chosen different tactics. Some came straight out with asking for a quote, others had gone for the sympathy vote: 'You know how it is, Kitty, the stress we're under here. The boss knows we're friends, he expects me to have something.' Others had randomly and spontaneously invited her out for dinner, for drinks, to their parents' anniversary parties and their grandfathers' eighty-fifth birthdays without mentioning the issue at all. She hadn't met or spoken with any of them but she was learning a lot and slowly crossing them off her Christmas card list. There was only one person who hadn't called her yet and that was her friend Steve. They had studied journalism together in college and had remained friends since then. His one desire had been to cover sport but the closest he'd got to that so far was covering footballers' private lives in tabloid newspapers. It had been he who had suggested she go for the job at *Etcetera*. He'd picked up a copy of the magazine in a doctor's waiting room while she'd gone for the morning-after pill after their one and only dalliance, which had resulted in the realisation they were destined only ever to be simply friends.

Thinking about Steve and her constantly ringing mobile gave

her a sixth sense and she stopped cycling and reached for her phone. It was him. She actually debated not answering. She actually *doubted* him. The consequences of the *Thirty Minutes* story had played havoc with whom she could and could not trust. She answered the phone.

'No comment,' she snapped.

'Excuse me?'

'I said, no comment. You can tell your boss that you haven't spoken to me, that we fell out, in fact we may be about to because I can't believe you have the nerve to call me up and abuse our friendship in this way.'

'Are you smoking crack?'

'What? No. Hold on, is this part of the story? Because if they're now saying I'm a drug addict then they can—'

'Kitty, shut up. I'll tell my boss that you, Kitty Logan, who he's never heard of anyway, has no comment to make on Victoria Beckham's new line because that is about the only thing that I am allowed to talk about to anybody today. Not the impending match between Carlow and Monaghan, which is critical because Carlow hasn't been in an All-Ireland final since 1936 and Monaghan hasn't been in a final since 1930, but nobody cares about that. Not in my office. No. All we care about is whether V.B.'s new range is a hit or miss, or hot or not, or two other words that mean the opposite but which rhyme, something I'm currently supposed to be inventing but I can't.' He finished his rant and Kitty couldn't help it, she started laughing, the first proper laugh she'd had all week.

'Well, I'm glad one of us thinks it's funny.'

'I thought you were allowed to write football stories now.'

'She's married to David Beckham, so apparently that qualifies it as a football story. Apart from needing help with the ridiculous piece I have to write, I was calling to make sure you weren't decaying inside your flat.'

'Well, you were right. I was rotting away in the flat but I had to leave to visit Constance. I'm going back there now to continue where I left off.'

'Good, I'll see you soon. I'm outside your door. Oh, and, Kitty,' his tone turned serious, 'I suggest you bring some bleach and a good scrubbing brush.'

Kitty's stomach churned.

'Journo Scumbag Bitch' was what Kitty found spray-painted across her door when she eventually made it to the top of the stairs with her bicycle in her arms. The studio flat was in Fairview, Dublin and the proximity to the city meant that she could cycle, sometimes walk, into the city. The fact that it was above a dry-cleaners made it affordable.

'Maybe you should move,' Steve said as they got down on their knees and started scrubbing the door.

'No way. I can't afford anywhere else. Unless you know of any available apartments above dry-cleaners.'

'That's a requirement for you?'

'When I open any of my windows day or night, I am showered in dry-cleaning chemicals called tetrachloroethene, also known as tetrachloroethylene, perchloroethylene, PCE or, most commonly, PERC. Ever heard of it?'

Steve shook his head and sprayed more bleach on the door.

'It's used to dry-clean clothes as well as degrease metal parts. It's considered a probable carcinogen by the World Health Organization. Tests showed that short-term exposure of eight hours or less to seven hundred thousand micrograms per cubic metre of air causes central nervous system symptoms such as dizziness, sleepiness, headaches, lightheadedness and poor balance. The red is difficult to get off, isn't it?'

'You do the green, I'll do the red.'

They switched places.

'Exposure to three hundred and fifty thousand micrograms for four hours affects the nerves of the visual system.' Kitty dipped her sponge into her bucket of water and continued scrubbing the door. 'Long-term exposure on dry-cleaner workers indicates biochemical changes in blood and urine. PERC can travel through floor, ceiling and wall materials, and there was a study on fourteen healthy adults living in apartments near dry-cleaners that showed their behaviour tests were lower than the average score of unexposed people.'

'So that's what's wrong with you. I take it from that verbal diarrhoea that you did a story about PERC.'

'Not quite. I researched it, then I told the landlord downstairs that I was doing a story on it and that I'd circulate it to all the neighbours and I'd tell their staff about the effects of working with PERC, so he reduced the rent by one hundred euro.'

Steve looked at her, shocked. 'They could just have got another tenant.'

'I told them I'd tell the next tenant and every other tenant they found. They panicked.'

He shook his head. 'You're . . .'

'Smart?' she smiled.

'A journo scumbag bitch,' he said. 'Maybe we should stop cleaning this now, they're right.' He continued looking at her as if he suddenly didn't recognise her.

'Hey! They're the ones using PERC!'

'Then move somewhere else.'

'It would be too expensive.'

'Kitty, you can't just threaten people like that. You can't use your job to get what you want. That's called bullying, you know.'

'Oooh.' She rolled her eyes, but dropped the sponge into the bucket in frustration and opened the door to the flat. She left the door open, sat at the kitchen table and waited for him to follow her. She bit into one of the cupcakes she'd brought back home. Steve closed the door behind him but he didn't sit down.

'Is there something you want to get off your chest, Steve?'

'I came by to make sure that you were feeling okay about the trial tomorrow, but the more you talk, the more I can't help but not feel sorry for you.'

The cupcake felt like a rock in her mouth. She swallowed it quickly. And then, finally, it came.

'You accused a well-respected PE teacher, who is married, with a young family, of sexually abusing two students and fathering a child. On television. In front of the entire country. And you were wrong.'

She looked at him, her eyes stinging. Her heart hurt from the way he was speaking to her, and though she knew she had been wrong, she had made a mistake, she still didn't feel that she deserved to be spoken to like that.

'I know all of this, I know what I did,' she said more confidently than she felt.

'And are you sorry?'

'Of course I'm bloody sorry,' she exploded. 'My career is destroyed. Absolutely nobody will ever hire me again. I've cost the network who knows what, if he wins his case, which he probably will, and God knows how much in legal fees, and *their* reputation. I'm over.' Feeling unnerved, Kitty watched her usually calm friend struggle with his composure.

'You see, this is what bugs me, Kitty.'

'What?'

'Your tone, you're so . . . flippant about it all.'

'Flippant? I'm *panicking* here, Steve!'

'Panicking for yourself. For "Katherine Logan, TV journalist",' he said, using his fingers as inverted commas.

'Not just that,' she swallowed. 'I'm really worried about my job on *Etcetera* too. There's a lot at stake, Steve.'

He laughed to himself but it wasn't a happy sound. 'That's exactly what I mean, you've just done it again. All I've heard from you is how *your* name, *your* reputation and *your* profession are ruined. It's all about you. When I hear of you doing stupid things like threatening your landlord with a story, then it bothers me.

You bother me.' He stopped pacing back and forth and fixed his eyes on her. 'You have for the past year.'

'The past *year*? Oh, okay, I think somebody has definitely been hanging on to a few issues,' she replied, shocked. 'I made a mistake in my story. The thing about the apartment? That was harmless! Hold on, I remember you pretending to find a *pubic hair* in your burger on the very last bite just so you could get another one for free. And you did too. That poor manager, you embarrassed him so much in front of the other customers, he had no choice.'

'I was eighteen,' he said quietly. 'You're thirty-two.'

'Thirty-three. You missed my last birthday,' she added childishly. 'It's the way I am; I find stories in everything.'

'Stories to use people.'

'Steve!'

'They used to be good stories, Kitty. Positive. A story for the sake of telling a good story. Not about exposing people, or setting people up.'

'I'm sorry I wasn't aware that your story about Victoria Beckham's new line was going to change the world,' she said cattily.

'What I'm saying is, I used to like reading them, hearing about them. Now you're just . . .'

'Now I'm what?' Her eyes filled.

'It doesn't matter.'

'No, please, please tell me what I am because I've only been hearing it on every single news station, reading it on internet sites and graffitied *on my own front door* for the last week, and I'd really like to know what my best friend thinks of me because that would just be the icing on the cake,' she yelled.

He sighed and looked away.

There was a long silence.

'How am I supposed to fix this, Steve?' she finally asked. 'What do I do to make you and the rest of the world not hate me?'

'Have you spoken to the guy?'

'Colin Maguire? No way. We're about to begin a court case.

If I go anywhere near him I'll get into even more trouble. We made an apology to him at the start of *Thirty Minutes*, when it was discovered he wasn't the father. We gave it priority to the show.'

'Do you think that will make him feel better?'

She shrugged.

'Kitty, if you did to me what you did to him, I would do a lot worse than they've done to your door. I would want to kill you,' he said sternly.

Kitty's eyes widened. 'Steve, don't scare me like that.'

'This is what you're not understanding, Kitty. This is not about your career. Or your good name. This is not about *you*. This is about *him*.'

'I don't know what to do,' she said, struggling. 'Maybe if I can explain what happened . . . The two women were so credible, Steve. Their stories matched up, the dates, the times, everything was so . . . real. Believe me, I followed it up over and over. I didn't just run with it straight off. It took me *six months*. The producer was behind me, the editor, I wasn't the only person who did this. And it wasn't just about him. Did you even see it? It was about the number of paedophiles and sex offenders in Ireland who occupy roles in schools and other jobs with direct contact to children who have been reported and who have been charged with the crime of abusing students in their care.'

'Apart from him. He was completely innocent.'

'Okay! Apart from him,' she said, frustrated. 'All the other stuff I covered was perfectly accurate! Nobody ever says anything about that!'

'Because that's your job, to be accurate. You shouldn't be congratulated for it.'

'Any other journalist in that room would have done the same thing, but the letter came to me.'

'It went to you for a reason. Those women set you up and they used you to set him up. You were covering bullshit stories so they knew you'd want to jump on this straight away, have your moment of glory.'

'It wasn't about me having my moment of glory.'

'Wasn't it? All I know is I've never seen you as excited as the day you got the job on the show. And you were doing a story about *tea*, Kitty. If Constance asked you to do a story about tea, you'd tell her to go and jump. Television made you excited.'

She tried to pretend it wasn't true but she couldn't. He was right. *Thirty Minutes* was made up of one large investigative story – the big one, the story everybody wanted to work on – and the remainder of the show was padded with smaller, local, not so ground-breaking pieces. Her first story had been to look into why consumers chose the brand of tea they bought. Numerous trips to tea factories, sweeping shots of supermarket tea aisles, and visits to morning community tea events led her to find that people simply followed the same brand their parents drank. It was a generational thing. It had been four minutes and fifty seconds long and Kitty believed she had a cutting-edge piece of art on her hands. Four months along in the job, when she received the letter, addressed to her, from the two women making claims against Colin Maguire, she had instantly, vehemently believed them, and she had worked with them and helped build a case against him. She had got lost in the drama, the excitement, the atmosphere of the TV studio offices, her opportunity to move from sweet harmless stories to the big time, and in her search for the truth had told a lie, a dangerous lie, and had ruined a man's life.

Steve was looking around the flat.

'What now?' she asked, completely drained.

'Where's Glen?'

'At work.'

'Does he usually take his coffee machine to work?'

She turned round to look at the counter, confused, but her phone interrupted them.

'My mum. Shit.'

'Have you spoken to them lately?'

Kitty swallowed and shook her head.

'Answer it,' he said, refusing to leave until she had answered.

'*Hello?*' She exaggerated the word for effect and then Steve was gone.

'Katherine, is that you?'

'Yes.'

'Oh, Katherine . . .' Her mother broke down in tears. 'Katherine, you've no idea . . .' She could barely get the words out.

'Mum, what's wrong?' Kitty sat up, panicked. 'Is it Dad? Is everyone okay?'

'Oh, Katherine,' Mrs Logan sobbed. 'I can't take it any more. We are just so *embarrassed* down here. How could you do it? How could you do that to that poor man?'

Kitty sat back and prepared for the onslaught. It was then she noticed Glen's plasma TV had disappeared too and, on further inspection, so had the clothes in his wardrobe.

CHAPTER THREE

A week later, after what felt like the longest seven days of her life, Kitty awoke in a sweat from a nightmare. She lay with the bedcovers in a tangled mess around her, and her heart beating wildly. She was afraid to look around the room, but as the nightmare faded from her memory she gained courage and sat up. She couldn't breathe. She pushed open her bedroom window and drank in deep breaths of air, but the steam pouring from the vents of the twenty-four-hour dry-cleaners was inhaled directly into her lungs. She coughed, slammed the window shut and made her way to the fridge where she stood naked before the open door in an effort to cool down. She was not ready for tomorrow. She was nowhere near equipped for tomorrow at all.

'Colin Maguire suffered irreparable damage to his reputation, his life was utterly altered and he was removed from his home and community as a result of the January tenth episode of *Thirty Minutes*. Katherine Logan confronted Mr Maguire outside his place of work and accused him of sexually abusing two teenage girls and fathering one child. Despite his repeated denials and an offer to take a paternity test, the programme was broadcast. Katherine Logan, Donal Smith and Paul Montgomery's careless actions and unprofessional behaviour had a devastating impact on Mr Maguire's life.'

Kitty sat in court alongside *Thirty Minutes* producer, Paul, and editor, Donal, as they listened to the lengthy terms of the four hundred thousand euro settlement for compensatory damage and aggravated damage. It took exactly seventeen minutes to read. With each word, each accusation, Kitty hated herself a little more. Near her, Colin Maguire and his family – his wife, his parents, his brothers and sisters – and everyone in his community who had come out to support him were staring at her, their eyes searing into her back. She felt their hatred, she felt their anger, but more than anything she felt Colin's hurt. He would barely lift his head, his eyes cast downward, his chin firmly lodged on his chest. He looked like he hadn't slept in a year.

The *Thirty Minutes* team and their legal advisors left the courthouse, swiftly pushing through the mill of photographers and cameras, some from their own network, which were shoved in Kitty's face as though she were one of the criminals she regularly saw leaving this very building on the news. The men walked so quickly she could barely keep up but she didn't want to run. Her sanity depended on surviving that moment. She did not want to put a foot wrong now after making so many mistakes to get them there. She kept her head down and then, thinking it made her look guilty, she lifted it again. *Chin up, take your punishment, and walk,* she repeated to herself, trying to keep her tears at bay. The flash bulbs dizzied her and she was forced to look down at the pavement again. The act of walking suddenly felt unnatural, like a mechanical movement that took great effort. She concentrated on putting one foot in front of the other, trying to swing her left arm with her right foot and not the other way around. She focused on not smiling, but didn't want to look upset. She knew these photos would be around for ever, she knew this footage would be played over and over, then would sit in the archives for reporters to root through. She knew because she did it every day. She didn't want to look cold, but she didn't want people to think immediately that she was guilty. People didn't always listen to the narrative, they just looked at the pictures. She wanted to look innocent but sorry. That was it, contrite. She tried to maintain her pride and dignity when inside she felt she had neither left, and all the while people were shouting at her. Mr Maguire's supporters had quickly exited the courtroom and spilled onto the street to give interviews to the press, and to heckle the *Thirty Minutes* team. She could hear them behind her hurling abuse and insults, and the journalists who were looking for a comment were trying to raise their voices above the tirades. The cars going by on Inns Quay slowed to watch the commotion, to see who was being surrounded by the media, literally being pressed by the press. Squashed and squeezed, drained and demoralised, everything being taken out of her, Kitty reflected that this was what she had done to Colin Maguire, as the reporters bumped against her, trying to keep up with her pace. Kitty kept on walking, one foot in front of the other; it was all she could do. *Chin up, don't smile, don't cry, don't fall, walk.*

Once they'd entered their solicitor's nearby offices and had escaped the reporters, Kitty dropped her bag to the floor, leaned her forehead against the cold wall and took deep breaths.

'Jesus,' she gasped, feeling her entire body flush with heat.

'Are you okay?' Donal asked gently.

'No,' she whispered. 'I'm so sorry, I'm so, so sorry about this.'

She felt a light pat on her back and was grateful for his support. She had caused this and he was perfectly entitled to have a go at her.

'This is absolutely ridiculous,' Paul raged to the solicitor in the next room, pacing before his desk. 'Four hundred thousand euro, *plus* his legal fees. This is nothing like you said it would be.'

'I said it *might*—'

'Don't you dare backtrack now,' he yelled. 'This is appalling. How could they do this to us? We've already apologised. Publicly. At the start of our show on February the eighth. Four hundred and fifty thousand people saw that we apologised, that we acknowledged he was not guilty, *millions* more saw it on the internet and God knows how many more after today. You know, I bet we were set up from the start. Those two women, I bet they and Colin Maguire are in on it together, and they're getting a cut of that money. I wouldn't be surprised. Nothing would surprise me now. Jesus. Four hundred thousand. How am I supposed to explain this to the Director-General?'

Kitty removed her forehead from where it was resting against the cool wall of the corridor and stood at the door of the solicitor's office. 'We deserved it, Paul.'

There was a silence and she heard Donal's intake of breath behind her. Paul spun round and stared at her as if she was nothing, which was a certain amount more than she felt right then.

'We ruined Colin Maguire's life. We deserved to hear every single word they said in there. We shouldn't have made such an enormous mistake and now we have to take responsibility for our actions.'

'*Our* actions? No. *Your* actions. *You* ruined his life, I was just the idiot who assumed you had done your job properly and had actually done your research. I knew we never should have given you this story. Mark my words, the network will never hire you again, do you hear me, Kitty? You don't know the first thing about covering a bloody story,' he yelled.

Kitty nodded and backed away. ''Bye, Donal,' she said quietly.

He nodded, and she left the building through the back exit.

She was afraid to return to her flat for two reasons. She wasn't sure if the court's decision would fuel the attacks on her home or if they would die down now that Colin had been further vindicated and financially awarded. The other reason was that she was afraid to be alone. She didn't know what to do; she couldn't spend another moment thinking about this, beating herself up about it, but she didn't feel it was right not to either. She deserved to be punished, she needed to wait out this feeling of absolute shame. She retrieved her bicycle from the backstreets of the Four Courts and headed in the direction of Constance's home. Paul may have accused her of not having the first clue how to cover a story but she knew someone who did know, and perhaps it was time to start learning again.

Constance and Bob's home was a basement apartment in a three-storey Edwardian house in Ballsbridge, the rest of which housed the magazine. The basement flat had over the years become an extended office, which they shared and lived in together and had done so for twenty-five years. The kitchen, never used as they ate out almost every night, was hidden beneath the clutter of memorabilia and items they had collected on their extensive travels. Every surface was littered with an eclectic mix of art: ebony carvings next to happy Buddhas and Venetian glass naked ladies, African and Venetian masks placed on old teddy bears' heads, and on the wall Chinese etchings and landscape paintings hung beside Bob's favourite satirical comic strips. The entire place felt like *them*. It had personality, it was fun, it was alive. Teresa, the housekeeper, had worked for Constance and Bob for twenty-five years and was now into her seventies. She didn't appear to do anything more than light dusting and watch *The Jeremy Kyle Show*, but Constance, who wasn't one for caring about a tidy home anyway, couldn't find it in her heart to let her go. Teresa was more than familiar with Kitty and so immediately welcomed her into the flat without question and returned to her armchair with a cup of tea to watch a man and a woman screaming at each other over a lie detector test that hadn't gone in anybody's favour. Kitty was thankful Teresa never watched the news and was completely unaware of the week's drama, sparing her an inquisition. She went into Constance and Bob's office.

Their desks were directly opposite one another and equally piled high with what appeared to be rubbish, but which was probably vital paperwork. Above Constance's desk were nude photographs of women in 1930s France, draped in provocative poses. She had put them there for Bob's viewing pleasure and in return he had placed African art of naked men above his desk for her. The floors were as cluttered as the surfaces, with rug after Persian rug of busy patterns overlapping one another, so that it was difficult not to trip on the lumps and bumps. As well as the continuation of art from the rest of the flat, there were dozens of porcelain cats in various positions on the floor all along the room. Kitty knew that Constance hated them, real ones and the porcelain kind, but they had been her mother's and when she passed away Constance had insisted on giving them a home. The room was so busy Kitty wondered how on earth they could concentrate at all, but they could and they were mighty successful at it. Constance had moved from Paris to Dublin to annoy her wealthy father and study English Literature in Trinity College. There she edited the college paper and her first job was writing for the Society section of the *Irish Times*, where she met Robert McDonald. Bob was ten years older than she, and was the *Times*'s business affairs correspondent. When she eventually tired of being told what to do, which never took long, Constance decided to frustrate her father furthermore by leaving her respectable job with Ireland's major broadsheet and instead start her own publication. Bob came along with her, and after cutting their teeth on various magazines, they set up *Etcetera* twelve years ago, their most successful venture yet. It wasn't the highest selling magazine in Ireland, as it failed to divulge tips on how to remove cellulite or how to get the perfect bikini body, but it was widely respected in the industry. To write for *Etcetera* was considered an honour, a great step on the ladder to success. Constance was a straight-talking no-nonsense editor with an impeccable eye for a story and for talent; *Etcetera* was where many of the country's successful writers had started out.

Kitty went to the filing cabinet and was immediately impressed by the neat system that Constance had developed. It was nothing like the rest of her home: every single article that had been written for *Etcetera* or any other magazine Constance had run, articles she had written for other publications and all ideas she'd had in the past and for the future were neatly filed on cards in alphabetical order. Kitty was unable to ignore her inherent nosiness and so read as many as she could before getting to N. And there it was, a simple brown manila envelope filed under 'Names'. It was sealed, and though she knew she shouldn't break the deal she had made with Constance, she couldn't contain her impatience and so sat down at Constance's desk to open it. Teresa appeared at the door and Kitty jumped like a naughty schoolgirl caught smoking. She dropped the envelope on the desk and then laughed at herself.

'Have you seen her yet?' Teresa asked.

'Yes, last week. I couldn't see her this week because I had this thing to attend,' she said, feeling guilty that the court case had once again kept her from seeing Constance. She knew she should have made the effort but the daily grind at the Four Courts left her feeling drained, self-pitiful, introspective and, quite frankly, rather defensive and snappy. She didn't think it was fair to bring that energy to Constance's bedside.

'I imagine she looks desperate. My Frank died from cancer. He had it in his lungs. He smoked forty a day but still, no one deserves what he went through. He was the same age as Constance. Fifty-four,' Teresa tutted. 'Would you believe I've spent almost as many years without him as I had with him?' She shook her head again. 'Do you want a cup of tea? It tastes a bit metallic. I found coins in the teapot. They used it as their piggy bank. Bob told me to take them to the bank. Seventy-six euro and twenty-five cent they had in there.'

Kitty laughed at their eccentricity and declined the offer of the metallic tea. Excited finally to have the envelope with Constance's idea in her possession, and overcoming the urge to open the envelope, Kitty called Bob straight away to arrange a visit. Three of her calls rang out to his voicemail, and then when she was tired of waiting and was en route to the hospital on her bicycle, she felt her phone vibrate. She spoke into her headset.

'Hi, Bob. I'm just making my way over, hope that's okay. I have the idea Constance was going to tell us about. I can't wait any longer.'

'It's not a good time,' Bob replied, his stress evident even above the sound of the traffic around Kitty. 'She's, er, she's had a bad turn.'

Kitty stopped cycling suddenly and a fellow cyclist almost ran into the back of her and swore her out of it. She lifted her bike out of the cycle lane and onto the pavement.

'What happened?'

'I didn't want to say anything to you – you've had a rough enough week as it is and I was hoping she would improve – but she's . . . she's gone downhill since you saw her. She was drifting in and out of consciousness, she couldn't recognise me for the past two days, she was confused, hallucinating, speaking mostly in French. Today she's, well, she's in a coma, Kitty . . .' His voice cracked.

'Do you want me to be there with you?' Kitty asked, feeling panic inside and genuinely with all of her heart wanting to be there, in that place, with that smell, with him, by Constance's side.

'No, no, you're busy, I'm okay.'

'I'm not, Bob. I've nothing to . . . I've got nothing, okay? I want to be there. Let me, please?'

Kitty hung up and cycled as though her life depended on it, which in a way, it did.

'Hi, Steve, it's me. I was just thinking of you and, well, I had a few things to say about what we last talked about. So here goes. "Rad or Bad". "Rad" is short for "radical", but cool kids shorten it for even cooler effect. It's a bit surfer dude language, though, so it's probably a bit dated. Then there's "Cool or Fool", or to make it a bit more modern you could say "Cool or Tool". And finally my favourite, and probably yours too as it brings in a football angle – "Score or Whore". Hope your boss likes them and I hope it's not too late. Okay, well, you're obviously not in, or you are and you're listening to this thinking I'm drunk or . . . I don't know what you're thinking. I'll go now. Oh, and one last thing. Constance passed away. Tonight. And, em, God, I'm so sorry to be crying on your answering machine but . . . I don't quite know what to do. Okay. Thanks for listening. 'Bye.'

CHAPTER FOUR

Though Kitty hadn't spent much time with Constance over the past few months, she had instinctively known she was there. There was a difference when somebody died. Their absence was felt, at every second of every day. Kitty would think of a question and would suddenly go to call Constance for the answer. She would think of an amusing story she would want to share with her or, more frustratingly, she would remember a half-finished conversation she would want to complete or a question that had somehow gone unanswered. Because Constance wasn't there Kitty wanted her more than ever, and she tortured herself over her lack of visits to the hospital and for not calling her more regularly, not just when Constance was sick but throughout her life. There were events Kitty could have invited her to, nights out they could have shared together; there was so much time wasted not spending it together. But in the end, she knew that if they were to relive their friendship all over again, they would do it exactly the same way. Constance hadn't needed Kitty in her life any more frequently than Kitty had been there.

Not having work to engross herself in, or a boyfriend to help distract her and show her the joys and beauty of her own life, or a functional family that lived in the same county or possessed the abilities to be understanding and show compassion, Kitty felt more alone than ever. The only place she felt she wanted to be was at

32

the offices of *Etcetera*. Being there was like being with Constance, who had been the beating heart of that magazine. It was founded by her, made up of her ideologies, inspired by her, and by simply holding an issue of the magazine in her hands, Kitty felt that in some way Constance still lived on. Kitty supposed it was like seeing the child of someone who had passed away; their looks, their mannerisms, their little quirks were passed down.

As soon as she entered the office Kitty felt the pang of loss she had been running from. It hit her like an icy breeze, like a slap in her face that took her breath away. Her eyes immediately filled up.

'Oh, I know,' Rebecca, the art director, said, catching sight of Kitty frozen at the door. 'You're not the only one who's done that.' She went to her and hugged her warmly, took her coat off and helped her move from the spot. 'Come on in, they're all in Pete's office, brainstorming.'

Pete's office. Calling it that immediately riled Kitty, and though it had absolutely nothing to do with Pete, she momentarily despised him, as if he alone had conspired with God to obliterate her friend. As duty editor he had taken over while Constance was ill, and Cheryl Dunne, an ambitious young woman not much older than Kitty, was acting deputy editor, while Bob spent the past months full time with Constance. Because of Pete and Cheryl's presence, the place felt different. Pete and Cheryl had found their own routine and natural rhythm, and while it seemed everybody else had learned to fall into step with that rhythm, Kitty had been struggling.

It was nine months since Constance had been at the helm of *Etcetera*, six months since she had stepped inside the offices at all, and in that time it was clear to see that the stories Kitty had written were not exactly her best. They were by no means below par or else Pete wouldn't have published them and Constance, who had been keeping a close eye on everything even until the end, would have dragged Kitty into the hospital kicking and screaming to put her in her place. She had been good at doing that. As well as wanting her magazine to be the greatest on the shelves, she never wanted anybody to fail to meet their potential. To her that was the greatest error of all.

Knowing that, after Constance's funeral Kitty had retreated to her flat, not to lick her wounds but to further pour salt on them by poring over her stories, trying to figure out where she had gone wrong, where she needed to go in the future, what her strengths and weaknesses were. As soon as she read her stories from the past six months she could see that they lacked sparkle. As much as she hated to admit it, and she never would to anybody out loud, there was almost a robotic painting-by-numbers feel to her writing. They were informative, emotional and possessed style and a little flair, and they met the standards of the magazine on all levels by covering similar themes with different angles – with a monthly magazine, having a unique angle to an already covered story was top priority – but, rereading them, Kitty felt a stale taste in her mouth. After the disastrous experience with *Thirty Minutes* she was aware that nothing she had ever written and would probably ever write again would please her as it once had. She knew she was deliberately finding flaw with everything about herself, and finding very little to celebrate. She second-guessed everything she said and did but, despite her self-doubt, she knew she was right about the deterioration of her writing.

Constance's method of motivation during brainstorming was not for everyone. It had been perfect for Kitty, but while she knew Pete and Cheryl appreciated Constance's methods, she also knew they couldn't wait to leave the office so they could return to their own sources of inspiration: other magazines, newspapers, internet sites and twenty-four-hour news networks to see what was new, current and hot. Constance's method was always about looking within for the answers. She had asked her staff to look at themselves for stories: what was moving them at that particular moment, what was challenging them, what were the issues not of the day in the world but of the day in their hearts and minds; mumbo jumbo to people like Pete and Cheryl. Constance always believed those subjects would make stronger stories. Instead of writing for the market, she wanted them to write for themselves. It was only then, she believed, that the readers would connect. She wanted her writers not just to be informative and stylish but she encouraged the artist within them to come out. How stories were decided on varied between Constance telling specific people to write particular stories that she knew they were suited to, or which would challenge them, and also by listening to ideas. She was very much an advocate of hearing people's ideas.

And that's what the problem was – Kitty had finally nailed it. In the six months of *Etcetera* stories that Kitty had pored over, she now realised she hadn't written a single article that had been an idea of her own. Each story had been proposed by Pete or Cheryl or by somebody else who had enough on their own plate and was unable to write it. She hadn't noticed it happening because she hadn't minded. She hadn't noticed or minded because she had been working on *Thirty Minutes* and each story she had covered for that show had been a story she had been told to cover. In a way, her method of storytelling for *Thirty Minutes* had trickled over into her writing. The stories on the show were stories that hadn't meant anything to her, stories that hadn't moved her, stories she hadn't tried to understand on any deeper level because there wasn't enough time, the filming conditions were suddenly right or not right, they'd lost a few minutes because of another story gaining momentum, they had an interview, they didn't have an interview, they had to fill a cancelled interview with something else, and she felt she was switching herself on and off like a tap. It was a less creative style of working for her; it was mechanical, her days were spent on her toes and less in her mind. For six months Kitty hadn't had an original thought of her own and in the week it took her to discover that, it terrified her so much she couldn't even think of anything when she tried. Now the final conversation she had

had with Constance in hospital was making more sense to her. When Constance had accused Kitty of writing a story because she was told it was interesting and not because she felt it, she had thought Constance had been referring to her stories on *Thirty Minutes*, but perhaps she had been talking about her articles for *Etcetera*. In fact now Kitty was sure of it.

Kitty walked towards the boardroom off Constance's office, feeling vulnerable after her recent humiliation, knowing she hadn't an original thought or idea in her head, completely alone without Constance and Bob's support. Though there had been many monthly brainstorming sessions since Constance had left the office there had been none that could not be overruled by her, and so with Pete in the hot seat, and Bob still not present, this was the first of its kind. Kitty opened the door and everyone in the room looked up at her.

'Hi.'

'Kitty,' Pete said, sounding surprised in a not-so-good way. 'We didn't expect to see you here this week. Bob said he gave you the week off.' And it sounded like he'd rather not have seen her this week either, or perhaps she was just being paranoid.

'He did,' Kitty explained, standing at the back of the room as all the chairs had been taken, 'but I just couldn't think of anywhere else I'd rather be.' She received sad and sympathetic looks from a few around her.

'Okay. Well. We were talking about next month's edition, which is going to be a tribute to Constance.'

Kitty's eyes welled. 'That's a beautiful idea.'

'So . . .' he clapped his hands and Kitty jumped. 'Ideas. I suggest an eight-to-twelve-page look at Constance's journey, stories that she's written for *Etcetera* and other publications throughout her career. A look back on her greatest exposés, the writers she helped discover, for example an interview with Tom Sullivan would be good, all about how she helped him find and develop his voice. Dara, I want you to interview Tom; I talked to him at the funeral and he's already agreed to it. Niamh, I want you to cover the other writers living and dead: who she found, how she found them, what they wrote, what they went on to write and so on.'

Dara and Niamh nodded and made notes.

Pete began dishing out pieces to the others around the table and Kitty couldn't help but think that it all felt rather wrong. Constance would hate this edition, not just because it was all about her, but because it was rehashing old material. She looked around at the others for their reactions but they were all concentrating hard, busy scribbling down Pete's orders in their notepads. And that's what they felt like: orders, nothing gentle or inspiring, nothing to try to coax out further ideas from the people sitting around the table. No questions about personal stories or memories about a woman they all deeply respected, just information from his own head on what he thought was a good idea. Kitty appreciated that it was difficult for Pete having to do this at all and she hadn't an original idea in her head to offer, so she kept her mouth shut.

'Okay, so that's that sorted out. Let's talk about the rest of the magazine. Conal, how's that piece on China in South Africa coming along?'

They began talking about the rest of the magazine, Constance's tribute piece already over. That made Kitty angry.

'Uh, Pete?'

He looked at her.

'I don't know, Pete. That all seems a bit . . . old?' Not a popular thing to say when people were discussing their work. Some tutted and shifted in their chairs. 'What I mean is, the Constance tribute. Constance hated republishing old articles.'

'We're not just doing that, Kitty. If you'd been listening properly you'd have heard that. And we have to look back, that's what a tribute piece does.'

'Yeah, I know,' Kitty said, trying not to annoy anybody. 'But Constance said it was like using used toilet paper, remember?' She laughed. Nobody else did. 'She wouldn't want to just keep looking back. She'd want something new, something that looked forward, something celebratory.'

'Like what?' Pete asked, and Kitty froze.

'I don't know.'

Someone sighed heavily.

'Kitty, this twelve-page spread is to celebrate Constance. We have the rest of the magazine to create new stories,' Pete said, trying to sound patient but instead sounding like a patronising father at the edge of his tether. 'If you don't have any ideas to offer then I'm going to move on.'

She thought long and hard, while all eyes were bearing down on her. Instead of coming up with ideas, all she could think was that she couldn't think of anything. She hadn't been able to think of anything for six months, so she surely wouldn't start now. Eventually people began to look away, feeling embarrassed for her, but Pete kept the spotlight on her, as if to prove a point. She wanted him to move on; why wasn't he moving on? Her cheeks burned and she looked down to avoid meeting anyone's eye, feeling that she couldn't possibly sink any lower.

'I don't know,' she eventually said, quietly.

Pete moved on but Kitty couldn't concentrate on a word he said thereafter. She felt as though she had let Constance down – she was sure she had let herself down, and though it still hurt, she was used to that now. She kept wondering what exactly Constance would want. If she was in this room, what story would she want to tell . . .? That's when Kitty thought of it.

'I've got it,' she blurted out, interrupting Sarah's feedback on how her story on contrasting nail varnish sales increases in a recession with lipstick sales during the Second World War was shaping up.

'Kitty, Sarah is talking.' Others looked at her annoyed.

She shrunk lower in her chair and waited for Sarah to finish. When she had, Pete moved on to Trevor. She sat through two more ideas pitches, neither of which Pete would probably use, and then finally he looked back at her.

'The last time I spoke to Constance she had an idea that she wanted to run by you. I don't know if she did or not. It was just over a week ago.' When she had been living and breathing.

'No. I haven't spoken to her for a month.'

'Okay. Well, she wanted to tell you an idea she had and that was a piece about asking retired writers, if they had the opportunity to write the story they always wanted to write, what would it be?'

Pete looked around the table and he could see that people looked interested.

'Writers like Oisín O'Ceallaigh and Olivia Wallace,' Kitty continued.

'Oisín is eighty years old and lives on the Aran Islands. He hasn't written a word for anyone for ten years and hasn't written anything in the English language for twenty.'

'They're the people she mentioned.'

'Are you sure?'

'Yes,' Kitty replied, cheeks burning again at being repeatedly questioned.

'And are these interview pieces about their stories or are we asking them to write their actual stories?'

'First she said I should interview them—'

'She said *you* should interview them,' Pete interrupted.

'Yes . . .' She paused, unsure what the problem was. 'But then she said you could ask the writers to write the stories they always wanted to write.'

'Commission them?'

'I suppose so.'

'Writers of that standard, that's a costly piece.'

'Well, it's a tribute to Constance, so maybe they'd offer their time for free. If it's a story they've always wanted to write, perhaps that's payment enough. It will be cathartic.'

Pete looked doubtful. 'How did this conversation come about?'

39

Everyone looked from Pete to Kitty.

'Why?' she asked.

'I'm trying to find a link between this idea you have and it being a tribute to Constance.'

'It was one of her final feature ideas.'

'But was it? Or was it yours?'

Everyone looked uncomfortable and shifted in their chairs.

'Are you accusing me of using this tribute piece so that I can use one of my own ideas?' Kitty had wanted it to sound bigger than him, superior, to make him seem small, but instead her voice came out battered and meek, and she sounded as if she was doing exactly what she was accused of.

'Why don't we call this meeting off for now and everyone can get back to their desks?' Cheryl added in the awkward silence.

Everyone quickly exited the room, glad to be away from the awkwardness. Pete remained standing at the head of the table, two hands spread on the surface, leaning over. Cheryl remained, too, at the table, which annoyed Kitty.

'Kitty, I'm not trying to be smart here but I want this to be authentically Constance. I know you knew her more personally than the rest of us but you're talking about a conversation you both had alone. I want to make sure it was something Constance really wanted to do.'

Kitty swallowed and suddenly doubted herself. What had once been a crystal-clear memory of the conversation now seemed fuzzy. 'I can't tell you if it was something she *really* wanted to do, Pete.'

'Come on, Kitty,' he laughed with frustration. 'Make up your mind, will you?'

'All I know is that I asked her what story she had always wanted to write but never did. She liked the question and said that it would be a good idea for a feature, that I should do a piece where I asked retired writers about the story they'd always wanted to write or, better yet, asked them to write the piece. She said she would talk to you about it.'

'She didn't.'

Silence.

'It's a good idea, Pete,' Cheryl said quietly, and Kitty was momentarily glad she'd stayed.

Pete tapped his pen on the table while he thought. 'Did she tell you her idea?'

'No.'

He didn't believe her. She swallowed.

'She told me to find it in her office, bring it back to her at the hospital and she'd explain, but when I brought it back to the hospital it was too late.' Kitty's eyes filled and she looked down. She hoped then for a bit of humanity but none came.

'Did you open it?' Pete asked.

'No.'

He didn't believe her again.

'I didn't open it,' Kitty said firmly, her anger rising.

'Where is it now?'

'Bob has it.'

Pete went quiet.

'What are you thinking?' Cheryl asked.

'I'm thinking it would be a great feature and tribute *if* we had Constance's story that she always wanted to write, to tie in with the other writers' pieces. If Bob gives us the story, you could write it,' he said to Cheryl.

Kitty felt angry at Pete for handing the story over to Cheryl.

'Maybe Bob would prefer to write it,' Kitty suggested.

'We'll give Bob first preference.'

'I have it here.' Bob's voice came from the adjoining room.

'Bob.' Pete straightened up. 'I didn't know you were here.'

Bob entered the room. He looked tired. 'I wasn't going to come in but then I realised there was nowhere else I'd rather be,' he repeated Kitty's line, which told Kitty he'd been there since the beginning and had heard it all. 'I needed to get something from Constance's office – her address book, God knows where she's put

41

it – and I couldn't help but overhear talk about covering her story.'
Bob smiled. 'Pete, I think that's a marvellous idea. Well done.'

'Would you like to write it?' Pete asked.

'No. No. I'm too close to it.'

'What is the story?' Pete asked.

'I have no idea,' Bob shrugged. 'The envelope is sealed, it's never been opened.'

Kitty was vindicated. She tried not to leap up and punch the air.

'Okay,' Pete looked at Cheryl, pleased with himself, and about to do the honours on her behalf but Bob sensed that and interrupted.

'I'd like Kitty to write it.'

Pete and Cheryl were surprised.

'I think she's better suited,' he explained gently, as ever thoughtful and apologetic to Cheryl.

Cheryl tried to look accepting.

'Even though you don't know what it's about,' Pete said, defending his number one.

'Yes. Even though,' Bob replied, handing the envelope to Kitty.

They all looked at her in suspense. Kitty carefully opened the envelope. A single sheet lay inside. She slid it out and was faced with a list of one hundred names.

CHAPTER FIVE

1. *Sarah McGowan*
2. *Ambrose Nolan*
3. *Eva Wu*
4. *Jedrek Vysotski*
5. *Bartle Faulkner*
6. *Bridget Murphy*
7. *Mary-Rose Godfrey*
8. *Bernadette Toomy*
9. *Raymond Cosgrave*
10. *Olive Byrne*
11. *Marion Brennan*
12. *Julio Quintero*
13. *Maureen Rabbit*
14. *Patrick Quinn*
15. *Gloria Flannery*
16. *Susan Flood*
17. *Kieran Kidd*
18. *Anthony Kershaw*
19. *Janice O'Meara*
20. *Angela O'Neill*
21. *Eugene Cullen*
22. *Evelyn Meagher*
23. *Barry Meegan*
24. *Aiden Traynor*
25. *Seamus Tully*
26. *Diana Zukov*
27. *Bin Yang*
28. *Gabriela Zat*
29. *Barbara Tomlin*
30. *Benjamin Toland*
31. *Anthony Spencer*
32. *Aidan Somerville*
33. *Patrick Leahy*
34. *Cyril Lee*
35. *Dudley Foster*
36. *Josephine Fowler*
37. *Colette Burrows*
38. *Ann Kimmage*
39. *Dermot Murphy*
40. *Sharon Vickers*
41. *George Wallace*
42. *Michael O'Fagain*
43. *Lisa Dwyer*
44. *Danny Flannery*
45. *Karen Flood*
46. *Máire O'Muireagáin*
47. *Barry O'Shea*
48. *Frank O'Rourke*
49. *Claire Shanley*
50. *Kevin Sharkey*

51. *Carmel Reilly*
52. *Russell Todd*
53. *Heather Spencer*
54. *Ingrid Smith*
55. *Ken Sheeran*
56. *Margaret McCarthy*
57. *Janet Martin*
58. *John O'Shea*
59. *Catherine Sheppard*
60. *Magdalena Ludwiczak*
61. *Declan Keogh*
62. *Siobhán Kennedy*
63. *Dudley Foster*
64. *Denis MacCauley*
65. *Nigel Meaney*
66. *Thomas Masterson*
67. *Archie Hamilton*
68. *Damien Rafferty*
69. *Ian Sheridan*
70. *Gordon Phelan*
71. *Marie Perrem*
72. *Emma Pierce*
73. *Eileen Foley*
74. *Liam Greene*
75. *Aoife Graham*
76. *Sinéad Hennessey*
77. *Andrew Perkins*
78. *Patricia Shelley*
79. *Peter O'Carroll*
80. *Seán Maguire*
81. *Michael Sheils*
82. *Alan Waldron*
83. *Carmel Wagner*
84. *Jonathan Treacy*
85. *Lee Reehill*
86. *Pauric Naughton*
87. *Ben Gleeson*
88. *Darlene Gochoco*
89. *Desmond Hand*
90. *Jim Duffy*
91. *Maurice Lucas*
92. *Denise McBride*
93. *Jos Merrigan*
94. *Frank Jones*
95. *Gwen Megarry*
96. *Vida Tonacao*
97. *Alan Shanahan*
98. *Orla Foley*
99. *Simon Fitzgerald*
100. *Katrina Mooney*

There was no summary, synopsis or anything to explain who these people were or what the story was. Kitty looked in the envelope for more but there was nothing.

'What does it say?' Pete asked, no longer able to stand the silence.

'It's a list of names,' Kitty replied.

The names had been typed and were numbered along the left-hand side from one to one hundred.

'Are the names familiar?' Pete asked, stretching his body so far over the table he was practically crawling on it.

Kitty shook her head, feeling a failure again. 'Maybe you guys will recognise them.' She slid the page down the table and the other three jumped on it like lions on a piece of fresh meat. They placed it in the centre of the table in front of Pete and huddled round it. Kitty watched their faces, hoping for some signs of recognition but when they finally lifted their heads, looking as confused as she had, she sank back in her chair both relieved and confused. Should she know what the names meant? Had she and Constance had a conversation about it before? Was there a hidden message?

'What else is in the envelope?' Pete asked.

'Nothing.'

'Let me see.'

He doubted her again, and she in turn doubted herself, despite looking inside it twice. Quickly seeing there was no further information he tossed the envelope back on the table and Kitty dived for it and held it protectively as if he had thrown a baby.

'Did she keep notes?' Pete asked Bob. 'In a book or on file? Maybe there's something in the office.'

'If there is, it will be downstairs,' Bob said, looking at the names again. 'My dear Constance, what on earth were you up to?'

Kitty couldn't help but laugh. Constance would love seeing them all huddled round, scratching their heads.

'It's hardly funny, Kitty,' Pete said. 'The feature won't make much sense if we don't have a story from Constance.'

'I disagree,' she said, surprised. 'It's the last piece Constance suggested for the magazine.'

'I'd still prefer to include Constance's story,' Pete said stubbornly. 'It's what I want the other stories to revolve around. If we don't have Constance's story, I'm not sure about the idea at all.'

'But Constance's story is just a list of names,' Kitty said, losing confidence in herself. She didn't want the entire tribute piece to rest on her ability to piece together what on earth this list meant. There wasn't enough time, and the time that they did have happened to be the worst time of Kitty's life. She was feeling far from inspired and her self-belief was at an all-time low. 'There's nothing to explain where Constance was going with it or how she was feeling about it.'

'Well then, Cheryl will do it,' Pete said quickly, taking them all by surprise. 'She'll figure it out.' He snapped his folder shut and straightened up.

'With all due respect, I think Kitty should do it,' Bob said.

'But she just said she didn't think she could.'

'She just needs a little encouragement, Pete,' Bob said, a little firmer then. 'It's a daunting task.'

'Fine,' Pete said suddenly. 'We have two weeks until we go to print. Kitty, keep me up to date with how you're getting on. I'd like daily feedback.'

'Daily?' she asked, surprised.

'Yep.' He gathered his things and made for Constance's, *his*, office.

With Pete's demand for daily updates, Kitty knew that her suspension from the television network, the vandalism to her flat, her relationship breakdown and the court case loss had just scratched the surface, and now the real repercussions of *Thirty Minutes* were beginning.

Kitty reluctantly sat behind Constance's desk in her home office, her hands up in the air as though she was being shot at, afraid to touch anything, afraid to ruin the order of how Constance had placed things, knowing they would never find their way back to their rightful place without their rightful owner to fix them. Last week she had loved the feeling of being there but now she felt like an intruder. Bob had given her free rein in the office; there was nothing she couldn't read, no territory she wasn't allowed to examine. The previous Kitty – the Kitty who had Constance in her life and who hadn't a court ruling against her for irresponsible journalism – would have jumped at the chance to be meddlesome and would have read everything she could get her hands on, whether it was related to the story or not, but now it was different.

She spent the afternoon doing fruitless but time-consuming searches through the filing cabinet, trying to see if any other paper-work matched up to the one hundred names. It was pointless because she had no idea what the names meant and how they could be linked to anything else. She Googled the names but nothing of interest came up; everything led her down deceiving paths.

By the end of day two, after an embarrassing meeting with Pete in which she had nothing to report, she returned home to find her flat with red-paint-splashed toilet paper hanging in strands across the front door as if to mimic a crime scene.

Despite going to bed without an ounce of hope and a blocked toilet from when she'd tried to flush away all the toilet paper at once, she managed to wake up somehow feeling vibrant and full of possibilities. A new day meant a new start to her search. She could do it. This was her moment to redeem herself, to make Constance proud. Her final thought of the night had been that the people on the list could be absolutely anyone – and where else do you find people who could be anyone? Not bothering to get dressed, she retrieved the phone directory and sat at the table in her pants.

She had made various photocopies of Constance's list, not wanting to damage the original, which she had placed back in Constance's filing cabinet. Kitty's own copy was now covered in thoughts, questions, cartoon squiggles and shapes and so she took a fresh copy, a new notepad, the phone book, a fresh mug of coffee – instant, as Glen had taken his coffee machine and fresh coffee beans – took a deep breath and prepared herself. She heard a key in the door and it suddenly opened and she was faced with Glen. Her hands went straight to her naked chest. Then, feeling vulnerable, she folded her legs, opened the phone directory and covered herself more.

'Sorry,' Glen said, still frozen at the door, key in hand, staring at her. 'I thought you'd be at work.'

'Do you have to keep staring at me?'

'Sorry.' He blinked, looked away, then turned his back. 'Do you want me to leave?'

'Too late for that, isn't it?' she snapped, marching to her wardrobe.

'Oh, here we go,' he said, politeness leaving his voice. The door banged and he followed her into the bedroom.

'I'm not dressed yet.'

'Do you know what, Kitty, I've seen it all before and I really couldn't care less.' He didn't glance at her as he rooted in her drawers.

'What are you looking for?'

'None of your business.'

'It's my flat, of course it's my business.'

'And I've paid my half of this month's rent, so technically it's mine too.'

'If you tell me what it is, I can help,' she said, watching him root. 'Because I'd really like for you to take your hands off my knickers.'

He finally retrieved a watch from her underwear drawer and strapped it around his wrist.

'How long has that been there?'

'Always.'

'Oh.'

How much more hadn't she known about him? That's what they were both thinking: how much more didn't they know about each other? They were silent for a moment, and then he looked around the room again, more gently this time, placing shoes, CDs and other miscellaneous items he'd left behind into a black bin liner. Kitty couldn't watch and went to sit at the kitchen table again.

'Thanks for telling me you were leaving,' she said as he passed her and made his way around the kitchen. He took the oven gloves, the *oven gloves*. 'It was very gentlemanly of you.'

'You knew that I was leaving.'

'How the hell did I know that?'

'How many arguments did we have, Kitty? How many times did I tell you exactly how I felt? How many more arguments did you want to have?'

'None, of course.'

'Exactly!'

'But this wasn't quite the outcome I was hoping for.'

He seemed surprised. 'I thought you weren't happy. You said you weren't happy.'

'I wasn't having a happy *time*. I didn't think that . . . anyway, it doesn't matter now, does it?' She was surprised to feel hope in her heart, hope that he would say, of course it matters, let's fix this . . . but instead he left a long silence.

'Why aren't you at work?'

'I decided to work from home.'

'Did the magazine fire you?' he asked, disbelieving her.

'No,' she snapped, tired of being second-guessed. 'They didn't fire me. It may surprise you to know that some people still believe in me.' Which wasn't entirely true with the way Pete was treating her.

Glen sighed, then walked to the door, bin liner over his shoulder. She looked back down at the directory. Her eyes jumped from one name to the next, unable to concentrate while he was there.

'Sorry to hear about Constance.'

Emotion flooded her and she couldn't speak.

'I was at the funeral, in case you hadn't heard.'

'Sally told me.' She wiped her eyes roughly, annoyed that she was crying.

'Are you okay?'

Kitty blocked her face with her hands. It was too humiliating to have him stand there while she cried, when before he would

49

have comforted her. She cried about that and she cried for
Constance. And she cried about everything else in between. 'Please
go,' she sobbed.

She heard the door softly close.

With dry eyes Kitty started afresh. She went to the first name on
the list, Sarah McGowan. She turned to the McGowan pages in
the directory. There were hundreds of McGowans in total. Eighty
Mr and Mrs McGowans, twenty S McGowans, eight Sarah
McGowans, which meant she would at least have to attempt to
call them all if the twenty-eight specific S's didn't work out for her.

She began by ringing the Sarahs. The first call was answered
immediately.

'Hello, can I please speak to Sarah McGowan?'

'This is she.'

'My name is Katherine Logan and I'm calling from *Etcetera*
magazine.'

She left a pause to see if there was any recognition.

'I don't want to take part in any surveys, thank you.'

'No, no, this isn't about a survey. I'm calling on behalf of our
editor, Constance Dubois. I believe she may have been in contact
with you regarding a story.'

She hadn't been. Nor had she been with six other S's she had
contacted, while two calls rang out and she left a message for another
two. Kitty started on the other McGowans in the directory, hoping
Sarah was listed as a Mrs Somebody Else McGowan. Ten calls weren't
answered and she made a note to call them back. There were no
Sarahs in the first eight Mr and Mrs' homes she called; on the ninth
there was, but at three months old baby Sarah was not the subject
of Constance's story, Kitty quickly learned. Twenty McGowans left,
not to mention ninety-nine other names on the list with at least one
hundred of each name to call. A possible ten thousand more phone-
calls awaited her, unless she began with the more obscure names.
Kitty didn't doubt that she could do it – nothing bored her about

research – but there were two factors working against her: time and money. She simply couldn't afford to make all of these calls.

She abandoned her work-from-home strategy and returned to the office at lunchtime. It was busy with everyone working flat out to meet their new deadline for Constance's tribute section as well as researching and writing stories for future issues.

Rebecca, the art director, came out of Pete's office pulling a face. 'He's in a mood today. Good luck.'

An unfamiliar woman was sitting in Kitty's usual desk, which wasn't all that rare as they had many freelance writers in the editorial section who came and went from the office. Kitty stood in the centre of the room looking for a free desk and when that proved fruitless she looked for a free phone. Pete opened the door and called her into his office.

'What are you doing?' he asked.

'Looking for a desk. I have a mountain of calls to make, do you think you could get somebody's phone for me for the day? And who is that lady at my desk?'

'You on to something?'

'I'm going to contact the names directly to see if Constance was speaking to them. Who is that lady at my desk?'

'How can you contact them?'

'From the phone directory,' she said, trying not to show that she was well aware it was a stupid idea.

'That's it?'

'Yes.'

'And how many people are on the list?'

'One hundred. Who is the lady at my desk?'

'One hundred? Jesus, Kitty, that will take for ever.'

'I've already worked my way through most of the first name.'

'And? Any luck?'

'Not yet.'

He stared at her angrily.

'Her name is "McGowan"; it might as well be "Smith" in this

country. I've made about one hundred calls already. Pete, what do you expect me to do? There's no other way. I started by googling them all and Archie Hamilton is either a clown available for kids' parties, he works at Davy's stockbrokers, he died ten years ago or he went to prison five years ago for assault. Which one do you think I should just guess it is?'

He sighed. 'Look, you can't work here.'

'Why not?' She looked out the window, then pointedly back at her desk.

'That's Bernie Mulligan. I've asked her to write a story in your place in this month's issue. The Cox Brothers called, along with a few other of our major advertisers. They've come under severe pressure to pull this month's advertising.'

'Why?'

Silence.

'Oh. Because of me.'

'They've been put under pressure for months but after the court case now they feel that they can't support the magazine without it been seen to at least reprimand you in some way.'

'But the television network have already suspended me. It has nothing to do with *Etcetera*.'

'Somebody is stirring trouble for them.'

'Colin Maguire's crowd,' she said. 'They're doing whatever they can to destroy me.'

'We don't know it's them,' he said, but with very little energy and belief behind it. He ran his hand through his hair. It was so glossy and perfect it fell straight back into place and reminded Kitty of a Head & Shoulders commercial. For the first time, she noticed he was actually quite handsome.

'So you're suspending me.'

'No . . . I'm asking you not to work in the office for the next three weeks while I try to convince them.'

'But what about Constance's story?'

He rubbed his eyes tiredly.

'That's why you didn't want me to write it, isn't it? That's why you asked Cheryl.'

'My hands are tied, Kitty. They're our biggest advertisers. We lose them, it's suicide and I can't afford to let that happen.'

'Does Bob know?'

'No, and you're not to tell him either. He doesn't need this on his plate. That's why Cheryl and I are here.'

'I want to work on the story,' Kitty said. She suddenly very much needed to do this story. It was all she had.

'If they do as they say then we can't publish your name,' he said, appearing tired. 'I don't see a way round it.'

Kitty suddenly liked this side of him. He seemed human, not like his usual bulldog self. 'I was thinking of writing under Kitty Logan from now on. You know, drop Katherine. Nobody but my mother calls me it anyway . . .' She swallowed. Katherine Logan carried such weight, she felt embarrassed saying it aloud, self-conscious when she phoned up the names on the list, paranoid about their reaction and what they must be thinking but not saying. She was ashamed of her own name. Kitty could be her fresh start.

Pete looked at her rather pityingly.

'Or even better,' she fought off his pity and brightened as a new idea sprung to her mind, 'we put Constance's name to it. It's her final story.'

'We can't do that, Kitty, not if it's your story.' He seemed surprised, but in a good way, impressed that she was suggesting not putting her name to her own hard work. He softened. 'We'll work something out. Just keep on working on it. Can't you work from home?'

'I can't . . . I can't afford to make that many calls.'

He sighed and leaned over his desk, hands flat on the surface like in the boardroom. He had a muscular back and, to her very great surprise, Kitty felt a crush developing. She just wanted to reach out and help massage the tension from his shoulders.

'Okay,' he said gently. 'Use your home phone and bill the office.'

'Thanks.'

'But, Kitty, you'll have to figure out another way to do this than working your way through the phone directory.'

'Yeah. I know.'

As Kitty was making her way downstairs, she noticed that the bird house in the front garden had a 'Junk Mail' sign and was overflowing with leaflets. She thought about Glen, hiding his watch in her underwear drawer. Bob and Constance hid things in bizarre places; surely the key to Constance's story lay somewhere inside that flat. She knocked on the door.

Teresa answered. 'He's having a lie-down, love.'

'I need to use Constance's desk. I need your help. I need to find the telephone directory.'

Teresa laughed. 'Well, good luck with that. You know I found the phone in the laundry basket the other day? Bob said it was ringing too loudly.'

They looked around the flat.

'Money in the teapot, passports in the toaster, junk mail in the bird house – where on earth would Constance put a directory?' Kitty asked.

'It's probably in the loo, she probably used it to wipe her bum,' Teresa said, shuffling off back to the kitchen where Kitty could hear the washing machine in action. Kitty was pleased to see that at least Teresa had upped her duties from light dusting and was looking after Bob now.

Left to her own devices, Kitty began looking around the flat for the phonebook, checking in the most obvious places and then straining her mind to think of the bizarre. She kneeled on the floor in Bob and Constance's office, on a sheepskin shagpile rug that was out of place next to its Persian neighbour, and examined the low coffee table on which sat the phone. She didn't know why but she felt compelled to look underneath the table, and there they were. Instead of on four table legs, the wooden surface stood on four pillars of phonebooks and Golden Pages, each five books thick, and going back over the last ten years. Kitty laughed

and Teresa appeared at the door to see what she'd discovered.
Seeing Kitty lift the wooden slab off the directories, Teresa rolled
her eyes, but couldn't hide her amusement before she wandered
back down the corridor to the kitchen. Kitty flicked through the
latest directory but there was nothing new. Then she studied last
year's. She went straight to McGowan, and as soon as she reached
the page she almost leaped for joy. It was highlighted in pink.
She flicked to the second name on the list, Ambrose Nolan, and
to her delight found that it too had been highlighted. Pulling out
the list from her folder, she went through every single name and
squealed happily to find each appeared highlighted in the directory. A lucky break at last. She punched the air in celebration
and accidentally toppled a lamp. It wobbled dangerously and a
small red leather address book came falling to the floor, the one
Bob had been searching for. Kitty laughed, hugged the directory
to her and lifted her head to the sky.

'Thank you,' she whispered.

CHAPTER SIX

So now Kitty had all the names, the addresses and the phone numbers. Everyone lived in Ireland, and her wild-goose chase was limited to one country. She was so close to Constance's story she could practically smell the ink on the freshly published magazine. With a deadline of only a week and a half to go, and with one hundred people to meet, Kitty was surprised at her lack of eagerness to begin contacting them immediately. As she looked at the phone directory, her eyes kept being pulled to search for one name, and that wasn't even on Constance's list.

Kitty took the 123 bus to O'Connell Street and then the 140 to Finglas. One hour after setting out on her journey, and constantly going over her words in her head, she arrived at her destination and she still didn't even know what to say. She stood across the green from Colin Maguire's house while kids raced around her on their bikes, almost knocking her over as if she wasn't even there. She suddenly wished she wasn't. At that hour the streets were busy with mothers and their children coming and going, but none seemed to take any notice of a stranger's presence. Not yet. She was sure it would be only a matter a time before one of the children alerted its mother to a strange woman lurking at the green. The green was a one-hundred-metre stretch of grass with a diagonal pathway going through it from one exit to another, surrounded by a small knee-high wall. She wasn't protected by anything, she was completely exposed, and all that stood between her and Colin's house was distance and her own terror.

As she looked around at the neighbours, she took in their faces, wondering if they had been at the courthouse, if they had been the ones shouting at her, if they were the people who came to her door with spray paint and toilet paper while she slept inside or while she slipped out to work. Were they watching her all the time as she was watching them now? With a hat pulled low over her face, she watched Colin Maguire's house and tried to decide whether to approach and, if so, what to say.

Sorry. Sorry for ruining your life. Sorry you were suspended from your job, sorry you were rejected from your community. Sorry that, for whatever reason, I'm sure related in some way to the story, you've had to put your house on the market. Sorry your marriage has suffered as a consequence. Sorry for putting your job in jeopardy. Sorry for embarrassing your family and destroying personal relationships. I know you mustn't think that I understand, that I'm a heartless bitch who couldn't possibly understand, but I do. Believe me, I do. I understand because I'm going through it too. That's what she wanted to say but she knew it was an apology that was full of self-sympathy and she needed to be selfless. Yet she couldn't bring herself to be so because she felt she was suffering so much. It was her fault, yes it was, but they were both suffering, and whoever loved him and was trying to protect him was causing her misery to continue.

She studied the house, which had a 'For Sale' notice in the garden. There was no sign of his children, no bikes in the garden, no toys on the windowsill, the car was still in the drive. It was Colin's car. She remembered chasing him to it after school with a camera in his face, his look bewildered and confused. She had thought he was a criminal then. She had been so sure he was, but to think of the things she'd said to him made her ashamed now. She wondered if the car in the driveway meant that he hadn't gone back to work yet. She assumed his job was still open to him now that his name was well and truly cleared. Or perhaps the stigma was too great for him to return.

Sorry.

Colin was thirty-eight years old. He started working in the Finglas Community Secondary School, for twelve- to eighteen-year-olds, as soon as he finished college at the age of twenty-four. He was popular with the students, to his detriment, often a regular at the end-of-year debutante balls, a supportive young teacher they didn't consider a proper teacher as he failed to dish out homework, and punishments other than press-ups while forced to sing the latest songs in the charts. He was the teacher whom students felt they could go to when in need, and as a reward for his popularity was made class tutor on many occasions, unusual for a physical education teacher in that particular school. When he turned down the advances of sixteen-year-old Tanya O'Brien, he suffered the consequences ten years later. For whatever reasons, choosing to direct her personal unhappiness at him, Tanya talked her old school friend Tracey O'Neill into becoming her accomplice. Tracey had truly believed that Tanya was abused and that her ten-year-old son was in fact Colin's son. Apart from wanting to support her friend, having been convinced that two people with identical stories would strengthen her case, Tracey also believed there would be a monetary reward for Tanya's trauma, with magazines keen to tell her story and possibly even television appearances to talk about the abuse she'd suffered. Tanya had shown her friend examples of previous abuse cases in which the victims were paid by the media. One evil young woman and the other bored and twisted had come together to target an overambitious one. Kitty was young and coming up the ranks. They'd known she would be hungry. And she was. She gobbled up their lies and came at them for seconds, talking the editor and producer of *Thirty Minutes* into allowing her to follow the story up, convincing herself that exposing this pervert was all for the greater good of society.

The front door of Colin's house opened and he appeared. Head still down as she had last seen him in the courthouse, his chin on his chest. Kitty's heart hammered wildly and she realised she couldn't do it. She turned and walked away quickly, hat low over her face, feeling once again an interloper in Colin's life.

Not one of her voicemails was returned. Those she had called hadn't answered, or weren't home, messages were to be passed on but she couldn't be sure if they would be. Besides, increasingly people screened their calls and refused to answer if they didn't recognise a number or it was withheld. Kitty decided that the best way to approach this story was not to contact all one hundred names via the telephone but to try a face-to-face approach.

On day one of her personal visits she went to Sarah McGowan's address in Lucan, a ground-floor red-brick block of flats built in the seventies, which looked like it belonged in a retirement community. The balcony door opened beside her at the front door to the flats and a woman in her twenties in a nurse's uniform stepped out.

'Are you Sarah McGowan?'

The girl looked her up and down. Made a decision. 'She moved out six months ago.'

Kitty couldn't hide her disappointment.

'No jobs for her here,' the nurse shrugged, 'which I understand, but she was supposed to give me three months' notice. Which she didn't.'

'Where did she move to?' Kitty asked hopefully.

'Australia.'

'Australia!'

'Victoria, I think. Or at least that's where she went first. She had friends out there working on a watermelon farm. They got her a job picking watermelons.' The nurse rolled her eyes.

'I don't know, that sounds kind of fun,' Kitty said, thinking picking watermelons on the other side of the world would be quite the remedy for her situation right now.

'For a qualified accountant?'

Kitty took her point. 'Do you have her new number?'

The nurse shook her head. 'We weren't exactly friends. She set up a forwarding address with the Post Office and I sold her crap on eBay. The least she could do for me.'

'Do you know her friends or family?'

The girl gave Kitty a look that answered everything.

'Thanks for your help.' Kitty backed away, knowing there was nothing more she'd get from this girl.

'Hey, are you that woman?'

Kitty stopped. 'Depends which woman you mean.'

'The TV woman. From *Thirty Minutes*.'

Kitty paused. 'Yes, that's me.'

'You left a message on my phone.'

It didn't warrant a response.

'I've never seen your show. I just know you from the court case.'

Kitty's smile faded.

The girl seemed to think about it. 'She's a good girl, you know. Sarah. Despite what I've said about her. Don't do anything horrible on her.'

'I won't.' Kitty swallowed and made her way out of the quiet apartment complex. Perhaps she would use the name Kitty in future after all.

On the bus to her next destination, Kitty tried to ignore the parting words of the previous exchange by making notes in her notepad.

Story Theory: People who've had to move abroad.
Recession story?

Kitty hoped that wasn't the case. She'd had enough of those stories – the media was inundated with the subject – and unless the situation was unique, she knew Constance had believed the same.

She stared out of the bus window. She had hoped to follow the list in the exact order Constance had catalogued the names, but as Kitty was cold calling door to door, and hadn't use of a car, she had decided to start with the Dublin addresses first. Sixth on the list, but second on Kitty's, was Bridget Murphy.

Number 42 was a terraced house in Beaumont, with nothing in particular to distinguish it from the line of identical pebble-dash houses on that row, opposite it, or around the maze that made up the estate. In an effort to inject colour into the estate some homeowners had painted their houses, though they clearly hadn't pulled together. There were clashing lemons and oranges, snot greens beside mint greens, pretty pinks beside unpainted murky pebble dash. The house number was displayed as a novelty happy-faced sticker on the wheelie bins out by the front gate, the driveway was littered with abandoned toys and bikes, but there was no car inside the gates or outside on the path. It was 5.30 p.m., people were returning from work and the evening was already closing in. Next door an old woman was sitting at her front door on a kitchen chair catching the last of the evening sun. She was wearing a knee-length skirt, thick tights on her bumpy bandaged legs, and tartan slippers on her feet. She watched Kitty closely and nodded at her when she caught her eye.

Kitty rang the doorbell to Bridget Murphy's house and stepped down from the doorstep.

'They're having their dinner,' the old woman said. On Kitty's displaced interest in her, she continued, 'Chicken curry. They always have it on Thursdays. I can smell it in my house every week.' She ruffled up her nose.

Kitty laughed. 'You're not a fan of chicken curry?'

'Not of hers, I'm not,' she said, looking away from the house as if the very sight of it offended her. 'They won't hear you out here, they're a noisy lot.'

Kitty could hear that from where she stood. It sounded like there was an army of squealing kids dropping knives and clanging glasses. She didn't want to be rude by ringing again, particularly as she was disturbing a family dinner and she had the old woman as her audience.

'I'd ring again if I were you,' the neighbour said.

Happy to receive permission, Kitty pressed the doorbell again.

'Who are you looking for anyway? Him or her? Because he's not in, doesn't get home until seven most days. A banker.' She rolled up her nose again.

'I'm here to see Bridget.'

The old woman frowned. 'Bridget Murphy?'

Kitty checked her notepad again even though she had memorised practically the entire list, but she did that now, checked everything twenty times and then still wasn't sure.

'Bridget doesn't live there any more,' the old woman said just as the front door opened and a flushed-looking mother of the army stared at a confused Kitty.

'Oh. Hello,' Kitty said.

'Can I help you?'

'I hope so. I'm looking for Bridget Murphy but I've just learned that she might not live here any longer.'

'She doesn't,' the old woman said. 'I told you that. I already told her that, Mary.'

'Yes, that's right,' the mother said, ignoring the old lady.

'See?'

'Do you know how I could contact Bridget?'

'I don't know Bridget at all. We bought the house last year but perhaps Agnes here could help.'

Kitty apologised for disturbing her dinner, the door closed and they heard Mary's ironic shout for silence rattle through the building.

She turned to Agnes. Kitty guessed Agnes knew the business of most people on the street. A journalist's dream. She contemplated climbing over the knee-high wall that separated them but decided Agnes might consider it rude so she walked down the path, out the gate, in at Agnes's gate and up the path again.

Agnes looked at her oddly. 'You could have just climbed over the wall.'

'Do you know where Bridget lives?'

'We lived next door to each other for forty years. She's a great woman. A bunch of selfish good-for-nothings her children turned out to be. To hear them talk you'd think they think they're royalty. Far from how they were reared, I'll tell you that. She had a fall is all,' she said angrily. 'She tripped. Who doesn't take a tumble now and then? But oh no, it was off to the nursing home for poor Birdie just so that lot could sell that house and spend the money on another skiing holiday.' She grumbled to herself, her mouth moving up and down angrily, her false teeth sloshing around inside.

'Do you know which nursing home she's in?'

'St Margaret's in Oldtown,' she said, sounding angry at the whole of Oldtown.

'Have you visited her?'

'Me? No. The furthest I can get is the shop at the end of the road and then I have to figure out how to get back,' she laughed, a wheezy sound that resulted in a cough.

'Do you think she'd see me?'

Agnes looked at her then. 'I know your face.'

'Yes,' Kitty said, not proudly this time.

'You did the show about the tea.'

'Yes, I did,' Kitty brightened up.

'I drink Barry's,' she said. 'So did my mother. And her mother.'

Kitty nodded solemnly. 'A good choice, I believe.'

Agnes's eyes narrowed as she made a decision. 'Tell her Agnes said you were all right. And that I was asking after her. We go way back, me and her.' She looked off into the distance again, reflective. 'You can tell her I'm still here.'

When Kitty was leaving, the door next to Agnes's opened again and four kids came firing out as if from a cannon, their mother quickly following to shout her orders. Agnes called out, 'And tell her they cut her rose bush down. Butchered it, they did.'

Mary threw Agnes a look of absolute loathing and Kitty smiled and lifted her hand in a farewell. En route to her next destination, Kitty looked at the two names she had visited that day. Sarah McGowan and Bridget Murphy.

Story theory: people who have had to move home against their will?

That was definitely a theme she could relate to. Her and Colin Maguire.

CHAPTER SEVEN

Due to a very limited bus service to Oldtown, Kitty had no choice but to get a taxi and with a driver hailing from the opposite side of the county, a fact he pointed out many times, they had to stop three times for directions as they drove down a series of country lanes that seemed to get ever narrower. In the heart of the countryside they finally reached St Margaret's, a 1970s bungalow that had been extended on all sides to meet its new requirements as a nursing home. The south-facing conservatory to the right was set as a dining room, an extension to the left and then further to the back filled with couches and armchairs. The gardens were extensively landscaped, with benches placed all around and colourful hanging baskets hung from the sides of the house. If she ever saw her again, Kitty would be sure to tell Agnes that her friend Bridget was in a good place. It was 7 p.m., only thirty minutes of visiting time remaining, and having not had the greatest luck so far with hunting down her subjects, Kitty was really hoping Bridget would agree to see her.

She asked at the desk for Bridget Murphy and waited while a stern-faced nurse, her hair in a severe bun, checked the visitors' book. Kitty squirmed as she watched her, trying to figure out how to tell her she wasn't expected and figure out her best way of manipulating the situation. To her right was the common room, busy with visitors, and on-going chess games. A middle-aged woman with dreadlocks was in the centre of the floor forcing three old men, one using a walking frame, another wearing hearing aids in both ears, to play Simon Says.

'No, Wally!' she screeched with laughter. 'I didn't say "Simon Says"!'

The old man with the hearing aids looked confused.

'You have to sit down now, you're out of the game. You're out of the game!' she shouted even louder.

She abandoned the two remaining men standing with their hands on their heads and came to the common room door. 'Molly,' she called, looking Kitty up and down as though surveying the competition, 'where is Birdie?'

'She's having a lie-down,' a young nurse with blue hair and blue nail varnish responded in a bored tone, without looking up from a chart.

'Should I go to her room?' dreadlocked woman asked. 'I've brought my angel cards I was telling her about.'

Molly looked at Kitty and lifted an eyebrow as if to say, 'No wonder she's lying down.'

Dreadlocked woman looked slighted at that, like a little girl who'd lost her playmate.

Molly sighed. 'Let me go check on her and I'll see if she wants to come to the common room.'

While waiting, dreadlocked woman turned round and spoke loudly to an old man near her. 'Seth, would you like to hear a poem I wrote this week?' Seth looked a little weary as she sat down anyway before he'd answered and began reciting her poem like a six-year-old at elocution lessons.

Kitty watched Molly wander down the hall, pause outside a bathroom, lean against the door where she studied her nails. Kitty smiled to herself. After the count of ten seconds Molly returned and called to the dreadlocked woman, 'She's having a nap.'

'Seth needs new batteries,' the nurse dealing with Kitty said to Molly when she returned to the desk.

Molly glanced up at dreadlocked woman reciting her poem. 'Why don't we leave him battery free for a few minutes?' Kitty liked Molly's style.

'I'm sorry, what did you say your name is again?' the plump stern-faced nurse finally looked up from the book.

'Kath—' she stalled, realising she couldn't bring herself to say her usual professional name. 'Kitty Logan,' she finally said.

'And you've made an appointment to visit Bridget?'

'Actually, no, I haven't. I just thought I'd call by,' she said as sweetly as she could. Though how anybody could just drop by this place was anybody's guess. A missile couldn't be programmed to target this place.

'We only allow visits by appointment,' the nurse said firmly, snapping the visitors' book closed without a smile, and Kitty knew immediately this one would be tricky.

'But I'm here now, and I've come all this way. Could you tell her that I'm here and ask if she'd like to see me? You can tell her that Agnes said I'm all right,' she smiled.

'That's against our policy, I'm afraid. You'll have to come back if Brenda wishes—'

'Bridget. I'm here to see Bridget Murphy,' Kitty said, her temper rising. She had had no luck with making contact with anyone on the list so far, time was running out, so was her patience, and she had no intention of leaving the building without seeing Bridget or at least without smacking somebody in the face, she didn't care who, but preferably the battle-axe in front of her.

'Well, now . . .' the nurse put her hands on her rotund hips and looked as if she was about to give Kitty a good spanking.

'Bernadette,' the blue-haired nurse interrupted, 'I'll deal with this. Why don't you go see to Seth, he much prefers you.'

Bernadette looked at her, annoyed she'd interrupted her telling-off, then backed down, gave Kitty a final snarl and went to Seth's aid.

'Follow me,' Molly said, and she turned and headed into the extension to the back.

Great, she was doing the walk of shame; they didn't even have the nerve to throw her out the front door. When they stepped out into the lush landscaped gardens Molly finally spoke.

'Don't mind her, she was an army sergeant in her last life and a frustrated one in this. Birdie hates visiting hour. That hippie inside annoys everyone but always seems to focus on Birdie. I'd punch her lights out if I could. She's nothing better to be doing with her time, she's either hugging trees or annoying old people, and if she annoys the trees as much as she hugs the old people, she's not appreciated all that much. Over here.' She led Kitty under an archway to a bench. 'Don't get me wrong, it's great that people come and visit,' she assured her so as not to insult her. 'Sometimes they do get a bit lonely here and, you know, sane people would be a good start.'

They heard the piano and then the dreadlocked woman starting up 'This Little Light of Mine'.

'Doesn't Bridget have visitors in the evening?'

'Her family can only visit on weekends. We're not exactly easy to get to, as I'm sure you discovered. But don't worry, that doesn't bother Birdie in the slightest, in fact I think she likes it. Make yourself comfortable and I'll bring her to you.'

She wandered off in the direction of some tiny adjoining bungalows. Kitty got her notebook and recorder ready, wondering what the story could be.

Bridget appeared. She was a graceful woman who moved slowly, aided by a cane, but appeared more like a ballet instructor than an old person. Her grey hair was pinned back neatly, not a strand out of place, she had a gentle smile on her pink lipsticked lips and a curious expression in her eyes as she studied Kitty and tried to figure out if she should know her visitor. She was well dressed, sophisticated and looked like she'd made an effort despite the fact she'd had no intention of meeting anybody that day.

Kitty stood to greet her.

'I'll be back with your tea, Birdie. Kitty?'

Kitty nodded yes please, and turned to Bridget. 'I'm so glad to finally meet you, Bridget,' Kitty said, surprised to discover she genuinely meant it. She had finally made contact with someone from Constance's list. She felt connected to her friend, ready to embark on the journey Constance had set out for herself but didn't have time to finish.

Bridget seemed relieved. 'Call me Birdie, please. Ah, so we haven't met,' she stated, rather than asked. There was a light Cork lilt in her accent.

'No, we haven't.'

'I pride myself on my good memory but there are times when it lets me down,' she smiled.

'Well, not this time. We haven't met. But we do have somebody in common who you have met, or at least been in contact with, which is why I'm here. Her name is Constance Dubois.' Kitty realised she was perched on the edge of the bench, her anticipation high. She waited for Birdie's eyes to light up but it didn't happen and again a cloud lowered over Kitty's enthusiasm. To jolt her memory she took out a copy of *Etcetera* from her bag. 'I work for this magazine, Constance Dubois was the editor. She had an idea for a story, a story which you were part of.'

'Oh dear.' Birdie took her glasses up and looked up from the magazine. 'I'm afraid you've got the wrong person. I'm sorry you came all this way. I haven't heard of your friend . . . '

'Constance.'

'Yes, Constance. I'm afraid I haven't received any communications from her at all.' She looked at the magazine as if trying to recall a memory. 'And this magazine, I haven't seen this before either. I'm very sorry.'

'You weren't in contact with Constance Dubois at all?'

'I'm afraid not, dear.'

'You didn't receive a letter from her or an email or a message of any kind?' Kitty's desperation was oozing from her pores and so was her frustration; she was just short of asking Birdie if she had any history of Alzheimer's in the family.

'No, dear, I'm sorry. I would remember that. I've been here for six months, so unless she contacted the battle-axe at reception who insisted she have an appointment, I certainly didn't receive any contact from her.' Birdie studied the magazine again. 'I would have remembered something as exciting as a magazine editor contacting me.'

Molly came with the tea and winked at Birdie as she handed it over. There was a smell that was very unlike tea to Kitty.

'She's my one accomplice in here, the rest are as rigid as anything,' Birdie smiled, sipping on her brandy.

Kitty was disappointed to learn her tea was in fact tea; she could do with something stronger. 'Constance would have been in touch with you over six months ago, a year or more ago, in fact, when you were living in Beaumont.' On her surprised reaction to the knowledge of her previous home, Kitty explained, 'I called to your house earlier today. Agnes told me you were here.'

'Ah, so that's the link with Agnes,' she smiled. 'Agnes Dowling. The nosiest old bat I've ever known, and the most loyal woman I've ever met too. How is she?'

'She misses you. She doesn't seem to be too happy with the new neighbours.'

Birdie chuckled. 'Agnes and I made a good team. We lived beside each other for forty years. We helped each other out a lot over the years.'

'She wants to visit you but she's not too mobile at the moment.'

'Ah, yes,' Birdie said softly.

It struck Kitty how, on coming to live in a home, it seemed almost as if each habitant had to say goodbye to life outside the walls. They would receive visitors and have day trips, perhaps weekends or holidays, but the life that they once knew, the people who once surrounded them, were no longer a part of them. She thought of Sarah McGowan, qualified accountant, now farming watermelons on the other side of the world.

Story theory – saying goodbye to old lives, hello to new lives. Castaways?

Birdie looked at Kitty's note nervously. Kitty was used to that: people were often afraid of speaking to journalists, afraid of saying something wrong.

'My editor, and friend, Constance, passed away a few weeks ago,' Kitty started to explain. 'She was going to do a story, one which she left in my hands but which she never had the opportunity to fully explain to me. Your name was on the list of people she wanted to write about.'

'My name?' Birdie seemed surprised. 'But why would I be of interest to her?'

'You tell me,' Kitty urged. 'Is there something that happened in your life that you think she would have been particularly interested in? Something she would have been aware of? Something you talked about publicly that she could have seen or heard from somebody else? Or perhaps your paths crossed along the way somewhere. She was fifty-four years old, French accent, tough as nails.' Kitty smiled to herself.

'My goodness, where would I even start?' Birdie began. 'I have never done anything particularly special in my life that I can think of. I never saved a life, won any awards . . .' she trailed off. 'I can't see why I would be of interest to her.'

'Would you be willing to let me write the story about you?' Kitty asked. 'Would you allow me to ask you questions and perhaps find the thing that Constance thought was so special?'

Birdie's cheeks pinked. 'Goodness, I was getting ready for a chess game with Walter, I didn't think a magazine would be suddenly doing a story on me.' She laughed lightly and sounded like a little

71

girl. 'But I would be more than happy to try to help you with your story. I don't know how much help I will be, though.'

'Great,' Kitty said, not feeling as happy as she should be. She had finally found somebody from the list but that person had no idea of the story. It was getting curiouser and curiouser.

Birdie sensed her hesitancy. 'How many are on the list?'

'There are one hundred names in total.'

'My goodness,' she whispered. 'And do none of them know what the story is about?'

'You're the first I found.'

'I hope you have more luck with the others.'

Me too, she thought, but didn't say it out loud.

With a lot of encouragement from Kitty, Birdie talked about her life, starting from her childhood and going all the way up to her current life. Kitty kept it general, making a note of where she would like to question her further on her next visit. Birdie was shy at first, as most people were when talking about themselves, leaving out information, talking more about others than herself, but she seemed to warm up by the end, the wheels of her memory bank moving up a gear with each new question.

Birdie was eighty-four years old and had grown up in a small chapel town in County Cork, in the southwest of Ireland. Her father had been a school teacher, as strict at home as he was in the school, and her mother had died when Birdie was a child. She had three sisters and one brother and when she was eighteen she had moved to Dublin to live with a family to mind their children. That same year she met her husband, Niall. They married and immediately started having children. She had seven children, six boys and one girl, ranging in age now between sixty-five and forty-six. Her daughter was the youngest. At the age of thirty-eight Birdie had her last child. This seemed less to do with family planning than with her husband having to sleep on the couch. The seven children were raised first in Cabra and then in Beaumont, in the home Kitty had visited earlier that evening, with Agnes sounding more like the second parent who helped raise Birdie's children, taking the place of the husband who was busy with his job in the Civil Service.

Though Birdie's life was indeed interesting, nothing jumped out to Kitty as being particularly extraordinary about it. Birdie seemed embarrassed by it all at the end, apologising for not being more exciting, while Kitty reassured her over and over that her life was more than interesting, that she was an inspiring woman who lots of women could look up to and relate to.

On the way home Kitty glanced at her notes and felt guilty for feeling that Birdie's beautiful rich family life was not enough.

From the bench in the now darkened garden lit by pathway lights and overhead lanterns, Birdie remained outside long after Kitty had left her, feeling aware of the lack of excitement in her life, feeling her simple answers had done nothing to inspire the lady who had spent an hour with her, though she had done her best to try to convince her her life was indeed interesting. Birdie had no doubt that it wasn't interesting to any other person. It had at times been barely interesting to her but it was her life and she had liked it; had never been in it for more than she could handle. Birdie couldn't help but retreat into her memory that evening and she stayed there for the entirety of the chess game, so that Walter had checkmate almost as soon as they started.

Birdie would be eighty-five years old the following week; of course she had stories, of course she had secrets, everybody did. It was a case of trying to decide which one she felt Kitty would like to hear and, after all this time, which one Birdie wished to tell.

Kitty ignored Pete's call on her way home in another expensive taxi. She didn't want to have to tell him she was nowhere with the story. She couldn't bear the condescending tone in his voice, the judgement, the doubt that trickled through each of his words.

She placed her phone on silent and as a result missed another call. When she picked up the voicemail it was a woman speaking so loudly the taxi driver gave Kitty a look, and she had to turn down the volume.

'Hi, Kitty, it's Gaby O'Connor, Eva Wu's publicity agent. We received your call today. Sorry we missed you, we've just been so busy. Eva would be only too happy to give you an interview. We're based in Galway but we'll be in Dublin tomorrow. In fact, Eva's doing an interview tomorrow in Arnotts on Henry Street if you'd like to come along and meet us there.'

Eva Wu. Number three of the one hundred names. She'd made contact with her second person, and this one had a publicity agent and was doing a television interview. Who on earth was she and how on earth had Kitty missed her?

When she arrived home after an exhausting day feeling a bit more upbeat about her story, she found dog turd smeared all over her front door.

CHAPTER EIGHT

'I'm so sorry to drag you over so late,' Kitty apologised to Steve as he got out of his car. She'd wiped her eyes roughly while she waited and now hoped it wasn't obvious that she'd been crying. 'I didn't mean for you to come over at all, I just didn't know who else to call. The dry-cleaners said they'd evict me next month if I didn't sort it out and I didn't want to call the guards and I didn't know who else to call. Sorry,' she repeated.

'Kitty, shut up saying sorry, okay?' he said gently, putting his arm around her shoulder and giving her as much of an embrace as his PDA-hating body would allow him, and though it was more the kind of hug a footballer would give another she appreciated that he even touched her. 'What did they do this time?'

She didn't need to answer, the smell hit as soon as they stepped in the stairwell.

'Oh God . . .' He pulled the neck of his sweater up over his mouth and nose.

It took them twenty minutes of much gagging and retching to clean the door and it seemed it would take eternity to get rid of the stink. As a further apology and thanks, Kitty treated Steve to dinner in a nearby bistro.

'I have to wash my hands again,' Steve said, rolling up his nose in disgust, 'I can still smell it on me. I don't think I can touch food.'

'You've cleaned your hands six times,' she laughed, watching him disappear to the bistro toilet.

'So how is everything with you? Is Victoria Beckham's new line Fit or Shit?' she asked as soon as he'd returned.

'Ha ha,' he said, without cracking a smile. 'I wouldn't know, seeing as I'm no longer a slave to her fashion.'

Steve wasn't a slave to any particular fashion but his own style, which wasn't especially bad but it was consistent, had pretty much been the same since their college days, though the fabrics were now more expensive and he tended to wash his clothes more regularly. He was thirty-four years old, with a mop of unruly black curly hair on top of his head, a style he'd had since college and which, like him, never seemed able to be tamed. His curls often hung in front of his blue eyes so that he was constantly jerking his head to move his fringe away, having long ago given up on brushing it away with his fingers. He was always unshaven, his stubble a designer length, but Kitty had never seen him freshly shaven or reach beard stage. He lived in leather jackets and jeans and would have appeared more at home reviewing the alternative music scene than as a sports journalist, or at least a frustrated sports journalist. Even when going to matches he never wore a jersey, his love for the game not having to be proved by his T-shirt. He was the eternal student, never seeming to have any money and sharing houses and flats with unusual characters, chopping and changing accommodation according to their recent behaviour. He was currently living in the suburbs in a nice semi-detached three-bedroom house with a married couple who needed help from a third party to meet the mortgage payments of their negative equity. Living in non-violation of the married couple's strict household code for the past six months, Steve found his lifestyle now mirrored theirs, and it was almost like he'd grown up a little.

'Actually,' he shifted in his chair, a movement that told Kitty he was preparing to say something he deemed interesting, 'I no longer work for the paper.'

'What?'

'I no longer work for the paper,' he said in exactly the same tone.

'Yes, I heard you but . . . they fired you?'

'No,' he said, insulted. 'I left.'

'Why?'

'Why? I thought that would be obvious. Because a million reasons, but mainly because you were right about what you said a few weeks ago—'

'No, no, no,' she interrupted, not wanting to hear whatever it was that she'd said. 'I was wrong. Completely wrong. Don't ever let anything I say be of any value to you in your life at all.'

He smiled. 'Mostly it isn't.'

'Good.'

'But you were right about one thing. I was hardly setting the world alight by writing the stories I was writing, and even then the editor would change them so much I could hardly call them my own. And the thing is, Kitty, I never wanted to set the world alight with my writing. I just like sports. I like to watch sports, talk about sports, I like to read about sports and I wanted to be one of those people who wrote about it. It was never about anything else.'

'So who are you writing for now?'

'No one.'

'I thought you left so you could write about sport?'

'I left because I *couldn't* write about sports. So what's the point in staying there? Writing ridiculous articles that aren't even true about people I have never met and have no interest in is not a job I want. It suits Kyle, who leaves meetings to watch breaking headlines on *E! News*. It's for Charlotte who wants to be in every VIP room in every club in the world so she can stand at the wall and write about people she has odd obsessions with. The morning after our . . . chat, I went into work and the first thing I was asked to do was write one hundred and fifty words on how a certain footballer was allegedly having an affair with a glamour model.'

'Oooh, who?' Kitty leaned in.

'It's not the point,' he said brusquely. 'I didn't want to write about it. It's not what I'm about. Never mind not writing ground-breaking stories, stories that do nothing but numb the human mind is not my gameplan either.'

'Yeah, but who was the footballer?'

'Kitty.'

'Okay, fine. Who was the glamour model?'

'Not. The. Point.'

She sat back, disappointed.

'How could I lecture you about your stories when that's the work that I was doing? I have more self-respect than writing that crap. That kind of journalism . . . it was killing my soul.'

Kitty tried not to wince at the constant digging in her ribs. 'I get it, it was an honest, self-sacrificing move, aimed to take a stance at the smut that the public are being forced to ingest, which is very honourable of you and I respect that, now cut the crap and tell me who the footballer and the slag were?'

'I'm going to throw this prawn cocktail at you.'

'You wouldn't dare.'

He picked up a prawn, which was more of a mini shrimp, placed it on his fork, held it back like a catapult and let it go. The prawn flew through the air and landed on Kitty's boob, the Marie Rose sauce splodging on the satin.

She gasped. 'You little prick.'

'Don't talk about the size of my prick.'

'My top is stained.'

'So take it to the dry-cleaners. I know one that's open all night.'

'I'm going to stink of fish.'

'Will go nicely with the shit.'

And they were right back at college lunch hour, having mean-ingless back-and-forth slagging matches.

She dipped her serviette in her water and ignored him for five minutes while she dabbed at her top, making it worse. 'So what are you going to do now? It's great timing to be an unemployed wannabe sports journalist.'

'A-ha. That's where you're wrong. I'm not unemployed. I'm working on the allotments.'

'No way.'

'Yes way.'

'Your dad's allotments?'

'Yes.'

'But you hate the allotments.'

'Hat*ed*.'

'And you hate your dad.'

'Hat*ed*. Again, there's a distinct difference. Besides, now that he's paying me a wage he's not so bad. He's needed help around the place since he put his back out, so I'm the go-to man. Looking for a rotavator? I'm your man. Looking for fertiliser? A tool shed? A polytunnel? Just give me a call. Instead of being cooped up all day in a sweat box, I get to be outdoors.'

'You hate daylight. It does something to your vampire skin.'

'Kitty,' he warned, lifting another prawn.

'Okay, okay, I'm just shocked. You've made some very big changes for a guy who I remember changed his underwear on a weekly basis, and this is a lot to take in.'

Another shrimp missile was fired but this time Kitty dodged it. 'What made you want to suddenly work with your dad? Last time you mentioned him, you said that was it, you had cut all ties with him.'

'It's been going on for a while. We've been slowly getting in contact with each other.' Steve distracted himself with more bread, avoiding her eyes; he was never comfortable talking about anything personal. He mumbled the next part quite well. 'Then Katja and Dad met and they surprisingly get along, and . . . '

He rattled on about the change in his life, none of which Kitty heard as she was still stuck on the word 'Katja'.

'Why are you looking at me like that?'

She realised he'd stopped talking.

'Oh. Well. I thought I heard you say the name "Katja" and I got confused.'

'I did.'

'*Katja*,' she repeated loudly as though he were deaf.

'Yes,' he smiled, amused at her.

'The girl you went out for dinner with a few months ago?'

'Yes, and who I'm still going out with,' he confirmed, his cheeks turning pink and giving it all away.

Their main course arrived – two beef fillets – but suddenly Kitty didn't feel hungry. 'Katja,' she repeated. 'You never mentioned you two were going out.'

'Well, we are.'

'Like boyfriend and girlfriend?'

He rolled his eyes. 'You never mentioned you'd broken up with Glen.'

'Because you found out before I did.'

'I did?'

'The coffee machine.'

Realisation passed over his face. 'He just left?'

'Something like that.'

'He was a prick anyway.'

'I thought you liked him.'

Steve shook his head, mouth full.

She sighed. 'Did anyone like him?'

He swallowed. 'You did.'

'I was hoping for more people than that.'

'Crusty liked him.'

They laughed. Crusty was Steve's fourteen-year-old dog who he'd taken in from a shelter four years ago. No one had known his name but he had looked crusty then and even after a wash, his appearance never altered very much. It was the perfect name. Despite getting on in years, Crusty always managed to find the energy to hump Glen's leg, which had always disgusted Glen and probably caused him silently to question his sexuality along with everything else in life he over-analysed, such as what kind of a woman he had found himself living with after the Colin Maguire case.

'So how long have you been together? Two months?'

'Five.'

'Five? Jesus, Steve, you might as well get married. I should buy a hat.'

'Don't. They give away your Spock ears.'

She laughed. 'This is the Romanian girl?'

'Croatian.'

'Right. She's a painter?'

'Photographer.'

'Right.' She studied him.

'What?' he laughed self-consciously as though he was a twelve-year-old boy who'd just been caught with his first girlfriend.

'Nothing.'

'Come on.'

'I don't know, Steve,' she cut into her meat, 'you've changed. You no longer write about Victoria Beckham and you have a girlfriend. I think . . . '

'You think what?'

'I don't know, I might be jumping the gun here, but I *think* there's a possibility you might not be gay after all.'

A chip was hurled at her head.

Kitty spent the remainder of the meal eating as though she had a chip stuck in the back of her throat. Food wasn't going down easily and she didn't know why. She used to find comfort in the fact that Steve had an appalling job that he hated and refused to settle down. His realising that changes needed to be made in his life, and then making them, was upsetting. She simply didn't want to be the only one with problems.

'How is your new story going?' he asked, finally filling the uncomfortable silence.

'Oh,' Kitty sighed, feeling drained by it already. 'I don't know. I met a very nice old lady tonight who told me about her very nice life and it's all sounding very nice, but nothing . . .' she scrunched her hands together, 'nothing meaty, nothing juicy. I need to dig around in her cupboard for a few skeletons or something. Something that's not so "very nice". This is my chance to prove myself to so many people – probably my *last* chance – and whatever it was that Constance saw, I'm sure as hell not seeing it. It's a little frustrating.'

Steve was quiet. She looked at him and his whole body had tensed up. His jaw had squared and he was looking at her as if he wanted to inflict physical pain on her.

'Have you spoken to Colin Maguire yet?'

'I will phone him right now if it stops you from saying whatever horrible thing is on the tip of your tongue.'

'So it's about you again,' he snapped. 'You apologising to him is all about you.' His sudden change of mood took her by surprise.

'I was joking, Steve, but go on, I see you're in the mood to rip me to shreds again.' Before he had the chance to do so, she dived in, 'Just so you know, I am truly sorry about what happened to him.'

'What *happened* to him? Something didn't just happen to him, Kitty, *you* caused it, you *actively* caused it, not some random unexplained unlucky event that just *happened*.'

'I know that! Okay, I phrased it wrong. I can't win with you. Of course I know it's my fault. I have a bloody conscience, you know. I will be sorry every single day for the rest of my life.'

'*After* the fact,' he said, confusing her. 'You're always sorry *after* you do something. You never think about how they feel or how you'd feel *before*. That's what annoys me. You've learned nothing from the Colin Maguire situation. Here you are interviewing a nice little old lady and her nice little story is not enough for you. You always want more.'

Kitty was so shocked by his mood swing that her eyes stung with hot frustrated tears. She looked around and tried to focus on everything else around her to stop the tears from falling. Kitty didn't cry easily but she was having an emotional time lately and she had never been so out of favour with Steve. His opinion was of high importance to her. She had heard her mother accuse her of everything under the sun since January but nothing – *nothing* – could affect her as much as one simple look of disappointment from Steve.

They finished their meat in silence, she paid the bill and they walked in silence to her flat.

'I'll make sure it's safe,' Steve said quietly, running up the stairs to check the area.

The door that led to the stairs up to her flat was always left open. As much as Kitty had pleaded with the landlords they couldn't lock it as it was the shared door to the second internal door, which led to the dry-cleaners. This meant that at any time of the day anybody could walk up the stairs to her door.

'It's okay,' he said, coming back down. 'Stinks of shit, though.'

'Thanks for coming over. I really appreciate it. Especially now that you have a girlfriend,' she teased childishly, elbowing him.

'She wants to meet you,' he said, softening.

'Yeah, cool, that would be great,' she said over-enthusiastically, and it was obvious. 'Well, I'd better get inside before somebody chucks a water balloon filled with vomit at my head. I'm glad you're happy, Steve.' She tried to make it sound jolly and genuine but all that she heard was her own voice saying, *Your happiness makes me jealous and unhappy, Steve. I am a bitter and twisted human being.*

She blocked her nose and mouth with her jacket as she ran up the steps to her flat and tried to convince herself that the unbearable stench was the reason for her crying.

CHAPTER NINE

'Here we are in Arnotts, on their new personal shopping floor, and with me is top super shopper to the stars Eva Wu and author of the internationally renowned blog, "Dedicated".'

Kitty stood to the side of the television camera along with Gaby, Eva's PR girl, and watched, along with the dozen other shoppers who had gathered at the sight of the camera. The first thing the head cameraman on *Thirty Minutes* had taught her on her first day of filming was that the camera was an 'asshole magnet'. As soon as you took it out in public it encouraged a plethora of ridiculous self-conscious behaviour from otherwise mostly normal people. Many of Kitty's pieces to camera had been destroyed by idiots standing behind her in her shot waving at their mothers.

Kitty was at the department store on Henry Street in Dublin to interview Eva Wu. Unable to sleep after her second confrontation with Steve, she had spent much of the night reading up about Eva and her blog. Gaby had been more than keen on her coming here today as she had phoned Kitty three times already that morning. As Gaby was a rather pushy, loud-mouthed, fast-talking stereotypical PR girl who made things happen even when nature and the universe conspired against making them happen, Kitty imagined Eva to be quite the opposite. She wasn't as loud as Gaby, and Kitty had to strain her ears to hear her voice. She appeared to be more reserved, quiet, but not shy.

Eva was being interviewed by one of the lead TV presenters of *The Scoop*, whose personal life was currently being played out on the front pages of the tabloid papers. *The Scoop* was a gossip and showbiz programme that also focused on beauty and fashion.

'So, Eva,' the presenter with the frozen forehead and overly plumped top lip said into her oversized microphone with *The Scoop*'s logo emblazoned across the front. 'Give us The Scoop, what was it like meeting Brad Pitt?'

Eva smiled politely. 'Sorry, Laura, but I, er, I didn't meet Brad Pitt.'

Laura looked down at her notes. 'Cut,' she said, her big smile fading immediately. She looked at the camerawoman. 'Let's start that again.' And on the count of three her smile was back on her face. 'So, Eva, give us The Scoop, what was it like meeting George Clooney?'

Eva looked rather nervously and a little angrily in Gaby's direction.

'I didn't actually meet George Clooney. What happened is that a company who were working with him contacted me and asked if I would buy a gift for him on their behalf.'

'Ooh, George Clooney, girls!' Laura pulled her microphone away from Eva's mouth and screeched into it excitedly, looking directly at the hand-held camera. The camera, almost in response to her excited squeal tilted and darted at an angle towards them both. Hoping to avoid an on-air collision, Eva jerked backwards on the high stool, not looking very cool in the process. Gaby held her head in her hands.

'So what did you buy him? An exclusive here on *The Scoop*.' Laura looked at the camera excitedly again and then back to Eva. 'Spill the beans!'

'I'm sorry to disappoint you,' Eva said pleasantly but coolly, 'but I declined the job, which really does explain my company ethos.' She brightened up then, excited to be talking about her baby. 'I developed "Dedicated" so that I can personally dedicate my time to finding the perfect gift for the perfect person. In order to do that, I like to spend time with the person so that I can really get a sense of what it is that their heart truly desires. I can't shop for someone I don't know or else how is it personal shopping?'

Gaby covered her head in her hands and cringed, directly in Eva's eyeline.

Laura's eyes had glazed over halfway through Eva's spiel and Kitty could bet her savings, not that there was much, that most if not all of what Eva had said would end up on the cutting-room floor. All Eva had to do was make a sexually derogatory comment about George Clooney and the producers of the show would have been delighted. Sincere as Eva sounded, to Kitty's critical and arguably cynical ear, she wasn't quite sure if she believed in Eva's ethos or if she really believed that Eva believed in her ethos, but her personal shopping idea was different and it stood out from the rest of the market. She supposed that's what companies were looking to do. It seemed quite a long way to go about doing something quite as simple as buying a present.

The man next to Eva was throwing her dagger looks at her last comment.

'Beside Eva, we have Arnotts' personal shopper, Jack Wilson. So, Jack, tell us about some of the things you'll be purchasing this year for your clients.'

'Well,' he looked directly at the camera, 'we have this Tom Ford iPad sleeve. Perfect for the man in your life who loves designer accessories. It will also keep the iPad protected from the sand on upcoming summer hols. It retails at one thousand five hundred euro, which is a great price for such a luxury.'

Eva's eyes widened.

'Stop it,' Gaby muttered under her breath and the sound man threw her a look.

'We also have this Coco Chanel umbrella. Perfect for the lady in your life who doesn't like to get wet.'

'Great for the frizzy-hair, girls,' Laura said to the camera, and the camera went wild in response, moving in so close to her face it almost headbutted her.

'And that retails at one thousand euro.'

Eva's mouth dropped, as did Kitty's, but Kitty wasn't currently on camera. She could feel Gaby raging beside her.

'What celebrities will you be shopping for?' Laura asked.

'Oh, we get them all in here.' Jack proceeded to list any stars who were known to be jetting into the Irish capital for summer concerts and Kitty noted his use of the word 'possibly' before he named anyone.

'Wow. Hear that guys? Madonna! Moving on, Eva, these sunglasses we see on the likes of Victoria Beckham and Katie Holmes, who would you see yourself buying these for?'

'Of my clients?'

'Come on, come on,' Gaby urged.

'Well, my client list is strictly private, I wouldn't—'

'Yes, but what *kind* of person would you buy these for?'

'Who would I buy sunglasses for?' She looked around as if someone was playing a trick on her.

'Worn by Victoria Beckham and Katie Holmes,' Laura said through gritted teeth. Eva's mouth opened and closed but no words would come out.

'Well, can I just say,' Jack jumped in, 'these glasses would be perfect for the women in your life who just love Victoria Beckham and Katie Holmes and who don't want the sun in their eyes this summer.'

'So there you have it, guys, top tips on how to buy the perfect gift for that extra special person in your life to help them feel like a celebrity.'

Cut.

Eva jumped off the stool.

'Jesus Christ,' Kitty heard Laura say to the camerawoman as they were packing up. 'What are we doing next? Vajazzling?'

'How to help them feel like a celebrity?' Eva said to Gaby

once they were outside on Henry Street. She wasn't shouting but her anger was obvious. 'Sunglasses? To make people feel like a celebrity? Jesus, Gaby!'

'Okay, so that was not the best booking I've ever made.'

'Not the best? Gaby, it was the worst. Of a very bad lot. How can I share what my business is about when you keep getting me publicity like this? The message is getting lost. Nobody is listening. They don't care about "Dedicated", they only care about my *celebrity* client list and *George Clooney*? What was that about?' Eva's voice was still quiet but her annoyance was clear. Knowing Eva wasn't yet aware of her presence, Kitty remained in the background, quite enjoying the display of Eva's true opinion of the show.

'It impresses people. It helps bookings,' Gaby shrugged.

'The fact that I did *not* buy a gift for George Clooney impresses people?'

'People mostly just listen to the questions.'

Eva closed her eyes and took deep breaths. 'I would rather not do interviews at all if these are the kind that we're getting.'

'It helps build your profile.'

'You think *that* helped?'

'Maybe not that.'

Eva groaned. 'All my hard work.' But Kitty could see she was calming down. 'We need publicity that allows me to *talk* about the gift of giving, how precious it is, how special it can be, particularly in these times when people are really struggling. It's not about how expensive something is – as a nation we've stopped giving lavish gifts – it's actually about *thinking* about what to give someone, how it can lift them when they're down, how they can feel loved and important and special just by one simple gesture.'

'I know, I know, you don't have to tell me all this, I know it all,' Gaby said, stuffing chewing gum into her mouth. If she wasn't talking it seemed her mouth needed to be moving up and down regardless.

'Do you?' Eva looked at Gaby.

'I'm shocked and appalled that you've asked me that,' she said dramatically, and Kitty felt that was for her benefit. 'How long have we been working together, Eva?'

'Too long?' Eva smiled.

'Anyway, your next appointment is here.'

'Where?'

'There.' She turned and looked at Kitty, who tried to move a few steps away to help save Eva's face but it was too late, Eva's cheeks pinked, embarrassed to have been overheard, particularly by a journalist.

'I'm so sorry, I didn't . . .' she looked pointedly at Gaby '. . . I *didn't know* you had arrived.'

Gaby took the heat again.

'That's okay, it was good for me to hear all that. I won't pretend I wasn't listening.'

'I'm so embarrassed. I'm a big fan of *Etcetera*. Huge. I read it every month. I was so glad when you called.'

'Thank you,' Kitty beamed. 'My editor was in touch with you last year I believe, Constance Dubois?'

'I'm familiar with Constance, but no, she wasn't in touch. Should she have been?' She looked at Gaby. 'Was she?'

Gaby shrugged. 'Not that I know of. I run everything by you.'

Kitty was new to their relationship but even she knew that wasn't true. Her heart dropped at the discovery that yet another person on the list hadn't been contacted by Constance. What was this list about? 'Well, would you be open to me doing a story on you?'

'Yes, of course. I mean, what's the story, or the angle, as you say?'

Kitty froze. That was an excellent question. 'The story is about you and, well, ninety-nine other people. It's about the thing that links you all together.'

'One hundred people?' Gaby seemed disappointed it wasn't solely about Eva. 'Who are the other people? Anyone we know?'

'No. Nobody you would know, I don't think. Though that's a

good question.' Kitty suddenly had a thought and rooted in her bag for her list of names. 'Are any of these names familiar to you?' She had been directing the question at Eva but Gaby pushed her head close to Eva's to check the names. Eva took her time reading through the names, Gaby was finished in three seconds.

'Nope,' Gabby said. 'Nobody. Can I have a copy of these names?'

'Why?'

'So I can look into who they are. I don't want to agree to this interview unless I know who my client is being associated with.'

It was actually a fair enough request but for all that, it took both Eva and Kitty by surprise.

'I have my moments,' Gaby smiled at Eva, in an 'I told you so' way.

'I don't think there's any need for that,' Eva said softly. 'Look, why don't we go for a coffee somewhere, just the two of us?' Gaby scowled. 'And we can talk about it all somewhere more relaxing than Henry Street at lunch hour.'

'Good idea,' Kitty said, relieved.

'The only thing is, I have an appointment with a client in thirty minutes in the IFSC, would you like to meet after that? Or we could walk and talk?'

'Or . . . I could come and watch you at work?'

Eva looked uncertainly at Gaby. If ever there was a time Eva needed Gaby to speak on her behalf it was then, as she clearly wasn't comfortable with the suggestion, but Gaby wasn't picking up on it. She was chewing her gum and staring at her blankly.

'What?'

'It would be a good opportunity for me to see how you really work,' Kitty said. 'You know, that you're not just a regular personal shopper.'

Eva smiled. 'You're good. Fine. Let's go.'

The IFSC, the Irish Financial Services Centre, was by the River Liffey along North Wall Quay and Custom House Quay. The centre employed fourteen thousand people and housed more than four hundred and thirty financial operations along with hotels, restaurants and shops. The address they were heading to was Molloy Kelly Solicitors in Harbourmaster Place, a large firm that dealt with banking law and commercial litigation, and the meeting Eva had lined up was with George Webb, partner in the firm. Kitty's Google told her that he was responsible for Banking Law, Insolvency, Bankruptcy and Corporate Recovery, Insurance Law, Defamation, Separation and Divorce.

'So are these usually the kinds of people you work for?' Kitty asked. 'Busy businessmen who don't have time to shop for their loved ones?'

Eva looked at her curiously. 'What makes you think that's the case here?'

'I've Googled him, I know his type. Work first, family second. They're so used to having people do things for them – their dry-cleaning, their shopping, their housework – that buying presents for their loved ones is not on their list of priorities.'

'Well, if that's the case, I won't be working for him.'

'Why not?'

'I would rather find someone who actually wants to find the perfect gift for a loved one as opposed to someone who couldn't be bothered. I choose my clients as much as they choose me,' she said, wide-eyed and sincere.

Kitty was immediately intrigued, both by Eva's philosophy and by her earnestness.

'I invest a lot of my time into my clients, Kitty,' Eva smiled. 'I need to know that they care about who they're giving a gift to, or else how can I possibly care? I'm sure it's like you writing a story. If you don't care, how can the reader?'

Kitty thought about that. The girl spoke the truth.

After a ten-minute wait in a sparkling marble reception, the elevator pinged and a young gentleman in a dapper suit with pink tie and handkerchief called them from the lift. Kitty immediately guessed that this was not George Webb; he reminded her more of a younger Julian Clary. His eyebrows were tweezed to perfection, his skin glowed as if it had been carefully exfoliated and nurtured since childhood, she didn't detect make-up but there was a sheen from his high cheekbones that made her jealous.

'I'm Nigel,' the camp dapper young man introduced himself to Kitty, though his words were clipped and his hand wasn't extended. 'I'll take you to the office. Who are you?'

'Kath— Kitty Logan,' she stumbled again, not yet used to using her nickname as her professional name.

'And what are you doing here today, Kath-Kitty?' he asked, mocking her mistake.

'Work experience,' Kitty lied sweetly for no particular reason other than to annoy him.

'For the mature student, I assume,' he preened, not believing her.

Eva just smiled and shook her head at the two of them.

He led them to a waiting room. 'Wait here, he'll be with you shortly.'

Eva sat down and Kitty wandered around the room examining everything. They were very different creatures, that was for sure. Eva was the type to do what she was told, follow orders and be polite. Kitty couldn't, she never could. She always felt there was something she wasn't being let in on, something further to what she saw, and she always wanted to know what that was. She had always been profoundly curious as a child, trying to see through façades and uncover secrets people hid away for no reason other than because *they* felt the secrets meant something, though in reality they probably didn't to anybody else. At college she would separate from her friends on nights out and usually end up sitting beside the person she considered to be the most interesting, challenging, complex person in the room, while she listened to their fascinating stories. She sought out unusual minds, loved hearing both the mundane and fantastical. She didn't believe that what you saw was necessarily all there was and she felt a burning desire to discover what was really beyond the layers of each person. It was this fascination and, indeed, love for people that she brought to her stories in *Etcetera* and perhaps this love for people had not transferred well in her stories on *Thirty Minutes*. While working there and covering investigative stories, her love had changed to distrust, a need to know what people were hiding from her. Her usual skills of simple conversation and understanding had been altered to game playing, trying to get people to speak without their realising it, trying to get quotes from people who didn't wish to be quoted. She went about telling stories in a completely different way.

She paused at this sudden insight into herself, thinking Steve perhaps had been right. Steve, her long-time friend, whom she rarely had a deep conversation with, had known more about her than she had known herself. She felt goose bumps on her skin all of a sudden and looked up to see what had caused them.

She noticed then that Eva was watching her as she moved around the room examining the art on the walls but really examining herself, and this all of a sudden made Kitty feel uncomfortable. Observing was *her* job, the cloak of invisibility that came when watching others was what helped her gain insight, and Eva was taking that role from her. It was unnerving, unnatural for a watcher to be watched and it put her on edge. Kitty gave up prowling around the room and sank into one of the leather chairs.

The door opened and George Webb entered the room.

'Hello,' he said, a big smile with perfect teeth greeting the women as he looked from Kitty to Eva. 'Ms Wu, I assume,' he said, looking at Eva. It was the obvious choice. She was oriental, her long hair thick and silky, and so black it almost gave off a blue hue where the light hit. Her skin was flawless, she barely wore any make-up, but she didn't need to: she was blemish free and strikingly pretty.

'Well, it's not me,' Kitty joked.

'This is Kath-Kitty Logan,' Nigel said, joining them in the room.

'She's a journalist for *Etcetera*.' He raised a perfect eyebrow at her as if to say she couldn't get one past him.

George Webb seemed confused.

'It's a magazine,' Nigel explained. 'Not one you'd read.'

'But *you* do,' Kitty smiled at Nigel.

'No. I Googled you.'

Kitty laughed. 'I'm doing a story on Ms Wu,' Kitty explained. 'But please don't worry, everything will be about her, not her clients. No names will be mentioned. I simply want to get an idea of how she works.' If the story was indeed about how Eva worked, or if it was about something else entirely. So far, Kitty had no clue whatsoever but she tried to sound confident in her sale.

George Webb thought about it. 'Okay,' he said. 'Sounds fine to me. You're a popular lady,' he added, sitting opposite Eva and studying her.

George was striking, extremely handsome, well groomed in that modern Irishman way, with two separate eyebrows, tweezed nose hairs, attention to the finer detail of his face without embarrassment. He wore a smart suit, nothing too elaborate, but stylish and fitted. Eva was looking at him with the face of somebody who was looking at something beautiful, just as he was looking at her. The mutual attraction was obvious. It was as if Kitty wasn't even in the room, which was how she liked it – when she was working, at least. She was going to enjoy this one.

'I got your details from Nigel,' George explained. 'He told me you were the best.'

Nigel, who was making them coffee, threw them a look, annoyed. Kitty knew he was the reason they were there when he had gone out of his way to be so entertainingly rude.

'Well, that's very nice of Nigel,' Eva said softly, genuinely moved.

'I also believe you worked with a neighbour of mine, well, a neighbour here at work. Elizabeth Toomey?' George continued.

'Ah, yes.' Eva's eyes lit up. 'She works across the road in PricewaterhouseCoopers.'

'Did you hear she got a promotion in January?'

'Yes, I heard. I was delighted for her.'

'Her boss must really have liked that gift you got for him.'

Eva immediately closed up. Kitty could see the transformation right before her, like an insect going into a cocoon. George could sense it too.

'I think she deserved it. It appeared to me that she worked extremely hard,' was all Eva said.

'I think your gift helped,' he laughed.

Kitty was surprised at him. He was clever enough to leave it alone but he couldn't, he was desperate to find out and his desperation showed. Knowing Eva's philosophy on client confidentiality, Kitty feared this did not bode well for the charming George.

Eva just smiled.

'So what was it?' he asked, and looked at Kitty. 'I bet you want to know.'

Kitty held her hands up as if to back out of it. 'I'm merely an observer here.'

A gift that could get someone a promotion? Of course she wanted to know, and she wanted to know where she could buy it too. The sound was so light she could have imagined it but she was sure she heard a light snort as Nigel put the coffee cup down before her.

Nigel stepped in to explain. 'What Mr Webb brought you here for today was to discuss his upcoming family gathering. They're having a big reunion. Lots of people coming together, it's very exciting for them all,' he said drily and Eva, Kitty and George couldn't help but laugh. 'His sister is also getting married, it's his grandfather's eightieth birthday and they've decided to put it all into the same wonderful celebration day. Mr Webb quite simply needs your help.'

'Thanks, Nigel,' George said, and on that note Nigel left the room. George looked at his watch and seemed concerned.

Kitty sensed their time was up. Nigel had done what he was

supposed to do, George had politely made time for the woman and now it was over. She drank her coffee quickly.

George looked at Eva. 'What do you think?'

'I'm sorry, what do I think about what?'

'About taking the job.'

'Where are your family based?'

George seemed confused. 'Cork.'

'When is the event?'

'Here's the thing, I haven't been terribly organised. It's next week. Friday. But Nigel – or I – can give you all the details you're looking for.' He leaned forward, his face intent. If Eva was any less beautiful, Kitty suspected George would have left the room a long time ago.

'That's very close. I usually take a few weeks at the very least.'

'Weeks?' George's surprise reflected Kitty's feelings exactly.

'How many gifts are you thinking of?'

'Oh, let's see, Nigel has all these details but . . . one for my grandfather's birthday, and one for my sister and her husband-to-be.' He concentrated on a bit of invisible fluff on his trouser leg and picked at it and flicked it to the ground before finding another. 'Oh, and there's one other for another person.'

Kitty felt genuine disappointment at that, not for herself – George had barely looked her way since he'd entered the room, his attention had been entirely on Eva – and not just for business reasons. Kitty had to bite the inside of her cheeks to stop herself from saying anything. It was obvious who the other person was, but he had been so charming, and though Eva was professional and a woman of few words she had clearly been responsive to him. Kitty could see that, and now there was a nice little connection between the two, which just made him saying what he had to say all the more awkward.

'For your girlfriend?' Eva asked, professionally.

'Yes.' He cleared his throat. 'It's a one-year thing,' he practically mumbled.

One final-year thing, Kitty thought to herself.

'An anniversary,' Eva said, making a note in her book. 'Let me just explain how I work, Mr Webb—'

'Call me George, please.'

'George,' she smiled. The connection was back and Kitty was invisible again. 'I like to spend time with the people I'm buying gifts for. I like to see who they really are, what it is they really want and I choose items designed solely for them. I'm not sure if your assistant explained that to you.'

'No he didn't.' George seemed uncomfortable with that. 'I could just give you a budget of say, three thousand? And you could find something for them within that budget. Do you work on an hourly basis? I'm not sure how this works, because if you do, it really doesn't matter about spending time with them, I'm willing to pay you a fee that makes it worth your while.'

'I'm probably not the person you need for this,' Eva said, which surprised Kitty. He was willing to pay her anything and she was turning it down. She wanted to throw her notebook at Eva's head. 'I think what you're looking for is more of a personal shopper. You describe the person, they find the gift. A nice perfume for your mother, perhaps matching luggage tickets and passport holders for your sister and her husband, that kind of thing?'

'Brilliant, that's brilliant,' he said, lighting up. Then he looked at his watch again and that frown returned; he was even later now.

'I'm sorry, George, this job isn't for me.' Eva smiled and stood.

He sat on the couch and looked up at her in confusion. Then he realised what was going on and stood too. 'Okay.' He shook her hand, a bit put out, a bit annoyed. 'Thanks for coming. I'll make sure Nigel shows you out. I'm late for a meeting,' he said. He took one last look at her, an intrigued one, he nodded at Kitty, said goodbye and left the room.

Nigel reappeared immediately and he, Kitty and Eva rode the elevator in silence.

'Why did you suggest Eva for George?' Kitty asked Nigel.

'Is this for your piece?' He said the word 'piece' as if it were a dirty word.

'If you want it to be.'

'I don't.'

'Fine, then, it's off the record.'

He gave her a sarky look, then looked at Eva to answer the question. 'I've worked for him for six years and for six years I've had to do all his lists. Birthdays, Christmas, christenings, you name it. I think it's time his grandfather stopped receiving handkerchiefs and ties, though they were of the finest quality, of course,' he said, complimenting himself.

'Does he have a nice family?' Eva asked, which Kitty thought was a rather unusual question.

'Nice? They'd make you sick,' Nigel said, which they both took to mean yes.

'As wonderful as I am.' He looked at Kitty, blinked his long lashes, then turned back to Eva. 'They deserve better,' he said seriously.

Eva nodded.

'And I,' he returned to his mock tones, 'am tired of patrolling the aisles looking for anti-wrinkle moisturisers. I've better things to be doing.'

'Like making coffee,' Kitty said as they stepped out of the elevator.

'Eddie will show you out, Kath-Kitty.' He nodded his head at the burly security guard standing in the corner.

The doors closed and Kitty laughed, and they found themselves back on the path outside the IFSC.

'Well,' Kitty looked at Eva, feeling that she had certainly witnessed something very unusual in there, 'that was interesting.'

'Was it?' Eva looked uncertain.

'Mr Webb certainly took to you,' Kitty said, and Eva's cheeks pinked.

'Mr Webb shouldn't be taking to anyone,' Eva said drily. 'Mr Webb has a one-year anniversary to celebrate.'

'Is that why you said no to the job?'

'No! If you think I'm in this job to find men then you're sorely mistaken,' Eva said, 'otherwise I would have said yes.'

They laughed.

'So why did you say no to the job, exactly?' Kitty asked.

'Would you like to go for a coffee?'

Kitty weighed up her options. Eva was very nice and her job made for interesting conversation but she wasn't sure there was anything there unless of course Constance's story lay in Eva's personal life. So far, to Kitty's journalistic eye, there was nothing dramatic or overtly interesting about Eva. Once again Constance had found a subject that Kitty couldn't yet identify. Kitty thought about the benefits of progressing with the other ninety-eight people on her list – people who had more immediate exciting stories to share – versus spending a few more hours with Eva to ask her about her life. Eva was a lovely girl, but Kitty was under pressure. She needed to move on.

'I won't take up any more of your time,' Kitty smiled politely, feeling guilty over Eva's fallen expression. 'But before I go, I just have one question.'

'Of course.' Eva brightened again.

'I was wondering, can you remember the first gift, really memorable gift, that you received that really meant something to you, that perhaps sparked something inside you? Perhaps it sparked this . . . this desire you have to buy people the perfect gift. That gift could be the reason you got into this . . . career.'

Eva looked sad and then her face brightened as the mask came back on again. 'Yes,' she said perkily. 'It was a My Little Pony stable and pony. It was from my grandmother. I was seven years old and I absolutely loved it. I played with it every second of every day.'

'Really?' Kitty asked, surprised, disappointed even.

'Yes.' Her mask didn't budge. 'Why?'

'I just thought that there was something, something with more meaning, or . . .' She looked at her for more but Eva's face was blank.

'Nope. I really loved that pony,' she said, her smile tight.

Eva watched Kitty Logan cycle away from her and she cursed herself. She could tell when she was being dropped like a hot potato. It had happened plenty of times before. Gaby would never forgive her for this one. Her one real opportunity to talk about her business in a way that she wanted and she had blown it. But she couldn't give Kitty what she wanted. Kitty wanted more, she wanted to get inside Eva's head, inside her heart. Eva knew she did that to other people, but she didn't feel comfortable allowing anyone to occupy that place within her. She barely went to that place herself.

Her phone rang and she sighed and answered it. 'Hi, Mum.'

'Eva, can you come get me?' Eva heard the whimper in her voice, the sniff, the weakness, and her heart dropped.

'What happened?' she asked, her voice thick with dread, knowing already.

'It's my wrist. I thought it was just a sprain but it's been hurting me all night. I couldn't sleep, and so I finally thought I should check it. They said it's broken.'

'Where are you now?'

'The hospital.'

'Where's Dad?'

Silence. Then a quiet, 'I don't know. I haven't seen him today. Bessie brought me to hospital but she had to go to help Clare. She's just had a baby, she needs help with the boys, and I can't ask Bessie to come get me again.'

Eva felt the anger surge through her. Hot, hopeless anger that she could do nothing with, standing on the quays in Dublin city. And it would stay with her, no doubt, all the way back on the train to Galway, until she would arrive at the station, exhausted and drained.

'I'm in Dublin,' she said. 'I won't be home until this evening.'

'That's fine, I can wait.'

'Why don't you get a taxi?'

'No. No, thanks. I'll wait for you.'

Eva knew she'd say that. She never wanted anyone to see her like that. She would sit in the house until she'd healed, no doubt.

'It will be hours, Mum.'

'I'll wait for you,' her mother said with a firmness in her voice. Eva wondered where that strength disappeared to when the time really called for it. 'I just hope I can get this cast off for your father's birthday. He's decided to have a party.'

'When?' Dread filled Eva again.

'Friday week.'

'Friday week? But . . .' she stalled. 'I can't make it Friday week. He could have given me some notice at least.'

'Oh, your father will be so disappointed,' Eva's mother said in a voice that made Eva's stomach churn.

'Well, there's nothing I can do about it. I can't turn down work – you know what it's like these days.' She looked up at the building she had just walked out of with Kitty. 'Besides, I'll be in Cork . . .'

CHAPTER TEN

The address of Archie Hamilton, sixty-seventh on the list of one hundred names, jumped out at Kitty as she made her way home after spending time with Eva. It was Friday evening; she felt it was a good time to call in, people would be home from work, they'd be sitting down to dinner, she would catch them unawares. Apart from Gaby, not one of her voicemails had had a response and she needed to keep moving. The clock was ticking on this story and as another day drew to a close, she was no closer to finding her subject. The thought panicked her far more than it should have.

Archie Hamilton lived in a block of flats a mere ten minutes' walk from her flat. There was a strong sense of community around these parts. The immediate neighbours were tight: if you were from around there they had your back, if you weren't . . . they didn't and Kitty lived just outside this zone. While Archie Hamilton operated three locks to open the door, she waited on the balcony of the fourth floor. A young boy with bright red hair and freckles, sitting on a basketball, watched her and a crowd of kids on the ground floor hovered a little too closely to her bicycle, which was tied up at the railings.

A final lock was slid and the door opened until a chain stopped it from going any further. A pair of eyes stared back at her, bloodshot, rheumy eyes that looked as if they hadn't seen the light of day for years. Kitty couldn't help but take a step back.

'Archie Hamilton?' she asked, and the eyes looked her up and down, then the door slammed in her face.

She looked around, unsure whether to knock again or leave. The boy sitting on the basketball sniggered.

'Do you know Archie?' she asked.

'Do you know Archie?' he responded in exactly the same voice, mimicking her perfectly, getting the high-pitched tone and the slight country accent. In fact she felt he exaggerated the accent a little too much but either way it had a disturbing effect, which she was sure was intended. She debated leaving but she suddenly heard a voice inside calling Archie's name and she stayed where she was. More locks turned, quicker this time, the chain slid across the door and the door was suddenly pulled open wide. A man, not the man who had first answered, but who replaced intimidation with anger and exhaustion, stared at her. He examined her as he put on his denim jacket, then, as though not liking what he saw, he stepped outside and she jumped back. He slammed the door and locked it. Then he put the keys in his pocket and charged off towards the stairs.

'Excuse me?' Kitty called out politely.

'Excuse me?' she heard her voice echoed behind her from the boy on the basketball.

The man kept on walking; she ran after him. He skipped down the concrete stairs. She gave up on politeness.

'Are you Archie?'

'What if I am?'

'Well, if you are, I'd love to talk to you,' she said, breathless as they started on the third flight of stairs.

'About what?'

'About . . . well, if you stop racing, I can tell you what.'

'I'm late for work.' He upped his speed just as she had managed to catch up with him.

'Maybe we can make an appointment to meet at a time that suits you better. Here's my card . . .' She rooted in her handbag, which slowed her down, and he was then a level ahead of her. She retrieved the card and jumped down the steps in twos and threes to catch up.

He didn't take the card. 'I don't talk to journalists,' he said, hitting the ground floor and walking away from the flats.

Kitty eyed the crowd of kids around her bike and chose to jog alongside Archie.

'How did you know I was a journalist?'

He looked her up and down as if to answer her question. 'You have that desperate look.'

She was only mildly insulted as, judging by their cat-and-mouse routine, he was correct.

'You left a message on my phone.'

'Yes.'

'Don't call me again.'

They rounded the corner and she expected him to keep walking but suddenly he stopped, took a sharp left and disappeared into a chipper. Kitty had to backtrack a few steps. She watched him through the window: he lifted the counter barrier, took off his jacket and disappeared in the back. There was a queue of two people inside the shop. Kitty glanced at the sign above the window: 'Nico's'. Archie Hamilton reappeared wearing a white hat and apron. His colleague filled him in on the orders and left him alone. She pushed open the door.

'You could be done for stalking,' he said, barely looking at her. A stalking offence to add to her woes was all she needed right then.

The two in the queue stared at her.

'I'll have a single of chips,' she ordered.

He stopped shovelling chips then and looked at her. She couldn't tell if he was impressed or if he wanted to throw boiling hot chip fat at her. There was a fine line. He made a decision and lowered the basket of frozen chips into the bubbling oil. Kitty debated waiting for the one customer ahead of her to leave, then thought against it. She didn't need super investigative powers of journalism to know that this was her one chance with Archie.

'I'm going to leave my card here,' she said, placing it on the counter.

He glanced at it, then back at his work. He made a burger, chips, bagged it, took money at the till and the customer left.

'I've never talked about it. Not then and I won't now. Nothing's changed.'

Kitty was most definitely missing a trick. 'I'm not sure who exactly you think I am but—'

'You're a journalist, aren't you?'

'Yes.'

'You're all the same.'

'I won't talk to you about anything you don't want to talk about.'

'I've heard that before too.'

He shovelled her chips into a small white paper bag, then he put the bag into a larger brown bag and shovelled extra in.

'Look, I'll be honest with you, I have no idea what you're talking about or what it is that you don't want to talk about. I have no idea who you are. I found you on a list of one hundred names as someone I had to interview for a story. I don't know you or any of the other ninety-nine people and I don't know what the story is. All I ask for is at least thirty minutes of your time, any time – morning, noon or night – so that we can talk. It may not be about the thing you think it is, or maybe it is, and if you don't want me to write about it I just won't write about it, but I can promise you that I'm an honest writer and I'll keep my word.'

For Constance, for her own sanity, more than anything Kitty wanted to do things right.

He seemed amused, or at least he was now something other than what he had been, which was threatening and intimidating. She guessed he was in his late fifties, maybe sixties, though he could have been younger and the stress was ageing him. He clearly *was* stressed; he carried it in bags around his body. His hair was completely grey, his skin was red, dry and unhealthy, he appeared overweight but his arms were muscular beneath his T-shirt. He was to Kitty the epitome of stressful living, unhealthy eating and not enough sleep. She wondered how far off she was from looking like that. She couldn't read him at all. Finally he looked at her and she felt a swell of relief that her words had made some kind of difference.

'Salt and vinegar?' he asked, and she sighed.

'Yes, please.'

He saturated the chips with vinegar, folded the top over and placed the sopping bag directly down on her business card.

'Two seventy.'

She paid and couldn't think of anything further to say. She took the chips and left the vinegar-covered card on the counter. At least she had dinner. When she rounded the corner her bike was gone, and so were the kids.

Kitty stood at the base of the steps that led to her flat and looked up into the darkness, dreading to think what might be waiting for her that evening.

'Kitty? Kitty Logan, is that you?'

She whirled around, trying to find the source of the voice. A man inside the dry-cleaners was squinting at her, head cocked to one side and then to the other as he tried to figure her out. She took him in: the smart suit, the respectable haircut, the polished shoes, the long face, the strong jaw. The small circular glasses were a new addition, though.

'Richie?' she asked. 'Richie Daly?'

He looked relieved and she knew she was right. She went into the dry-cleaners to meet him, usually a no-no for her as the owner was only ever a moment away from throwing her on the ironing board and steaming her to death.

'I knew that was you!' he laughed, holding his arms open for

Kitty to fall into. She hugged him warmly and then stepped back to study him.

'My God, you look like you but you're completely different,' she said, unable to believe her eyes.

'For the better, I hope,' he said with a grin. 'The ripped cords and Converse weren't a good look.'

'And your hair! It's all gone!'

'I could say the same about you,' he replied, and her hand immediately went to her bobbed hair, which had always been halfway down her back in college.

'Listen to us – you'd swear we hadn't met in fifty years,' she laughed.

'Well, twelve years is a long time.'

'Is it twelve? Scary. So what are you doing here?'

He signalled his surroundings, 'Uh . . . dry-cleaning.'

'Of course.' She rolled her eyes.

Her landlord cleared his throat, interrupting their conversation, and looked at them like he wanted to kill them both.

'I live just upstairs, would you like to . . . I mean, do you want a coffee or something?' Half-way through her sentence she realised there could be a possible wife and two point four kids waiting in a car outside the dry-cleaners, wondering why Daddy was hugging a strange woman. She looked outside self-consciously.

'A coffee?' Richie asked, appalled. 'Forget it, let's get a proper drink.'

They went to Smyths pub on Fairview Strand, it was seven o'clock and busy on a Friday. They managed to find a table with two stools, and they shared the chips and caught up on old times.

'So what are you doing?' Kitty asked after filling him in on her work history since college, leaving out the disastrous Colin Maguire débâcle, of course, and though she was guessing he already knew, as she felt the entire world knew, he was polite enough not to bring it up.

'Me?' He looked down at his pint. It was his fourth already

and Kitty, after her fourth glass of wine, was already feeling woozy. 'I'm currently writing a book.'

'A book? Wow, Richie, that's fantastic.'

'It's funny to hear you call me Richie, you know. They all call me Richard now.'

'Well, of course, any decent self-respecting author wouldn't settle for anything less. What's the book about?'

'It's a novel.'

'That's exciting.'

'And that's it,' he said coyly.

'Ah, come on, you have to tell me more. Is it romance? Historical? Mills & Boon?'

He laughed. 'Mills & Boon, definitely Mills & Boon.'

She was suddenly aware of their closeness, how they'd gone from innocent catching-up to flirting, and more importantly, of how much more handsome he seemed now.

'It's a crime novel,' he explained, their heads closer now, their knees touching. 'I'm about a quarter of the way through. It's something I've always wanted to do but never did. With work and everything it's hard to find the time to do things for yourself. So I just thought one day, fuck it, Richie, do it. And I did. Or at least I'm trying.'

'Good for you. It takes a lot for people to follow their dreams. You could be the next Susan Boyle,' she teased.

'What about you? Is *Thirty Minutes* the dream?'

She looked down at her glass and was surprised to see it was empty again; hadn't she just started it? Richie signalled for another. 'I don't know,' she said, her head spinning nicely and her tongue feeling oversized. 'I don't know what the dream is any more.'

'You don't like working in TV?'

'I . . .' she hesitated, feeling that at any moment she could explode about all that she felt for the show and its process, but she was guarded. She hadn't spoken to anybody about it, but Richie genuinely didn't seem to know. His eyes were soft and welcoming, non-judgemental, and a little bloodshot, and she felt like she was twenty again, back in the college bar, missing lectures at a time when nothing, at least to her now, felt serious. She trusted him. 'I don't work for *Thirty Minutes* any more,' she finally admitted.

'No?' He drained his glass. 'What happened?'

'You really don't know or are you just trying to be nice?'

'How would I know? Is it something I should know? Kitty, I'm sorry, I've had my head in my book for the past few months. I've no idea what's going on. Somebody just told me today that those Chilean miners were all rescued.'

Kitty laughed. 'That was two years ago.'

'Well, there you go,' he smiled. 'I'm a slow writer. Seriously, you don't have to tell if you don't want to. We're just here for a nice time.' He smiled supportively.

'I fucked up a story. I fucked up a story really badly and it ended up going to court, the network lost a load of money, and they suspended me, which is code for *never hiring me ever again*. Now the magazine that I work for are thinking of doing the same thing because they're under pressure from advertisers who feel they have a responsibility even though it's been rumoured they've been using child labourers on boats to make their crap products, but in the meantime I'm still working on a story for them even though they can't publish it and it's the only thing I truly care about now, but I have a week to my deadline and I still don't know what the story is and while I'm trying to do that I return to my apartment every evening to find dog shit, paint, toilet roll and whatever vile thing Colin Maguire's four hundred and fifty thousand euro and his little posse can throw at me.'

When she finished, Richie was looking at her open-mouthed. Kitty did the only thing she could think of to do, the thing she'd needed to do since this all began: she threw her head back and laughed. Hysterically.

*

When the bar lights were turned on full and last orders were long finished, and a loud man wearing black began to patrol the bar shouting for them to leave, Richie's hand moved to the small of Kitty's back, one finger circling above the waist of her trousers, another creeping downward.

'Let's go back to your place,' he said quietly.

'No. We can't, it's booby-trapped,' she giggled.

'I like the sound of that . . .' He groped her and they laughed.

'Let's go back to yours,' she said, moving in to kiss him.

He was a long way away in Stoneybatter, and as the lights blurred past and she had to lower the window for some air, she did recall wondering why on earth he had been doing his dry-cleaning on the other side of the city.

If she'd had her notebook with her she would have made a note to ask him. Later, she wished she had.

CHAPTER ELEVEN

'Shit, I'm late.'

'Late for what?'

'Birdie.'

'You're still pissed.'

They both laughed and Kitty got a whiff of his morning breath and rolled away from him.

'It's a story I'm working on.'

'I thought you weren't working.'

'I am, I just don't know what the story is.'

She sat up and her head pounded so she lay back down again. 'Are you feeling better today?'

'What do you mean?'

'You were crying about a stolen bike.'

Kitty groaned, then she threw the covers off and wandered around his bedroom looking for her underwear. 'Where the hell are my knickers?'

He pinched his eyes closed, then opened them again suddenly. 'The kitchen.' He rubbed his eyes. 'Shit, my head hurts.'

Kitty found her underwear and the rest of her clothes scattered around his tiny kitchen. She looked out the window. 'Where are we again?'

'Stoneybatter,' he called groggily from the bedroom.

'You know a guy named Dudley Foster?'

'No, why?'

'He's on my list.' She pulled her jeans on.

'What list?'

'My story.'

He appeared at the door in his underwear, and her vision of him now and the memory of how he looked last night were not one and the same. She felt slightly repulsed. She wondered if she should use his shower but then she was worried he'd want to join her and she just couldn't go there again. Not now. Possibly not ever.

'Want me to call you a taxi?'

'Eh. Yes, please.'

He disappeared into his room to make the call and Kitty brushed her hair with a fork, wiped smudged mascara from under her eyes and stole the deodorant from the bathroom. The second apartment bedroom contained a desk with a computer, and pages scattered everywhere: the book. She heard the shower going and was about to go snooping into the novel when the intercom rang. It was the taxi driver, waiting downstairs. She went into Richie's en-suite and knocked awkwardly on the door but he didn't hear her. She pushed the door open and was faced with his naked self. Again, not something she could stomach that early in the morning with a dreadful hangover.

'Taxi's here,' she said loudly.

He looked up suddenly and soap went into his eyes. She could tell it was stinging as he tried to wipe his lathered face.

'Uh, I'd better go,' she said, handing him a towel, but he couldn't see as he was rubbing his eyes in a frantic effort to get the soap out. It wasn't the coolest of looks.

'Okay,' he said, water dripping from his nose and mouth. 'Thanks for . . . last night.'

'Yeah, you too.'

The most awkward goodbye ever? Definitely in her top five. She stole a banana, let herself out of the apartment, and it was at least thirty minutes more before she stopped cringing.

It was a beautifully bright and hot sunny May Saturday. Anyone with any sense would not be sitting in traffic unless it was for something worthwhile like going to the beach or the park. Seaside villages would be overcrowded with sun-worshippers, their shops lined with queues for ice creams, any restaurant or café with so much as a chair outside would be the most popular place to be for the day. Instead of joining these people on the sand, or on the grass, or al fresco with her frappuccino, Kitty found herself in a smelly taxi wearing yesterday's clothes, the faint smell of sweat drifting from her armpits when she lifted her arms. She kept her pits firmly clamped down by her side as she tried not to listen to football match commentary at full blast on the M50, her eyes straining to stay open in the sunlight, her head pounding, her mouth cotton wool from the wine, watching with absolute horror as the meter moved at what she questioned was a legal pace. She read the standard sticker on the window that told her that she and every other passenger was entitled to a journey in a clean, hygienic car and not to be pestered by the driver. The driver smelled like he hadn't washed in a week, the car was filthy and she couldn't hear herself think over the noise of the radio. Still, at least he wasn't talking to her and that was something. She made a note of the phone number.

It was midday by the time she arrived at St Margaret's Nursing Home, and she had promised Birdie she would be there at ten to follow up on their first interview. She had listened back to Birdie's story so far and had some more in-depth questions to ask.

'I'm so sorry,' Kitty apologised to Molly, the first person she saw when she entered reception.

'Hoo hoo,' Molly chuckled at the sight of her. 'Somebody had a good night.'

Kitty smiled coyly. 'Do I look that bad?'

'Not if he was worth it,' Molly winked, coming around the other side of the desk. Her hair was still blue but her nails had been painted a luminous coral.

'Is Birdie going to kill me?'

'Birdie? Birdie wouldn't hurt a fly, unless the fly is perhaps Freda, the hippie. She's outside, teaching them a movement class. Last I saw they were pretending to be leaves.'

'I don't know her well enough but I can't imagine Birdie doing that.'

'You know her just fine. She's not, but she'd probably rather be. She's on the lawn with her family. Don't look at me like that, you're not intruding, she'll be thrilled to see you.'

Kitty followed Molly out to the lawn where families had gathered for tea and scones. Umbrellas had been opened to protect them from the searing sun, and that is where Kitty found Birdie, sitting while the rest of her family were sprawled around her, chatting. Children were running around – Kitty wasn't sure who belonged to whom – and teenagers were out of the circle playing with their iPhones and listening to their iPods, preferring to be absolutely anywhere but there.

As Kitty walked towards Birdie's family she couldn't help but notice how distant Birdie seemed. Conversation was flowing all around her but not *to* her or even in her direction. Now and then somebody would deliver part of the sentence to her and she would momentarily snap out of her trance to smile and nod, but at the soonest opportunity she would drift again.

'Sorry to interrupt you,' Molly said cheerfully. 'You have a visitor, Birdie.'

They all looked up at Kitty. Kitty looked at Birdie apologetically and made her way round to her. 'Birdie, I'm so sorry I'm late.'

'Not at all.' Her face seemed genuinely to light up and Kitty was pleased.

Birdie stood and held Kitty's hand warmly as she introduced her to the family.

'This is Kitty Logan, a friend of mine. Kitty, this is my daughter, Caroline, this is her daughter, Alice, and she has a son, Edward, but he's studying for his finals at Trinity at the moment.'

Caroline looked proud so Kitty mouthed a wow.

'This is Alice's son, Levi, my great-grandchild. This is my eldest son, Cormac, his son, Barry, and Barry's two children, Ruán and Thomas.' Two young boys barely looked up from their game consoles. 'This is Seán, his wife, Kathleen, and their youngest son, Clive. Their daughter, Gráinne, lives in Australia with her husband doing . . . what is it now, Kathleen?'

'Computer software analysis.'

'That's it.' And Birdie continued through the group, two more sons, one wife and one partner and some of their children, some of whom were polite and others who couldn't care less if she were the Queen of Sheba. Soon Kitty had no idea who was who, and as soon as she sat down beside Birdie, a position she was honoured to hold, Birdie's daughter – her only daughter, Caroline – started talking. And she didn't stop. Not for one second. Not for a breath. She commanded the conversation, telling anecdote after anecdote, *long* anecdotes, without bringing anyone else in at all. Occasionally a son or two would pipe up with something and a daughter-in-law would fill in gaps, refresh their memories, correct a mistake, but all the conversation, if it could be called that, was directed, produced, edited and starred in by Caroline. She was an elegant, well-dressed, well-spoken woman, with a wonderful turn of phrase and language skills, and had an impressive amount of knowledge on various topics. She was used to speaking, comfortable with her anecdotes and recanted them in an interesting way, but it was so constant that her voice – the sheer Caroline-ness of it all – began to bother Kitty. Birdie was quiet, rarely referred to; she was merely the reason for the visit, not the subject of it. Kitty kept waiting for the attention to turn to Birdie, or for one of the grandchildren or great-grandchildren to say something, until each time Caroline started a new subject, Kitty wanted to leap across the table and strangle her. She wasn't sure if it was the hangover, the searing heat, and the irritating wasps circulating about their heads that made it all worse, but the only thing she could hear were words jumbling around that didn't make any sense at all.

Molly appeared by Birdie's side again, and without a word handed Birdie a small cup of brightly coloured pills and a glass of water. It was only then that Caroline chose to stop talking to turn her attention to her mother. When Caroline looked, every-body else looked, which made it rather uncomfortable for Birdie. Molly noticed them all staring.

'Lovely day, isn't it?' Molly said, and despite the fact that it was an ordinary comment, everything she said in her Drogheda accent sounded brash, almost sarcastic, as if she meant something else but wouldn't say. Perhaps it was the way her eyes glistened mischievously, her confident air, that gave the idea she didn't feel anyone was better than she was, which of course she was right to believe, but she came across as defiant, as though she knew everyone thought they were better and she was constantly fighting it.

'What are you giving her?' Caroline asked, and it bothered Kitty that she hadn't asked her mother that question.

They carried out a conversation about Birdie's drugs, why she was taking them, and then Caroline in turn suggested other drugs she should be on and happily debated with Molly on how she was right. Caroline, it seemed, was either well up on her drugs or else she was a doctor. She was one who knew all about the craft but had no bedside manner. Kitty had her summed up already.

Caroline looked away from her mother, finally allowing her to take her pills in peace without an audience, and she began a story about a new vaccine on the market and a conversation she had had with somebody in the World Health Organization about it. At least some of the brothers were doctors too, because they seemed to understand the terminology, even added to it when they had the rare opportunity.

'Molly, is there any chance I could get some of Birdie's special tea?' Kitty asked.

Birdie, who had been drinking water at that exact moment, snorted with laughter and her water spluttered down her top. Caroline stopped her story to look at her mother in surprise. In fact, everybody did. Even the teenagers looked up from their electronic equipment and one even cracked a smile to the other as they watched their grandmother giggle. Kitty handed her a napkin to wipe her face.

'Thank you,' Birdie said, composed, though her eyes were moist. 'Excuse me for interrupting you, Caroline. Please do continue.'

Caroline studied her mother for a split second before continuing her conversation but she made sure to direct her speech at her mother so as to avoid another interruption or so she wouldn't miss the next inside joke. They were the kind of family who, when one person spoke, kept all eyes and ears on that person until the story was finished. Pockets of conversations couldn't break out among the others or else the entire story would come to an abrupt end until the narrator had everyone's full attention again.

Kitty wondered why on earth nobody asked her or Birdie how they knew one another, and why Kitty was there interrupting their family get-together. Birdie couldn't have told them who she was before she'd arrived – Kitty was due to have been there and gone two hours previously – but if she had told them, hadn't they any follow-up questions? Hadn't they any interest in their mother at all? Kitty was angry on Birdie's behalf; she felt like she was standing on a busy motorway with cars speeding past her while she waited for a gap in the traffic to run across.

The gap came when Alice's baby, Levi, choked on something, which sent both Caroline and Alice into a panic. Caroline took over without asking Alice for permission, which Alice succumbed to without a fight.

Kitty saw her opportunity.

'I don't know if you're aware but I'm a journalist with *Etcetera*,' Kitty said to the group, then turned to a surprised Birdie. 'Did you fill them in?'

'No, I didn't.' Birdie seemed a little embarrassed, if not slightly nervous.

'What did she say?' one son asked.

'*Etcetera*,' a daughter-in-law replied. 'It's a magazine.'

'A kind of social and cultural magazine, would I be right?' another asked, and Kitty agreed.

'Did I read in the *Times* that the editor passed away recently?' a son asked.

'Yes, she did,' Kitty replied. 'Constance Dubois.' She still wasn't used to saying it, that Constance was gone, dropping it into casual conversation over scones and tea as if her friend was just a topic, like hypochondriac patients and new vaccines.

'Oh, yes, she was the woman who gave that dreadful man a voice. That anti-medicine man, what's his name.'

'Bernard Carberry,' Kitty said, her blood boiling. He was a nice man, a very well-respected and highly educated man, who also happened to send her a Christmas card every year.

'That's it, the man who preaches against the evils of GPs,' Caroline continued, laughing to belittle him, though her disdain and rage was clear. 'He believes we should be eating grass and drinking more water.'

'He believes GPs unnecessarily prescribe antibiotics and other medications without actually getting to the root of the problem, whereas the other drugs he recommends are less damaging and can build up immunity.'

'Utter tosh,' Caroline said dismissively. 'So do you work for this man then?'

'We work for the same magazine and our paths have regularly crossed.' Kitty was determined to stay polite.

'And do you agree with his conspiracy theories?'

'I believe Constance Dubois was an incredibly progressive figure who had the ability to see what the new and interesting were before other publications. She recognised Dr Carberry's studies were of great interest to a wide audience twenty years ago before the topic was really being discussed and now he is among the world's leading lecturers on homeopathic and new-age medicines, with many GPs actually agreeing with his findings, so yes, I think a lot of heed must be paid to what he says.'

Kitty used her firmest voice, and, as Caroline opened her mouth to speak, she took a risk and jumped in front of the traffic and hoped they would slam on the brakes in time.

'But that's not why I'm here. I have nothing to do with Dr Bernard Carberry; I don't work in that department. My mentor and friend, Constance Dubois, has once again had the great foresight to find another person of interest to the public, a person that the country needs to read about, the kind of person who is inspiring and warm-hearted and who has a long and wonderful story to tell us all. Your mother is helping me with my story.'

Kitty realised she wasn't just trying to give Birdie's family a kick up the backside but that she genuinely meant what she was saying. It didn't matter that she couldn't yet find the link between the people she had so far met, their stories alone were interesting to her. She saw they were all staring at her in silence. Confused, she looked at Birdie and back at them, unsure what they were waiting for.

'So don't leave us in suspense,' Caroline finally spoke. 'Who is it you're writing about?'

'But . . .' Kitty turned to Birdie with a frown. Birdie's cheeks had pinked and she was looking down at her skirt, fixing the hem. Kitty thought she had made it perfectly clear. Anger filled her heart. 'I'm here for the same reason as you are.' She reached out and took Birdie's hand. 'To spend time with this wonderful woman.' And when they still didn't get it, she said, 'I'm writing about your mother.'

'That was a nice thing you did for Birdie,' Molly said as Kitty was leaving the home that evening. They had sat outside in the sun most of the day, spending a few hours with Birdie and asking her more about her life, delving a little further, getting a little more personal as they grew to know one another better and as Birdie learned to trust her. Kitty felt she had a good insight into Birdie's life growing up in the chapel town with her father as principal and only teacher of the local school. With no mother for Birdie to turn to her life was strict, regimented. Her father took care of the family in every way he could but there was no physical love. No hugs at bedtime, no whispers of affection. Birdie came from a prominent family in the village and as the daughter of the principal she had a certain sense of duty and expectation. As soon as she could, she left for life in Dublin. Her one caution to herself had been not to marry her father's type and, to her credit, she hadn't. She had married a kind and supportive yet traditional man in Niall Murphy, a civil servant, and they in turn had bred a family of doctors.

'What do you mean?' Kitty asked.

'You know what I mean,' Molly replied. 'Word gets around here quickly.'

'I meant it, you know. She's an interesting lady.'

'That's an understatement.'

This comment intrigued Kitty and she wanted to find out more about Birdie from Molly. 'Are you heading back to the city, by any chance? Fancy splitting a taxi?'

'I'm going the other way, but I can drop you to Oldtown, if you like.'

Kitty would take whatever she could get.

'It's Birdie's birthday on Thursday,' Kitty said. 'I overheard her family asking her out for dinner.'

'Yeah, that's right.'

'She says she won't go.'

Molly shrugged and a smile appeared briefly on her lips.

'What?'

'Nothing.'

'Something I should know?'

'No.'

Kitty didn't believe her. 'She'll be eighty-five. *Eighty-five*. She should celebrate. Is there something you can do for her here?'

'We usually have a cake. A chocolate one with candles. We bring it in during dinner and everyone sings. It's nice. Birthdays don't go unnoticed.'

'I'd like to do something for her.'

Molly looked at her. 'You're growing fond of her, aren't you?'

Kitty nodded.

'Well, she won't be here that day,' she said, grabbing her leather jacket. 'She's taking a trip.'

A swarm of residents arrived through the front door, conversation buzzing, and more piled out of the bus parked out front. The bus, an eighteen-seater, had St Margaret's stencilled across the side.

'They won the bowling match,' Molly explained. 'They play against teams from surrounding homes once a fortnight. You wouldn't believe how serious they take it. I love being on driving duty, just so I can hear their tactics, and because I always wanted to be a bus driver when I was a kid, but they rarely let me. Fancy a lift to town?'

Kitty took her up on her offer and as she sped along the potholed roads that led to the small village of Oldtown, on the back of Molly's motorbike, she quickly understood why Molly wasn't often allowed behind the wheel of the bus.

Sitting in Oldtown, Kitty had over an hour to wait for a bus to the city. Pulling out the list of one hundred names, she pored over it and set to work.

Magdalena Ludwiczak did not speak enough English to enable Kitty to have a decent conversation with her so she struck her off her list. Number five, Bartle Faulkner, was on holiday for the next fortnight, and she could hear the water lapping on the beach in the background. No, he hadn't heard from Constance at all, and yes, he could meet up in two weeks when he was home, by which time it would be too late for Kitty's story. Eugene Cullen, an old man, by the sound of it, told her in no uncertain terms never to call him again, and she left a message for Patrick Quinn.

Kitty went back to the seventh name on her list.

'Hello?' The phone was answered in a whisper.

'Is that Mary-Rose Godfrey?'

'Yes,' she whispered. 'I'm at work. I'm not supposed to be on the phone.' The girl sounded about sixteen.

'Okay,' Kitty whispered, and then realised she didn't need to and cleared her throat. 'My name is Kitty Logan. I'm a journalist for *Etcetera*. Perhaps my editor Constance Dubois was in touch with you?'

'No, sorry,' the girl whispered.

Kitty sighed and cut straight to the chase. 'Can we meet?'

'Yeah, sure. When?'

Kitty straightened up, surprised. 'Tonight?'

'Yeah, cool. I'll be in Café en Seine at eight. Good for you?'

'Great!' Kitty couldn't believe her luck.

Mary-Rose hung up before they could arrange anything further like what Mary-Rose looked like or what Kitty looked like. When the bus arrived, Kitty jumped on with a spring in her step. Sitting down next to a man picking his nose and rolling the snot on the ball of his fingers couldn't even dampen her mood. She examined her phone and contemplated sending Richie a message. She thought of the fun they'd had the night before and she smiled, then used her hand to block her face so that she wouldn't look like a lunatic. But then she remembered how she'd felt that morning, awkward and cringing at the sight of his naked body. She decided against texting him. She took her notebooks out again; there was much work to be done. Though she had done it before, she Googled Archie Hamilton again, knowing a bit more about him now and what to focus on.

By the time she reached Café en Seine, she knew exactly why

he didn't want to speak to her, and exactly why she wanted to speak to him more than ever.

Kitty kissed the list before she entered the pub and thanked Constance again. She was beginning to enjoy this.

CHAPTER TWELVE

Café en Seine on Dawson Street was a series of bars spanning three floors, a three-storey atrium with glass-panelled ceilings with forty-foot trees reaching to the glass. The style was Parisian art nouveau and it was situated on a bustling street in central Dublin that consisted of restaurants, bars, cafés, the Lord Mayor's residence and St Anne's Church. Just a stone's throw from Stephen's Green, it was a popular choice for all ages, particularly then, on a Saturday night. Kitty had no idea where she was to meet Mary-Rose, nor how on earth she was to find her in such a gigantic place with numerous bars and darkened hidden corners and alcoves. You could spend a night there not realising that somebody you knew had also been there the entire time. Taking a seat at the main bar on a stool closest to the entrance – which also made her feel like she was in prime position to want to be chatted up – she sat with a glass of wine watching the door.

Her mind drifted again to the previous night's exploits. She couldn't help feeling disappointed that Richie still hadn't contacted her, not even a text. She wasn't even sure if she wanted him to, but she was sure that he should. She had definitely given him her number. She remembered little about the night but she did remember that. They had been perfectly sober when that had happened, and his number sat in her phone as proof that he'd existed at all. She thought about calling him, about how perhaps he was waiting for her and thinking exactly the same thing, when she heard her name being mentioned down the other end of the bar.

'Are you Kitty Logan?' she heard a man ask.

'Are you Kitty Logan?' she then heard a woman ask.

She leaned back in her stool to get a look at the people behind the voices but couldn't see anyone through the crowd. She examined the mirror behind the bar to find their reflection, trying to get a glimpse of them before they found her.

'Are you Kitty Logan?' she heard more loudly this time, and she leaned back in her chair to see a young man in his twenties asking a smooth suit-wearing stockbroker-type man. Stockbroker boy wasn't overly impressed with the question. 'Are you sure?' The young man looked him dead in the eye, all serious.

The group with stockbroker boy laughed and he seemed to relax then.

'No little operations the boys don't know about?'

'No.' His smile faded.

'Okay, Sam, let's move on,' the female voice said and a delicate hand appeared on his forearm as she moved him on.

'Are you Kitty Logan?' she asked the middle-aged woman sitting with a group of women.

'I might be,' the lady responded.

'I think you're lying,' Sam said. 'She wasn't Kitty Logan last night, were you, baby?'

The group of girls howled with laughter and Kitty felt they would stay with them for ever if she didn't interrupt.

'Excuse me?' she leaned forward on her stool. The group next to her along with Mary-Rose, Sam and the group of women all turned to look at her. She raised her hand. 'I'm Kitty Logan.'

'No, *I'm* Kitty Logan,' a deep voice came from the tables across the bar, followed by laughter.

'You have a contender!' Sam exclaimed, and as if they were part of a pantomime, people oohed.

Kitty laughed and stood to meet her contender, who stepped out from his table. He was four stone overweight, had a beard and he stood with his shoulders back, his fingers twitching as if he was a cowboy in a face-off. Kitty couldn't keep a straight face.

'I am victorious!' the man declared, arms punching the air, and the small audience applauded. The cool stockbrokers looked at them as if they were all a bad smell and they turned their backs. 'I *am* Kitty Logan,' the man declared and he celebrated one final time and returned to his seat. While Sam went to his table to shake his hand and continue the good fun, Mary-Rose approached Kitty.

'Hello,' she said. A smile transformed her face and her eyes lit up. She was an extremely pretty young woman, and though she was dressed in skinny jeans, the highest shoes Kitty had ever seen and a simple tank top, she looked a million dollars.

'I'm Mary-Rose,' she said.

'Nice to meet you. I was worried I wouldn't be able to find you in here but I see that my concerns were in vain.'

'Oh, trust Sam.' She rolled her eyes. 'He makes a scene every-where we go.'

'He's your boyfriend?'

'Hell, no.' She scrunched up her face. 'We're just friends. Have been since we were kids. Our moms were best friends, *are* best friends, blah blah blah,' she finished quickly.

'Kitty Logan,' Sam joined them. 'We're going for dinner, would you like to join us?'

Kitty looked to Mary-Rose expecting her to try to make a face at him to disinvite her but there was nothing but warmth emanating from her, from the two of them. They were exactly what she needed right then.

They walked five minutes to Frederick Street to a small Italian restaurant. Inside, a table of eight people awaited them and Sam insisted on dragging Kitty around and introducing her to all of their young, attractive and incredibly fashionable friends. Still wearing her clothes from the day before, Kitty felt like a hillbilly next to them all. She sat opposite Mary-Rose, perfect position for her interview, but she doubted that would happen with the lively banter at the table. They were an exuberant lot, friends from childhood with inside jokes that were funny to Kitty because of how they were delivered, despite her not actually understanding their meaning. They knew each other well, tirelessly teased one another, and Kitty couldn't help but feel it was the best-scripted sitcom she had ever seen, with their flawless hair and clothes. And that was just the boys.

Kitty didn't have friends like that. She grew up in County Carlow, in the south-east of Ireland. After school she left to go to University College Dublin and had lived in Dublin ever since, choosing to go home only on holidays or if somebody got married or died. She had two brothers, one who'd remained in Carlow and married, the other who'd moved to Cork to study in Cork University and was living very happily with a man named Alexander, whom she'd never met and had only learned about through Facebook. She couldn't remember the last time they had all been together in the same room at the same time – probably a family member's funeral – and she couldn't remember the last time she phoned either of them for a conversation that wasn't related to putting funds together for their parents' dodgy immersion heater or their dysfunctional boiler. Her father managed the same bar in Tullow Street as he had done all through Kitty's youth. Her parents were quiet, socially odd people, not quite knowing or learning the art of conversation and so they stayed away from most social events apart from close friends and family gatherings, where it appeared they mostly listened and did little talking, sat in a corner and didn't leave for the entire event.

Kitty had grown up with two best friends, both named Mary: Mary Byrne and Mary Carroll, who were always called by their full names to avoid confusion. It had always been Katherine and the two Marys; nobody called her Kitty in Carlow. It was a name she had been proudly baptised with once she reached university and she was only too happy to embrace it, a new name for a new beginning. The two Marys had been irritated by the use of a name they hadn't invented and refused to call her by it on the rare nights they came to join Kitty and her college friends on a night out in Dublin. Her Carlow friends and college friends had never mixed. The two Marys ended up rallying together in a staged intervention at the end of one particular night to drunkenly tell Kitty how much she'd changed since she'd moved to Dublin. Eventually Kitty couldn't take the arguments over the same thing each time and the trips to Dublin were reduced to one a year, and then eventually stopped completely. As Kitty returned home less and less, their friendship had eventually whittled away to nothing. If a meeting on the street wasn't cleverly avoided, the chats were increasingly difficult with nothing much to say. Mary Byrne had moved to Canada and Mary Carroll had lost two stone and was working in a clothes shop in Carlow, which Kitty now made a habit of avoiding after having the most awkward conversation of her life and having to buy two dresses Mary had recommended but which Kitty somehow couldn't find in her heart to tell her she despised. Her politeness had cost her over one hundred euro.

Now, her solid never-changing friends were Steve and Sally. Apart from them, Kitty had never been able to keep friends, not because she was disloyal in any way, she just felt that she hadn't connected with anyone deeply since her school friends and so it was easy to drift away as life moved on, as college finished and as she found new jobs and created new friendships that lasted as long as the jobs had. This – she looked around at Mary-Rose's friends – this she did not have and had never had.

'So you work for a magazine,' Mary-Rose finally left the conversation at the other end of the table and turned her attention to Kitty. Kitty was momentarily disappointed about having to get back to work.

'Yes. *Etcetera*. Do you know it?'

Mary-Rose thought about it. 'Yes, I think so,' she said unconvincingly.

'My editor was Constance Dubois. Was she in touch with you, this year or last year?' Kitty had long ago given up the hope that Constance had questioned any of these people.

'No, I don't think so,' Mary-Rose said again uncertainly.

'She passed away a few weeks ago,' Kitty explained. 'But before she died she was working on a story. You were part of that story.'

Again, the same reaction as from Birdie, Eva and, to a certain extent, Archie. Surprise, confusion, embarrassment.

'Do you know why she would have wanted to talk to you and write about you?'

Mary-Rose looked stunned. Kitty could see her eyes moving left and right as she searched both sides of her brain for the answer.

'No,' she responded, confused. 'I'm the most boring person you could possibly meet.'

Kitty laughed. 'I seriously doubt that. It has been fun so far.'

'That's Sam. Me? Honestly, I'm so boring. I've never done anything interesting, thought anything interesting, known or seen anything interesting.'

Kitty laughed further. 'I find you very interesting.' And she wasn't lying. It was a pleasure to be in Mary-Rose's company, to be invited into her world. 'Well, how would you like to be part of the story I'm writing? Don't you think that would be interesting?'

Again there was the same look that Kitty had seen from the others: shyness, embarrassment, flattery, but overall the feeling that they simply weren't good enough for a story.

'What's the story about?'

'About the people on a list.'

'How many people are on the list?'

'One hundred names in total.'

Mary-Rose's eyes widened. 'How big is your story?'

Kitty smiled. 'How big is yours?'

*

Mary-Rose repeatedly pressed her finger against the crumbs on the table and released them again, while shyly answering Kitty's questions.

'I'm sure that these other people are very interesting, I'm sure they have exciting lives. I'm just a hairdresser. I work two days in a salon in Booterstown where I've lived all my life and the other two days I'm freelance. The rest of the time I'm at home with my mum.'

'Where do you freelance? Magazines? Television?'

'God, no. Debs' nights and hen parties are about as exciting as I get, but mostly I'm in hospitals.'

'Hospitals?'

'Yeah, they call me whenever they need me. There's no hair salons in the hospitals and often people who are sick really feel better when their hair's done. Sometimes I do make-up for them too, but that's less popular. It gives them a bit of dignity, at least it did for my mum.'

'She spent time in hospital?'

'She had a stroke. She was only young, forty-two. She's forty-four now and still needs full-time care but getting her hair done always made her feel better. Not *better* better, but better on the inside. I do nails too, if they ask me. I'm not a qualified nail technician but I bring a selection of colours. To be honest, I think a lot of them are just glad of the company and chat.'

'That's a beautiful thing for you to do. It's not something I'd ever thought about before.'

'I'm not that nice. I do charge them,' she said, embarrassed by the compliment.

'How is your mother now?'

'Not great. She lost the use of the left side of her body. She has to be helped to do most things, she had to learn to speak again.'

'That must have been very difficult for you?'

She smiled sadly. 'Not as hard as it was for her.'

'Who helps her?'

'We have home help for a few hours a day and then . . . well, me when I get home.'

'Any brothers or sisters?'

'Nope.'

'Dad?'

'Nope.'

'That's a lot of responsibility.'

'Ah. It is what it is. I love my mum. I'd do anything for her.'

And just when Kitty was about to tell Mary-Rose she was far from boring, her life got much more interesting.

Sam tapped his glass with a spoon and attracted the attention of those at their table along with the few surrounding tables too. The friends at Mary-Rose and Sam's table looked at each other with big smiles, knowing what was in store.

'Oh God.' Mary-Rose shrunk in her chair, her cheeks already pink.

'What's happening?' Kitty asked.

'You'll see.'

Sam stood, continued to tap his glass until he had the attention of the entire restaurant. Not sure how to react to this disruption, the manager and the waiters viewed him warily nearby.

'I'm very sorry to interrupt your evening,' Sam said politely, as if butter wouldn't melt. 'I promise I won't take up too much of your time but there's something that I just have to do. There's somebody important in this room who I'd like to say something special to.'

He cleared his throat and a twitter of excitement gathered in the room. He was no longer annoying anybody; he had their full attention.

Sam ran his eyes over everyone on his table, resting for a moment on Kitty, which got her heart rate up, and then moved on to Mary-Rose, whose face was now puce. He smiled at her lovingly.

'Josephine Quinn,' he said softly, and Kitty looked around in confusion. Had she been duped? Was she sitting with the wrong person? How on earth had Mary-Rose suddenly become Josephine?

'Yes,' she said softly.

'You and I have been friends for a long time, you were there for me every day of my life, every single second. I never needed to call for you, you were always there, like a shadow, behind me, following me, stalking me.'

One of his friends snorted and was thumped in the arm by his girlfriend.

'You have always been there exactly when I need you, ever since . . .' his voice cracked and he looked down, and Kitty wasn't sure if he was going to be able to continue. He looked up again and his eyes shone with tears '. . . ever since I had my operation, you know, Josephine, the operation where I had my—'

'Yes, yes, I know the one,' Mary-Rose said hastily.

'Well,' he took a deep breath and came around the table to her.

A few women in the restaurant yelped excitedly, Mary-Rose covered her face in her napkin. Her friend beside her pulled her arm down. The chefs came from the kitchen to the door to watch. Everything was still and silent. Sam got down on bended knee and one woman yelped in excitement. The diners and staff all laughed and then a hush resumed. Sam reached for Mary-Rose's hand and she was forced to face him, removing her hands from her flushed cheeks. She shook her head at him as though she couldn't believe he was doing this.

'Josephine Quinn,' Sam said proudly and clearly, delivering his words to every corner of the room. 'I have loved you since the very moment I met you and I will love you every day until the day that I die, and beyond.'

Kitty spied a woman wiping her eye with a napkin. She caught another rolling her eyes.

'Will you do me the honour of being my wife?'

Despite the fact all knew this was coming, there was another rumble of excitement, which again was quickly hushed as all eyes were on Mary-Rose, waiting for her answer.

She looked at Sam, smiled that beautiful perfect smile and said, 'Yes.'

That was all everybody needed. The room erupted in celebration, the manager was quick to join the table and offer his congratulations, where he announced they would all receive drinks on the house. A friendly man at the table beside them sent a glass of champagne to the bride- and groom-to-be, and Sam, who had previously been sitting at the head of the table, bumped up a friend so that he could sit beside his new fiancée. He wrapped his arm around her shoulder, and she leaned in and covered her face.

'I'm going to kill you,' she said so quietly that only Kitty could hear.

'Just smile and wave,' Sam said, a grin on his face, and she finally looked up and waved her thanks at the neighbouring tables offering their congratulations.

'Guys, I don't mean to rain on your parade,' Kitty said finally, 'but I'm so confused. I thought your name was Mary-Rose Godfrey.'

Sam laughed.

'Oh, Kitty, I'm so sorry.' She turned to Kitty and kept her voice down. 'It *is* Mary-Rose. Don't mind him, he's always doing this.

'Always doing what?'

'Proposing! It's just this weird *thing* that he does. It's not real.' She became serious. 'You do know it wasn't real?'

Kitty's mouth dropped.

Sam howled.

'But it was so beautiful,' Kitty said, disappointed.

'You see?' Sam exclaimed, looking at Mary-Rose. 'Other people find it touching.'

'Then do it to someone else for a change.'

'It's more fun with you, *sweetheart*.' He squeezed her even tighter and she scowled. 'My little shnookums here doesn't always appreciate it.'

Kitty looked from one to the other. 'So you just randomly propose to people when you're out.'

'Not just people. Just Mary-Rose. I know she secretly likes it.'

'I hate it.'

'She doesn't always know how best to express it, though.'

Kitty laughed. 'And you do this when you're out.'

'Restaurants, bars, cafés, you should try it sometime. You will always get a free drink. One time our entire meal was complimentary, another time we got that bottle of champagne, remember?'

Mary-Rose nodded.

'So you do this for free food and drink?'

'And to bring sunshine to Mary-Rose's days. Now, now, don't look so angry, sweetheart, we just got engaged. People are looking and here come our free drinks. If you don't perk up I'll kiss you.'

Mary-Rose pasted a smile on her face so quickly Kitty was in hysterics.

The free drinks arrived with a complimentary dessert plate for the happy couple with 'Congratulations' written in balsamic dressing at the bottom of the plate.

'Last time we got a free meal,' Sam said quietly so that the manager wouldn't hear. He handed Mary-Rose a spoon.

'You've proposed here before?' Kitty asked.

'Oh, no, always a different place,' Sam explained. 'A criminal never returns to the scene of the crime.'

'Actually they do,' Mary-Rose said. 'That's the saying. A criminal always returns to the scene of the crime.'

Sam frowned. They were almost nose-to-nose, they looked so comfortable together, so at ease and yet it was all fake. Kitty doubted that. Somebody must have felt something. She thought about her and Steve, how so often people commented that there must be more to their relationship, despite her persistent denials. They wouldn't say it any more now he had Katja. She swallowed, feeling a shocking sadness sweep over her.

134

'But that's stupid,' Sam said. 'Why would they go back to the scene?'

'That's the point. They are stupid. They make mistakes and they go back or else it's for self-gratification. They get cocky. Just like you wanting to come back here and do this again.'

'I wouldn't do that.'

'In about a year I bet you'd risk it.'

They continued their debate and Kitty turned to watch everyone around her. It was undeniable that the atmosphere had completely transformed since Sam's proposal. Everyone resumed their conversations but this time it was with more gusto. The energy had picked up in the room, it was louder, there was more laughter, people had fed off their happiness, and whether they believed in love or not they were willing to celebrate on the young couple's behalf and bask in the glow of those who did. Sam had done more than get a free drink or a free meal, he'd done more than embarrass his friend, he'd lifted spirits, he'd brought everyone around them together, at least if only for a few minutes. He had done something very special.

Mary-Rose returned home to the sound of the television on upstairs as usual. She dumped her bag and coat on the stairs and went straight upstairs to her mother's bedroom. She was sitting up in bed, propped up by cushions, watching late-night infomercials. Her new obsession was with the kitchen knives, not the knives themselves but she loved watching the chefs chop at top speed. Mary-Rose read into it that her mother missed being able to be so agile, to chop and cook as she used to, but it could simply be nothing more than a fascination with the speed of professionals. She didn't like to think about it too much, though she was sure she probably would as she dedicated much of her day to thinking about what her mother could no longer do.

She greeted her with a kiss. 'Do you need to go to the toilet?'

Her mother nodded and Mary-Rose took her arms and lifted

them over her own shoulders, pushed back the bedclothes, scooped her arms under her mother's legs and lifted. Her mother was heavy; it always surprised her how much heavier she was than she looked each time she picked her up. Trying to stay steady, she slowly made her way to the en-suite bathroom and lowered her mother to the ground, where her mother held on to the safety bar on the wall while Mary-Rose pulled her panties down and lowered her to the seat. She turned her back then, her mother liked her to, and she tried to drift away in her mind to give her as much privacy as she could.

Her mother's muffled words snapped her out of her tired trance. Nobody but their care worker and her closest friend, Sam's mother, would understand what she had said – her words were like that of a child – but Mary-Rose smiled, then laughed.

'Yes, Mom, he proposed again.'

Her mother spoke again, and Mary-Rose shook her head. 'No. Don't be silly. It's just a bit of fun.'

But for some reason, that night, of all the nights that Sam had proposed, tonight her mother's comment made her think. A startling thought that for the first time didn't quite repel her.

CHAPTER THIRTEEN

Three things happened that Sunday to make it officially the worst day of Kitty's life.

First, after Kitty had got home from the restaurant she'd showered and fallen into a deep sleep when she was awoken at 2 a.m. to what sounded like an air-raid attack on her home. Outside her door, she learned afterward, a firecracker roll containing five thousand firecrackers had been lit and proceeded, with the loudest noise Kitty had ever experienced, to explode. When Kitty finally came out of hiding and opened the door, the floors and walls were black, stained with smoke and her landlord, Zhi Cheng Wong, was standing on the stairs surveying the damage.

He glared at her angrily and it was only then that she realised she could be held partly responsible for this.

'I'm sorry,' she said, trying to hide behind the door and pull her T-shirt down lower to protect her modesty. 'I'm sorry.'

'You must stop this.'

'I'm sorry. You're right. I'm sorry. It will. You won't even know this ever happened. I'll make sure it's all cleaned and painted. Promise.'

He barely stayed till the end of her sentence and went back downstairs to work. Kitty found it an odd time to wonder when he ever slept.

Fully dressed and still shaking from head to toe, she downed three cups of camomile tea and sat at her kitchen table, jumping at the sound of everything around her. It was 3 a.m., it was still pitch-black outside and she was absolutely terrified. She called Sally, whose phone was off, and then she phoned Steve.

'Can I stay with you tonight?' she asked, her voice still shaking.

'What's wrong?' He was suddenly awake.

'I'm fine,' she said, trying to be strong. 'It's just another stupid joke. Firecrackers. Outside my door. The place is a mess and Zhi wants to kill me but I'm fine. It's no big deal. Actually, I should probably stay here – it's not as if they're going to come back – but—'

'Uh shit, did they hurt you?'

'No, I'm fine, honestly, I'm fine. I'm just a little shaky.'

'You need to call the guards.'

'No, I can't do that.'

'Why not?'

'I just can't.'

'Okay. Fuck. Okay. Well, there aren't any spare beds here, everyone's home.'

'What about the couch?'

'They're not like the other guys I shared with, Kitty, they'd go mad if they found you on the couch. We have fucking house rules here.'

'Oh. Well, what about the one in your room?'

'No. Eh. No. Em. Can't really do that.'

'Stevie, who's that?' Kitty heard a groggy voice in the background.

'Oh, of course, I'm sorry. Katja is there. How silly of me. I'm fine, Steve, I'm sorry for disturbing you, I shouldn't have called, I just—'

'Kitty, shut the fuck up for a second and let me think,' he snapped.

She shut up.

'Okay. Come over here. You can sleep in my room. Katja and I will go to her place, okay?'

She heard Katja say something, then the phone was moved and a muffled conversation continued in the background.

'Yeah, that's what we'll do,' Steve said into the phone. 'Come on over here.'

'I can't let you do that, Steve, I don't want to kick you out of your own house.'

'Well, have you any other ideas?'

She hadn't. She hadn't had a good idea for over six months; she was all out. She couldn't call Bob. He would be distressed enough as it was without her landing on his doorstep. Sally wasn't answering her phone and she didn't want to just turn up at 3 a.m. when she had a husband and an eighteen-month-old child asleep. Kitty's family were hours away in Carlow and she had never gone home crying to them over anything. She contemplated a booty call to Richie but very quickly changed her mind. Steve was all she had right then, her only option.

'Okay,' she whispered.

It was not how she'd planned their first meeting: Kitty red-eyed and exhausted at 3.30 a.m., Katja, clearly exhausted from being woken in the middle of the night and then tossed onto the street by some idiot woman who was a friend of her boyfriend's, though she still had enough energy and politeness to hide whatever anger she was feeling and replaced it with a sympathetic look. They were whispering at the foot of the stairs, barely a conversation, just a handover of a bed.

'You okay?' Steve asked.

'Yes, I'm so sorry about this.'

'It's fine. I'm not sure when I'll be back tomorrow so . . .'

'I'll let myself out early, they won't even know I was here. I'm really sorry about this.'

'If you see Alice and Dave, don't tell them anything. It's none of their business. Tell them I'll talk to them later.'

'I won't see anyone, I'll be gone before they're awake. I'm so sorry about this.'

'Okay,' Steve quietly opened the door. It made a difference from his other rental properties, where coming and going at 3 a.m. and having randomers over to stay was the norm. She guessed he was growing up. What bad timing for her and her crises.

'It was nice to meet you,' Katja said, and gave her a sad smile before closing the door behind her.

Kitty stuck her tongue out at the closed door.

And so for the second bad thing of that day. At only 4 a.m., Kitty found herself in Steve's unmade bed, though someone clearly had made the effort to tidy it. The window was open but there was still a smell of sex in the room. Kitty avoided the bed and sat on the couch, wrapping herself in a blanket, where she remained sitting upright, watching the sunrise and listening to the birds awaken with the rest of the world. She must have fallen asleep for a short time as she woke up with a crick in her neck. It was seven o'clock and she was parched. It was Sunday and outside everything was still. There was no traffic, no car doors slamming, no postmen, no deliveries. The house was as silent as it had been four hours earlier. She folded the blanket and placed it back exactly where she'd found it, she freshened herself up in the en-suite bathroom and tiptoed downstairs. She crept towards the kitchen and opened the door, and there at the table a woman, Lisa, looked up at her, expecting to see Steve, and was forced to do a double-take.

'Who are you?' she asked.

A man in jogging clothes and a sweat-stained back and pits turned round and took headphones out of his ears. Dave.

'Uh, hi,' Kitty said, wishing she had gone straight for the front door.

'You're Kate,' Dave said. 'We met her at the Christmas party, Lisa. She's Steve's friend.'

'Oh,' Lisa said, clearly not remembering. 'Did you stay here last night?'

'Er . . .' Kitty was afraid to say the wrong thing as Steve had clearly stated that she didn't tell them anything, and he was intensely private. 'Steve told me to tell you that he'd talk to you later. Do you mind if I get a glass of water? I'll leave straight after.'

'Sure,' Dave said.

'Is Steve okay?'

'Yes.' Kitty tentatively opened cupboard after cupboard, not wanting to intrude in their space any longer and wishing she had just walked to the shop for a bottle. 'He said he'd explain later.' It really sounded more mysterious than it actually was.

'Is he upstairs?'

'No.'

Dave opened the cupboard behind her and handed her a glass. 'Thanks.'

She self-consciously went to the sink and they watched her.

'Are you sure he's okay? I heard him go to bed last night. He must have left in the middle of the night.'

'He's fine.'

'Do you know what he wants to talk to us about?'

Kitty was confused. They were making a big deal out of something very simple. She wasn't sure whether to stick to her line or explain. Instead she gulped down her water and they eventually looked away. Dave resumed buttering his toast and Lisa picked up her newspaper and what Kitty saw on the front almost stopped her heart as the third bad thing of that day happened. It also caused her to choke on her water and she circled her little spot in the kitchen coughing, spluttering and banging on her chest.

'Are you okay?' Dave asked.

Tears were streaming down her face.

'Wrong way,' she squeaked before convulsing with coughs again.

He watched her, not knowing whether to help her and choosing not to. Finally the fit eased and it was just the occasional cough here and there, mostly when she spoke.

'Can I see that?' She pointed at the Sunday tabloid.

141

Lisa closed it over and handed it to her. She took it in her hands, looked at the photograph of herself smiling sweetly to the camera with nice make-up, nice hair, nice lighting, the network's official press shot. Below the photo was '"My Year of Hell." *Thirty Minute* star Katherine Logan's exclusive interview with the *Sunday World* by Richard Daly'.

'What?' she shrieked, opening the newspaper to get to the article. On the inside, a double-page spread, there was a photograph of Colin Maguire and his wife leaving the courthouse, another photo of Donal, Paul and Kitty leaving with their team of lawyers looking like the Sopranos, the big nasty TV people, the big bad wolves, guilty as hell. But what took up most of the page was a photograph of Kitty leaving the Four Courts after Colin Maguire had been awarded damages, her face squeezed and pinched as though there were a bright sun glaring in her face. She had been caught mid-blink as though she were doped on methadone, not looking at all as she was trying to appear, and certainly not as she felt, which was contrite, apologetic and full of self-loathing. Elsewhere on the page, in contrast, was another official photo of Kitty looking sweet and innocent, honest and trustworthy. What that girl didn't know then. What that girl hadn't known two nights ago. Her old college friend had double-crossed her. Her eyes jumped across the words, barely able to read a full sentence and take it all in. She kept hopping from subheadings filled with tacky adjectives such as 'shocked' and 'appalled', to the photo of the journalist who got the scoop looking smarmy and as awful as she remembered him and his disgusting naked body from the previous morning. Richard Daly.

Colin Maguire and his crew of supporters are possibly behind the abusive attacks which Katherine has had to endure. The victim of a bully campaign, Katherine, known to some friends as Kitty, has been suspended by the network, cast aside at a time when she needed them most.

There was a pretty headshot of her and beneath it the caption said 'Scapegoat'.

> She now has been suspended from *Etcetera* magazine. Though the case had nothing at all to do with the magazine, terrified advertisers coming under pressure, possibly from Maguire's crew, are withdrawing their support in the face of such shoddy and careless journalism, leaving the magazine in uncertain times.
> Despite all that, Logan insists she is working on the most 'exciting project of her life' though she was reluctant to say what that was, leaving those who know her to speculate if there's such a story at all.

Beneath the article there was a poll taken with the public to see if Katherine Logan deserved the abuse she was getting. Seventy-two per cent said yes, eighteen per cent said no, ten per cent didn't care.

Kitty narrowed her eyes and stared at Richie's ugly face again. She wanted to do such violent things to him, it scared her.

'Writing a book, my hole,' she said aloud, then remembered she wasn't alone. She looked up and the couple were watching her, a little disgusted by her words and presence. She dropped the paper down on the table and left the house.

'Hey, is that her?' she heard Alice ask before she closed the door behind her.

And then one good thing happened that day, the first good thing, the only good thing, but sometimes you only ever need one good thing.

Archie Hamilton called her.

CHAPTER FOURTEEN

They met in the Brick Alley Café in Temple Bar, a charming café on Essex Street that seemed to be the only place that wasn't a pub or chain sports bar or establishment without a shamrock or leprechaun emblazoned across the front, Ireland's version of the childcatcher to lure in the tourists. It was a low-key place with friendly staff, and when Kitty entered she saw Archie sitting alone at the back of the café. He was the first customer of the day and had been successful in finding a table alone. Later, customers would be encouraged to sit at large wooden communal tables. He looked up when she entered, seemed slightly amused, and then he looked back down at his paper again. He appeared even more exhausted than he had before, as though he hadn't slept, but after two nights of very little sleep Kitty dreaded to think what she looked like herself. After calling Richie's phone sixteen times and getting no answer, she'd leaped on her phone as soon as it rang. She was lucky it was Archie.

She sat beside him on a high stool at a counter that was a wooden bench secured to the wall. Above the counter was a blackboard with the daily specials, and above that it said, 'Every table has a story to tell'. She knew that was certainly true of this table. She was just hoping Archie was going to tell it.

'Hi,' Kitty said.

Archie was sitting to the side of his chair so that his elbow was

144

resting on the counter and he could have a full view of the ro
Perhaps not wanting to turn your back on a room is what came
of doing time in prison. Or, in Kitty's case, it was pure nosiness.

'I just ordered breakfast,' he said into his paper. 'Do you want
to order some?'

She could tell the paper was the Sunday tabloid with her story.
So he had seen the article and for some reason that was probably
why he had called her. He didn't seem like the gloating kind, so
she waited for his reasoning to be revealed.

'No, thanks. I'm not hungry.'

'You should eat,' he said, still not looking at her.

'No.' She felt sick, sick by what she had read, by how she had
been lied to, humiliated, by the fact she had slept with Richie. She
felt disgusting and used and like she could never trust anyone ever
again, and the last thing she wanted was food.

'You need to keep your strength up,' he said. 'Or those fuckers
will get you down.'

She sighed. 'Too late for that.' She heard her voice tremble; he
did too and looked up from the paper. She was thankful his food
arrived at that point, though the smell of it made her queasy. A
large plate of tomatoes, eggs, bacon, sausages, mushrooms, black
and white pudding and enough toast to tile a roof with. The waitress placed it down before him and he finally set his paper aside
and transferred his concentration to the food.

'Are you ready to order?' the waitress asked.

'I'm not eating, thank you.'

'Tea, coffee?'

'Still water, please.'

'And a plate of fruit,' Archie said, cutting into his sausage. 'She'll
have a plate of fruit. Fruit stays down okay.'

'Thanks,' Kitty said, touched by how he cared. 'I suppose you're
the expert on this.'

He nodded his head in a horse-trying-to-get-rid-of-a-fly-on-his-
nose kind of way.

'What did you want to speak to me about?'

He didn't answer, he just shovelled the food in his mouth, massive amounts that puffed out his cheeks and he chewed merely a few times before swallowing. Then he spoke as though she never asked the question. 'Did you know the guy?'

She knew who he was talking about straight away.

'An old college friend.'

'Ha. That old chestnut.'

'They did that to you?'

'The entire family. And friends. They know how to catch people out. People who don't know better. People who aren't trained in how they work. People who believe what they read. Regular people.'

'I'm not regular people.'

'You're different. You're one of them, you weren't expecting it.'

'I'm not one of them,' she said, disgusted. 'Never have, never will. I made a mistake on a story; he did this deliberately.' Her blood boiled. She really wanted to run from this meeting straight away and confront Richie at his house but she was afraid of what she might do to him. She couldn't face assault and battery charges on top of everything else.

'You're angry,' he said, watching her. Her foot was bouncing up and down; she felt like putting her fist through the wall.

'Of course I'm angry.'

'That's why I phoned you.'

'You like talking to angry people?' she snapped.

He smiled. 'I wanted to speak to one of them who I knew would never be one of them. That fella, your old college friend, he did me a favour.'

'Well I'm glad he made one of us happy. So you trust me now.'

He didn't respond, kept tucking into his breakfast. Kitty's fruit and water arrived and despite feeling nauseous she picked at it and began to feel a little respite.

The café door opened and the third customer of the day entered. She was a mousy-looking woman, small face framed with dull brown chin-length hair and a fringe. She was meek-looking, thin and frail, as though a strong wind would blow her over. She looked around the café hopefully, as though expecting to see someone, and then her face fell and she sat at the communal wooden table. Archie actually looked up from his breakfast, took her in, and watched her cross the room and sit down. From that point on his eyes rarely left her.

'Know her?' Kitty asked.

'No,' he said bluntly, and turned away to down his tea. 'So what do you know about me?'

'A lot more than I knew about you on Friday.'

'Go on.'

'Ten years ago your sixteen-year-old daughter went missing. She was last seen on CCTV leaving a clothes shop in Donaghmede shopping centre. The gardaí issued a search for her, you and the family began a public search and a rather big campaign. A month later she was found in a field. She'd been strangled. Four years later you assaulted and viciously beat a twenty-year-old man believed to have been her boyfriend at the time and you went to prison for four years.'

There was a silence.

He chewed on the rind of his bacon, then threw the leftovers down on the plate.

'It was eleven years ago, it was one week before her sixteenth birthday.' He took a moment to compose himself and when he spoke again his voice was quieter. 'She was last seen by a witness in the car park of Donaghmede shopping centre telling that lad, Brian "Bingo" O'Connell, to leave her alone, a lad who was not her boyfriend but who was in fact her friend's boyfriend. He'd developed a fascination with her and wouldn't leave her alone. I told the gardaí all this the day she didn't come home. I told them countless times but they kept insisting they had nothing on

147

him. If it wasn't for a cabbage farmer who came across her body they never would have found a thing. They kept barking up the wrong tree.'

'More specifically, you,' Kitty said.

'They wouldn't leave me alone, they just couldn't get it out of their heads. The only person they fully investigated was me, and I was the only one with the slightest bit of information on the last place she was seen.'

'Maybe that was why.'

'My friend Brick was the guy in the car park. They were so obsessed with pinning it on me, they didn't believe anything I told them.'

'Don't they always look to the family first?'

'Not like that they don't. Brick wasn't exactly the most reliable of witnesses. He'd been in some trouble.'

Kitty supposed he didn't get a nickname like 'Brick' for any good reason.

They were silent. Archie watched the woman again. She was wringing a tissue around her finger, spiralling it till it pushed the skin up between the tissue and then unwinding it again. The café was filling up and the chef was busy behind the counter cooking fry-ups on a hot plate. The food sizzled and the smell filled the small room. Kitty's stomach churned and she reached for another grape.

'What made them eventually stop looking at you?'

'When they found the body.'

He was silent.

'She was raped, you know,' he said suddenly, and Kitty had a hard time swallowing her grape.

'No, I didn't know that.'

'I wanted to keep that out of the papers. Give her a bit of dignity. Her body had been left out too long and there wasn't enough evidence.'

'And you're sure it was that guy? Brian O'Connell.'

'Bingo,' he said firmly, confident as hell. 'As sure as I live and breathe. I used to see him around and he'd give me a look, a look like he'd got away with it and he found it funny.'

Kitty shook her head. 'I don't blame you for what you did to him.'

'I'd do it again if I could,' Archie said straight away. 'Only blessing is I didn't kill him, because it means I could do it again if I wanted.'

'You wouldn't.'

He dropped the bravado. 'I went far enough to see the fear in his eye and that was enough for me. I'll remember that look for ever. Keep it right here.' He tapped his temple. 'That was for Rebecca.'

Kitty thought about his life since then, family man, life torn apart by a tragedy, suffering twice as a consequence.

'You don't live with your wife any more?'

He shook his head. 'She moved to Manchester. She's with a good man. She's found a way to live again. She deserves it. It's not right to be living with such anger. It's unhealthy. It destroys things. Destroyed our marriage, my friendships. Needless to say my job wouldn't take me back. Having a record doesn't make you a desirable candidate for employment.'

Tell me about it, Kitty thought. 'So you work at the chipper.'

'And I'm a bouncer at a club around the corner. That's why I end up here for breakfast most mornings.' He looked at the woman again. 'Have to make ends meet. Work as many jobs as I can. Build my life back up again, as much as I can.'

'Any other jobs going?' Kitty asked.

He gave her that amused look. 'Nah. You're not looking for a job. You've got one.'

'I'm not so sure about that.' She thought about Pete and how the shit was really going to hit the fan after her supposed exposé in today's paper.

'Well, you make sure,' he said, standing up. 'Because you have a story to write. *My* story.' And with that, he left with his rolled-up paper, leaving Kitty to ponder that, and pay the bill.

Archie left Kitty Logan at the Brick Alley Café and followed the woman who'd been sitting inside. As always she'd had a pot of tea and a fruit scone with butter and jam, stayed for twenty minutes and then left. She was like clockwork; every single morning that Archie had been there for the past nine months she had also been there. She never acknowledged his presence despite the fact they were always the first two people in the café. She would walk in looking for somebody else, not see anybody who was really there, sit and wait for the ghost of someone else, and then leave. Though he only ate in the café on weekends after night duty in the club, he had started going a few times during the week just to see if she was there and sure enough she was. Eight o'clock on the dot she would enter the café with the same expression.

He followed her down Wellington Quay, across the Halfpenny Bridge to Bachelor's Walk, and watched her go into the Blessed Sacrament Church. He thought about following her, then changed his mind, not because it was inappropriate but because he couldn't bring himself to go in there. Not in there. Not with what was going on with him.

He turned round and made his way back to his flat.

CHAPTER FIFTEEN

Colin Maguire's sister, Deirdre, put a pot of tea down in front of him, with a blueberry muffin, his favourite. Anything to cheer him up, despite the fact the weight he was piling on was obvious. She just wanted to make him happy. Her poor baby brother had been through enough already and now that his wife, Simone, and the kids had moved out 'for a break', he needed her more than ever. Since the day it all happened he hadn't shown any sign of anger. She was waiting for it to happen, she was waiting for the day that he would explode. She didn't want to be here when it happened but she knew she would have to be. He didn't have anybody else. Plenty who supported him were there to give him the thumbs up on the street, or a slap on the back in the pub, but they weren't there for him, not really.

'Thanks, Dee,' he said gently, keeping an eye on the television.

'No problem. Are you sure you don't want to come out with us for lunch? It's a nice carvery. Neil says they put the football on a big screen. The kids will be there and they'd love to see you.'

'Nah. Thanks, though.' He gave her a small smile. 'I'll just watch it here.'

Deirdre stood up and stretched, she looked out the window. 'She's there again.'

Colin didn't need to ask who. He looked out the window briefly, seeing across the road to the green and beyond.

151

'Did you know that already?' she asked.

'Yeah.'

'Why didn't you tell me?'

'Because I'm not in the mood to run chasing after you across the green with a frying pan in your hand.'

'Frying pan? I'd do a lot better than that, believe me,' she fumed, hands on hips, looking out. 'How many times is this? The second? Third?'

'Fourth, I think.'

'What the hell is she doing?' She moved closer to the window to watch her.

'Don't, Dee, she'll see you.'

'I want her to bloody well see me. I don't know what she's planning but I swear to God I want to go out and deck her.'

'Dee, stop.' He said it so gently it made her drop her angry stance immediately. He was like their daddy: just didn't seem to be able to have any anger in him at all. Too soft, too gentle, too ready to be there to listen to other people's problems. That's what had got him in this mess in the first place. He should have let that stupid schoolgirl go off home with whatever problems she had that day instead of trying to console her. She'd taken him up wrong, read into his kindness too much and he'd paid for her embarrassment.

She sighed, 'I don't know how you do it, Colin. If I was you I'd want to go out there and do God knows what to her. Okay, I'll be late if I don't go now. If you change your mind about lunch let me know. We'll be there from two on, okay?' She kissed her brother on the head and left.

Colin made sure his sister drove the other way, not trusting her not to mow down the reporter. When she was gone and the house returned to the quiet he still couldn't get used to since Simone said she needed time to herself to think about their future, he took the paper from behind the cushion in the couch and he laid it out on the coffee table before him. He looked at the photo of Katherine

Logan on the front of the paper, the happy smiling face, and then inside, the woman who left the courthouse and he read the article again.

When he looked out the window again, she was gone.

CHAPTER SIXTEEN

The door to *Etcetera*'s offices was left open when Kitty arrived, which added to her anticipation and overall impending sense of doom. It said to her, come on in if you dare, the door's open, you have no choice now. The office was deserted – it was Sunday morning – and Pete could do anything to her here and nobody would hear her scream. She was pinning all her hopes on Bob coming to her rescue but the article was probably enough to send him over the edge too, as *Etcetera* were implicated as losing advertisers and being in financial trouble. Not good press.

When she entered Constance's office, Pete was standing, as usual, at the desk with the phone glued to his ear. He was wearing his weekend casuals, a look Kitty wasn't used to seeing on him, and again it struck her that he looked younger, more attractive than the jacket-wearing stressed-out egomaniac who patrolled the offices. He looked up at Kitty's approach and his face darkened.

'Gary, can I call you back?' He hung up abruptly. 'That was Gary. A solicitor that I've been on the phone to all morning trying to figure out where we stand on all of this.'

'What do you mean, a solicitor?'

'You did read the paper this morning?' he asked sarcastically. 'But I forgot, you didn't need to, you already knew what the story was before it was printed. You see, there's a little bit there about *Etcetera*'s advertisers apparently pulling out if you are not suspended.'

'Yes, but—'

'And so the other advertisers who weren't going to pull their money are now in a panic as to whether they should do the same or not, because paying for advertising in this magazine apparently makes them look bad,' he ended in a shout.

Kitty's eyes widened and she jumped a little at the volume of his voice. She had never seen him this angry before. Bitching, stressed and bad-tempered, yes, but never like this.

'You think I did this deliberately?' Her voice cracked. 'Jesus, Pete, if I wanted to tell my side of the story, I'd have done it a whole lot better, don't you think? I was on my way home from working on the story when I ran into an old college friend who seemed to have no idea about what happened with *Thirty Minutes*. So we went for drinks to catch up and in the space of an entire night – yes, an entire night, Pete, because it wasn't enough that he used me for a story, he had to go and degrade me and make me feel like a complete whore in the process – I talked about what had happened, of course I did, because I was upset. It's all been very stressful and I decided to talk to somebody about it, somebody who was totally unrelated to this world, a man who told me he was writing a novel, for Christ's sake, and who seemed to care, and when I woke up this morning I find that crap splashed all over the paper and I'm really exhausted because I had to sleep on a friend's couch so I am humiliated and mortified and extremely sorry, okay? I'm really sorry.' She hadn't realised she was crying until Pete held out a tissue to her and she felt her wet cheeks and her nose running.

'Okay,' he said gently. 'Okay, that's a different story entirely. I'm sorry for getting the wrong idea.'

Kitty simply nodded her thanks and continued wiping her streaming eyes.

'Is it true about the attacks on your flat?'

'Last night it was firecrackers. A firecracker roll, apparently. Five thousand of them. Hence the sleep on a couch.'

'Jesus, that could have been dangerous,' he said, face full of concern.

'I'm fine.'

'Did you call the guards?'

She shook her head.

'Why not?'

She shrugged but she knew exactly why.

'You haven't had an easy time of it, have you?'

Her tears started up again at the sympathy. 'I made a stupid mistake, Pete, a really bad, unprofessional mistake, and I ruined a man's reputation, possibly his life, and for that I deserve to be punished, but,' her tears took over again and she struggled to speak, 'I've had enough now. I just want to write nice stories about good people, I want to get back to doing what it is that I love, what makes my world normal again. And I want people to believe in me again. I want you to look at me and listen to me without the doubt that I can see so obviously. I'm second-guessing myself enough as it is, Pete. I don't need it from everyone else too.'

Pete looked at her, full of sympathy. 'Would it be unprofessional to offer you a hug?'

'Would it be unprofessional to accept?' she sniffed.

Though when she thought of it after, it was rather unprofessional behaviour, but sometimes when people are involved, business has to stop being business and the human must win. However, Kitty couldn't ignore the underlying truth that they both hung on to that hug for a little too long.

The curtains were still closed in Bob's flat when she left the office and she contemplated calling in to give her version of events before he heard it from someone else but she decided against it. If her sleepless nights were anything to go by, she was certain he needed his rest.

'I'll tell him,' she heard Pete say from the top of the stairs as he locked the door.

'Thanks.'

He looked around the car park. 'No bike today?'

'It was stolen.'

He looked at her with a half-smile in disbelief. 'Jesus, Kitty, the same people?'

'No, no, other people. I'm a popular lady.'

He shook his head. 'So it seems.' He looked at her as if he had never seen her before, as if this was their very first meeting. As if it just occurred to him that she was a person in the world he had an interest in getting to know. And to her surprise, she liked it. She liked him looking at her like that. He came down the steps and they started walking together.

'Can I give you a lift?'

'No, thanks, I'll walk.'

'To Fairview?'

'No, I'm just going as far as town.'

They reached his car and he opened the passenger door, extended his arm like an old-fashioned gentleman.

Kitty laughed. 'I forgot that you don't take no for an answer.'

It felt strangely intimate sitting next to him in his car.

'Where am I driving you to?'

'Busáras, please.' It was the main central station for bus routes nationwide.

'Is this your attempt to run away?'

'Not a bad idea. No, this is just a day trip. I'm interviewing another person on Constance's list in Straffan. A woman named Ambrose Nolan who runs a butterfly museum and conservation site.'

'A butterfly museum? Never heard of it.'

'Well, then, it will make a good read.'

'So how is this butterfly woman linked to the others you've met?'

'I thought I had until Friday to tell you that,' she said in mock indignation.

'It's only a week until we go to print,' he shot back. 'I was hoping to know what the story is before then.'

Me too, thought Kitty.

'You know, Oisín O'Ceallaigh and Olivia Wallace have agreed to write their stories for Constance's tribute.'

'Really?' Kitty's eyes widened. 'I can't believe you talked them into it. Did they ask for much money?'

'They're doing it for free. For Constance.'

Kitty nodded. Constance had so much respect for the writers, she was glad to see them returning the support she'd given them over the years.

'It's a really big scoop to get stories from them, Kitty,' Pete said. 'No one has seen or heard from Oisín for almost ten years. Olivia hasn't written for over five years and has turned down every publishing deal offer imaginable to return to writing.'

'I know, I agree.' Kitty replied emphatically, wondering why he felt he had to tell her the importance of this. These were big-name writers; it was obviously a huge deal for *Etcetera* to get the opportunity to publish their original stories.

'They're only doing this because it's for Constance's tribute and their stories can only be included in Constance's tribute section if we also have Constance's last story. Do you understand?'

Kitty swallowed. Nodded.

'So you need to keep thinking, Lois Lane,' he warned playfully.

'No pressure then,' she said, trying to hide her nerves with a smile.

'Welcome to my world,' he said and gave her such a vulnerable look she wanted to reach out to him. Instead she cleared her throat, severing their eye contact, and climbed out of the car.

When she reached the ticket desk they refused to let her buy a ticket. Her bus was driving off.

'Jesus,' she fumed, her phone starting to vibrate in her pocket. 'What next?' She looked at her screen: it was Steve. She had thrown the man out of his bed in the middle of the night and had probably caused his housemates to think he was terminally ill. She couldn't ignore this call.

'I'm sorry, I just said what you told me to say, then they read way too much into it and made it a bigger deal than it actually was. I'm sorry but I was just doing what you told me to do.'

There was a silence. 'What are you talking about?'

'Your housemates. They saw me this morning.'

'Never mind them, I haven't been home yet. Did you know he was a journalist?' He spoke quickly, with a sense of urgency.

She sighed and sat down on a chair. 'Steve, I know you don't think very highly of me and my moral standards but—'

'Did you know he was a journalist?' He sounded like he was running and out of breath.

'Where are you?'

'Answer the question, Kitty.'

'No. He told me he was writing a book. A fictional thing. A novel. He didn't mention anything about being a journalist. I feel such an idiot.'

'What happened?'

'Are you running or something because you really sound like—'

'What happened?'

'Jesus! Okay! He showed up at the dry-cleaners like it was the biggest coincidence in the world, even though he lived on the other side of the city. I should have known. Then we went for drinks, caught up on old times, he knew nothing about *Thirty Minutes*, didn't even pretend to be all that interested, which, again, I should have been suspicious of, but I'd had a few drinks, so I talked a little . . . then . . . it doesn't matter. Then that was it. We left.'

'No, that wasn't it. Then what?'

'No, it's embarrassing, Steve. I—'

'Tell me,' he practically shouted at her.

'I ended up in his place.' She felt physically sick. 'Oh God, I feel so . . . crap. What do you think I should do?'

He was quiet. Then just when she thought he'd gone, he said, 'What do you mean, you ended up in his place?'

'Jesus, how else can I put it? I stayed over, you know?'

'Okay,' he said quietly, and he hung up the phone.

Kitty stared at the phone in shock. He hung up on her, probably for the first time ever. He must have been so disgusted by her.

Kitty's phone rang again and, assuming it was Steve to tell her their connection failed, she answered it immediately. It wasn't.

'Kitty, are you okay?' Sally asked.

'No.'

'Where are you?'

'BusÁras.'

'Why?'

'I was going to Kildare but I missed my bus.'

'I'll drive you.'

'You don't even know when I'm coming back.'

'When are you coming back?'

'Never.'

'Perfect. I'll be there in twenty minutes.'

Kitty had met Sally at a television presentation course five years previously. Sally was a meteorologist who had attained an honours degree in Mathematical Physics and, at the time, was working in Met Éireann and preparing to stretch her wings by moving into television weather presentations in the Irish language. Along with writing for *Etcetera*, Kitty, at that time, was preparing to make her move into television journalism after presenting a few small but successful shows on a small city channel. She had set her sights on bigger stories on a bigger network and was fine-tuning her presentation skills, which meant slowing down her speech and trying to stop looking so concerned or, in Steve's words, constipated, when she was concentrating on remembering her words.

Sally arrived at BusÁras with the top down on her convertible, and her long blond hair tied back. Kitty quickly scuttled away from her hiding place by the vending machine with her head down and as much hair in front of her face as possible.

'Everyone around me is reading the paper,' Kitty explained, after embracing her friend. 'I'm probably just being paranoid, though. I'm sure they're not paying the slightest bit of attention to my story, they're too busy reading about the earthquake. Aren't they? Tell me they're all reading about the earthquake.'

'There was an earthquake?' Sally asked without a hint of irony.

Kitty sighed. 'Isn't it your job to know about things like that?'

'I don't work weekends.'

'Obviously not.' Kitty looked up at the grey clouds they were headed towards. 'Maybe you should put the roof up; it looks like it's going to rain.'

Sally laughed as if she had the inside scoop, which she believed she had. 'It's not due to rain today.'

'Thought it was your weekend off.'

'I pay attention,' she shrugged, and they laughed.

'So, where are we going?'

'Straffan, to a butterfly farm.'

'Why?'

'I'm interviewing the woman who runs it. Kind of. She doesn't know she's going to be interviewed yet.'

'Be careful. Are you trying to get your own back?'

Kitty smiled but it faded quickly. 'At least I won't sleep with her for her story.'

Sally gasped. 'You slept with him?'

Kitty covered her face in her hands and slid down the chair. 'I'm a despicable human being.'

'Not really, but you know you could have got some money for the story, or were you desperate for sex?'

Kitty laughed. 'I'm kind of desperate for both.'

Sally gave her a sympathetic look and Kitty explained what had happened that night.

'Have your parents called?' she asked, after getting over her initial anger.

'Yes. To tell me once again how embarrassed and ashamed they are of me. I just let Mum get it out of her system. It seems to help her to have a go at me but there's nothing new there.' She looked up at the sky as she felt a drop of rain fall on her face.

'Did you feel that?'

'What?'

'Rain.'

'It's not going to rain today,' Sally said confidently.

Ten minutes later they had to pull over by the side of the road while Sally manually closed the roof.

'That's unusual,' Sally said, glancing up at the sky, and Kitty tried to hide her smile.

An hour and a quarter later they were fully updated on each other's lives and they had reached the butterfly museum in Straffan. It was situated just outside the village: a charming house beside the museum with plenty of land stretching all around it. Open seven days a week during the summer months, it was composed of a tropical house with a bridge over a small pond, with butterflies fluttering all around them.

Kitty asked a young girl at the customer desk for Ambrose Nolan and was instead diverted to a bow-tie-wearing man named Eugene, who told her that Ambrose didn't do tours. On learning Kitty was a member of the media he proceeded to take her and Sally on a personal tour of the museum, which was busy, on this reasonably good-weathered Sunday, with families and children. He was so jolly and full of such *joie de vivre* that Kitty couldn't bring it upon herself to stop his excited chatter about the butterflies he seemed to love and know so well. He certainly was up with his knowledge of the various species, and she wouldn't have been surprised if he was on a first-name basis with every butterfly in the tropical room.

'Many of the tropical butterflies breed here so you will able to observe the entire life cycle of a butterfly,' he explained as they stepped out to the tropical room. 'Here you will see where they have laid eggs, caterpillars eat the food plants, then they become well-camouflaged pupae, and if you're lucky you can watch a butterfly emerge from a pupa to start a new life with wings and set off on its first flight.'

Sally widened her eyes sarcastically at Kitty.

Kitty ignored her and looked around for Ambrose. 'So you said Ambrose doesn't do guided tours, but does Ambrose work here?'

'Oh, indeed, Ambrose has been working here for the past . . . well, since she was a child. Her mother and father opened the museum and when Ambrose was old enough she helped run the family business. She has been instrumental in developing what was initially just a small museum into this great centre. She extended the museum, which used to be in what is now the gift shop, into this great big exhibition room, she introduced the café and picnic area, which as you can see was a marvellous idea, and five years ago she opened the tropical room. If it wasn't for Ambrose, these facilities just simply wouldn't be here today,' he said proudly.

'Is *she* here today?' Kitty tried again.

'She's here every day,' he laughed. 'She lives next door but she doesn't see visitors. Now let me bring you through to the museum and I can show you what we do in more detail. The framed butterflies are from surplus captive-bred butterflies; they are not collected in the wild,' he explained seriously as he led them to the gallery.

Sally gave Kitty a withered look but Kitty prodded her and they followed him, while Kitty looked around for a way to get to the house next door.

The gallery consisted of dried butterflies exhibited in sealed timber frames with an internal mount and brass plate.

'These are perfect specimens,' Eugene explained, and a few customers drew nearer to them to listen to the talk. 'They haven't been altered in any way. Specimens last for fifty years but must not be hung in direct sunlight. Many of the butterflies are over one hundred years old and are still as bright as the day they were originally flying.'

He looked at them, his face flushed with the thrill of the idea.

'Fascinating,' Kitty said, looking at the wall and wondering how to change the conversation. 'Is it possible for me to speak with Ambrose today?'

'I'm afraid Ambrose isn't working in the museum today.'

'Is she at home? Could I call to her there?'

'Oh, I doubt she's in there on a day like this,' Eugene chuckled. 'Ambrose is working on a butterfly conservation garden on her land. She really is extremely dedicated to protecting our butterflies and making sure we don't do damage to their natural populations or environments.'

Kitty looked out at the picnic area and saw the 'Private. Staff Only' gate leading from the premises.

'She sounds like a wonderful woman,' Sally said.

'Oh, yes indeed, she is,' Eugene became a little flustered and he blushed. 'She has dedicated her life to conserving butterflies. Ms Logan,' he lowered his voice so that the people listening to his lecture wouldn't overhear, 'Ambrose is . . . very private, you see. If there's anything you would like me to ask her for you I promise I will do so and get in immediate contact with you. It's just that . . . well, Ambrose is private,' he repeated and then he resumed his normal tone. 'This beautiful butterfly here is called the Dark Green Fritillary from the Nymphalidae family, also known as *Mesoacidalia aglaia*. It is a large, powerful, bright orange butterfly, which you often see battling with the breeze on a cliff top, limestone pavement or sand dune. Startlingly visible yet frustratingly evasive, it is a grassland species that breeds on common dog-violet. Both sexes have a greenish underside on the hindwing.'

As more people gathered around to hear Eugene speak, Kitty

slowly backed away from the group while he was distracted. She headed straight to the picnic area, and when she noticed Eugene looking in her direction warily, she pointed discreetly to the ladies' toilet and he nodded and continued his talk. As soon as he looked away Kitty hurried to the gate that said, 'Private. Staff Only'. She pushed it open and stepped into a wonderland, a long lawn bursting with colour, butterflies fluttering to and fro, skimming her nose as they hurried to get out of her way. At the end of the garden Kitty saw a stooped figure.

'Excuse me,' Kitty called.

The figure stood up straight, turned round, then turned her back on Kitty. She pulled her hair down, long wild red hair, like fire, that fell to the small of her back.

'Stop!' she called, and her voice was so adamant that Kitty immediately halted.

'I'm sorry,' Kitty called. 'My name is—'

'You're not allowed in here,' the woman shouted.

'Yes, I know, I'm very sorry, I—'

'This is private premises. Please go back!'

Her voice was authoritative, but Kitty discerned a note of panic at the periphery of her words, and her posture showed she was afraid.

Kitty took steps back and then changed her mind. She had one chance to do this.

'My name is Kitty Logan,' she called. 'I work for *Etcetera* magazine. I wanted to talk to you about your stunning set-up here. I'm sorry to have frightened you. I just wanted to talk to you.'

'Eugene deals with press,' she barked. 'Out!' Then she added more gently, 'Please.'

Kitty backed away but when at the gate she tried one more time. 'I just need to know one thing. Did Constance Dubois contact you at any stage in the past year?'

She expected to be shouted at again, to find the gardening fork being flung at her head, but instead there was silence.

'Constance,' she said suddenly and Kitty's heart started racing. 'Constance Dubois,' she repeated.

Ambrose still wouldn't turn around.

'Yes. Do you know her?' Kitty asked.

'She called me. One time. She asked about a caterpillar.'

'She did?' Kitty asked, in shock, her mind racing. Had these names got to do with her initial interview? 'An Oleander caterpillar?'

'That means something to you?'

'Yes,' Kitty said breathlessly, trying to take it in and process what this could possibly mean for a story.

Ambrose finally turned round but all Kitty could see was her wild hair. 'You can wait for me in there.' She pointed the gardening fork at the open door that led to her house.

Kitty looked at it in surprise. 'Thank you.'

She stepped inside and found herself in the kitchen. It was a modest home, a charming country cottage that had been updated but kept true to its roots. The Aga took over the room, its heat still emanating from breakfast time. She sat at the kitchen table and watched the woman finish up work, make her way towards the house, head down, all wild red hair covering her, still not meeting Kitty's eye even as she stepped into the house and asked her if she'd like a cup of tea.

Kitty thought of Sally being lectured on butterflies of Ireland by Eugene and guiltily said yes to the tea. Ambrose did most of her talking with her back turned, and when she finally sat at the rectangular table, which seated eight, she chose to sit not opposite Kitty but at the end of the table, at the corner, looking away. It took a long time and an awkward warming-up conversation for Kitty finally to be able to make eye contact with Ambrose, and when she did she noticed something unusual. Ambrose had eyes of different colours, one a striking green and the other a deep dark brown. And it wasn't just that: when her thick hair finally did move a centimetre from where it had been strategically placed,

Kitty could see the discoloration that spread from the middle of her forehead and went down her nose, over her lips, half her chin, and disappeared beneath her high-collared blouse. The burn, if it was that, looked like a flame licking unevenly at the right side of her face, and as quickly as Kitty had seen it, it disappeared again as the thick veil of red hair was closed, and one bright green eye remained staring out at the kitchen table.

CHAPTER SEVENTEEN

If Kitty had been told that Ambrose had never before spoken to a human being, she would have believed it. She wasn't rude but she had no real understanding of how a conversation worked. There was no eye contact, or at least only an accidental one, enough for Kitty to see the disfigured face and the varying eye colours. Perhaps Kitty's reaction had been reflected in her face because Ambrose had chosen not to look at her again. Apart from failing to look her in the eye, where she positioned herself at the end of the table, she could turn her body away from Kitty. Kitty was looking at Ambrose's right side. At least the hair there had been tucked behind her ear to show pale porcelain skin. She really was the most unusual person Kitty had ever met, not just physically, but characterwise too.

Her conversation was as unsettling as her demeanour. Her voice was quiet but, as if conscious of it, she spoke up on certain words and then forgot again, other words disappearing in whispers. Kitty had to listen hard to hear.

'She called me. Yes it was. Last year. I remember. Because it was. Unusual.' She shouted the word 'unusual', and then as if she'd given herself a fright she continued in a whisper, 'She wanted to come to see me. To interview me. Yes, that's what it was. I told her no. That I don't. Do interviews.'

'Did she say what the interview was about?'

'Eugene. I told her to talk to Eugene about the museum. He deals with the public. Not me. She said it wasn't about the museum. She didn't know about the butterflies.'

'It was about you personally?'

'That's what she said. I told her I didn't want to. The list. She said she would keep me on the list anyway. I don't know what that means.'

'The list of people she wanted to interview,' Kitty explained. 'She left a list of one hundred names of people she wished to speak to and write about.'

'She called me again. A few days later. She had a question about a caterpillar.'

'The Oleander,' Kitty smiled.

'Laughing. She was laughing. She thought it was funny. In a nice way. She was nice,' she said gently, and finally her eyes lifted and flicked to Kitty for a split second and looked away again, as if she knew Constance was gone. 'She asked if she could visit. To talk to me. To see the museum. I told her she could visit. Not me. The museum. But it was only open for the summer months. Spring. She called me last spring. She never came.'

Kitty didn't need to look away to hide her tears. Ambrose would not look at her anyway.

'She got sick,' Kitty explained and her voice came out as a croak. She cleared it. 'She was diagnosed with breast cancer last year and she passed away two weeks ago.'

'Daddy died of cancer.'

It wasn't the usual sorry but it was full of empathy.

'Are you here to collect her order?'

Kitty's tears automatically stopped. 'What order?'

'Oh. I thought that was why you were here. I kept it for her. On display. I put it on display and nobody else bought it. A framed one. An Oleander moth. She said it was a gift.'

Ambrose suddenly upped and left the room, her long hair and loose clothing giving her a fluttering butterfly effect, and while Kitty waited, she wiped her flooding tears and smiled.

'I ran the museum with Daddy,' Ambrose explained after Kitty had gone into further detail about why it was she was really there. Ambrose, like most people, had been reluctant to talk to her at first, but when Kitty had suggested, quite honestly, that it would also be good for the business, as well as a personal adventure, and promised there would be no photographs of Ambrose, she agreed to start talking and Kitty kept writing as she talked, her mind racing as she tried to piece everything together.

Story Idea: People intrinsically don't believe that they are interesting.
   or
People who believe that they are not interesting, usually are the most interesting of all.

Kitty was aware of the threatening text messages she was receiving from Sally, who was still stuck in a lecture with Eugene and a group of tourists who kept asking too many questions, but Kitty couldn't let this opportunity pass her by. She still had no idea why Constance had chosen Ambrose for the story, though she knew it was not for the butterfly museum, and she was determined to discover what it was Constance had already found. Kitty was personally and not just professionally interested in hearing this intriguing woman's story.

'Mammy and Daddy had opened it together but Mammy died and Daddy took over.'

Ambrose must have been in her forties, but it was difficult to say. She often sounded childlike, and held the shyness of a child, but equally often stooped her body and appeared like an old woman.

'How did your mother die?' Kitty asked gently. She expected her to say a fire or something that would help explain Ambrose's appearance. She couldn't figure out how to broach that subject. It was fascinating to her and yet it was the one question she felt she probably would never be able to ask and possibly the one issue that would never be broached.

'Childbirth. Complications. She had me here. In the house. They probably would have saved her if she'd had me in a hospital but it's not what she wanted. So. 'Twas to be.'

'I'm sorry.' Kitty took a slug of her tea. 'Eugene seems to be a great help and certainly very knowledgeable,' she said.

Ambrose looked up then and smiled. Not at Kitty but out the open door into the garden, which was alive with butterflies and nature. She seemed to light up. Then she faded again. 'Eugene loves butterflies. I didn't think it would be possible to find someone who loved them as much as Daddy did. I couldn't do this. Not without Eugene.'

'He says the same. He said that none of this would be here if it wasn't for you,' Kitty told Ambrose, who smiled shyly. 'How did you find him?'

'His mammy was my tutor. He came to my house with her for my classes. He was always bored stiff. Sometimes he'd sit in on the classes, other times, most times, he wandered around the museum. That's how he knows so much. He's been looking at those butterflies in frames for over thirty years.'

'You were homeschooled?' Kitty prompted.

'Yes,' Ambrose was silent but Kitty waited, sensing more was to come and beginning to understand her way of stop-start communication. 'Children can say the cruellest of things. Isn't that what they say? I was, well, I was unconventional.'

That was an understatement.

'Daddy thought it best I stay here.'

'Were you happy with that?'

'Oh, yes,' she said firmly. 'This place is all I've known.'

'Do you mind me asking how old you are?'

She looked like she did mind. Shoulders hunched, more face disappeared behind yet more hair to have a long discussion with herself, which Kitty could see taking place. 'Is it important?'

Kitty thought about it. In some cases it wasn't, in this it was. 'If you don't mind.'

'Forty-four.'

Kitty's phone continuously vibrated, four, five, six missed calls in a row. As soon as it would stop it would start again. Sally was mad, and Kitty didn't want to miss her lift home.

'Excuse me, do you mind if I use your toilet?' Kitty asked.

Like being asked about her age, Kitty thought she would mind but Ambrose seemed relieved to have some respite from being questioned. One of Kitty's favourite things to do was to snoop. She looked into every room she passed, then instead of going right as she was instructed, she took a left. Judging by the other rooms she passed, this must have been Ambrose's bedroom and it took her breath away. One entire wall of the room, the wall facing the bed, was covered from floor to ceiling with magazine cut-outs of supermodels, actresses, singers, models. Some images were specific – of their hair, their eyes, their noses, their lips – others were of their entire faces. Some faces had been made up entirely of a collage of different women's features. Just as her museum was covered in framed collections of butterflies, her bedroom was equally such a museum, a celebration of beauty. However, it felt less like a celebration than the museum, one that caused a shudder to run down Kitty's spine. She quickly left the room.

When Kitty Logan finally left, Ambrose felt exhausted. She hadn't had that much contact with anybody, apart from Eugene, of course, for a very long time, and she felt drained, tired from trying to cover her face, hide her emotions, work hard at appearing normal, sounding sane, all of the things that she was by herself in the comfort of her own home but which she struggled with when she came into contact with anyone who wasn't inside her trusted circle. Those people consisted of Eugene; Harriet, the cleaner; and Sara, the young lady who worked in the museum. She rarely spoke to any of them, only when she absolutely had to, and it was only with Eugene that she could truly be herself because he *was* only Eugene, and what did he care? He had seen her all her life. The irony was that with everybody else she let her hair down and he was the only person for whom she could truly tie her hair back and look him in the eye.

She made her way to her bedroom and retrieved the magazine she had been reading that morning. Summertime, apart from the butterflies and her business, wasn't her favourite time of year. Summer meant revelation, magazines were covered with photos of celebrities and pretty women on beaches in their bikinis, the museum was filled with pretty women who never questioned being able to tie their hair back and wander without self-consciousness through the rooms or down the street. Ambrose liked the winter when she could layer up and disappear. She hadn't travelled much in her life but if she had her way she would book a holiday to somewhere cold, only she couldn't leave the business or her butterflies in the summertime.

She carefully cut out a photograph of a soapstar she didn't recognise who had been snapped on the beach in a tiny bikini after apparently shedding all the weight after having her baby a mere six weeks ago. She stuck the photo on the wall, making sure it wasn't blocking any of the others she needed to see and she proceeded to sit on the end of her bed and examine it for fifteen minutes. She looked at her eyes, her nose, her lips, her long neck, the arch of her back, her pert bottom, the way her thighs were firm and tanned, the way her toes were perfectly painted and wore little shoes of sand. She got lost in the photograph; for moments Ambrose was that girl, she was on that beach, she was getting out of the water, feeling eyes on her and feeling the heat on her body, feeling the sea water tricking down her body but knowing that she looked great, feeling light and happy and relaxed as she made her way to her sunbed to sip a cocktail. Ambrose lived it so vividly in her head.

Kitty Logan had asked her why she collected butterflies, why the fascination? Ambrose hadn't lied, but hadn't answered her truthfully as her response was incomplete. Why did she love butterflies? Because they were simply beautiful. And she wasn't.

It was the same reason she had always loved the story of 'Beauty and the Beast' when she was a child, and despite the fact she was

173

twenty-three when the Disney film was released, she went to see it in the cinema time and time again, watching it every day when it was out on video, knowing every word, every look, every single gesture each character made. Her daddy had been bewildered by her childish fascination with a cartoon, but he had misunderstood her love for it. It wasn't for the romance, it wasn't because she wanted to see a beast become handsome again, she watched it because, like the Beast capturing Belle, she knew what it was like to recognise beauty, to be so fascinated by it and to feel so alive when around it that she wanted to trap it and keep it locked up inside for her to see and celebrate every day.

'Who on earth is texting you?' Sally asked as they drove home from Kildare. It was the first thing she had said in a while and Kitty guessed she was slowly being forgiven.

'Why?' Kitty frowned.

'Because you've had that stupid smile on your face since you started that little textersation.'

'Textersation? No, that is not a word.'

'Stop trying to change the subject, who is it?'

'It's no one, it's just Pete.' She said it way too nonchalantly.

Sally's eyes widened. 'Pete, the prince of doom duty editor whom you despise Pete?'

'I never said I despised him.'

'Oh. My. God.'

'What?'

'Oh dear. You know what's happening, don't you?' Sally jested.

'Shut up, no, it's not. Be quiet, okay?' Kitty attempted to place her hand over Sally's mouth to stop the words coming out. Sally giggled and the car swerved so Kitty took her hand away immediately.

'Okay, fine, I won't say it, but you know you know it,' she said in a singsong voice.

'He's just seeing if I'm okay,' Kitty said, closing her phone and putting it away in her bag, and as soon as she did that she regretted it because she wanted to see if he'd responded to her rather witty and well-planned last text.

They settled into silence again and drove towards the darkening night, the sky red in the distance.

'Red sky at night,' Kitty said, 'shepherd's delight.'

'Oh, don't be silly,' Sally said. 'That doesn't make any sense. It's supposed to be torrential rain tomorrow.'

They fell into silence again and Kitty's mind drifted from Pete and on to her story. She thought of all the people she had met so far: Birdie Murphy, Eva Wu, Mary-Rose Godfrey, Archie Hamilton and Ambrose Nolan. She tried to find the link between them all but just couldn't see any. She twisted their life stories around in her head, tried to compare and contrast each and every little thing she knew about them, and while similarities could be found, there was no real link, no real story, but each was so strong in its own rights. She needed to start with a fresh mind and listen to their stories – perhaps constantly trying to find a link was stopping her story from flowing. She reached for her bag and Sally teased her about going for her phone but Kitty had already forgotten about that. She took out her notepad and pen and Sally realised she was in the zone and left her alone.

She thought of Ambrose, of the framed butterflies and the pictures on her wall.

Name Number Two: Ambrose Nolan
Story Title: Kalology – The Study of Beauty

CHAPTER EIGHTEEN

Kitty slept in Sally's house that night.

When they returned from Straffan to Kitty's flat, that day's newspaper article was rewarded with horse manure trailing up each step to her door on which it had been used to write the words 'Dirty Sell-Out Whore'. Even after so much abuse, Kitty still managed to feel hurt. She contemplated taking a photograph of the door and sending it to Richie along with a note of thanks, but decided against it as it would probably be tomorrow's news. The one thing she could be thankful for was that the attacks were never inside her home and never on her physically.

Kitty grabbed a change of clothes, in fact enough to last her a week, and then she turned on her heel to escape to Sally's car.

Zhi, the landlord, blocked her path.

'I'm sorry, Zhi, I'm in a massive rush. Can you please just—' She stepped to the right to pass him but he blocked her, so she stepped to the left and he blocked her again. She gave up and sighed. 'I'll arrange for this to be cleaned as soon as I can.'

'It is not good enough. Last week paint, toilet paper and shit, last night firework, today more shit. It is not good for my business.'

'I know, I know. I really don't think it will happen for much longer. They'll eventually get tired and stop it.'

He wasn't having any of it. 'The end of month I get new tenant. You out. You find other place to—'

'No no no no no,' Kitty interrupted, hands together and desperately pleading. 'Please, please don't say that. This is just a blip. I have been a good tenant, haven't I?'

He raised his eyebrows.

'I won't tell anyone about the PERC.'

His face darkened. 'You threaten me?'

'No! I said I *won't* tell anyone about the PERC. I *won't*.'

'Then why you it bring up? End of month you out,' he said, and stormed back down the stairs.

While Kitty was still on the stairs contemplating how much worse her life could get and where on earth she was going to find a place to live on a much lower income, Zhi reappeared with an item of clothing on a hanger, wrapped in plastic.

'And your friend,' he added, coming back up the stairs. 'He no pay for his suit jacket. He supposed to pay this morning. You pay. Ten euro.'

'No, no, he's *not* my friend. I'm not paying for that.'

'He your friend. I see you all kissy kissy. You pay. Ten euro. You pay.'

'No way. It's not mine. No way.'

He started to back away.

'Okay, let's make a deal. I'll pay for his jacket if you let me stay in the flat.'

He thought about it. 'You pay for jacket and I think about it.'

Kitty tried to fight her smile. 'Perfect.' She rooted in her bag for the money and handed it over. He gave her the jacket. 'So I can stay?'

'No,' he barked. 'I say I think about it and I think about it and answer is no.' On that note he stormed back down the stairs leaving Kitty open-mouthed.

After leaving Sally's responsible Rathgar home, with responsible furniture, her responsible husband with a responsible car and job, who'd talked to her over a responsible breakfast about his responsible golf trip away the previous weekend, Kitty left the responsible child-minder with Sally's eighteen-month-old and walked with Sally into the city. At 7.30 a.m. it was already warm, with a light breeze in the air. Though there was no need for a coat, Sally was wearing a thick sweater, had a raincoat hooked over her arm and was holding the largest umbrella Kitty had ever seen.

'Are you planning on providing housing for the homeless?' Kitty asked, eyeing up the umbrella.

'It's Douglas's golf umbrella.'

'I see that. Do you also hire it out for marquee events?'

Sally ignored her.

'It's warm today.' Kitty took off her cardigan.

Sally looked up at the clear blue sky. 'Supposed to have torrential rain today.'

'Not likely, though, is it?'

Sally smiled a knowing secret smile as if she alone held the country's weather secrets in her head. 'So what are you doing today?'

'I'm having breakfast with an ex-convict, brunch with a personal shopper, an afternoon with a hairdresser to the sick, an evening at a nursing home and then a date tonight with manure and a bucket of bleach.'

'Well, you can't say your life isn't boring.'

'No, it's definitely not that. And somewhere along the way I need to find a new place to live.'

'You know you're very welcome to stay with us for as long as you like,' Sally offered.

'I know that, and thank you, but I can't. I need to sort myself out.' Kitty tried to hide her worry. She wasn't going to be able to afford anywhere by herself, she would have to revert to sharing accommodation, and just when she thought she was moving forward in life with a larger salary and a shared rent, she found herself with little money to survive on alone. She wasn't sure if her job at *Etcetera* was in jeopardy, but assumed that it was despite the fact that Pete had been surprisingly kind and supportive the past two days, if not a little cosier than usual. She knew that the magazine was under pressure from advertisers not to print her stories. If she didn't publish stories, she didn't get paid, it was as simple as that, and she didn't think there were many other publications queuing up for her freelance services.

Sally's cheeks were flushed, she puffed a little and then rolled up the sleeves of her sweater. Kitty tried not to smile. Before they parted ways, Sally reached into her pocket, retrieved a business card and handed it to Kitty.

'Daniel Meara. That name's familiar,' Kitty said, reading it.

'He works at Ashford Private College.' The college where Kitty and Sally had met five years previously. 'He recently got in touch with me asking if I'd be interested teaching some night classes. I told him I couldn't but that I'd send some people to him who were equally qualified.'

Kitty looked at the card and swallowed. It was as close to a handout as she could get and she didn't like it, but knew that Sally, with her breezy attitude, was trying to make it sound like anything other than that.

'I don't have experience in teaching,' Kitty said, still examining the card.

'Doesn't matter, you have experience in television. That's all they need: someone who has first-hand experience and can tell them exactly what goes on behind the scenes. Besides, who cares? Let them be the judge of your teaching skills. It's good money.'

Kitty nodded.

'Just call him, give it a go, see if it's for you. It might not be but you know, it's worth a try.'

Kitty nodded again and finally looked up from the card. 'You're sure you don't want to do this yourself?'

'I can barely cope as it is,' Sally smiled. 'With work all day, and the occasional weekend shift at the station, I'm not seeing Finn enough already. Not to mention Douglas. You go for it.'

'Thanks.' Kitty hugged her friend.

'Don't worry,' Sally hugged her tight in return, 'we all have our blips. Remember when we first met?'

Kitty recalled Sally had just learned that Doug had had an affair, she was piecing her marriage back together, trying to do something new for herself in television and every day was a struggle for her.

'See, we all go through it, now it's your turn. It's only fair.' Sally kissed her on the forehead and they parted.

Kitty made her way to the Brick Alley Café in Temple Bar, excited to hear the remainder of Archie's story, and found him sitting at the same counter on the same stool, half-turned so that he could keep an eye on the room and eat at the same time.

'I suppose you expect me to pay for that again today,' she said, sitting beside him.

He smiled.

'Fruit and water?' the waitress from the previous morning asked.

'Yes, please,' Kitty replied, surprised she remembered her order.

'They're a dying breed,' Archie said, chewing the rind of his bacon. 'Not enough places like this. They know what you want and they leave you alone. A winning combination.'

The door opened and the mousy woman from the previous day entered.

'It's like Groundhog Day in here,' Kitty remarked.

The woman looked around, the hope visible on her face, then sat down, disappointed.

'The usual?' the waitress asked her, and the woman merely nodded.

'Why don't you just go over to her?' Kitty asked.

'What?' Archie snapped out of his trance and pushed his plate aside, embarrassed to be caught.

'The woman,' Kitty smiled. 'You're always looking at her.'

'What are you talking about?' His cheeks flushed. '*Always.* Sure, you've only been here twice.'

'Whatever,' she smiled, and let the dust settle before she moved on to more serious topics.

'I came prepared today,' she said, taking out her notepad and recorder.

The way he looked at the apparatus made her nervous he would back out, and she could have kicked herself for her error. Many people became uncomfortable around recording equipment. If the camera was the asshole magnet, her recorder often brought the shyness out of people. Nobody liked the sound of their own voice – well, most people didn't – and the recorder brought out the self-conscious realisation that their words were being listened to, less like a conversation and more of an interview.

'I don't have to use this if you don't want me to.'

He waved his hand dismissively as if he didn't care.

'So we were talking about your daughter's death—'

'Her murder,' he interrupted her.

'Yes. Her murder. And how the guards focused on you during the case, and you felt that it distracted them from finding the real killer.'

He nodded.

'I thought we could talk a bit more about that. How you must have felt, how frustrating it must have been to have vital information that wasn't being listened to.'

He looked at her with that amused gleam in his eye again. 'You think that would interest people?'

'Of course, Archie. It's everyone's worst nightmare and you went through it. People would be fascinated to hear about the reality of living through it, and I think it would help people to change their opinion of you too. You know, workwise, instead of seeing an ex-prisoner, they'd understand who you really are. That you were a father protecting his daughter.'

181

He looked at her and his eyes softened, his jaw, his shoulders, everything. 'Thank you.'

She waited.

'But the thing is, that's not the story.'

'Pardon?'

'My daughter's murder – sure that's part of it, I think it has a lot to do with what has happened and it was my story then – but it's not my story now.'

Kitty looked down at all her notes. She'd stayed awake working until three thirty that morning in Sally's responsible spare bedroom. 'So, what's the story?'

He looked down. 'I never believed in God. Not even at school when my priestly teacher drummed the fear and the guilt into us. I believed that he believed it, all right, but I thought he was mad. Delusional. I thought if somebody had to force you that much to believe in something then it wasn't worth believing, that it wasn't natural, you know?'

Kitty nodded.

'I prayed at night before I went to bed as routinely as brushing my teeth. I believed in God as much as I believed in germs. It was something adults just scared you about, just habit, something I had to do. I didn't believe in God when I was six years old and we buried my mother, or at seven when I made my first Holy Communion, or at twelve when I made my confirmation. I didn't believe in Him when I stood in His house and promised Him I'd forever be faithful to my wife-to-be, but,' he looked at Kitty, his eyes glassy, 'I thanked Him the day my daughter was born.'

He went silent.

'Now, why did I do that? How can you thank someone you don't even believe in? But I did. Without thinking. Like it was natural.' He pondered that for a while. 'But then the sleepless nights began and I forgot about Him again. Occasionally, when she fell ill, ran a high temperature or bumped her head as a toddler and we had to fly her in to Temple Street for stitches I remembered Him again. But as quickly as her tears would dry and that beautiful smile of hers would come back to her face and light up my whole world, I forgot about Him again.

'It was only when she went missing for one whole week and we started a public campaign to find her that I remembered Him again. I started praying to Him. Every morning just at first, at home, the very second I woke up. I'd pray for that day to be the day she came home. Then it became more regular, most minutes of every day. Then I started going to church. Every day. Thoughts of Him came as frequently as thoughts of her. I invested so much time and energy making pacts and promises, trade-offs: if You bring her back, I'll do this; if You help us find her alive, I'll do that. If You even help us find her at all I'll be the best bloody person You've ever known. I begged Him. A grown man, down on his hands and knees, begging. I believed in Him so strongly, more than I ever had in my whole life.

'But when her body was found battered and bruised, I not only stopped believing in Him, but believed so strongly in His non-existence that I felt sorry, irritated even, at those who did. I couldn't spend a minute in their company, not one single second, and believe me they all came out of the woodwork when Rebecca was found, to *help* us. Their belief, their naïvety, their openness to such ridiculous theories reduced me to blood-curdling anger. I felt their belief was a cop-out, a passing of the buck, a failure to be able to achieve anything completely by themselves, a lack of responsibility and a carelessness. Their idea that they had a saviour, that somebody else would guide them, was reckless to me. They were weak, why couldn't they just accept that their lives were *their* responsibility? I wanted nothing to do with them. Do you understand what I'm saying?'

'I do. That you don't believe in God.' She offered him a small smile.

'No. I *didn't*. I *didn't* believe in God. Then I did, and He let me down and I spent seven years hating His guts, hating the very idea of Him. But it's the same as thanking Him, isn't it? How can you hate somebody if you don't believe in them?'

Kitty had been so lost in his words she hadn't noticed her breakfast being placed before her. She took a drink of water, trying to assess where they were, trying to guess where this was taking her.

Archie watched her.

'You're not going to believe me.'

'I believe you,' she said.

'I promise you, you won't believe me.'

'Let me be the judge of that.'

He looked down at his tea, which must have been cold by then; Kitty could see the thin layer of hard water from the kettle on the surface. He didn't speak for a long time.

'Do your family know about the thing you don't think I'll believe?' She tried to get them back on the subject again.

He shook his head. 'No one knows.'

'So I've the exclusive.'

'Ah, there she is, the old hack is back.'

Kitty laughed. 'Are you in contact with your family?'

'No,' he said softly. 'Well, they're in contact with me but . . . I've a brother in Mayo. Frank. He's fifty years old and he's getting married, can you believe that?'

'There's no age limit on love.' Kitty tried not to sound sarcastic but failed.

'You don't believe in love?'

'This week I don't believe in very much at all.'

'And you're telling me you'll believe in me?'

'You've been very open so far. Plus, my future depends on you.'

He smiled. 'What do you think about God?'

'I don't believe in God,' she replied honestly.

He accepted that. 'Do you know what I think about love? I

think love can change us beyond recognition, we become love-sick, soft-eyed jelly-bellied fools.'

'You were never that,' Kitty teased.

'I was too. When I met my wife. Gorgeous, she was. I was a right eejit at the time too. Love can soften people, I believe that. But in me, now, love riles up an anger, a red-hot rage that crawls on my skin, seeps into my blood and brings out the worst in me. That's why everyone I love is better off loving me from afar. From Mayo. From Manchester. Wherever.'

Kitty pushed him to talk about it more.

'My love for people takes on negative forms,' he explained. 'Shadowy, threatening, it's far from the soppy crap you read in cards or the sweet nothings that people whisper in each other's ears. Love makes most people soar. For me it pulls me down. I'm a demon ready to defend, to protect, to do anything for the people that I love.'

'That's understandable considering what you've been through.'

'Is it?' He looked at her, surprised.

'Of course it is.'

'For the past seven years, I've felt like a monster that doesn't know how to love in the right way. And I know that, and yet . . .' he disappeared into his mind. She could see him building his barriers again, the tension was returning, the tough guy was coming back.

Kitty had to talk before she lost the loose-tongued Archie completely. 'Archie, tell me what it is.'

He studied the blackboard for a long time and then he turned round to check on the woman in the café again. He sighed, conflicted.

'Tell me,' Kitty said firmly.

'Sometimes,' he paused, 'I hear people's prayers.'

Kitty raised her eyebrows and waited for him to laugh, to tell her he was joking, but his expression didn't change. She analysed it all in the seconds she had to win or lose this story. The woman stood up and left the café and Archie's eyes followed her. Then he turned back to Kitty, probably waiting for her to do the same. She took a gamble.

'And what do you hear her pray about?'

For the second time he seemed surprised that her first question hadn't been anything more negative, that she'd got straight to the point.

'"Please",' he said, settling back down. 'She sits here for twenty minutes every morning and says "please" over and over again.'

Kitty massaged her temples as she sat on the bus to her next destination. A man who hears people's prayers? What on earth was she supposed to think of that? She could drop it right now, move on from Archie and speak to somebody else on the list. Someone normal. With such a tight deadline and Pete breathing down her neck, it was probably what she should have done, but it wasn't her list to play with, it was Constance's. Kitty remembered her old self, who used to crave meeting people like Archie and stories like his. She thought about Constance's teachings and realised this was exactly the kind of story Constance believed in covering. This was the kind of story that twenty-three-year-old Kitty, just out of college, would have brought to her job interview, and one that Constance would have been intrigued by. Anything unusual and non-traditional would be the first thing she would want to investigate. Her heart raced as she thought about the possibilities. Perhaps Archie had heard Mary-Rose's, Birdie's, Eva's or Ambrose's prayers, perhaps he had a link to everybody on the list. She desperately needed to find out more.

She stared at the words she had written on her notepad.

Name Number Sixty-seven: Archie Hamilton
Story Title: Man of Pray – from the hunted to the
haunted, to the hallowed

CHAPTER NINETEEN

With less than a week to Pete's deadline, and no more leads, Kitty was conscious of a mounting panic. A phone call to Archie established that he was not familiar with any of the names on the list. He impatiently snapped 'No' after each name she called out and informed her time and time again he didn't know the names of anybody whose prayers he heard, and she managed to reach reading out only as far as number eight before he hung up on her. Being realistic, if you could be when dealing with the issue of a man who believed he heard prayers, if it was possible he could have heard the prayers of each person on the list and simply not know it, then how could Constance possibly know? The answer was, she couldn't. The link between them did not lie in him hearing their prayers.

Kitty needed to meet more people. She needed more clues. She sat on a step in Temple Bar Square and rang name number four on her list.

'Mr Vysotski, my name is Kitty Logan, I write for *Etcetera* magazine and I'm contacting you regarding—'

'You received the press release?' a man with a foreign accent shouted excitedly down the phone.

'Excuse me?'

'The press release. We sent it on Friday. I am so happy you received it. You will come to our press conference?' He was so eager, so excited, talking a mile a minute, that she had to smile.

'Yes, Mr Vysotski, but—'

'Call me Jedrek, please!'

'Jedrek. Where is your press conference?'

'It was on the sheet! Today at noon! Erin's Isle GAA Club. Don't miss it now, will you?'

'I won't. I won't miss it.'

'You promise? We'll have cakes and tea. It will be nice, yes? Mrs Vysotski is the most excellent baker.'

'I'll be there, Jedrek.' She hung up, excited about her new intriguing addition to her growing list of quirky characters.

Kitty had a dilemma on her hands. She had made an appointment to meet Eva Wu at a brunch in the Four Seasons where Eva was to meet George Webb's family for the first time at a pre-wedding family meet and greet. Eva or Jedrek . . .? Eva or Jedrek . . .? She quickly made the call and let Eva Wu down for the second time. Then she took out the business card that Sally had given her. She dialled the number and waited.

'Hello. I'm calling about the teaching position for Television Presentation. My friend Sally Collins told me to call you . . .'

Kitty arrived at Erin's Isle GAA Club at twelve fifteen, fifteen minutes late for the press conference. She was anxious travelling through Finglas, Colin Maguire's home turf, and kept her head down low on the bus while at the same time she was constantly on the lookout for him. She pushed open the door quietly, hoping to sneak in unnoticed, without disturbing the event. However, that didn't go according to plan. As soon as she opened the door she was faced with a long hall with two men sitting behind a big head table, before which rows of chairs had been set up. In the front row sat one single person and a photographer who stood by a table of food with his camera around his neck, eating cake.

They were all looking at her.

'Sorry I'm late,' she apologised, making her way to the pews under their stare. 'I'm Kitty Logan from *Etcetera*. I spoke to Jedrek on the phone.'

'Ah, yes! Miss Logan.' A rotund man jumped up from the table and she immediately recognised his voice and his energy as the jolly man over the phone. He appeared to be in his fifties, a large pot belly as big as a six-month pregnancy on his cuddly frame. He came round the table, his hand extended, his head shaved to even the baldness, but a dark goatee around his mouth. He took Kitty's hand, practically crushed it in his and violently shook it.

'You're very welcome, Miss Logan. I knew you would come,' he said enthusiastically like a great big happy Buddha. He pointed a finger in her face in a 'gotcha' way. Kitty couldn't help but laugh. 'Alenka,' he called to the woman at the table of cakes, 'a cup of tea or coffee for our reporter.'

'Coffee, please.'

'Sit, sit!' He practically took her by the shoulders and pushed her down in her chair. Kitty felt giddy. She looked at the journalist sitting beside her.

'Are you Katherine Logan?' the woman asked, eyes narrowing.

'Yes,' she cleared her throat. 'And you are . . .?'

'Sheila Reilly from the *Northside People*,' Jedrek introduced her. 'And this is her photographer, Tom,' he said grandly, presenting the photographer. The photographer pinked as they all turned to look at him with a sandwich stuffed in his face. He mumbled something and then waved.

'Miss Reilly, you know our new arrival? She is a star reporter?' Jedrek asked excitedly, eyes bright.

'Er,' Sheila looked at Kitty uncertainly. Kitty held her stare, kept her head up, confidently. 'Yes . . .' She mumbled something and turned her attention back to Jedrek.

'Excellent!' Jedrek clapped his hands. 'Miss Logan, you must meet this man beside me. Achar Singh.' A man of similar age to

Jedrek, of Sikh religion, wearing a bright orange turban, nodded and smiled at Kitty.

Kitty was served a mug of coffee and a shortbread biscuit by a friendly Polish woman.

'My wife, Alenka,' Jedrek announced happily. 'The best cook in Poland.'

The table was filled with food and by the number of chairs set up, they had had high expectations for the turnout. And though only three people had attended, their spirits seemed to be high. Kitty looked up from dunking the home-made biscuit into her coffee to find them all looking at her. She closed her mouth and aborted biting into her biscuit. The soggy end fell into her mug, splashing her chin. She wiped it. 'Sorry. Aren't we waiting for more people to arrive before we start?'

'It actually already started,' the reporter from *Northside People* said, rising from her seat. 'And finished. I have to get back to the office, so if you'll all please excuse me . . .' The two men stood and extended their hands, and she moved along, wishing them the best of luck. 'See you later, Tom,' she said to her photographer, and he lifted his cup to her in farewell.

'When will the article appear?' Jedrek shouted.

'Oh. Uh. I'll have to speak with my editor first and I'll be in touch,' she said quickly and closed the door behind her. The two men looked at one another, downhearted, then turned their attention to Kitty.

'Okay.' She put her fresh coffee down on the chair beside her and took out her pen and paper. 'So I didn't receive your press release, I'm here on an entirely different matter, but I'm intrigued by what's going on. Could you please fill me in?'

Jedrek, the spokesperson, was only too happy to jump in.

'I am from Poland and my friend Achar is from India. We both came to Ireland in search of a better life and we found it. Sadly we lost our jobs when the company we worked for, SR Technics, moved out of Dublin. We were among over one thousand staff

190

who lost jobs within one month. It has been very difficult for us to find more work.'

'What kind of work did you do?'

'SR Technics is an aircraft maintenance company which provides turbine engine hot section component repair services for blades and vanes on large commercial airline engines. Our plant was based in Dublin airport. The company lost major contracts, and that, together with the high cost of operating in Ireland, meant there was no future for them in Ireland. However, *our* future was in Ireland. Our children and families are happy here, our children are in school, our life is settled here. Achar's son is a star on the under-fourteens' hurling team, which is why they kindly allowed us to use the hall for this occasion.'

Achar looked proud. The club caretaker standing by the door with a set of keys in his hand looked bored.

'Congratulations,' Kitty said.

'Thank you.'

'So . . .' Kitty tried to get to the point. 'Have you some kind of statement to make about your situation . . .?' She was interested and moved by their woes but inside she was crying, *not another recession story, please, not another recession story.*

They looked at each other and then back at her. 'If you would like us to . . .' Jedrek said uncertainly. 'If you think it would help . . . but we are really just here to talk about our record attempt.'

'Record attempt? You're making music?'

'No,' Jedrek leaned in over the table, his eyes lighting up. 'We are attempting to get into *Guinness World Records* by being the fastest two men in a one-hundred-metre pedalo dash, and we are looking for people's support to come and join us and cheer us on. This country needs a positive story. We have been training every day – well, as much as possible as Achar is busy with his taxi – but we have been in training for nine months. The local yacht club donated a pedalo in support of our efforts and we would very much like to achieve this. We have held cake sales, garage sales, all kinds of community events, but sadly we could only raise four hundred and twenty-one euro and nine cent, not enough, so we will do it alone but we need people's support.'

'Why do you need the money?'

'The cost of the adjudication service is between four thousand and five thousand per day, depending on the location. We would have to fly the adjudicator over from London. We have decided not to go through with this idea and so will attempt the record alone.'

'But isn't the adjudicator necessary?'

'No. We can still attempt to make the record and send our evidence to them but they reserve the right not to get back to us.'

'But we do know of an adjudicator who will be in Ireland this Thursday,' Achar finally spoke. 'A friend of ours who works in Cork tells us he knows of a record attempt where a judge will be present.'

'Achar, we talked about this,' Jedrek interrupted. 'We cannot accost a judge for another attempt. It does not work that way.'

'And I say we at least *try*, Jedrek.'

They stared at one another.

'We will discuss this later,' Jedrek said firmly, then turned his attention back to Kitty. 'So. Will you write our story, Miss Logan?'

Kitty looked at Tom the photographer. He popped a cherry bakewell into his mouth and examined what else he could eat on the table. She wasn't even sure if he'd listened to any of that.

'Let me get this straight,' Kitty said. 'You are both unemployed airplane engineers who lost your jobs and as a result of being unable to find work you are attempting a world record at being the fastest two men in a one-hundred-metre pedalo dash?' She looked from one to the other.

'Yes, that's correct,' Jedrek said sombrely.

Kitty started laughing.

'I knew she would not take us seriously.' Achar stood up, angrily.

'No! Wait! I'm sorry for laughing. You misunderstood. I'm laughing because I'm happy, excited, *relieved*,' she grinned. 'Of course I would love to write your story.'

'You would?' Achar asked, surprised.

'And I think you should attempt your record bid this week, in Cork.'

'I told you.' Achar looked at Jedrek. Jedrek didn't look convinced. 'What is wrong, Jedrek? This is exactly what you were hoping for.'

He narrowed his eyes at Kitty. 'Miss Logan says she did not receive our press release and that she was here for other matters. Before I agree to her writing our story, I would like to know what exactly brings her here.'

Jedrek watched the journalist from his seat in the pedalo. She was one of only two reporters who had bothered to show up despite their sending a press release to almost every publication, news and radio board in Ireland. She was standing on the edge of Malahide Estuary surrounded by swans, which were begging her for bread. She was wafting them away and continuing to speak into her phone.

'What do you think?' Achar asked, watching his friend. 'She seems to be interested in us.'

'Yes,' Jedrek replied, distracted. She was currently arguing with somebody on the phone – her editor it sounded like – and this was not a good sign to Jedrek, though he didn't want to worry his friend Achar. She was insisting she would tell her editor something on Friday and not a minute before. Jedrek liked that she was fighting for them – it was about time things moved in his and Achar's favour – but this lady wasn't just fighting for them, that much was obvious.

Achar looked at Jedrek with concern. 'She wants us to break the record by the end of this week. Are we ready to do this in three days?'

'Achar, we are more than ready. How long have we been training for this, my friend?'

'Nine months.'

'And how many days a week have we put into this?'

'Five days.'

'Exactly. Did we let the wind or rain, the ice or hail set us off course since we began our training?'

'No, Jedrek.'

'Even illnesses. I recall you and I both with flu and coughs and near fever out here in the boat. We have dedicated every free moment we have to this training. Our families, our friends, the boys in the pub and club, the sailing club, they are all supporting us. We are ready for this, Achar.'

'Yes, Jedrek.' Achar seemed to raise a few feet in the air as his back straightened and he pulled his shoulders back.

Achar was easily boosted in this way and Jedrek was good at motivational speeches. He had exercised this skill in the long cold winter when they had questioned their motivations and when the pedalo they had trained in had been destroyed by a mob of teenagers. It had been Jedrek who made sure they raised the funding to fix it and continue on. It had set them back three weeks but they had done it.

Jedrek knew that, to many, their goal was laughable, ludicrous even, but there was more to it than there seemed on the surface. Jedrek hadn't worked properly for three years. A qualified engineer, he had made a good honest living for his wife and three children. He had loved his job, valued the friendships there and felt comfortable in his role as provider for the family. It was what he felt he was supposed to do, but not only that, it was what he was good at. When that duty was taken away from him, he lost his spirit, lost a sense of who he was. He felt useless to his family, a disappointment, as week after week he failed to get another job. He could forget searching in his field of qualifications, for there was nothing, but that had taken him a while to realise. He had fallen into a depression; he recognised that now, though at the time any mention of it from anyone had sent him into a rage. He had been extremely difficult to live with, moody, irritable, always looking for a fight, always feeling everyone and the world was against him, sensitive to every comment and problem in the world. But he was searching all that time for his role, any authoritative role at all he could find in the family.

An acquaintance in their local had innocently suggested, without malice, that he go back home if there was nothing here for him. But what that man didn't understand was that this *was* Jedrek's home. He had lived in Ireland for fourteen years, his three children had been born in Ireland, held Irish passports and even had Irish accents. They were in education, had friends, their entire lives were in Dublin. To go back to Poland would not be returning home for any of them any more. Much of his family were dispersed across the world: his brother in Paris, his sister in New York. His parents had passed away so there was no focal point for them in Poland any longer, just his and Alenka's memories, which they tried so desperately to share and recreate with the children on annual summer holidays back to Poland. But their eldest, at thirteen, was now tired of the forced pilgrimage to a place that held no memories, no connection and no excitement for him. Of course they had been unable to afford the flights home for the past three years and so family holidays and Jedrek's quest for connection with his roots were lost.

Their first Christmas without work he took a job stocking shelves in a supermarket at night. He had been ashamed, had told no one, but had felt a slight relief when he found himself working beside a reputable architect who similarly had swallowed his pride and saw the act of providing food for the family as the main goal as opposed to the job itself. This brought a little light to Jedrek's situation, but having to watch his wife go to work in another home in an affluent area, to clean and do other people's laundry had filled him with a guilt so deep, their own marriage had suffered. His wife was ever-patient, though they had their bad days. It seemed when one was up, the other was down, a seesaw marriage, which survived only if at least one person's feet were dangling in the air.

Since that job in the supermarket Jedrek had found jobs here and there – driving a van, furniture removal – but nothing solid, nothing that allowed him to use his skills and knowledge, or to breathe a single sigh of relief that his family was safe. But nine months ago, something had changed inside him. Nine months ago, when he met up with his friend Achar at Erin's Isle Football Club, his spark, which had so obviously gone out, was ignited again.

Achar had been a colleague of his in SR Technics and when they met again the friendship between their two families brought happiness and joy back to their homes. Their children were similar ages and enjoyed playing together, their wives got along and it made days out more pleasurable, plus Jedrek had the added support and conversation of a man who was going through exactly the same thing as Jedrek. He'd been unable to talk about it before but here was someone who understood.

It was while on a family day out in Malahide Sailing Club, when Achar and Jedrek were racing their eldest sons in a pedal boat, that they attracted the attention of other families who had gathered that fine day. To everyone's surprise the unfit fathers won. Then when challenged by the other fathers they beat them too. And anyone else who dared take them on. This simple fun day out made both men feel as though they had accomplished something, they were good at something, they had made their families proud. They had a skill and they wanted to be recognised for it. They both had time, they both had hunger, they both needed acknowledgement and a pat on the back from society, from people other than their wives. This record attempt was a great deal more than it appeared on the surface.

Kitty finally ended the phone call to her editor. She looked strained, and Jedrek knew what a person under immense pressure looked like.

'Ready?' he called.

'I'm sorry for keeping you,' she replied, holding the stopwatch in her hand. 'Ready now.'

'On three,' Jedrek said, and he and Achar prepared. 'One, two . . . three,' he said, and their legs started pumping wildly.

When they reached the buoy one hundred metres away they turned to find her jumping up and down on the grass in celebration, two thumbs up high in the air.

Jedrek and Achar laughed and gave each other a high five.

Kitty sat on the bus, her adrenalin rushing inside her so much that she wanted to jump up and dance in the aisles. Instead she took out her notepad and wrote:

Name Number Four: Jedrek Vysotski
Story Title: Guinness World Records

CHAPTER TWENTY

From outside the door in the Mater Hospital, Kitty could hear a hair dryer blasting, and when she entered the room she found Mary-Rose standing over a head of hair, hard at work, a mop of blond flying around the room. She saw Kitty and turned the hair dryer off.

'Ah, just on time, my assistant has arrived.'

The woman beneath the hair peeked out from the strands that had been blown across her face. Her eyes were big and brown, huge in her shrunken face. Kitty felt a wave of dizziness pass over her, but she smiled and waved, then wanted to kick herself for smiling, and then again for not speaking. She found she was like one of those people who didn't know what to say to children; when it came to people who were ill, she simply hadn't the words, couldn't think of anything remotely in common to chat to them about, all her mind kept telling her was: *they are sick, they are sick.*

'Diane is the beautiful bride today,' Mary-Rose introduced them.

Congratulations? Should she say that? Was it appropriate? She was getting married but she was also about to die – how could she be congratulated for that? So instead she said, 'Ah,' and nodded her head.

'Well, I'm not beautiful yet,' Diane said. 'Hopefully I will be after Mary-Rose is finished with me.'

Kitty still hadn't said anything.

'Do me a favour and hold these clips?' Mary-Rose asked, handing her a container to hold.

Delighted to have something to do, Kitty jumped into action and stood behind Diane so she wouldn't have to look at her, then made it her job to be completely helpful, offering clips when Mary-Rose still had two in her hand, one in her mouth and was manoeuvring another firmly in Diane's head.

Mary-Rose began chatting casually without any uneasiness, without awkwardness, as if this was a normal day, just like any other.

'Will you have a bridesmaid?' Mary-Rose asked, a clip between her teeth.

'My daughter, Serena, she'll be here any moment. She's getting her hair done too. She's sixteen and loving all the excitement.'

'I bet,' Mary-Rose said. 'Her mum is getting married, *I'm* excited for you!'

Excited? All Kitty could feel was misery for the poor sixteen-year-old who was going to lose her mother.

'I know, I'm excited too,' Diane laughed. 'I'm trying to figure out why her dad and I didn't do this years ago!'

'Will you make a speech?' Mary-Rose asked, and Kitty wondered why she couldn't think of questions like that to ask. She was a journalist, she was supposed to be able to ask all kinds of questions, but her head had dried up, which wasn't a new experience.

Mary-Rose picked up strands of hair and moved them, twisted them, pinned them, manipulated them to look silkier, thicker, beautiful and healthy. The way she pinned each section before moving on to the next was hypnotic to watch.

'I'll speak if I can,' Diane said. 'Serena wants to speak.'

'She's a brave girl.'

'She's been the bravest.' There was a silence and Kitty felt awkward, but then Diane laughed. 'She sat me down to help me choose a coffin, would you believe?'

Mary-Rose laughed. 'I hope you picked a nice one.'

Kitty almost fainted at the conversation.

'Apparently there's new personalised coffins which you can have themed to suit your taste – football club emblems and that kind of thing.'

'And what did you choose?'

'Well, she wanted me to choose the sunset-themed one – the sea, the palm trees, the beach. I used to surf, you see.'

'It sounds beautiful.'

'Too good to be burned,' Diane joked. 'I'm being cremated.'

'Well, they could always cremate you and keep the coffin,' Mary-Rose said, and the two women burst out laughing. Kitty couldn't believe her ears; she watched the two of them in shock. How could they joke like this about death?

'Oh, stop.' Diane wiped the corners of her eyes. 'You'll ruin my make-up.'

'It's okay, I can do it again,' Mary-Rose said. 'I once had a client who told me she was choosing a dark oak because it would bring out the colour of her eyes.'

And with that they both started laughing again.

The door opened and an excited member of staff announced the arrival of the bridesmaid.

'Oh, darling.' Diane immediately stopped laughing as she took in the sight of her daughter wearing a pretty and simple dress for the low-key affair. 'You look beautiful.'

'Stop, Mum,' Serena said, embarrassed. 'We're not crying today, remember?' She went to her mother and embraced her, and Mary-Rose immediately stopped working and stepped back. Kitty followed her lead. As soon as they pulled away, both of them in tears, Mary-Rose chose the right moment to work again. She worked silently, quickly, almost becoming invisible in the room.

'Nearly there,' Mary-Rose said, reaching for another pin. 'This is the last one.' She twisted the final strand of hair around her finger and expertly pinned it in place so that the pin was invisible.

'Wow,' Kitty finally spoke.

'I want to see,' Diane said excitedly.

'You hold this mirror for me.' Mary-Rose gave Kitty a mirror. She went round the front with another mirror so that Diane could see the back and front.

Diane was silent but her face said it all. Her hands went slowly up to her hair but didn't touch it, instead hovered tenderly around her face. Her face, which had seemed lost in the big blond hair, now looked more at home.

'It's beautiful,' she whispered.

'Mum,' Serena warned.

'I'm not going to . . .' Diane tried not to cry. 'It just looks like . . .'

'Like . . . ?' Mary-Rose asked nervously.

'The way it used to be.'

And finally Kitty understood.

They all watched Diane's face go through some kind of transformation. It was difficult to know what she was thinking; who knew what on earth she could be thinking at a time like that? Nobody. Apart from Mary-Rose, apparently.

'But it's not you,' Mary-Rose said, surprising Kitty.

Diane looked at her in surprise and it changed to apologetic.

'It's okay, we can take it off.'

'But all your hard work . . .'

'Never mind my work, this is your day. Would you like me to take it out?'

Diane looked at Serena.

'I think it's stunning, Mum, but it's up to you.'

Diane thought hard. 'I just think, it's my old hair on a . . . new face and it feels wrong.'

'No problem.' And with that Mary-Rose lifted up the hair and revealed a bald Diane.

Diane swallowed.

The colour difference between her made-up face and her pale head was evident.

'I'll just use my magic brush,' Mary-Rose said chirpily, 'but be warned. It may tickle.'

Diane smiled as Serena laughed. 'Can I help?'

Kitty took a few steps back as she watched Mary-Rose and Serena dusting Diane's head, the three of them laughing.

'Well, our work here is done,' Mary-Rose said with a look of satisfaction as the door closed behind Serena wheeling her mother to the marriage ceremony in the hospital boardroom. The nurses excitedly followed after them, delighted to have such a positive event in the ward.

'How long do you think she has?' Kitty asked.

'I didn't ask but I'm guessing a few months.' Mary-Rose started to tidy things away.

'How do you do this?' Kitty sat down, drained.

'It's not easy, I suppose, but it's not all bad . . . I usen't to believe in marriage. My mum and dad separated when I was young, it was nasty and so I didn't have a good example of marriage, but a lot of my friends are getting married now and mostly I do their hair. All brides are nervous for different reasons, whether they're sick or not. You just have to judge if they want to chat or not. Some don't. The main difference is my friends are panicking about the "for ever" part. They have to stay together for ever whereas Diane's worried because she knows that it can't be. When I get married I want to be like Diane and hope beyond all hope that it can be for ever.'

Mary-Rose brought her mother into Dublin city once a week for afternoon tea. It was something she insisted on doing despite her mother's health, and this week she'd chosen Powerscourt Townhouse. Powerscourt Townhouse was a speciality shopping centre in a Georgian house off Grafton Street. It had once been the party home to Richard Wingfield, Third Viscount Powerscourt, and his wife, Lady Amelia, and was a popular place to eat and shop. The courtyard had been covered over and a large ground-floor restaurant sat in the centre overlooked by the balconies of each side of the building. A piano played softly beside them. As if Kitty hadn't had enough awkward moments with sick people she now faced a meal with Mary-Rose and a woman whose speech was near impossible to understand due to the paralysis of one side of her face. Mary-Rose, as she had done in the hospital, acted as their mediator.

As Kitty was in the middle of explaining to Mary-Rose's mother what exactly she was doing with her daughter a loud male voice interrupted everyone's conversations.

'Oh, no,' Mary-Rose said, looking up at the main staircase into the courtyard shopping area and seeing Sam standing there with a microphone in hand.

'Ladies and gentlemen, if I could please have your attention . . .' He tapped the microphone. There was an immediate hush. 'I won't take up too much of your time, I appreciate you're all trying to have an enjoyable break, but there's somebody I need to say something special to.'

Again that twitter of excitement began to build among the crowd.

'Margaret Posslewaite, are you here?'

Mary-Rose groaned.

'Maggie, are you here?' he asked again.

Mary-Rose's mother nudged her and Mary-Rose's hand shot up in the air at the same time as her other hand went to cover her face.

'There she is!' he exclaimed. 'Maggie. There's something I have to ask you in front of all these people.'

There it was, the gasp from some, the whoop of excitement from others, the cheer from some, the cynical eye roll of a few. Sam nodded to the piano player, who began to play 'Moon River'.

'Remember this song, Maggie? It was the first song we danced to on our first date.'

The crowd oohed.

He slowly made his way down the steps singing the first line of the song.

'Oh Jesus,' Mary-Rose said. Her mother laughed.

'Ever since our first dance on our first date, I knew I wanted to be with you. Ever since you wowed me with your merengue and cha-cha when we met at the YMCA dance class.'

Mary-Rose snorted and covered her face, trying not to laugh.

'But it was the salsa,' he made a little move with his hips and the crowd cheered, 'that made me realise I wanted to spend the rest of my life with you.'

People whooped.

'Margaret,' he came closer, stole a rose from a nearby table and swooped down to his knee beside her to thunderous applause, 'my huckleberry friend. Will you marry me?' Only Kitty was close enough to hear the snort from Mary-Rose as she tried to contain her hysterical laughter while her face was fighting hard to stay calm.

'Yes,' she said, but the crowd were too busy cheering to hear. Somebody shushed and that was sent around the shopping centre.

She and Sam were almost nose to nose.

'I can't hear you,' Sam said into the microphone and then pushed it close to her lips. She gave him a warning look. He gave her a cheesy smile.

'Yes,' she said into the microphone and the whole of Powerscourt Townhouse erupted.

They hugged and the manager brought over the menus and told them drinks were on the house.

'That was a good one,' Mary-Rose chuckled, her pretty face lighting up. 'Okay, you got me there, Sam. That was possibly one of your best. Your huckleberry friend?'

He shrugged and laughed. 'I had to impress the mother-in-law.

Hi, Judy.' He gave Mary-Rose's mother a kiss on the forehead. Judy said something intelligible to Kitty and Sam laughed, understanding her perfectly.

A young woman, whom Kitty had assumed was a member of staff standing by and watching it all, made her way over to the table.

'Am I allowed to join you now?' she asked, a big grin on her face. 'Is it safe?'

'Of course,' Sam said, lighting up. 'Guys, this is Aoife. I hope you don't mind her joining us today.'

Mary-Rose looked slightly confused but covered it up quickly. 'Yes, I mean no, I mean, no I don't mind.'

'Aoife, this is Kitty, a friend of Mary-Rose's. In fact you and me need to have words later, I have a few stories to share.' He winked and Kitty laughed. 'Aoife, this is my best friend and wife-to-be, Margaret Posslewaite, also known as Mary-Rose.'

'Congratulations,' Aoife laughed, leaning over and giving Mary-Rose a half-hug and kiss.

Mary-Rose seemed uncomfortable by the closeness.

'Aoife and I met a few weeks ago at work. I thought now would be a nice time for you to meet,' Sam said, a little embarrassed.

'Ah, yes, of course,' Mary-Rose said, still trying to gather herself together.

'I've heard so much about you,' Aoife said, bright-eyed and bushy-tailed, eager to please.

'Well, I . . .' Mary-Rose was at a loss for words.

'Don't worry, I didn't tell her about the baths we took together,' Sam jumped in, and Aoife laughed.

'What have you not done together?' Aoife laughed. She meant it innocently but it carried more weight with Mary-Rose, who immediately looked awkward, which Sam picked up on and who then also looked awkward. But Aoife didn't notice. Eager to impress her boyfriend's friend she continued, 'Speaking of baths, have you ever tried to wash Scotty? He's impossible!' Aoife launched into a story about how she and Sam had tried to clean Sam's dog, but Kitty wasn't listening to the story. Instead she caught the quick glance between mother and daughter, her mother reaching for her daughter's hand beneath the table.

Name Number Seven: Mary-Rose Godfrey
Story Title: The Proposee

CHAPTER TWENTY-ONE

After meeting with Mary-Rose, Kitty made her way to St Margaret's Nursing Home to meet Birdie again. She enjoyed spending time with Birdie, loved her simple stories of years gone by, her elegance, her gentleness, her openness to everything around her. Kitty had spent more time with Birdie than with the other people on her list, but, listening back over the tapes, Kitty realised that there was one question that needed to be asked. The day was still bright and sunny despite coming into a chillier evening at six o'clock. Many of the nursing home inhabitants were outside sitting in the shade, which was where Kitty found Birdie, looking as elegant as usual, her feet resting on a pillow on a garden chair, her face lifted up to the heat, her eyes closed.

'Hello, birthday girl,' Kitty said gently, not wanting to surprise her.

Birdie's eyes opened and she smiled. 'Well, hello, Kitty. It's lovely to see you again.' She took her feet down from the chair. 'It's not quite my birthday yet,' she said. 'Not that I'll be celebrating it. Eighty-five years old, can you believe it?' She shook her head, unimpressed.

'You don't look a day over eighty,' Kitty said, and Birdie laughed. 'You are celebrating it somewhere, though, aren't you?' Kitty probed, trying to get to the bottom of the mystery. It had been playing on Kitty's mind for the past few days: where on earth was an eighty-five-year-old woman planning on spending her birthday if it wasn't with her family, and she was intent on not telling them where she was going?

'Well, no, I'm not exactly celebrating it.' She removed an invisible piece of fluff from her skirt. 'Isn't it a smashing day?'

Kitty smiled, loving the challenge. 'Your birthday is on Thursday, isn't it?'

'Yes.'

'And you'll be somewhere other than here for your birthday?'

'That's right, I won't be here, but we can meet again on Saturday or Sunday, if that suits you. Even Thursday morning will be fine but I'm afraid I'm probably boring you with all of these stories.'

Kitty smiled. 'Birdie, can I ask, where are you going?'

'Oh, it's not important, Kitty, it's just . . .'

'Birdie,' Kitty said in a warning tone, and Birdie finally cracked a smile.

'You don't take no for an answer, do you?'

'Never.'

'Well, all right. I'm afraid I haven't been entirely honest with you, Kitty, and I do apologise.'

Kitty's ears pricked up and her adrenalin surged. 'Yes?'

'But only because it's a silly little thing and nothing you would want for your story.'

'Let me be the judge of that.'

She sighed. 'I told you that when I was a young girl I was very sick.'

'You had tuberculosis.'

'It was an incredibly fatal disease then. It was like being handed a death sentence. Four thousand people died from it every year.' She shook her head. 'There was a terrible stigma attached to it. I was only fourteen and was sent to a TB sanatorium on the edge of town where I stayed for six months before my father, God rest his soul, decided to take me out of there and go with me to Switzerland. They thought the fresh air would help me.

After a summer my father got the position of headmaster and we moved back home, but with my poor health there was very little I could do. So many people died in those sanatoriums. But because of my condition, my father wrapped me up in cotton wool. He had plans for me, he was very controlling of me – who I played with, who I talked to, eventually who I loved.' She looked sad at that. 'Even when I was improved, he couldn't change. I was his sick little girl, his youngest, and he wouldn't, couldn't, I suppose, let me go.'

She was silent.

'This is so silly, Kitty.'

'It's not. Please tell me.'

'I suppose I got used to being treated as if at any moment I could break. Not to run too fast, not to jump too high, not to laugh too loud, not to do anything too much, just take it nice and easy, but I never liked it. The whole town knew that I was the headmaster's sick daughter and many of them thought the TB would come back. I was brittle, I was fragile, I was not to be treated the same. I was the one who could drop dead at any moment, the one who wouldn't live to see her eighteenth birthday. When I moved away it broke my father's heart but I needed my own space and my own identity. I forgot about all those feelings over the years as I got married, had my babies, reared my children, and I could look after people for a change. But I see that is all I did. As though it was my way of rebelling against my adolescence. I became a childminder and cared for other children, never wanted to be cared for in that way again.

'But coming here to this place has brought it back to me. That feeling of . . .' she thought about it and looked as though she'd a bad taste in her mouth '. . . of being mollycoddled. Of being powerless. My children, as beloved as they are, have almost written me off already. I'm old, I know that, but I still have fire in my belly. I'm still . . . alive!' She chuckled at that. 'Oh, if the village could see me now.'

When Birdie looked at Kitty, her eyes sparkled mischievously. 'On my eighteenth birthday I made a bet. I used the birthday money my father had given me and on the day I left the village for ever I made a bet.'

'What was the bet?'

'That I would reach the age of eighty-five.'

Kitty's eyes widened. 'Can you make a bet like that?'

'Josie O'Hara, the meanest man in town, had the bookies in his family for what seems like for ever. He thought I was on my way out, just like all the others, and he was only too happy to take the bet.'

'How much money?'

'I bet one hundred pounds. A lot of money back then. And so confident was the bookmaker on my demise that he gladly offered me odds of one hundred to one.'

'So that means, to the bookie's dismay, you'll be collecting . . .' Kitty calculated it.

'Ten thousand pounds,' chuckled Birdie.

'Birdie!' Kitty gasped. 'That is phenomenal! Ten thousand!'

'Yes,' Birdie raised her eyebrows. 'But it's not just the money.' She turned serious. 'Not that any of those old codgers are alive now. I just need to go back there for myself.'

'You have unfinished business,' Kitty smiled, loving this story.

Birdie thought about that. 'Yes. I suppose I do.'

'So here's the plan,' Molly said, leaning in towards Kitty and Birdie conspiratorially around the garden table. 'Now that you're in on it, we could use your help.'

'Oh, don't drag poor Kitty into this,' Birdie interrupted.

'Are you joking? I wouldn't miss this for the world.'

'Really?'

'This is the most exciting thing I've heard all day. Apart from a man who hears prayers and a woman who gets proposed to every week.'

'What?' Molly asked.

'Never mind.'

'Okay, so the bus is out of action from Thursday morning, when the Oldtown Pistols return from their semi-final with the Balbriggan Eagles, to Friday evening, when the Pink Ladies go to bridge. Which gives us a window of opportunity to take the bus Thursday at 10 p.m., drive to Cork, stay the night, pick up the money and drive back the following morning to be home by Friday evening.'

'Hold on,' Kitty interrupted. 'You're taking the nursing home bus?'

'Unless you have a car or any other ideas, it's all we can do.'

'Are you allowed to take the bus?'

'It's strictly for nursing home activities.'

'So you're not allowed to take the bus.'

'Exactly.'

'So you're effectively *stealing* the bus.'

'We're *borrowing* the bus.'

'Birdie,' Kitty said in surprise, 'did you know this?'

'The woman is going to collect ten grand – what does she care how we get there? So I'll get slapped on the wrists if they find out, it's no big deal, but Bernadette won't find out. We'll be gone and back before they even notice we're gone.'

Kitty thought about it – it seemed innocent enough when she put it like that – but she didn't need vehicle theft on her record to top it all off. 'But what about you, Molly? They'll notice you're gone.'

'I don't work that shift. I don't start work until Friday evening, and before you ask, as far as the old battle-axe knows, Birdie is going out with her family on an overnight trip for her birthday.'

'You two have thought this all through, haven't you?'

They chuckled mischievously.

'Well?' Molly asked. 'Are you in?'

'I'm in,' Kitty replied, and the three reached into the centre of the table and held hands.

On the way home, Kitty took out her notepad.

Name Number Six: Bridget Murphy
Story Title: Birdie's Nest Egg

After a long day working on her subjects for the story, Kitty finally felt like she was getting somewhere. She had scratched the surface and was getting glimpses of the people beneath, the underneath part everyone hid from everyone else, the part of a person beneath the mask, beneath social politeness, beneath insecurity. She felt that she was beginning to get to the juicy parts of her list. Despite that, she had only met six of her one hundred names, had less than a week left of her deadline and she was no closer to establishing a solid link. Could it be hidden secrets, like Birdie and Archie's? She was going to have to dig a lot deeper with Eva, Mary-Rose and Jedrek, if so.

She called Pete for the second time that day.

'You better have something for me, Lois Lane.'

She laughed. 'Not that I'm ready to reveal yet. I told you, *Friday*. I forgot to ask, how long is the piece?'

He paused. 'Kitty, considering you should be finished and merely going over the article for perfection right now, I'm a little surprised to hear you ask that.'

'Have we gone back to bad Pete again?' She moved to the vacated back row of the bus for privacy.

'Bad Pete,' he laughed. 'Am I really that bad?'

'At times you are horrendously scary.'

'Well, I don't mean to be horrendously scary,' he said, and she almost felt his breath on her ear, one of those conversations when every pause, every word, breath and sigh meant something. 'Not to you, anyway.'

She smiled and then looked around to make sure no one was catching her obvious silly smile.

'So how many words have you written?' he asked more gently.

'You can't answer a question with a question, Pete. I asked you first.'

'Okay.' He sounded like he was stretching and she pictured his broad muscular shoulders and then her hands running over them. She surprised herself with this fantasy: this was Pete, bad Pete, duty editor Pete, who had often given her nightmares, not sexual fantasies on buses. What was happening?

'It's the main feature so you have five thousand words. However, I could reduce it to four if you're having problems. You could draw matchstick people to take up space or something,' he teased.

'I'm not having problems – well, okay, I am but in the opposite way. It's just that there is so much material. One hundred people's stories in five thousand words is near impossible.'

'Kitty . . .' He was warning her now.

'I know, I know, just listen.'

'No, I've heard you. This is your baby, you drove this thing forward. If this was Constance's idea for a feature then she would have figured out a way to do this. You knew her better than anyone, you're a great writer, Kitty, you'll figure it out.'

Kitty smiled at the praise; she hadn't had much of that for the past year. 'Thanks.'

'It's true, but I don't want to ever have to tell you that again.'

'I know, I'm sure it hurt you to say it.'

'You think I hate you so much.' She heard the smile in his tone. He lowered his voice so nobody could hear him. 'What can I do to make you believe that I don't?'

She heard herself say, 'Hmm,' and they both laughed.

'Actually, what are you doing tonight?' he asked.

'Oh, you don't want to know.' She thought of the manure lining the stairway to her flat, an impatient Zhi and a long night ahead of her, cleaning.

'So you're busy.'

'Why?' She sat up, her heart beating faster. She wanted to

213

backtrack, say no, she had no plans. What had she been thinking? That had been a deliberate lead on from her previous suggestive comment and she was too stupid thinking about manure to have realised it.

'Oh, no reason.' Pete cleared his throat. 'I've been working late here to get this done. I've been here most nights till ten or eleven; if you wanted any help or a meeting about anything, just drop by.'

'Thanks, Pete.'

'Otherwise, putting my bossy hat back on, you know Friday is the deadline, we're having a staff meeting and I need you to be there to present the story. No excuses.'

Kitty hopped off the bus, feeling lighter than before. When she reached her apartment she expected the smell of manure to greet her but it was clean. In fact, it smelled of turpentine, which was actually a welcome scent compared with the last. She pushed open the door to the dry-cleaners with a big smile on her face.

'Zhi, thank you so much. I can't thank you enough for cleaning that up. I fully intended on—'

'My wife. She do,' he snapped, and a scowl-faced woman bending over a dry-cleaning press looked up to glare at her.

'Ah. Mrs Wong, thank you so much.'

She grunted.

'We no do for you. We do for tenant. We show flat. New girl move in two week.'

'You showed my flat to a tenant?'

'My flat. Yes.'

'But you can't do that without my permission, Zhi. You can't just let someone wander around my home without telling me. It's . . . it's . . . against the rules of our tenancy agreement.'

He looked at her, unimpressed. 'So you write in newspaper,' he snorted.

She looked at him helplessly but he didn't care. She slowly backed away from the counter and retreated from the shop. Just as she was closing the door behind her he shouted, 'Two week from today. You out.'

Kitty sat at the kitchen table with the names of her six subjects spread out before her. Each name was written on a card of its own and beneath each name was her story idea for each person. She laid them out neatly and then studied them slowly, one by one, hoping a link could be sparked in her mind. She drummed her fingers on the table, looking at the ninety four other names, many of whom she had contacted and hadn't had time to meet, many of whom she barely had time even to think about as they lived so far out of Dublin. Her stomach rumbled as she hadn't eaten since tea with Mary-Rose, but she had no food in the fridge, no time to shop and no desire to steer off course. She was lost in the stories of the men and women who were taking over her mind: Archie, Eva, Birdie, Mary-Rose, Ambrose and Jedrek. Their worries were her worries, their problems were her problems, their delights her delights, their successes and their failures all hers too.

But – and there was a big but – no matter how much she stared at their names and how intrigued she was by their individual stories, they did not and could not make up one single combined piece for Constance's tribute, one that would join their stories together seamlessly, unite them under one great glorious banner. Kitty laid her forehead down on the cool surface of the kitchen table and groaned. Pete had named Friday as the final day for her to present the story and he meant it. He had put up with her procrastination for long enough. He had somehow managed to ease the worries of the panicking advertisers, allowing her to write for the magazine, and for that she owed him a lot. He had fought hard for her and it was time she repaid him by delivering on her promise, but she had been so busy being on the move, meeting with the people on the list, that she had barely had time to face the truth. The truth being, she was in big trouble.

It was time now that she admitted it, not just to herself but to someone of far greater importance.

Kitty knocked on Bob's door. He was the only person she could bring herself to talk to honestly about Constance's story, and she hoped that his understanding of the woman would help shed light on her problems.

Bob opened the door with a tired smile. 'I've been expecting you.'

'You have?'

'Though you're later than I thought you'd be. Days later, my dear. Never mind, come on in.' He opened the door wider, and made his way down the hall.

He sounded good-humoured but he looked so tired. He walked with a weariness that Kitty felt also, a weariness that came from a constant sadness, a hollowness in their hearts. The heart knew that something was missing and it was having to work extra hard to make up for it.

The living room was as cluttered as it always had been. Constance's death had not changed that, though it may have helped add to it. Teresa had not managed to change Bob and Constance's filing system, though Kitty was sure Bob would have fought her to the death if she'd tried to introduce a more linear, pedestrian form of living. Somewhere among all of that mess lay an order nobody else could decipher. It was impossible to sit at the kitchen table. The surface was covered in paperwork and miscellaneous items that spilled onto each of the six chairs that hugged the table.

'Coffee?' Bob asked, from the small kitchen.

'Yes, please.'

Kitty knew she could do with getting some sleep that night, but a cup of coffee or two was certainly not going to prevent the inevitable from happening. She hadn't slept properly for weeks, she doubted tonight was going to improve for her, and she needed to be alert for this conversation. She needed to defog her cloudy mind, a mind that felt it had scoured every avenue of possibility for the story, ransacking every home along its path as though it were leading a manhunt. She needed to view those pillaged avenues with a fresh eye and rewind, start afresh, and she needed Bob's help to do this. What stalled her from asking outright was his gallant support in her ability to write Constance's last story in the face of the doubting Cheryl and Pete. Now she had to tell him she had failed to deliver on her promise. There was no doubt that she had let herself down, that she was about to let Bob down was a sure thing, but as she stood in Constance's home, feeling and smelling her friend as if she were just in the next room, more terrifying and heartbreaking to her was the unbearable feeling she had let Constance down. She was supposed to be Constance's voice while Constance had been silenced, but what was she doing? Stuttering and stammering, humming and hawing, not being nearly as eloquent as Constance was somehow continuing to be in death.

A moment had passed in which Kitty had been studying the array of items cluttering every surface, then she realised she wasn't smelling the anticipated aroma of coffee, nor was there a sound of Bob moving around in the kitchen. She found him standing in the middle of the small space, frozen solid, looking at the cupboards but not seeing them, looking more lost than she'd ever seen him. Though Bob was ten years Constance's senior, they had always seemed to be the same age. Kitty wasn't sure if it was Constance who acted older than her years or if it was Bob who seemed more youthful, but whatever it was they were just perfectly matched, always the same, always in sync, never seemed separated by anything as large as a decade, apart from the occasional viewpoint. It was as though they had arrived on the planet at the same time and accompanied each other through every day as though they were made to be that way. Kitty found it difficult to imagine Constance's life before Bob, or Bob's life before Constance, that there had been an entire ten years of his roaming the earth before she'd arrived. Kitty wondered if he'd felt it, the day she was born, but never knew why, a moment when the life of a ten-year-old boy growing up in Dublin suddenly felt right because of the arrival of a little soul in Paris.

But now, looking at Bob, Kitty could see the Bob without Constance and he was almost like a body without a soul. A little light had gone out.

'Bob,' Kitty said gently, placing a hand on his shoulder.

'Yes,' he straightened up, came to, as if suddenly remembering he had company.

'Why don't I make the coffee, you sit down and relax?' she said casually, moving him aside gently and opening cupboards to get the coffee started.

'Yes, yes, indeed,' he said, distracted by who knew what memory or sudden thought he'd had, and sat in the only armchair free of a pile of newspapers and magazines.

Kitty opened the cupboards and was faced with books, crammed in as a regular bookshelf would be. Every single shelf in every press was filled; not a cup or saucer or plate, or even food was in sight. She frowned, searching for the coffee pot, for the cups, but failed. Trying to use Constance and Bob's logic, she made her way to the living room to search the bookshelves for mugs but there weren't any. No logic and no mugs, but plenty more books. Giving up momentarily on the mugs, she moved on with her task but there was no sign of a coffee pot, or of coffee granules, just a lone kettle that had once been their piggy bank of coins.

'Bob,' she said, a laugh catching in her throat, 'where do you usually keep the coffee?'

'Oh,' he said suddenly as though the thought had never occurred to him. 'We usually go out for coffee but Teresa is always drinking something from a mug. We must have something in there.'

Kitty looked around the cluttered kitchen. The calendar for that year was a Kama Sutra calendar. Stuck to the fridge with sticky tape, it displayed position number five for May: 'Raised

Missionary'. Kitty opened the fridge and was disappointed to find it empty; she had been hoping for something exciting after the presentation on the door. 'Maybe she brings her own . . .' She surveyed the empty shelves.

'We have wine in the evenings.' Bob spoke on behalf of himself and the empty armchair before him.

Which made sense. Constance was known to have at least a bottle of red wine every evening, and right now it sounded like a much better idea than coffee to Kitty.

'And where would the wine bottles be hiding?' Kitty smiled at Bob fondly.

He met her smile and the light returned to his eyes. 'Ms Green Fingers herself liked to store them in the potting shed.'

Kitty wandered out to the still bright evening, across the grass to the potting shed, unslid the lock and stepped inside. It smelled of damp and soil. She switched on the stark white light, which dangled dangerously from a thin wire in the centre of the ceiling, and was faced with shelves of single bottles of red wine, each sitting in a terracotta pot of soil.

'She liked to keep them warm,' Bob said suddenly, appearing behind her. 'She insisted they all have their own beds, kept to a temperature of no less than ten degrees.'

Kitty laughed. 'But of course. And what are these?' She examined the dozens of other pots with Post-it notes impaled by sticks stuck into the soil.

'Her ideas.'

Kitty frowned. 'I thought her ideas were all in the filing cabinet.'

'They were the developed ones. Most of them began here. She called them her little seeds. As soon as they would pop into her head she would write them on a Post-it note and skewer them into these pots. Then occasionally, when she was short of an idea or two, she would come out to the shed to see if her ideas had grown.'

Kitty looked at him in surprise. 'Why did I never hear about this?'

'Because, my love, if I told anybody about this, Constance would be in a mad house.'

'She already was in a mad house, Bob. With you.' They both smiled. 'So perhaps there's something about her "Names" story here . . .' She moved along the line of potted Post-its, reading the messy scrawled animated words and feeling an overwhelming urge just to be with Constance, to see her, to touch her.

'There wouldn't be anything here about that if it was in the filing cabinet. It may have started here first as one name, or five names or maybe not even a name at all. If it was in the filing cabinet, it had become something. This was the nursery for them all.'

'Her babies,' Kitty smiled, eyes running along the sporadic, spontaneous thoughts that had all at one stage popped into Constance's mind. She thought about what Bob had said: the idea wouldn't have appeared in the filing cabinet if it hadn't *become something* and it was so frustrating not knowing what that something was. *Come on, Constance*, Kitty silently wished, taking a last look around the shed, *give me a clue*. She waited a moment but the potting shed remained still and silent.

Kitty grabbed a bottle of wine, thought better of it, took a second and followed Bob back to the house. She removed the pile of photo albums from the armchair facing Bob, a French-style armchair with a metallic gold flower design. She could see Bob and Constance sitting by the roaring fire, discussing issues, theories, far-off, outlandish stories to cover, both arguing and bonded by their love for the unusual and fantastical, and equally so by the ordinary and seemingly mundane.

'How are you, Bob?' Kitty finally asked. 'How are you doing?'

He sighed. A long heavy sigh that carried more weight than any words. 'It's been two weeks. One shudders to think that it's been that long. The day after her funeral I woke up and said to myself, I can't do this. I cannot get through this day. But I did. Somehow. And then that day was over and I was facing the night and I said to myself, I cannot face this night. But I did. Somehow. And then that night was over. I have said the same thing to myself every day and every night since. Each second is rather torturous, as though it will never move on, and as though it will never get any easier, and yet when I look back on it, look where we are. Two weeks on. And I'm doing it. And I still believe I simply cannot.'

Kitty eyes filled as she listened to him.

'I expected the world to end when she died.' He took a bottle from Kitty, opened it swiftly with a bottle opener that had been on the side table next to the *Irish Times* crossword, a biro and his reading glasses. 'But it didn't. Everything kept going, everything is still going. Sometimes I go for walks and I find that I have stopped moving, and everything else is still shifting and evolving all around me. And I wonder, don't they know? Don't they know about the terrible thing that has happened?'

'I know how you feel,' Kitty said gently.

'There are good widowers and bad ones. You hear about the good ones all the time. Gosh, isn't so-and-so great, so strong, so *brave* for doing whatever so soon. I fear I'm not a good widower, Kitty. I don't want to do anything. I don't wish to go anywhere. Most of the time I don't want to even be here, but you're not supposed to say that, are you? You're just supposed to say insightful meaningful things that surprise people so that they can tell other people how brave you are. Brave,' he repeated, his eyes filling. 'But I was never the brave one. Why it should fall upon me to become that now is beyond me.' Bob swiftly reached for the second bottle, opened it as quickly, deftly, and then handed it back to Kitty. 'I don't know where we keep the glasses,' he said, then clinked his bottle against hers. 'To . . . something.'

'To our beloved Constance,' Kitty said, lifting the bottle to her lips and drinking. The red wine burned her throat on the way down but left a delicious warm sweet coating in her mouth. She quickly followed it up with another mouthful.

'Our beloved Constance,' Bob repeated, thoughtfully studying the bottle.

'And to getting through tonight,' she added.

'Ah, now that is one I will drink to,' he said, and raised his bottle in the air. 'To getting through tonight.'

They sat in a comfortable silence, Kitty trying to figure out how to broach the subject, but Bob beat her to it.

'I sense you've run into some trouble with the story.'

'That's an understatement,' Kitty sighed, then took another swig. 'I'm sorry to admit it, Bob, but I'm lost. Totally and utterly lost. Pete is expecting the story by Friday, or at least to *know* what it is, and, well, unless I figure this out I have to go up there and tell him that there is no story, that I have ruined the entire Constance story. Yet another failure on my part.' Her eyes felt hot as they filled up with frustration and guilt.

'Ah. Well, perhaps there's something I can help you with,' Bob said, maintaining his good nature in spite of what she had revealed. 'I'm afraid I know no more about the names than you do, and after a week of your investigations I now know even less, but what I do know is Constance, so allow me to give you a lesson in Constance.' He looked upward at the light, his eyes shining as he brought her to life in his mind. 'Do you remember that awful murder around fifteen years ago on Ailesbury Road, where the multimillionaire business mogul husband was suspected of bludgeoning the wife to death with an odd cleaning implement?' Kitty shook her head. 'You were probably too young to remember it but it was rather big news. They never caught him, by the way, though all assumed it was him. He moved away, sold the house, and not much has been heard of him since, but Constance pored over every word of that case and something about it resonated with her, excited her, really, and not just because it was the usual educated wealthy man who should know better accused of murdering his wife. Constance, like every other journalist, was desperate to get an interview with the young maid who had found the wife in the bedroom, alerted the police and who had been the star of the trial that he walked away from. She was a young

222

beautiful thing from the Philippines or Thailand – I can't remember where exactly – but Constance kept going to the house to try and speak to her, and whenever Constance was busy meddling in something else, which was often, as you know, she sent me around to the house to try to convince the maid to speak to us. I assumed, like everyone else, it was to talk about the case, what she saw, what she had found, what kind of a man her boss was, what kind of relationship the husband and wife had, what were her personal suspicions, that kind of thing . . .' Bob stared into the distance and laughed, thinking of what came next. 'It turned out that what struck Constance as interesting was not the murder story but the item that the husband had used to murder his wife. It was an old cleaning implement – I can't remember what it was called – which had been brought to Ireland by the housemaid and, doing a story about old traditional cleaning methods, Constance had been desperate to speak to the young woman about the implement.'

Kitty smiled, shaking her head.

'And she spoke to her too. Ours was the only magazine that year to get an interview with the most popular housemaid, and we didn't even mention the murder at all. So the point is, my dear, you may think Constance is leading you down one track but in reality, it is most likely a completely different track altogether. With Constance, it's never about what you think it's about. Whatever *you* think is logical, forget about it, it is not logical to Constance. Start trying to see it from her eyes, try to feel it from her heart, for it was a big and complicated one, but it will find you her story.'

Kitty sat back in the armchair and took another slug of her bottle. Bob watched her while her mind ticked over the story he had just told her and then over the new stories Constance had led her to.

And then she got it. She finally got it.

CHAPTER TWENTY-TWO

After spending a further few hours with Bob and another of Constance's homegrown bottles of red wine, Kitty felt far more relaxed about approaching Pete. With a plan in her head, she was ready to pitch to him how she was now going to focus on the people she had met so far and *only* the people she had met. That particular part had been Bob's idea. He had helped her to see that despite the fact she had figured out what the link was, she didn't need to meet ninety-four more people in order to reach the same conclusion. There simply wasn't the time to do all that dear Constance had planned for them to do. And she had really done it this time: Constance had come up with something grand and wonderful, so entirely full of her teachings, which made Kitty both excited and emotional. It was almost as if this was Constance's parting message, her final words from the grave, and what perfect words to leave behind.

Kitty wasn't so nervous about going to Pete with her pitch, knowing Bob was behind her all the way, and also their relationship had evolved so much over the past few days. She smiled again to herself, that schoolgirl feeling of butterflies in her stomach. She was suddenly aware of how she looked, the flush in her cheeks from the wine, the jeans, the blouse, the flats she'd been wearing all day. Should she have changed? She fixed her hair and quickly rooted in her bag for her lipstick and powder.

The door to the office opened and the two cleaners stepped out, having finished their work for the evening.

'Can you keep that open for me, please?' Kitty called to them, putting her make-up away. She rushed up the steps and went inside the office. It was silent inside, nobody working late apart from Pete, who as usual was bearing the brunt of responsibility. He didn't have a girlfriend but she could imagine the frustration of sitting at home waiting for him to return at ten at night. She checked herself in the mirror at reception, fluffed her hair, opened another button on her blouse, and then ran through the story in her head, how she was best going to sell it to him.

She heard furniture moving in Constance's office and she headed in that direction. She was about to call out when she heard a woman laugh. Then sigh. She looked around, wondering if somebody else was in the office but it was quiet, eerily quiet. Then she got that feeling, that uh-oh feeling, and debated turning back and leaving. But it wasn't in Kitty's nature to leave a suspicious situation and so she moved forward, continuing to hear the furniture moving now and then, as if somebody was pushing a chair back and forth. She didn't bother knocking. She knew instinctively that to do that would be to miss out on what she already knew in her heart. She pushed the door open and was faced with Cheryl, her grey office skirt up around her thighs, which were wrapped around the man pole she was currently gyrating against. Hands were all over her back, moving up and down, to her thighs, to her bottom, squeezing and pinching, looking so unromantic and clumsy that Kitty leaned against the doorframe and ruffled up her nose. They were not the hands of an expert.

The sloppiness of their kisses was audible, along with an occasional sigh, and when she heard the duty editor's voice, husky with desire, tell the acting deputy editor what exactly he planned to do with her in a rather vicious tone, she felt it was the right time to clear her throat. Cheryl jumped so far off the table Kitty wondered if it could be considered actual human flight.

'Jesus, Kitty,' Cheryl said, pulling her skirt down from her waist and pushing it back round her thighs. The buttons on her blouse were open and her fingers trembled as she tried to button them and then deserted the idea and instead pulled them closed and folded her arms. 'We were just, I was just . . .'

'About to screw your boss,' Kitty said. 'Yeah, I know. Sorry to interrupt you both. It does sound like Pete had proposed a good plan for you both but I popped by, as invited, to share my break-through with you. But maybe it's not the best time for that.' Her eyes fell on Pete and she suddenly felt emotional. She knew she had very little reason to feel that way but she genuinely felt betrayed. It had been only a few days' flirtation but it had meant something to her, particularly after the disastrous weekend she'd had with Richie. Her love life was not going well, she was feeling sorry for herself, victimised, when really she should probably blame herself for her own ridiculous choice in men. But she wasn't going to, not yet. Now she was going for self-pity just because of the way he was looking at her, the soft sorry expression in his eyes. She knew then that she was right to feel betrayed because she could see that *he* felt as though he had betrayed her.

Pete had barely budged an inch from where he'd been caught. He stood at the desk, his hair a tousled mess, while he looked at Kitty expectantly, uncertain and nervous as to what she'd do next. He at least had the decency to show shame on his face.

Cheryl sensed something was up too because she glanced from Pete to Kitty in confusion. 'What's going on here?' Her two hands clasped her blouse closed so tightly her knuckles were white.

'Nothing,' Kitty said, and her voice mistakenly came out as a whisper. She cleared her throat and spoke loudly. 'Absolutely nothing.'

And on that note, she left.

Apart from feeling a little humiliated, deflated and victimised, in a professional sense, Kitty was empowered now because she suddenly felt that it didn't matter what Pete said about her article, she would write it exactly how she wanted, how she felt Constance intended it to be, and she wouldn't bend or be changed in any way, despite his temper, authority or threats. It was what she needed for her work. It had lacked confidence and now she felt nothing but. The ball was in her court, the story was hers to own. She hurried back to Fairview and at 10 p.m. now knew that going to Archie's home at the flats was not the cleverest idea she'd ever had. Still, she was on a mission. She ran past the kids crowding the footpath and up the four flights of stairs to Archie's flat. She banged on the door, moving from foot to foot, wanting to do this all now, not wanting another day to be wasted. She cleared her throat. She heard someone do the same and when she turned to the right she saw the young boy sitting on the basketball.

'Hi,' she said.

'Hi,' he imitated her.

'Is he in?'

'Is he in?' he repeated.

She rolled her eyes. He did the same.

She backed away from the flat and ran back downstairs, through the crowd of kids who jeered after her and she ran around the corner to Nico's chipper. Monday night and there was a long queue ahead of her. She spotted Archie behind the counter flipping burgers.

'Archie,' she called, pushing her way through the queue to get to the counter.

He turned around, giving her that familiar amused smile as if the joke was on her and she entertained him. 'You'll have to wait in the queue,' he said, then turned back to his burgers.

'I'm not here for food, I just want to talk to you.'

She was trying to keep her voice down but even with the news report playing on the radio it was impossible not to be heard in the chipper. Archie's colleague gave him a dark look and Archie was clearly annoyed. She was getting him into trouble.

'Fine,' she said, backing away from the counter. 'Chips, please.'

His colleague nodded and got to work, lowering a basket of chips into the hot oil. Her stomach rumbled. 'And a cheeseburger,' she added.

Archie slapped another cheeseburger on the hotplate and it sizzled.

Twenty minutes later she had made it to the cash register. Archie left his place by the hotplate to personally serve the food to her.

'I haven't been able to stop thinking about you all day,' she said, the excitement building in her again.

'It's a common complaint from women,' he said, dousing her chips in salt and vinegar.

'You have to help her,' Kitty said.

He looked up at her, finally met her eyes.

'The woman in the café, you have to talk to her. Maybe you're supposed to help her, maybe this is why it's happening to you.'

He looked at the others in the queue nervously, hoping they weren't listening.

'Five eighty,' he said.

She took her time searching for her money. 'Meet me at the café again tomorrow morning. She'll be there, won't she?'

He squared his jaw while he thought about it, then gave her a single nod.

'Okay.' She left the counter and pulled the door open.

'Do you think it will stop then?' he asked.

'Do you want it to?'

She left him with something to think about while she made her way in the cool night, the vinegar chips making her mouth water. Passing Archie's flats she saw a boy cycling a familiar bike. She stopped, looking around to make sure he had no one to back him up. The crowd that had been hanging around were now gone, either on to a new destination, inside to their homes or were lingering in the shadows.

'Hey,' she said.

'Hey,' she heard a voice imitate her four floors up.

Both her and the boy looked up to the source of the sound and then back at each other again.

'That's my bike,' she said.

'That's my bike.'

The boy cycled up the kerb to the footpath and circled her. He couldn't have been older than thirteen yet he intimidated her.

'If it's yours, how come I have it?'

'Because you stole it.'

'I didn't steal anything.' He continued circling her.

'I left it locked on the railings on Friday. Somebody took it.' As soon as the words started coming out of her mouth they were immediately repeated by the freckled face boy on the basketball. He was speaking over her so that she could barely concentrate on what she was saying.

'Must have been a shit lock.'

'True.'

'True.'

He went down the kerb to the road, stood up on the pedals and braked hard, causing the back wheel to lift. He did a few more moves in the middle of the road.

'Do you want it back?'

'Well, of course. Yes.'

She heard, 'Well, of course. Yes.'

He stopped abruptly and hopped off the bike. He stood a few yards ahead of her, holding the bike upright by the handlebars. 'All you had to do was ask.'

She looked around, thinking there must be a catch, that a crew were somewhere ready to jump out at her.

She slowly walked towards him, her burger and chips in hand, the light an orange glow from the streetlight. She reached the bike and waited for something to happen. Nothing did. She took the bike by the handlebars and the boy walked away.

'Thanks,' she said, hearing the surprise in her voice.

'Thanks,' she heard the patronising echo back at her.

All she had to do was ask.

Kitty was about to get on her bicycle when she had an over-whelming desire to do something. 'Hey!' she called out.

'Hey!' she heard the voice repeat.

'You up there on the basketball,' she said, and there was no response, just a little head appearing above the wall. 'Want to play?' she asked.

He didn't repeat her. The head disappeared instead and she heard his steps coming down the flights of stairs. On the basketball courts beside the block of flats, Kitty was brought back to her youth as she and the young boy battled it out in the dark, neither of them saying a word.

When she got home she was so busy concentrating on carrying her bike up the stairs that she got a fright when a figure at the top appeared in her eyeline.

'Jesus.' She dropped the bike, thinking it was Colin Maguire's crew ready to pounce on her. She might have preferred that because facing her was Richie, evil tabloid journalist. She would have slapped him across the face right then had his eye not resembled a rotten plum, half-closed and purple, and his lip was busted. She wasn't sure what to say. All of her preprepared nasty comments went out of her head.

'What happened to you?'

'Don't pretend you don't know,' he said bitterly. 'Just give me my jacket and I'll get out of here.'

Her blood pumped. 'Excuse me?'

'My jacket. I came to collect it. The fella downstairs says you have it.'

'Your jacket,' she repeated. 'And what about an apology? Hello, Kitty, I'm sorry? I'm sorry I was a lying scumbag rat dickhead?' She didn't bother trying to control her rage – it all just came tumbling out.

'Ah, come on, don't get like this.' He held his hands up. 'You know how this game is, you know how it works. I was sent to get the story from you and I did my job.'

'You did your job? Sleeping with me was part of your job?' She had her hands on her hips now and was so close to his face she could see her spit landing on his skin with each word. He had the audacity to look slightly embarrassed about that.

'Look that, that wasn't . . . I had too much to drink. That shouldn't have happened.'

She couldn't believe her ears. So many times she had played this conversation in her head, how it was supposed to go, her being extremely angry but incredibly eloquent in her insults and also having life-changing effects on Richie, he hanging his head low, so sorry, so very disgusted by his behaviour that he could barely express it, yet he did, in equally eloquent language. But here she was, in reality, listening to somebody who could barely apologise and, when pushed, the only thing he was sorry for was sleeping with her. The sex had been the only decent – well, half-decent – thing that had occurred that night. Her rage was so great she felt her body shaking. She just didn't want to cry, anything but show this insensitive little shit how much he'd hurt her. She tried to think of the most hurtful thing she could possibly say to him, she racked her brains, conscious of the time that was passing her by as she stared at his beaten face and she realised he was talking.

'But that was still no reason to send your bodyguard after me. That was ridiculous, Kitty. You're lucky I didn't press charges or tell anyone who was responsible for this because, believe me, you could be in a whole lot more trouble.'

'Bodyguard? What the hell are you talking about? I didn't "send" anyone after you. I would have been far more than happy to do that to your face myself so you can stop accusing me and start thinking of the numerous amount of people you have managed to insult doing your dirty little job.'

He actually smiled and when his lip stretched and fresh blood drew from the cut, he immediately stopped. 'First of all, my dirty little job, as you say, is exactly the same as the one you have, so we're in the same boat, Kitty Logan. And secondly, bodyguard or boyfriend, I'm not sure which, but did our night out get you into trouble, Kitty?' he said smugly. 'The last time I annoyed Steve Jackson was when I accidentally knocked his pint over you in the college bar so you can be sure I know exactly who it is that came after me and why.'

'Steve? Steve did this to you?'

'Are you going to pretend you didn't know about that like you pretended you didn't know a whole pile of other things on *Thirty Minutes*? I don't have much more time to waste on this so, my jacket?'

Kitty wanted to punch his other eye but she was so shocked by his behaviour and the revelation that Steve had hit him that she simply unlocked the door, retrieved his jacket from the couch where she'd thrown it and brought it back to him.

'Never come here again,' she said firmly as she handed it back.

He gave her an amused look as he slithered down the stairs. 'Hold on,' he paused and came back up the stairs. 'My USB, where is it?'

'What USB?'

'It must have been in my pocket. It's what I'm here for. My novel is on it.' He suddenly came over all worried little schoolboy as he stood before her, checking the pockets in a panic.

'Well, I don't have your USB so perhaps you should ask the dry-cleaners about it. Maybe they put it through the steamer for you.'

He genuinely looked panicked about that. 'Seriously, have you got it? It's the only version I have.'

'Well, you should have backed it up.' She folded her arms, enjoying watching him suffer.

'That was my back-up, my computer crashed . . . shit! Kitty,

232

have you got it?' he asked desperately. 'Seriously, have you got it?'

'No,' she said firmly, the anger returning. 'I do not have your stupid novel, nor do I want it. Please do not come one step near me ever again or I'll call the police,' and she slammed the door in his face.

She sat at the kitchen table, head in her hands, taking in deep breaths, slowly in and out, going over their conversation so many times that she wanted to open the door and challenge him once again, properly this time.

Finally she had a moment of clarity. She walked to the couch where she had thrown Richie's jacket before leaving to stay in Sally's house, and she searched around the floor, then the couch, then, when she didn't find anything, she felt around the cushions. Her hand hit something. She pulled out the cushion and laughed as she was faced with Richie's USB.

'Payback time,' she said.

CHAPTER TWENTY-THREE

Kitty and Archie sat in the Brick Alley Café in Temple Bar in silence. He held a cup of tea in his hand, she a mug of coffee, and they sat half-turned in their stools, facing one another so that they could see the rest of the café behind them. The mousy woman arrived a little after 8 a.m., on cue as usual, stayed for twenty minutes, drank a pot of tea and ate a fruit scone with butter and jam, as she always did, and then she paid and left. Kitty was the first to hop off her stool. Archie was a little more hesitant.

'Come on,' she said, and he grudgingly stood as if a child scorned by his mother. 'Hurry.' She rushed him along out of the café and on to the street while he shuffled his feet behind her. 'We'll lose her.'

By the time they got outside with all of Archie's faffing around there was no sign of the woman either end of the street. 'Ah, Archie, we've lost her. You did this on purpose. I should have made you approach her inside.'

'You can't make me do anything,' he said firmly. 'And we haven't lost her.' He shoved his hands in his pockets and turned left, walking without purpose up the road, as if he had all the time in the world.

'But she's not here. What do you mean, we haven't lost her? Why are you walking like that? Archie, believe me, I have enough going on in my life right now without having been dragged here to be fooled.' She continued her rant while he walked and eventually she fell into a silence and just walked with him, thinking of all the things she could have done that morning that would have been far more beneficial. When they took a sharp right and another right on to the quays they saw her crossing the Halfpenny Bridge.

'There she is!' Kitty exclaimed, grabbing his arm excitedly.

Archie didn't seem at all surprised.

'You've followed her before,' she accused him, eyes narrowing.

He didn't respond.

'How many times?'

'Once or twice.'

'Where does she go?'

'See for yourself.'

They crossed the bridge over the River Liffey and arrived on Bachelor's Quay. The woman disappeared inside a church. Archie promptly stopped.

'This is as far as I go.'

'Let's go in.'

'No. I'll wait here.'

'Why? We'll see what she does in there.'

'What do you think she does? It's a church. I'll stay here, thank you very much.'

'She could go to confession, she could meet somebody in there, pass a briefcase or two, she could sing or cry or strip naked and cartwheel across the altar, for all we know.'

He looked at her intrigued. 'The way your mind works.'

'I'm more interested in yours. If you hear prayers like you say you can, maybe there are more people in there that you could help.'

'Are you doubting me?'

'I am now, yes,' she replied truthfully.

He thought about it and then went inside the church.

Kitty watched Archie's face as he entered. The church was quiet, with a dozen or so people scattered across the pews. It was silent but for the occasional cough and sniffle, which, when started, seemed to flow like a tidal wave through the small gathering and then silence again. Archie closed his eyes and tilted his head to one side, seeming pained. He finally looked around, studying each person. His eyes rested on the mousy woman. She was lighting a candle, then she moved to a pew and kneeled. Archie slowly made his way down the left-hand side and self-consciously shuffled into a row to sit behind her. Kitty stayed where she was at the back. She did this for a few reasons – she wanted to give Archie space, she wasn't entirely comfortable in churches but mostly because, on the rare chance that Archie did possess the ability to hear people's prayers, she didn't want him to hear hers. Kitty hadn't been lying when she said she didn't believe in God. She had been christened Catholic but, like most Catholics she knew, didn't practise her religion. Church services for her were confined to weddings and funerals. She didn't pray either, not in the sense of getting down on her knees by her bedside each night in a ritual, but occasionally when she felt lost she prayed for whatever crisis she was in to pass quickly and never gave any thought as to whom exactly she was sending these thoughts to. She understood that Archie believed he could hear people's prayers, that after spending time thinking nobody was hearing his prayers for his daughter he had to somehow manifest the idea that somebody somewhere, if not a god, might have heard him and now he was that person. Perhaps this was to help him believe his prayers weren't wasted, but that whoever heard them was powerless, just as he was, to act on them. Or perhaps he was simply bonkers. Kitty tried to think of anything but her prayers as she stood down the back of the church, but it was difficult. She had much on her mind, much to worry about. It was so quiet, so peaceful, that the silence was like a wave on a shoreline, pulling her into her mind.

She was worrying about Pete, about Richie, about thinking Steve had been ignoring her instead of the fact he had been defending her honour and how that made her feel, about her story presentation on Friday and then, *if* approved, having a mere weekend to write it, about having to find a new place to live by a fortnight's time, about the upcoming job interview, about possibly being involved in the theft of a nursing home bus. But mostly what occupied her mind was how she was ever going to figure out how to apologise to Colin Maguire. At least she was confident on one thing. She had found the way to write Constance's story and, with or without Pete's permission, she was going to write it.

After fifteen minutes the mousy woman stood and exited the church. She didn't glance at Kitty, showing no recollection whatsoever that they had been in the same café three mornings. Archie stood up and left too, passing Kitty and walking towards the bright light of outside existence. They both squinted in the sun.

'Where does she go now?' Kitty asked.

'Don't know, I never lasted this long.' He sighed. He seemed weary.

'How was that for you?' she asked gently.

'It's one thing being in a crowd or on the bus – you hear the occasional thing that someone's praying for, like people not wanting to be late, praying for good results in school or college, praying for something to happen at work or a mortgage or loan to be approved – but in there . . .' he blew air out of his mouth '. . . it's pretty hardcore.'

'What did you hear?'

He looked at her uncertainly. 'It's kind of . . . private, isn't it?'

'I have to know this stuff,' Kitty said simply. 'Otherwise how can I write about it? And it's not like you have some priestly confidentiality clause that says you can't tell anyone.'

'Still,' Archie shrugged. 'I'd rather not. It wasn't exactly pleasant. People don't usually pray when they're happy. And if they do, they don't go in there at nine in the morning on a weekday to do it.'

They stopped walking on the Liffey boardwalk, a promenade hanging over the river, a south-facing set-up for al fresco lunch and coffee. The mousy woman went to the coffee kiosk next to O'Connell Bridge and started setting up for her shift.

'What do you think I should do?' Archie asked.

'I think you should help who you can. I think it will help you. And I think you should start with her.'

They watched her.

'People are going to think I'm crazy when this comes out.'

'Won't it be better than what you say they think of you now?'

He pondered that, then watched for a gap in the traffic and hurried across the road to the kiosk.

'I just think you should give her another chance,' Gaby was saying to Kitty over her second espresso in the Merrion Hotel in Merrion Square.

Kitty had called her the previous night to arrange a meeting, Gaby had chosen the venue and so far had done all the talking, and Kitty was hoping Gaby planned on picking up the tab too for what seemed like the most expensive coffee she'd ever drunk. They were sitting outside in the garden, meetings going on all around them, and Gaby had one eye and ear on everybody else's conversations and the other on her and Kitty's. She lit up another cigarette. Gaby appeared to be under the illusion that Kitty had the intention of dropping Eva from her story and had launched into a tirade of Eva's career history, starting with celebrity clients and magazines she had been featured in, and while that was partly correct, as Kitty was reluctant to waste more of her precious time on Eva after being fobbed off with the My Little Pony present response, this wasn't actually something she had yet shared with either Eva or Gaby. However, they weren't foolish women. Kitty had turned down an opportunity to meet Eva twice over the past few days, unsure that she was ever going to get anything from Eva about herself as a person as opposed to her business. Kitty simply didn't have enough time to spend with such a closed book.

'She's been mentioned in *Vogue* on their "Who's hot" list and was in *Cosmopolitan*'s "Young and Happening" slot. She really is *incredible*.' She shut her eyes and squeezed her entire body to emphasise the word, then opened her eyes and took another puff of her cigarette.

'She's a closed book, Gaby. Each time I ask her a question she either refuses to answer or she brings it back to work. I know that she is a hard worker and that she is passionate about her company ethos but I have to have more to run with than that. The other people that I'm interviewing are more . . .' she tried to think of a polite way of saying it but realised it was Gaby she was speaking to and politeness counted for nothing '. . . substantial. They intrigue me. I want to find out more and when I dig a little deeper, I discover more. Eva isn't willing to open up to me and I don't want to force her into talking about anything she doesn't want to talk about. That's not the kind of journalist I am.'

Gaby raised one eyebrow, thinking otherwise.

'At least, I'm not any more.' Kitty raised her chin haughtily.

'She's difficult to get to know, I realise that. The problem with Eva is that she is . . .' Gaby paused for dramatic effect, which worked as Kitty hung on every word '. . . *creative*.' She said it like it was a bad word. Then she lowered her voice so that nobody could hear the dirty secret to come. 'She's one of these types who thinks that their *art* speaks for themselves.' She rolled her eyes. 'Honestly. I deal with this crap all the time with my writers. They think their work is their voice, they don't understand that *they* have to give it one. They don't realise that it's people like me and you who help them sell their bloody *art*. Do you know how long it took me to get Eva to start that "Dedicated" blog? They

239

think that stuff is in the way of whatever it is they think they're channelling. Think about it, if James Joyce were alive today, don't you think his tweets could make his stuff more accessible?'

Kitty really hoped nobody was listening to their conversation.

'Anyway,' she waved her hand dismissively, 'Eva is an interesting person, she's got a great heart, you just need to spend a lot of time with her to really open her up and when you see inside, well then, you'll understand it all.'

'You know something about her?'

'I know more than most, which isn't saying a lot, but I've seen in there once or twice. She went out with my brother for three years. He was an idiot but she was adorable. We've been close ever since. I vowed to help her out and I won't let her down.'

Kitty had wanted to talk to Gaby about something that had nothing to do with Eva Wu at all, but while they were there and talking about her she was interested in new insights on the girl she couldn't quite find a story on.

'It would help if I could at least talk to her clients, hear how she's helped them, learn what she's done for them. She's so secretive about it all.'

'Not so much secretive as protective of her clients. She insists on discretion. She sees what she does as more than giving a gift and she's right really. What she does is very special.'

Kitty shook her head, confused.

'I know. It will all make sense when you're in Cork.'

'How did you know I was going to Cork?'

'To the wedding? I just assumed.'

'The wedding, on Friday.' Kitty gasped. 'Of course.' With all the excitement of Birdie's impending road trip she had forgotten about the wedding where Eva was due to present the Webb family with their gifts. 'How does Eva usually travel?' Kitty asked.

'She drives, why?'

'Ask her if she'd like to catch a bus with me on Thursday to Cork. There's something I have to do there that I think she'll like.'

'Sure,' Gaby said, looking over Kitty's shoulder towards her next appointment arriving. 'Here's Jools Scott. The writer. Great on a page but can't put two words together in person. If I manage to get him one interview I'll be doing well,' she said out of the side of her mouth, and then waved at him happily.

'Before you move on, there's something I have to ask you. I'm sure everyone asks you this but I wonder if you could do me a huge favour.' Kitty got to the real reason she'd asked for the meeting. She placed Richie's USB down on the table before her and fixed Gaby with her sweetest smile.

To Kitty's great relief Gaby took care of the bill with her publisher's credit card, her final bribe to Kitty to write a positive piece on Eva. Feeling that she owed Eva for letting her down twice, Kitty called Nigel at George Webb's office.

'Molloy Kelly Solicitors.'

'It's Kitty Logan. I'm outside your office. Eva Wu is incredibly protective of her clients and won't tell me a thing. If you want the piece to be as favourable as possible then I need you to start talking.'

He was quiet, then: 'Fine.'

Five minutes later he was outside with her in another of his dapper suits. When he saw her bike his lips curled at the edges. 'How twee. Walk with me, Judy Bloom, I don't want anybody to see me with you in those last season's pumps.'

Kitty smiled and they walked to the famine memorial and leaned out overlooking the rather murky Liffey.

'Let's get straight to the point. I'm gay.' He looked at Kitty but she wasn't in the mood for smart comments. 'I'm from a small parish in Donegal where everybody knows everybody's business. As soon as I could talk I knew that I was gay and in my family that kind of thing is completely unacceptable. My father is a dairy farmer, like his father before him, like his father before him. I'm the only boy in the family and it was expected that I would go into the family business. It wasn't a life that appealed to me. My parents are fanatically Catholic. Hell, for them, is a very real place. Sex before marriage would have my sisters kicked out of the house, if my parents ever knew the truth. They live in a world of religious rules and they do not break them. They can't see beyond them; it's all they've ever known. Homosexuality,' he laughed bitterly, 'you can imagine what they thought of that. If my father couldn't understand why I wouldn't want to be a dairy farmer for the rest of my life, he certainly wouldn't understand the fact that I just happen to love men. When I told him I didn't want to be involved in the family business he didn't speak to me for almost a year. Imagine how he felt when I told him I was gay. But I'd no choice but to tell him. I'd met someone, he was a huge part of my life, it felt like I was living a lie not being able to talk about him or my life in Dublin, or not being able to bring him to family occasions. I finally told them and, well, my mother could deal with it as long as we never discussed it again and she prayed every day for me to be healed, but my father refused to be in the same house as me. He wouldn't look me in the eye, he wouldn't speak to me.'

'It must have been very difficult.'

'It was.'

He was silent.

'He was like that for five years. We didn't speak a word for five years. Well, I tried but . . . but then it was his sixtieth birthday and I suppose having that come up and me not being there didn't feel right. I wanted to get him something, a gift that he would be able to look at in his own time to understand what I was trying to tell him. So I hired Eva.'

'How did you hear about her?'

'She'd helped out another friend of mine,' he smiled. 'But that's another story for another day. She stayed with us in Donegal for a week, because that's what she insists on doing. It was the most awkward time for her but she was fantastic, she fit right in.'

Kitty had noticed that was what Eva seemed to do best.

'My mother was convinced that she was my girlfriend, that I'd been "healed", and she couldn't have made Eva feel any more welcome.'

'What about your father?'

'He managed to sleep in the house when I was there, which was progress, but he made sure to be gone at meal times and throughout the day. My sisters bought him a motorbike – it had been his lifetime ambition to have one – but I wanted him to have a present that meant something more to me, to him. I thought, there's no way in the world this girl can find the gift that can do everything I want it to.'

'And did she?'

To her surprise Nigel shook his head. 'No, it wasn't everything I wanted. It was far more. She made a photo album. She found photographs of his grandfather and his father working the farm, photos of him and his father working the farm, and then photos of him and me from the day I was born to the day I left the house. Photos of us together on the farm, of him pushing me on the tyre swing that he'd made for me, photos I'd never seen before. Dad had had to cut down one of the oak trees on the land. He'd been devastated about it because it was one of the trees we'd all played on as children, that he and his father had played on. It was the one with the tyre swing. But because of the heavy snow that year, it had suffocated the roots and the tree couldn't survive. Eva had taken the chopped wood from that tree and used it to form the back and cover of the photo album. On the front she'd carved his name and birthday message from me. She charged me sixty-five euro for the carpentry and forty euro for the printing of the photos and stationery. That was the cost of the gift.'

'Did it work?'

'Mother said she heard him crying while he was looking through it when she'd gone to bed. He didn't say anything to me for weeks and then out of the blue one day he called me.'

'What did he say?'

Nigel laughed. 'He started telling me about a problem he was having on the farm. Something about one of the cows in heat. I was just so surprised to hear his voice on the end of the phone, I could barely take in what he was saying. There was no mention of the five years we hadn't spoken, it was like he'd picked up where we'd left off.'

'So Eva is incredibly thoughtful.'

'She's more than that. She understood how my father thought, what exactly it was that upset him or disappointed him, what would move him, what would shake his belief. She lived with us and asked us questions and listened to our stories and she came up with a solution. My father is a sensitive man, but he's a closed man, he would never show or discuss emotions, yet she found a gift that touched his heart.'

Kitty thought about that. 'Okay.'

'You get it?'

'I got it.'

'Good. Now don't disturb me at work again,' he said cheekily, and left her alone on Custom House Quay.

CHAPTER TWENTY-FOUR

Kitty got off the bus in Kinsealy, North County Dublin beside the garden centre early on Wednesday morning. In the fields beyond, families gathered to pick strawberries and behind that field Steve's father's allotment was in full swing as the summer weather attracted garden lovers to their patches. All of the land belonged to Steve's father: the garden centre, the strawberry fields, the allotment, and to most people's surprise and frustration, for over a decade he had managed to fight off planners from buying the land to develop houses. Those offers had stopped in recent years but he had turned down millions, happy to keep his businesses going. He was a farmer at heart, as tough as they came, and he wouldn't know what to do with twenty million in his bank account. His days were best spent toiling the earth, finding new gadgets for gardening. And snapping at people.

'Thought you'd be hiding under a rock,' he said to Kitty as she walked into the clubhouse.

'Thought you'd be the best man to see about the right rock.'

'The biggest one you could find, I'd say,' he eyed her warily.

'I'm open to anything,' she smiled back, which further annoyed him. 'How's everything going? Business good?'

He looked at her and then back down at the paperwork on his desk. 'If you're looking for Steve, he's rotavating allotment fifty.'

'Steve is rotavating?' Kitty laughed. 'What does he know about rotavating?'

'A lot more than you know about journalism, that's for sure,' he barked back.

That put her in her place.

'He has a girlfriend, you know.'

'I know.'

'Katja.'

'I know.'

'Nice girl.'

'I know.'

'Does well at work.'

'I know. She takes pictures.'

'She took that one.' He eyed her warily again and Kitty's eyes moved up to the beautiful landscape of Skellig Rock off the coast of County Kerry on a misty day. It had the desired effect: the sheer beauty of it, and knowing Katja had taken it, made her uncomfortable.

'Which is number fifty?'

He waved his hand at a map on the wall and ignored her.

Kitty made her way through the fifty-metre square patches and smiled at families in their gardens. Some were busy at work, others were sitting out in deckchairs, drinking from tea flasks, children running around, soaking one another with watering cans. Each plot had a different scene, which reminded her of the black-board of specials in Brick Alley Café: 'Every table has a story to tell.'

She found Steve in the allotment, alone with a rotavator, noise so loud he couldn't hear her call out to him. She stood at the fence and watched him, his face etched in concentration on the soil ahead of him. To her surprise his skin was visible. He'd lost the leather jacket and instead wore a T-shirt and jeans, thick work boots on his feet. He was entirely covered in mud and grass, stains that she couldn't recognise, his hair even more of a tangled mess than usual as he'd worked outside all day. Finally he lifted his gaze from the soil and saw her.

She smiled and waved. He turned the machine off immediately.

'Kitty,' he said, surprised.

'Thought I'd come down and surprise you.'

'How long have you been here?'

'A few minutes. I was watching your concentration face.' She frowned and pouted, the same way his lips went when they were studying in college or when she caught sight of him in exams.

He laughed.

'Dad greet you at the door?'

'The best welcome committee a girl could have.'

'Sorry about that,' he said, genuinely concerned.

'Don't worry, I'd rather that than manure on my front door any day.'

'They've done more?'

'Just that. It's stopped since Sunday, actually,' she said, realising. 'Maybe they got into trouble. And speaking of trouble,' she made her way round the fence and inside the allotment, 'I came here to give you this.' She opened her arms and threw them around Steve, wrapping him so tight and squeezing him. She could tell he was shocked, his body stiffened, not comfortable with human contact, but she didn't care, she needed to thank him for what he had done for her. Finally his body relaxed and he surprised her by wrapping his arms around her waist. It felt oddly comfortable. She hadn't expected him to react that way, she had expected him to push her away but appreciate the gesture anyway, but now she found them both in the allotment hugging tightly and she was suddenly self-conscious. She loosened her grip and he did too, but he didn't pull away from her. Their faces were close when they looked at one another. His blue eyes bored into hers. She swallowed.

'That was supposed to be a thank you,' she said quietly.

He frowned. 'Thank you for what?'

'For cleaning spray paint off my apartment door, for cleaning dog shit off the steps, for giving me your bed, but most of all for making Richie's face look like a rotten tomato.'

'Oh. Right.' He let go suddenly and took a few steps back – a lot of steps back – and then separated them entirely by standing behind the machine. Back to his usual self. 'So you found out about that.'

'He came to my flat to get his jacket. He thought you were my boyfriend and that you'd caught me out. He was thrilled.'

Steve's face hardened. 'That fucker. I swear I could hit him again.'

Kitty was surprised by his reaction. Steve wasn't that kind of guy. He was never aggressive. He wasn't soft but his first method of defence was to get out of a situation because he was never that bothered by anyone, not to pounce.

'Well . . . you did it once and I appreciate that.'

'Twice, actually,' he smiled. 'Almost broke my fist too.' He lifted his hand and that's when Kitty saw the swollen bruising on his knuckles.

'Oh, Steve, I'm so sorry.' She went towards him to touch it but, true to character, he pulled it away.

'It's fine. No big deal.'

'I thought you weren't speaking to me.'

He looked confused.

'Just the way you hung up the phone the other day, I thought you were angry at me. About the story in the Sunday paper. About messing up again.'

'No, no, Kitty, no,' he said gently. 'No way. I was so angry. At him. Why would I be angry at you?'

She shrugged and looked around, suddenly feeling so vulnerable in his company, so eager to please, so . . . no! She couldn't be feeling like this *with Steve*?

'So how are you, how's the story going?'

248

'I am *loving* it,' Kitty said, pushing her feelings to one side and responding ecstatically.

He laughed.

'I have met the most amazing people and I can't wait to tell you all about them.'

'Sounds good,' he smiled. 'It sounds like you're back to your best.'

'Does it?' she said, genuinely touched.

'Yeah. Back to all the stuff you used to bore me with before. It's good to see you so . . .' he looked at her '. . . happy.'

Happy. She thought about it. Yes, she was happy. Despite all the crap going on in her life, she was actually happy.

'Do you want to go for something to eat or drink, or . . .?'

'I'd love to but I have to get to Kildare, to the butterfly woman. I really need to learn more about her. She is so fascinating, like a creature from a Tolkien novel or something. And then I have a job interview,' she winced.

'Where?'

'Ashford night school for their media studies course. Though I'm half-thinking of cancelling.'

'Don't you dare,' he warned. 'You'll knock them dead.'

'That's what I'm afraid of.'

'Kitty,' he fixed her firmly with his blue-eyed gaze, 'you'll be wonderful.'

She was genuinely moved by that and felt ridiculous as tears sprung to her eyes. She hadn't received any praise lately, particularly not from Steve, and she hadn't realised how much she desired his praise. She looked down at her feet in the soil and cleared her throat. 'So I'm going on a trip tomorrow and I was wondering if I could use the assistance of your girlfriend.' The words felt like chalk in her mouth but she was trying, she hoped that he could see she was trying.

'Katja? Why?'

'The most exciting story of all.' She smiled then. 'Birdie, one of the names on my list, made a bet that she would live to the age of eighty-five and she turns eighty-five tomorrow. We're driving to Cork to pick up her winnings.'

'You're kidding. How much winnings?'

'Ten grand,' Kitty grinned. 'Or its euro equivalent, at least. So I need a photographer. It will be an overnight trip and there's a couple of things along the way I'll need her to do too.'

Steve thought about it. 'I'll let her know.'

'Thanks. I'll text you the pick-up details from the bus. If she can't come let me know so I can organise someone else. I'd better go.' They stood still in the allotment and Kitty all of a sudden very desperately wanted to be back in that embrace with him. Stunned by her feelings, she turned round and left awkwardly.

'But, Eugene, I don't understand why you told her about that?' Ambrose shouted at her friend and colleague.

Eugene's cheeks flushed. Ambrose's temper was as fiery as her hair. He had faced her wrath before and wasn't particularly good at dealing with it. It reduced him to a stammering wreck. 'It just came up in conversation,' he said meekly.

His meekness gave her more confidence to have a go at him. 'How could something like that just come up in conversation? It has nothing to do with the business. Oh, I knew I shouldn't have let you be interviewed by her,' she fumed, pacing her kitchen.

However, they both knew the opposite was true. If Eugene didn't speak to the reporter there would be no article, there would be no publicity for the museum, of which they were in dire need, and there would certainly be no better way to air their shared opinions and worries on the extinction of many butterflies. Eugene was better with people, everybody knew that. Apart from when she was with him, Ambrose had a complete inability to deal with most people. She became too conscious of her appearance, too obsessed by what they were thinking about her to be able to formulate a proper thought, never mind do business or promote her museum. She was okay over the phone but was all too aware of the local mystery surrounding her and so preferred not to deal with anyone at all. That way she couldn't add to the whispers and tales of 'the time they met Ambrose Nolan . . .' Truth be told, she was getting worse. She shopped online for clothes and groceries, making sure that anything that needed to be signed for would go directly to the museum so that Eugene, or Sara in the shop and café, would take care of it. But the one thing that nobody knew was the very thing Eugene had splurged to the reporter. Well, there were two things really. The first Eugene had broken to Ambrose, thinking she would be mildly annoyed, but she had exploded when she'd heard, and the second was simply unforgivable. He'd known it as he was telling the reporter but he couldn't help it, it had just come out. The reporter was good; she had a way of weaselling things out of him, which bothered him. He had said things he didn't even know to be true until he heard them come out of his mouth.

'I apologise about telling her about the operation,' he stammered. 'I shouldn't have done that. I don't know why I did, in fact, I'll ask her to make sure she doesn't write it in the article.' He referred to the fact that Ambrose had been saving for a very long time to have the birthmark on her face removed. She had visited various doctors about it and it would take many laser treatments to have it removed, but it was possible. This piece of information was not something she expected to be shared. The idea that Eugene had discussed her appearance with anybody humiliated her. 'But I didn't know you didn't want anybody to know about your report,' Eugene said more firmly, confidence in his voice, and Ambrose believed him.

'Who else have you told?'

'Nobody.'

'So you see, you did know not to say anything otherwise you would have told people.'

'Look, Ambrose, calm down. What you've done is terrific. You should be proud. I've read your report over and over again and it's the most wonderful thing I've ever read. I'm proud of you; you should want to tell the world about your findings. The fact that the symposium has asked you to speak about it is a huge honour and confirmation that your studies are remarkable. This symposium is your golden opportunity and you know it. It's not every day or even every year that it comes to Ireland.' He was referring to the upcoming event in Cork University where Sir David Attenborough, President of Butterfly Conservation, was to open this year's symposium. There would be reviews and news of the latest initiatives to reverse the decline in butterfly and moth numbers and how to conserve habitats. The symposium would also provide researchers from all around the world with a forum to present papers on practical conservation work. It would look at the future challenges, including the impact of climate change. Ambrose was one of the people who had been invited to speak. Eugene had confirmed the engagement on her behalf, much to her anger, but that had been another day's argument. Whether she would bite the bullet and attend the conference was unknown at this point but Eugene wasn't giving up on her.

'So you told her deliberately,' she snapped, face hot, eyes bright, one green and burning bright, the other as fearsome though dull brown, 'to force me to do it. If she writes about it then I have to do it, is that your plan?'

'I think your work is something to tell the world about,' he said firmly, trying to keep the stammer out of his voice. 'I doubt anybody else in the world has studied the Peacock butterfly as closely as you have. You have the data, the experience to prove it. Why spend five years studying and writing a report if you're not going to show it to anybody?' He realised his voice had risen louder and louder. Ambrose seemed surprised. Amused, even.

'You told her I was going to Cork and now she wants to come with us,' she said, frustrated.

'Correction. She wants *us* to go with *her*.'

'I don't understand.'

'You will soon. She'll be here soon to talk to you. She wants to spend the afternoon with you.'

The doorbell rang.

'That will be her,' Eugene said. Shaking from his confrontation he left an open-mouthed Ambrose quickly pulling down her hair from its clip, covering her face in a panic.

He took a deep breath and smiled before opening the door. 'Ah. Ms Logan, how lovely to see you. Please do come in.'

'She ties her hair back when she's around you,' Kitty said to Eugene after her interview session with the increasingly intriguing Ambrose was finished.

Eugene looked up in surprise from his paperwork where he was sitting in a small cubbyhole office. 'She told you that?'

'No, I saw you two talking through the window before I rang the doorbell.' Which translated to: 'I was snooping before I rang the doorbell.'

'Oh,' he said. 'Well then, I've nothing further to add to that.'

'I'm not going to write about that,' Kitty said, leaning against the doorframe, making him feel trapped. 'It just must be nice for you to know that.'

'Nice? Why would it be nice?' He fidgeted with papers. His cheeks flushed and the colour ran down his neck and stopped at his bow tie.

'Because she obviously feels very comfortable around you,' Kitty smiled and watched the corners of his mouth twitch as he thought about it.

'Well, I've never considered it. I mean, that's no reason to . . . It's not . . . She's not, we're not . . .' he stammered, unable to finish a single sentence he'd started.

'So I'll see you both tomorrow afternoon,' Kitty said.

'She said she'd go?'

'No, but I'll leave it up to you to convince her. I have a feeling

253

she listens to what you say.' She winked at him and left the museum.

Ashford Private College was situated on Parnell Square beside the Irish Writers' Centre, which faced the Garden of Remembrance and other such important venues as the Gate Theatre and Rotunda Maternity Hospital. It was a Georgian square and the college filled four floors of classrooms, advertising subjects from cookery to technology, interior design, business studies, marketing and media. Part of that media course was a television presentation class that taught the student how to speak properly and slowly, how to speak to the camera, getting rid of any habits or tics they unknowingly had and becoming comfortable with presentation and the sound of their own voice. Kitty had taken the class five years ago and was now attending an interview to teach it. It didn't escape her that she had no teaching credentials but she had gained plenty of experience actually working in the field, and in addition to being keen to share her knowledge, she really needed the money. Pay for two and a half hours a week would go a long way in her current situation.

She sat before Daniel Meara, the captain of the ship, former principal-turned-businessman, who had opened up the college to teach part-time and night courses, making money on handing out diplomas and certificates for employment opportunities that no longer existed.

'Katherine,' he looked down at her résumé and back up at her with a smile. It was an awkward smile, one that immediately had Kitty questioning why on earth she had come at all. If she didn't believe in herself, how on earth was she going to convince this man that she was good enough for the job? She braced herself.

'I appreciate you coming in to us today. And here is the thing,' he said, placing the palms of his hands down flat on the surface of the table. His fingers were sweaty and made a sticky sound each time he lifted them from the table, which he did to emphasise certain words. 'You are a past student of ours, which we appreciate greatly, and so that's why I told Triona to ask you in, so I could see you myself.' He moved his fingers and they made that sticky noise. 'And you have gone on to work in the field you studied, which we admire greatly and are most proud of.' He cleared his throat. 'However, under the current circumstances, *your* current circumstances . . .' They were the only words Kitty needed to hear to understand where this was going, and the rest disappeared before it reached her head apart from the memorable: 'The students are studying your case in Media Law and we feel this would be a conflict of interest and very uncomfortable for you.'

She would have preferred to have heard it over the phone. She had spent time getting dressed up, doing her make-up and hair, wearing shoes that cut off her circulation, and was now being smiled at patronisingly. At least with the phone she wouldn't have had to cycle home with tears streaming down her face. The one thing she could be grateful for was Sally's predicted torrential rain, which suddenly fell as she made her way through the miserable dark night.

CHAPTER TWENTY-FIVE

Kitty couldn't sleep the night before Birdie's excursion. She couldn't even close her eyes. She had pushed the humiliation of the job interview to the back of her mind, to be dealt with at another time on another day when she had the resources, and right now her mind was on the story, on the people and the trip. She felt nervous. Excited tingles rippled through her stomach, and then the all-too-familiar negative thoughts would immediately follow. What if she had made a mistake in throwing them all together? What if her entire plan of action regarding the angle she was taking was wrong? She felt an overwhelming duty to Constance, and also to Bob, to get it right. Her desire to please Pete no longer existed. He would have to employ some of Constance's belief and spirit and trust that his writer knew what she was doing. The thing was that she *felt* that she knew what she was doing; she was back to following her instincts instead of reacting to somebody else's. That outcome alone from this entire process was enough to celebrate. She had found the confidence to listen to herself again, she was simply worried that her instincts were wrong, that this trip would be a disaster.

As she lay in bed looking at the apartment bathed in blue moonlight she began to think about having to leave it. She had lived there alone for five years, and for four months with Glen. She loved her apartment, was so fond of the space and didn't want to leave it. She had been lucky to find it, cheeky to threaten her landlord into giving it to her cheaper and now her dastardly ways had come back to haunt her. She was going to be out on her ear in less than a fortnight. Wide awake at the thought of her uncertain future, she threw off the bedcovers and immediately began packing, afraid about the impending trip and afraid to be moving on. By three thirty her clothes were all in suitcases; by 4 a.m. she was fast asleep dreaming of her adventure with six of the one hundred names.

The plan was for Kitty to collect Birdie from the nursing home in a taxi, where the battle-axe had been informed she would be taking Birdie away to stay overnight with her family. In the meantime, she saw the Oldtown Pistols return right on cue, victorious from their win against the Balbriggan Eagles. While on duty, Molly had arranged for the bus to be serviced, concocting a lie about hearing it make a funny noise and that a 'Pistol' had reported a funny smell and noise. This was taken seriously and the nurses had agreed to Molly's arrangements of local man Billy Meaghar to take the bus for a check-up, with strict instructions that it be returned for the Pink Ladies' bridge night the following evening. For an extra fifty euro Billy had agreed that Molly could take the bus and have it back on time for him to return it to the nursing home the following day.

So far so good.

Birdie and Kitty waited anxiously in the Oldtown café for Molly to arrive with the bus, both waiting for their plan to be overthrown by the battle-axe in the nursing home.

'How are you feeling?' Kitty asked Birdie.

'About the bus?'

'About the trip,' Kitty smiled. 'About going home.'

She sighed, long and hard, and Kitty couldn't tell if it was contented or loaded with anxiety, or both.

'I feel excited, but I feel nervous. I only went back there once, for my father's funeral, and that was forty years ago. This trip has got me thinking. Funny, really, how the mere thought of going back has me disappearing into the memories . . .' She trailed off as if getting caught in another web of thoughts of the past. 'There are so many things I'm remembering that I had completely forgotten.'

'Are you sure that it's okay for me to bring others on this journey? I know it's a very personal one for you.'

'Kitty, I'm more than happy to meet these people,' Birdie smiled. 'It will be intriguing to see who else has been "listed" with me.'

'Intriguing is one word for it,' Kitty laughed nervously.

'You've figured it out, haven't you?' Birdie asked. 'The thing that links us all.'

'Yes,' Kitty replied, 'I think I have.' She respected Birdie for not asking.

'That's okay, I have a little secret of my own,' Birdie chuckled, her eyes sparkling mischievously again. 'Molly doesn't know it yet but we have one extra stop to make along the way.'

That stop was Trinity College, Dublin where Birdie's grandson, Edward, was studying for a law degree. Kitty remembered seeing him visit as she was leaving one time. He was a handsome man in his twenties, responsible and diligent, by the sounds of it, and a fine match for Molly in Birdie's eyes, though they couldn't be more like chalk and cheese in Kitty's.

'You little romantic,' Kitty teased.

'Molly will kill me, no doubt, but Edward needs a kick up the backside. He's Caroline's son,' Birdie said, as if that explained it all. 'His head is so far in those books, he wouldn't see a good thing in front of him if it stripped naked and writhed in front of his eyes.'

'I wouldn't put that past Molly,' Kitty said, and Birdie laughed heartily.

Suddenly there was a loud honk of a horn, which made them both jump in their seats, along with the other customers, and they looked out the café window to see Molly behind the wheel, two enthusiastic thumbs up.

'That's nice and subtle,' Kitty mumbled as they made their way out to the bus.

'I love doing that,' Molly said happily, closing the doors again and savouring the feeling. She pulled a lever and the doors opened again and then she closed them.

'Please stop playing with the bus,' Kitty said nervously, looking around the town. 'I don't want to be arrested for theft until after we've completed the trip.'

Birdie and Kitty sat in the front row behind Molly, though Kitty had no intention of staying there very long if Molly's driving skills on the motorbike were anything to go by.

'There's even a microphone,' Molly said excitedly. 'Next stop,' she said into the mic, 'the foothills of the Boggeragh Mountains.'

'Actually, we also need to stop at Trinity College,' Kitty interrupted her announcement.

'I thought we were collecting your gang under the clock at Clerys and going straight to Cork,' she frowned. 'Oh, don't tell me . . .' She looked back at Birdie.

'Keep your eye on the road, child!' Birdie exclaimed. 'I want to make it to my eighty-fifth birthday. He doesn't know he's coming yet, but he is.'

Molly rolled her eyes and they left Oldtown before anybody else could report seeing them.

They pulled in at Clerys department store on O'Connell Street, and numerous cars and buses behind them sounded their horns in protestation of Molly's irrational driving.

'Oh, shut up,' Molly muttered, putting her hazard lights on. 'Are they here, Kitty?'

Kitty's stomach churned as she surveyed the pathway outside of Clerys and spotted them all, some standing in small groups and others alone. Her heart lifted when she saw Ambrose and Eugene standing together, Ambrose's mop of wild red hair covering her face as she stood side on, looking at her feet, and Eugene lifting his face to the sun happily, no doubt doing his best to distract Ambrose into forgetting she was out in the big bad world surrounded by strangers, distanced from her precious butterflies.

Eva Wu was the first to notice Kitty standing at the open door of the bus. She looked at 'St Margaret's' boldly emblazoned across the side of the bus and threw her a quizzical look. Despite the fact she had numerous gifts to give people at the wedding, she had only an overnight bag and one small carrier bag with her. Kitty guessed the presents would be arriving in another way.

'Hi, Kitty,' she said, greeting her with a hug at the door. When the others spotted Kitty they made a move towards the bus and lined up behind Eva. What really surprised Kitty was the sight of Steve, who deliberately waited around to join the end of the queue. She looked at him confused, then continued greeting her guests. 'What's with the nursing home sign?' Eva giggled, stepping on to the bus.

'All will be revealed,' Kitty said. 'Archie!' she smiled and hugged him as he stepped up next. He stiffened at the personal display of affection.

'Er, I brought someone, hope you don't mind. Her name is Regina.' Archie stepped aside to reveal the mousy woman from the café. 'I told her about, you know, everything.'

Regina looked up at him with a shy smile and then back to Kitty nervously. She still had that slightly haunted look, afraid that something was going to happen, or wishing it would but afraid it wouldn't.

'You're very welcome, Regina,' Kitty smiled, shaking her hand, trying to hide her shock but failing miserably.

'Thank you,' Regina blushed, looking at Archie nervously.

'Sit wherever you like.' Kitty held her hand out and they made their way down the aisle, choosing to sit three rows back. Archie gave Regina the window seat.

Next were Eugene and Ambrose. Kitty gave Eugene a hug and kiss but knew better than to touch Ambrose. She also knew not to make a big deal of her presence. Eugene looked pleased as punch, dressed in his jumper, shirt and bow tie with butterfly images, and Ambrose barely looked Kitty in the eye as she climbed aboard and went straight down the back of the bus. At the very back was a row of five seats, which faced two small tables and two seats on opposite sides. Ambrose unsurprisingly avoided the more social seats and instead sat in the last row of two seats at the back.

Next were Mary-Rose and Sam.

'Hope you don't mind her bringing me,' Sam said.

'I didn't expect her to come any other way,' Kitty teased, noticing Mary-Rose blush, and embracing them both. They went straight to the back of the bus, Sam saying hello to everybody and introducing himself, and immediately the mood picked up.

Next were Jedrek and Achar, and to Kitty's delight and to the passers-by on O'Connell Street's amusement, they had brought their pedalo. It took Sam, Jedrek, Achar and Steve to carry it to the boot of the bus, where they managed to turn it sideways and slam the door.

'What are you doing here?' Kitty asked Steve as they followed the others onto the bus. 'Where's Katja?'

'She couldn't make it so I thought I'd be photographer for the next two days.'

'Steve,' Kitty said, panicking, 'you should have told me she couldn't make it. I need a real photographer for the magazine.'

'Hold on, before you completely insult me, we both studied photojournalism, remember? I know what I'm doing.'

'That was ten years ago and you were crap.'

'I wasn't crap, I was creative. There's a difference.'

'Well, at least get people's heads in, will you?'

'Jesus, thanks so much Steve for taking a day off work and offering to help, I really appreciate it,' he said, insulted.

'Sorry. Thank you,' she said sincerely, sitting down. 'But do not fuck this up.'

He sat beside her in the front row and surveyed the bus of eclectic people. 'So this is all your hard work. Hey, Kitty, this is cool. I'm really glad you're doing this.'

She couldn't think of anything nasty to say at that so instead she smiled and thanked him, genuinely delighted he was here with her on this trip. It felt right.

'Okay, be quick,' Molly said a little nervously, looking in her rear-view mirror as she pulled in on Nassau Street. 'I can't stay here long.'

'What do you mean, be quick?'

'You have to go and get Edward. I can't leave the bus.'

'Can't you ring him?' Kitty asked. 'He doesn't even know me.'

'His phone is off,' Birdie explained apologetically. 'He's studying in the Berkeley Library.'

Kitty and Steve ran from the bus and entered Trinity College through the side entrance. They made their way to the Berkeley Library and asked for Edward Fitzsimons.

'He can't be disturbed, he's working on an assignment with a group and specifically asked not to be disturbed.'

Kitty sighed and stepped back. 'Let's go,' she said to Steve. 'We'll have to tell Birdie he's busy.'

'What, and break that old woman's heart? She's going on an adventure of a lifetime – I'm excited and I don't even know her – and if she was my grandmother I wouldn't want to miss it.'

'But you heard what she said.'

'Come on,' he looked at her. 'Can't hard-hitting reporter *Katherine* Logan come up with something clever to get him out here?'

'Not any more,' Kitty said firmly. 'That's not who I am any longer. Besides, you hated that part of me.' She didn't mean to turn this conversation so serious, not now, not when there was a nursing home bus filled with eleven people and a pedalo waiting for them on double yellow lines, but she couldn't help it.

Steve fixed her with that look again, the one from yesterday that sent shivers running down her spine. She tried to shake it away, suddenly uncomfortable. 'Anyway, it doesn't matter.' She turned and left the library.

'Kitty,' she felt his hand on her arm, 'I didn't mean all of those things.'

'Yes you did.'

'Okay, some of them. I meant some of them. But I don't *hate* that part of you, I just didn't want it to be *all* of who you are and I felt that's what was happening.'

'So I've taken that on board and I'm never going to be like that again.'

He looked at her disbelievingly. 'Of all the days . . . Can't you be the wicked lying reporter one last time?'

'So you're giving me permission now?'

'There's a time and a place. Do your worst,' he smiled.

'Okay.' She straightened up and went back to the desk. 'Hello again, I'm very sorry to bother you but it's vital that I speak with Edward. I didn't want to have to do it like this but we're here about his grandmother, Birdie. She passed away and we really need to tell him in person.' Kitty heard an audible gasp from Steve behind her and she tried not to smile as the librarian quickly made her way down the hall to get Edward.

Fifteen minutes and dozens of apologies later, they were back on the road and Edward had sat beside his grandmother and was asking twenty questions about the trip ahead.

'So you're sure you're okay?'

'Yes I'm fine.'

'You're not . . . dying.'

'Well, we're all dying, dear, and I'm probably a lot closer to it than you,' she teased.

'I wouldn't say that,' Molly interrupted. 'He could go any second.'

'Especially with your driving,' he shot back. 'So whose great idea was it to steal the bus?'

Molly looked away from the mirror and whistled loudly.

'Did you even think to ask me to drive?' Edward asked.

'Oh, yes, there is nothing more I'd love than to spend four

263

hours to Cork in your honky-tonk of metal.'

'Just because your motorbike is so much more elaborate than mine.'

'At least it doesn't break down every five minutes.'

'At least I actually know how to drive without putting other people's lives at stake.'

'What?' Molly asked, eyes narrowing at Edward in the rearview mirror. 'What are you looking at me like that for?'

'I'm just wondering why it's blue. Of all the colours. Blue.'

'I chose it to match your personality,' she shot back.

So Edward and Molly were well acquainted with one another, then. Kitty caught Birdie smiling to herself before she turned to look out of the window.

Kitty stood and made her way to the microphone at the front of the bus. Sam immediately started to whoop and shouted for her to sing, everyone laughed and she had all eyes on her.

'I'm definitely not going to sing,' Kitty said.

'Trust me,' Steve called out, and they all laughed.

'I just want to say a few words to you about the trip. I know most of you have no idea what exactly is going on here and I really appreciate you turning up and coming on the journey with me. In fact, to be truthful, it's all of you who have taken me on a journey.' She cleared her throat. 'Sadly, I lost my friend and editor to cancer a few weeks ago and it fell to me to write the story that got away from her. The only clue I had as to what this story is about was all of your names – plus ninety-four other people who couldn't fit on the bus today.'

They laughed.

'I had no idea what it was that Constance wanted me to write but the more I speak to you, the more I get to know you, some so far better than others, the more I feel the story is writing itself because you are all remarkable people with fascinating stories and I thank you for sharing them with me. Particularly at a time when . . .'

She heard the shake in her voice and she stopped to compose herself.

That got the complete attention of everyone, all eyes on her, even Molly's. 'Keep your eyes on the road,' Kitty said, which broke the tension and she was able to finish. 'Particularly at a time when I really needed this. I know that I have pestered and annoyed many of you, that I've showed up in your lives when you haven't wanted me to, to talk about things you may not have wanted to talk about, but again I appreciate your patience and hope that you understand that I have invested everything into you, into getting to know you, into hearing your stories, into doing your stories justice. I have learned a lot from you all, you have moved me and, dare I say it, made me a better person and helped me back on track.'

She could see Ambrose in particular staring at her with that powerful stare.

'So, let me introduce you all. We have a long way to go so I'm sure you all will have the opportunity to speak to one another and discover each other's stories, apart from this man.' She pointed out Steve. 'He is not here for his story, he has none, he's just my friend so don't talk to him.'

They all laughed and Steve threw her a face.

'Maybe he'll tell us your story, Kitty,' Jedrek shouted from the back, and they laughed.

'No, believe me, you don't want to hear that.'

'You should have read the paper on Sunday,' Steve shouted down, and those who understood the joke laughed.

'Thank you for that, Steve. But first I'd like to introduce you to the main woman. Our birthday girl, Birdie Murphy.' There was a round of applause and everybody started singing 'Happy Birthday to You'.

The atmosphere couldn't have been any more special as everybody mixed, mingled and there was a real sense of celebration and jubilation on the bus. When she sat down next to Steve, Kitty couldn't hide the contented smile on her face.

'Look at you, happy head,' he said, ruffling her hair affectionately.

CHAPTER TWENTY-SIX

Most of 'the names' had gathered at the back of the bus to hear Jedrek and Achar speak about their record attempt.

'It is a two-man one-hundred-metre pedalo dash,' Jedrek explained seriously. 'The current world record is one minute fifty-eight point six two seconds. We can do it in one minute fifty.'

They received many pats on the back for that.

'You're going to attempt the record in Cork?' Eva asked.

'Our desire was always to do this with our families as witnesses,' Jedrek said a little sadly. 'They have been with us for the entire journey, for them not to be here . . .'

Achar stepped in, more enthusiastic. 'Unfortunately they could not come with us on this trip but the reason we are with you now is because we know of an adjudicator who will be here in Cork. If we can convince him to come to view our record attempt we can be officially accepted into *Guinness World Records.*'

'Though we do not need a judge to make a record attempt,' Jedrek was quick to jump in.

'No,' Achar conceded, 'but their presence is the only way we can immediately know our record attempt has been successful. If you want instant approval of your record, to boost the status and news appeal, then the adjudicator is the way to go. They can give you the official presentation of a framed *Guinness World Records* Certificate. We enquired into getting an adjudicator but it costs five thousand euro to fly one over for the event. We learned that there is an adjudicator in Cork today at a corporate event. If we can convince him to witness our attempt then we will have instant confirmation.'

'Yes, but it is not compulsory to have a judge at the event,' Jedrek said again. 'I just do not want you to get your hopes up for no reason.'

'What is wrong with getting my hopes up? It seems it is you who has no hope at all already,' Achar said.

They argued this in front of the others until Archie spoke up. 'But it's worth a try, fellas, isn't it? And if you can't get the judge? You can do it for all of us as witnesses.'

'I'll film it on my iPhone so you can have video footage of you completing the challenge,' Sam offered.

'And I'll be taking plenty of photos,' Steve added. 'And it will be backed up by the presence of a journalist who is going to write about it.'

Jedrek, ever the sentimental one, seemed moved by their kind words of encouragement, though he remained cynical over the possibility of acquiring the adjudicator.

While Steve was talking to Eugene about butterflies and how best to grow butterfly-friendly flowers in his allotment, Kitty sat in the seat next to Ambrose.

'The devil's-bit scabious will grow in damp and dry situations, the Ragged Robin, primroses, violets, the common dandelion . . .' Eugene listed off as Steve nodded his head but didn't say a word.

'I really appreciate you coming today,' Kitty said gently. 'I know it's not . . . easy for you.' Kitty had meant it in a kind way but it seemed to anger Ambrose.

'Because of my face,' Ambrose snapped, turning to Kitty and fixing her with that angry green eye. 'I know about the conversation you had with Eugene. He shouldn't have told you what he told you.'

Kitty had to cast her mind back to figure out what she shouldn't know but she instantly guessed it was the surgery Ambrose was saving for to have the birthmark removed. Eugene had told Kitty that all of Ambrose's savings were going towards multiple laser surgeries, which would be needed to remove what they called a disfiguring birthmark, though Kitty thought the opposite was true: if anything it did not mar her beauty in any way but added to it; she was like some exotic-looking butterfly that she had framed on her walls. But she doubted Ambrose would believe her if she told her this.

'We weren't talking about you in the way in which I think you think we were,' Kitty said slowly.

Ambrose frowned, confused. 'Yes, I'm sure you weren't having a laugh at my expense, or discussing poor Ambrose's disgusting face. I don't want you writing about it. I don't want any mention of my appearance in the article.'

'The article is about you, Ambrose. If I can't write about you, I can't write the article.'

'Well then, we might as well pull the bus over here because I will not give you permission to mock me in public.'

'Why do you think I'm planning to mock you? On the contrary. If you must know, and I think you must, the only reason Eugene told me about the laser surgery is because he *doesn't* want you to have it done.' Kitty knew she was speaking out of turn but felt it would be harmless to smooth over the obvious misunderstanding between her and Ambrose, and obviously between Eugene and Ambrose. Ambrose couldn't see how he felt about her.

'What?'

'He was comparing you to the butterflies that you both adore and cherish, and he said you were special for all the same reasons: you were rare, exotic and entirely you. He said he thinks you're beautiful exactly the way you are now. That's the only reason we were talking about you, I promise,' Kitty said.

Ambrose's mouth opened and closed as she tried to process the information. She wanted to be angry, Kitty could tell – any discussion or comment on her appearance immediately made her so – but for once, this didn't. She eventually closed her mouth and Kitty saw the hint of a small smile.

Kitty had wanted to use this journey to do as she'd promised Gaby, by getting to know Eva better, but quickly after they'd left Dublin, Eva was seated beside Birdie and the two were deeply engrossed in conversation. Edward was sitting in the tour guide's chair beside Molly and they were arguing about the route to take to Cork to best encompass everyone's destination. After the city, they could make it to Birdie's hometown of Nadd by the afternoon, and Eva's wedding was tomorrow. Kitty had it all planned out, but it was this that caused her to worry: things never went according to plan. Kitty desperately wanted to get in on Birdie and Eva's conversation but she couldn't. Instead, Mary-Rose made her way from the back of the bus to where Kitty was indecisively hovering.

'Kitty, do you mind if we have a word?' She seemed anxious and so they sat in a row of two vacant seats where Kitty could still hear Steve being lectured by Eugene on how better to help conserve butterflies on his father's land.

'Is everything okay?'

'Yes, everything's great. Everyone is so polite and very welcoming. It's lovely to hear their stories, but, em, I'm not really sure why I'm here. You see, everyone has a purpose, they're all going somewhere or doing something. I really have no idea why I'm here.'

'I just wanted you to meet everybody. You're all part of the same reason I met you all. Please don't feel like you need to do something.'

'But I feel so useless.'

Suddenly Kitty had an idea. 'Did you bring your kit with you?'

'I bring it everywhere,' she laughed.

'How about making the birthday girl look pretty for her big day?'

Mary-Rose's eyes lit up, delighted to be able to do something, and having Birdie distracted by her makeover would also give Kitty an opportunity to speak to Eva.

'Anyway, you never know, this whole experience might inspire another proposal,' Kitty joked.

Mary-Rose's face darkened. 'Oh, I'm not sure about that.'

Kitty picked up on her mood. 'Are he and Aoife serious?'

Mary-Rose swallowed. 'Yeah, I think so, I don't know, we haven't really spoken about . . . her.'

There was a silence.

'What about your friend?' Mary-Rose asked, nodding at Steve.

'What about him?' Kitty immediately felt uncomfortable, irritated, even. Did Mary-Rose have a crush on Steve? That couldn't be allowed, surely? Mary-Rose was at least ten years younger than he, better-looking, youthful . . . she couldn't possibly be interested in Steve.

'Does he have a girlfriend?'

'Oh, yes,' Kitty said over-enthusiastically. 'For quite a while now. They're crazy about each other,' she said, not knowing if this was true exactly but feeling ill inside at the thought of Mary-Rose with Steve. What on earth was wrong with her?

'Oh, that's a pity,' Mary-Rose said, crestfallen, and Kitty was secretly relieved. 'I really thought you two would be perfect together.'

This surprised Kitty so much that she didn't know what to say. It went unnoticed, though, as Mary-Rose approached Birdie and asked the birthday girl if she was ready for her makeover. There was a girly whoop and Regina even moved away from Archie to watch it take place.

Kitty got lost in her head imagining the possibilities of her and Steve together, picturing them together, how it could be, even recalling the one clumsy drunken time they'd shared a bed in college, and Kitty's heart began thumping and her stomach fluttered. She couldn't possibly . . .

'Well, I escaped that little lecture, thanks for the introduction,' Steve said slipping in beside her. 'If I ever need to know anything more about butterflies be sure to shoot me,' he whispered conspiratorially, close to her ear. Shivers ran through her body at the closeness of his breath. 'What's wrong with you?' he asked then. 'Your face is all red.'

Kitty's mouth opened and shut like a codfish until the bus suddenly swerved and got everybody's attention. The rendition of a Polish song ended swiftly from the back.

'Left! I said left!' Edward raised his voice. 'Are you trying to kill us?'

'No, just you, college boy,' Molly growled.

'Everything okay there?' Eva asked as Mary-Rose wiped the long line of lipstick that had run along Birdie's cheek as the bus swerved.

'Yep, fine thanks. Head Smurf here has got it all figured out,' Edward said.

Kitty caught Birdie once again smiling with glee as her nurse and her grandson battled for power.

Kitty was torn when it came to their arrival in Cork. The only way they could stay on schedule was by splitting up. While Ambrose and Eugene went to the butterfly symposium at Cork University, Achar and Jedrek went to Cork English Market where the Irish food board, *Bord Bia*, had arranged a corporate adjudicator from *Guinness World Records* to recognise the largest number of people dressed as eggs ever to gather in the same place. This was part of a scheme to promote the local organic egg farmers. Kitty knew that she needed to be at both events, and that Steve needed to be too, and so she quickly hopped off the bus on a mission to push her way through the people dressed as eggs, their faces popping out of holes in the egg costumes, their legs in gold spandex leggings, to find the adjudicator. Jedrek and Achar were searching just as anxiously.

'Do you see him?' Achar asked, his head darting around.

'What does he look like?' Sam asked.

When an egg became unbalanced and bumped against Mary-Rose, Sam immediately reached out to steady and protect her.

'Not like that anyway, I hope,' Jedrek said, and they laughed.

Birdie linked Edward's arm and looked around with delight, and despite Molly's declaration of not being able to get far enough away from the college boy, she stayed close. They all decided to split up in search of the judge, unsure if the egg record attempt had officially been logged yet.

'Look, Jedrek,' Achar said, surveying the scene. 'This is what we need.'

Local media, crowd support and an official adjudicator, it was all Achar had dreamed of for their event.

'Yes, Achar, but there is no water,' Jedrek poured cold water over Achar's dreams.

'I found him!' Eva called, and Kitty followed Eva's voice to a bewildered-looking black-suited man who was surrounded by Kitty's odd bunch of people.

Jedrek and Achar pushed through the crowd, looking like they'd found the Holy Grail when their eyes fell upon the adjudicator. Jedrek walked towards him, hand extended the entire way. The adjudicator looked at Kitty's gang, who had circled him, back to Jedrek's hand as if this was some kind of joke, then finally he shook his hand, sensing the seriousness.

'Mr Adjudicator,' Jedrek addressed him as though he were royalty, holding his hands up and looking him up and down as though greatness were in this very market. 'We have travelled a long way to see you today, myself and my friends.'

The judge looked at the group.

'Well, hello,' he said unsurely. 'I'm James.'

'James!' Jedrek announced as if that was fascinating. 'My name is Jedrek Vysotski and this is my friend Achar Singh. This, James, is Kitty Logan, the great journalistic reporter who we are blessed with writing our story.' Kitty nodded enthusiastically and James said another awkward hello.

'James,' a man behind him interrupted, 'we're about to get things started here.'

'Okay, just a minute,' James said pleasantly, turning back to Jedrek, intrigued.

'We, Achar and I, are going to make the great record attempt to be the fastest two men in a pedalo for a distance of one hundred metres. The current record is one minute fifty-eight point six two seconds and Achar and I can do it in one minute fifty. This is going to happen, James. In Cork. And we would like to invite you to be our adjudicator.'

This time an egg interrupted. 'We're ready now, James.'

'Okay, just a second,' he said, a little panicked.

'We will not let you down, James,' Achar pushed.

Jedrek placed a gentle hand on his friend's shoulder. 'Let the man speak.'

'Thank you,' James said, sweat breaking out on his brow. 'I'm afraid I can't come to your event, as delightful as it sounds.' He spoke in an English accent. 'But according to the rules you must have registered your details with Guinness World Records already.'

'Yes we have, we have,' Jedrek said enthusiastically.

'And what did they say?'

'They told us the cost of adjudication and we could not possibly afford that,' Achar said immediately, to Jedrek's annoyance. 'That is why we have sought you out here. We have come to you, to save you having to come to us,' he said as if they were doing James a big favour.

'I'm sorry, gentlemen, I'm afraid it doesn't work like that,' he began.

'They've been training for months,' Archie interrupted. 'Surely you could just turn up and watch them.' Archie's tactics weren't as gentle as the others' and it sounded a little threatening.

Eva sensed this and joined in. 'We'll be at Kinsale Pier tomorrow, at 2 p.m., all you have to do is come and watch them, witness it for yourself and then they can do the rest of the work. What do you think?'

'I have a flight back to London in the morning . . .'

'Change it,' Sam said.

'I'll cover the cost of your flight,' Kitty butted in. 'They really deserve to be seen by you,' she urged.

'They've a jolly good spirit,' Regina added from somewhere outside of the circle. 'We believe they can do it.'

'I'll pay your fee,' Birdie said suddenly, and everybody looked at her in shock.

'No, no,' Achar and Jedrek protested. 'It is too much. We cannot allow you to pay.'

'After today I can pay whatever I want,' Birdie smiled mischievously, then looked at the adjudicator. 'Name your price and I will pay you,' she said, chin high.

'It's not about the fee,' he said starting to break out in a sweat. 'It's about the protocol. Your record attempt must be cleared in advance so that I can have the certificate ready to present to you—'

'You can send us the certificate when it's ready,' Achar interrupted. 'You don't have to give it to us tomorrow.'

Suddenly everybody started talking at him, trying in their own way to convince him, but he couldn't possibly make out everybody's pleas and instead they all bled into one. He held his hands up in defence.

'I'm very sorry, I can't,' he apologised sincerely. 'But I wish you the best of luck with your attempt tomorrow.'

There was a silence, an awkward one, and it was obvious he felt awful.

'Kinsale Pier, 2 p.m. tomorrow,' Kitty said firmly. 'Please come.'

And he was finally dragged away to the small stage where he prepared to present the certificate for most people dressed as eggs in one area. As everybody gathered to face the podium, Kitty and her crew pushed in the opposite direction, making their way back to the bus, their spirits crushed.

Across the city, Kitty and Steve arrived just in time, breathless, sweating and dizzy, to hear Ambrose's name announced in a lecture theatre to speak about her much-anticipated report. Five hundred applauded. But there was no sign of her. People looked around, the speaker looked behind him, confused.

Kitty saw Eugene stand up from the front row and make his way backstage. He returned and climbed onto the stage and had a word in the speaker's ear.

Kitty's heart fell. 'Oh, no,' she whispered, and to her surprise felt tears welling in her eyes.

Steve, the man who hated personal contact, put his arm around her shoulder and gave her a squeeze.

'Ladies and gentlemen, I believe we'll be a further two minutes, if you wouldn't mind bearing with me.'

People relaxed a little and fell into conversation with each other. Five minutes passed and the speaker was looking uncomfortable.

'Should I go back there?' Kitty asked Steve, worriedly. Just as she stood to make her way towards the stage, the speaker looked behind him and nodded.

'And I believe we are ready to go now. So once again, speaking on one of our most beautiful butterflies, the Peacock, known to most of you as *Inachis io*, our treasured member of Butterfly Conservation, Ambrose Nolan.' There was polite applause.

Ambrose, her hair down in front of her face, head down, made her way to the podium.

She stood up and cleared her throat, which reverberated around the room loudly through the microphone.

'My apologies for the delay. My partner told me to tell you I was very much like the *Aglais urticae*, most commonly known as the Small Tortoiseshell, which is fast, vigilant, but extremely wary and difficult to approach closely.'

Everyone laughed at the inside butterfly joke, and the atmosphere became much more relaxed. Ambrose looked up, saw Kitty, and took a deep breath. And then she began to talk.

CHAPTER TWENTY-SEVEN

Ambrose and Eugene were on a high, and despite the failed adjudicator kidnap, spirits were buoyant on the bus as they listened to Eugene's proud retelling of how Ambrose had entranced them all with her discoveries, and Steve was able to show his photographs on the camera, which Ambrose swiftly put an end to. When Eugene had told the story enough times, they turned to Birdie's impending win.

Birdie hadn't been exaggerating when she said she was from a small town. Nadd was in the foothills of the Boggeragh Mountains and had a population of just over one hundred and seventy people. It consisted of two pubs, one which doubled as a guesthouse, the other which tripled as a shop and betting office, and also a church and a school. On the outskirts of the village a housing scheme to encourage and attract young families into the area had begun and stopped halfway, leaving pastel-coloured summer houses standing unfinished with smashed windows.

'Ooh, there it is, Birdie,' Mary-Rose sang as they passed the bookies and added more hairspray to Birdie's perfect hair-do, much to Edward's disgust as another coughing fit took him over.

Molly took delight in seeing this.

It was decided that everybody would wait in the guesthouse garden to give Birdie privacy while she went inside the bookies, but Kitty was honoured to be asked to go inside with her. Birdie linked arms with Edward, while Kitty and Steve waited in the background, Steve subtly taking photos.

The bookies, attached to the pub, was a small room that resembled a living room. On the right-hand side of the O'Hara pub was a newsagent shop, on the left was the bookies. Inside, two men were sitting on stools and watching a small television in the corner of the room. They were wearing tweed caps and suit jackets, and smelled like they hadn't washed for a few weeks. Behind the protected glass was a man in his thirties. He looked up and when Birdie laid eyes on him she took an audible intake of breath. Kitty assumed she knew him and waited for a flicker of recognition to pass his face but it never came and Birdie composed herself.

'My name is Bridget Murphy,' she said, a slight shake in her voice, which definitely had more of a hint of her Cork accent than before.

The two old men looked away from the television screen to stare at her. Edward put his hand supportively around his grandmother's body.

'Sixty-seven years ago I placed a bet with Josie O'Hara and I'm here to collect my winnings,' she said.

Kitty almost felt emotional hearing Birdie say those words. How often had Birdie said them to herself, as a teenager desperate to leave the town but equally desperate to prove she could come back, as a young mother, as she hit middle age, and then in her old age? How often had she thought of this moment, and now it was here?

The young man stood from his stool behind the counter. 'Have you got the slip?'

She retrieved a plastic sleeve from her handbag and with shaking fingers slid it under the counter. Kitty wasn't sure if the shake was from nerves or old age, but she hadn't noticed it before. The young man studied the slip, looked back up at her, at Molly and Edward by her side, then back down at the slip again. He smiled, then he laughed.

'I can't believe this,' he said. 'Sixty-seven years ago!'

Molly and Kitty grinned but Edward's voice showed concern.
'You'll give her the money?' he asked.

Birdie's not receiving the money had never entered Kitty's mind.
It had always been a question of how much they would give her
with the changes in currency in all of those years. Her original
bet surely no longer followed the ordinary rules.

'A bet's a bet,' the man said, his smile large on his face. 'You
know, Josie was my great-grandfather,' he sounded excited. 'He
died when I was young but I'll never forget his . . . hold on.' His
smile quickly faded and he brought the old slip closer to his face.
'One hundred to one?' he read the odds, shocked.

Birdie nodded. 'That's what Josie gave me.'

'I'll have to . . . I'm not sure I can . . . I don't have the authority
to . . . hold on just a minute, please.'

He took the slip and disappeared out the door, leaving them
standing there. One of the old men was staring at them.

'Are you Thomas's girl?' he asked.

Birdie turned and examined him. 'I am.'

'Jaysus, Sean, would you look at that, Thomas's girl.'

'Ha?' the old man shouted.

'She's Thomas's girl,' the man shouted.

The old man fixed his eye on Molly. He immediately distrusted
her with her blue hair. 'Is she now?'

'Not her, the other one.' He waved his crooked finger. 'You're
the sick girl,' he said.

Birdie's cheeks flushed and Kitty could see that still the stigma
lived on.

'And who are you?' Molly asked, protectively.

'Paddy Healy. Una and Paddy's son.'

Birdie's eyes narrowed as she thought about it, her mind casting
back all those years to a time lost or forgotten, deliberately and
some naturally. Suddenly her eyes stopped moving from left to
right and lit up. 'From down the road?'

'Aye.'

'Rachel's baby brother.'

'That's me.'

Kitty took in his appearance and found it hard to imagine this old man as a baby brother to anyone.

'Rachel and I were in school together, the times that I was in school.'

He softened. 'She passed away some ten years ago.'

Birdie's smile quickly faded. 'I'm sorry to hear that.'

The door behind them opened and they heard a loud voice coming from their side of the glass.

'We're not giving you the money,' the voice announced. The source was an old lady in her eighties but time had not been as kind to her as it had been to Birdie. She was badly hunched over a cane, and her hair was almost woollen-looking it was so thick and dry. Dog hairs covered her smock and her swollen legs and ankles had been stuffed into a new pair of Ecco shoes.

'Excuse me?' Molly replied, her tone harsh as she stood up to the old woman half her height.

Birdie looked the old woman up and down. 'Mary O'Hara.'

The woman sniffed. 'Fitzgerald. So you're still alive then.' She looked Birdie up and down in turn.

'Alive and well,' Birdie said, straightening up. 'I assume it is your decision not to give me the money.'

Josie's great-grandson looked at them apologetically.

'I'm the authority around here and I say so.'

'It was a valid bet,' Birdie said firmly. 'Your father, at least, was a man of his word.'

'And you, it turned out, were not.' She sniffed again and it was clear there was a lot more going on here than a bet made over sixty years ago.

'I hope this isn't personal, Mary. That was a long time ago.'

'You broke my brother's heart. Once broken, always broken. I don't care how much time has passed.'

Birdie seemed to pale at this. 'Is he . . . how is . . .?'

'He's dead,' Mary snapped, and even the man behind her bristled at how harshly it had been delivered.

Kitty noticed how Edward held on to Birdie tighter as if she had suddenly lost her power to stand alone.

'Why, did you expect him to be here?' Mary asked, then laughed, a wheezy thing that turned into a cough. 'Did you expect him to still be waiting for you? Well, he didn't, he left, moved on, married, had children, grandchildren.'

Birdie gave a small but sad smile at that. 'When did he . . . pass away?'

When Mary responded her tone was less harsh but still carried the loathing she felt for Birdie. 'Last year.'

Birdie's face was etched with pain and sadness. Without another word, she turned and left the bookies.

'Well?' Mary-Rose pounced on her immediately as they stepped outside.

Kitty shook her head at everyone so they knew not to ask any more questions.

Birdie seemed disoriented. Both Edward and Kitty looked to Molly for guidance.

'Why don't we get some fresh air?' Molly said, taking Birdie's arm and leading her gently away from the bookies.

The others decided to go back across the road to the guesthouse and order dinner. It was a cool evening but they chose to sit outside in the beer garden while Edward and Steve filled them in on what had happened and they debated legally what was the right thing. Edward, with his knowledge of the law, and Steve, with his knowledge of bookies, between them agreed that it was merely a gentleman's agreement, and while it could be honoured, there was no legal standing for it to be. The mood dropped even more in the group. Feeling frustrated, upset for Birdie and embarrassed that she had taken everyone on this wild-goose chase, Kitty tried to figure out a way to excuse herself from the table. The O'Hara great-grandson from the bookies gave her the perfect excuse as she saw him enter the beer garden and look around the area.

She left the table to meet him.

It wasn't difficult to find Birdie. She was sitting on a bench on the main street staring across at the small school where her father had been the headmaster and only teacher, and the nearby house, which she must have grown up in. Kitty could imagine all the days Birdie spent looking out the window and watching the children playing in the yard, unable to join them as she was sick, or at least thought of as being too delicate to play.

Kitty joined her on the bench. 'I'm sorry, Birdie, I didn't think.'

'Why are you sorry?' Birdie snapped out of her trance.

'For bringing everyone here, on your trip. I should have known it was a bad idea. This was personal for you. I shouldn't have intruded.'

'Nonsense. Kitty, I've had the most wonderful day. When else can I say I spent the day with four hundred people dressed as eggs?' she laughed. 'It's rare I get invited to go on as many exciting adventures all in one go. The same for all of us. You've done something very special for us all, Kitty, don't forget that. You brought us all together. Nobody is blaming you for when things don't go our way.'

Kitty appreciated the kind words but they had no real effect. She felt as though she had let everyone down: no adjudicator for Achar and Jedrek, no winnings for Birdie, though at least the day had been a success for Ambrose.

'Remember, it wasn't about the money,' Birdie said, a small smile on her lips, though the argument didn't sound as credible as the first time Kitty had heard it. Kitty believed it wasn't about the money, it had been to come and face old ghosts, but those old ghosts had won yet again on a day when Birdie had imagined victory.

'What have you got there?' Birdie asked, looking at the bunch of wild flowers Kitty had gathered before coming over to meet her.

'Ah. Yes. The young O'Hara came to see me,' she said. 'He wanted me to tell you something.'

In the foothills of the Boggeragh Mountains, a light mist falling all around them, Birdie finally stopped searching the gravestones and settled next to one, her search over. Next to the church, the small school and schoolhouse she had grown up in, she laid flowers on the grave of her first true love, Jamie O'Hara, who she'd loved but hadn't been allowed to love as she wished, who she'd had to leave behind to move to Dublin to escape her father's clutches and a small town's prejudices. She'd made a promise and she'd made a bet, and she had finally come home. For both, unfortunately, it was too late.

Kitty joined the group outside and picked at her battered fish and chips with mushy peas and tartare sauce, and wondered how on earth she could recover the mood of the group. How on earth she could recover her own? Conversations were light and quiet but lacked the jovial joyfulness from the bus.

'It's not your fault,' Steve said quietly, breaking her silence.

She looked at him uncertainly. 'I feel embarrassed.'

'What for?'

'For bringing everyone here, for—'

'It's not your fault, Kitty,' he simply repeated, and gave her a glass of wine. 'Now get this into you so you can be more fun. 'You'd better not snore tonight or I'll suffocate you with a pillow.'

'I don't snore.'

'Yes, you do. When you've had a drink, you snore as loudly as my dad.'

'I do not. You don't know that.'

He fixed her with that look again, that froze her outsides but turned her insides to mush. 'I know that at least on one occasion you did.'

She swallowed. 'No one's ever told me that before,' she said quietly.

'Maybe they were never awake when you were asleep.'

It was a simple comment but it went straight to her heart again, and all she could think of was lying in that student accommodation beside him, sleeping on his chest while Steve, with those long black eyelashes and messy mop of hair, watched her. Suddenly there was a tinkling sound as Sam stood and tapped his spoon against the glass.

'Oh, no, Sam,' Mary-Rose said, her face meaning business without an ounce of a smile this time.

'Esmerelda,' he said in a warning tone.

'Esmerelda?' Jedrek said, confused. 'I have been calling you Mary-Rose,' he leaned over the table and shouted down to her.

'Just ignore him,' Mary-Rose said, covering her face with her hands. 'Sam, I mean it, stop it.'

But Sam wasn't picking up on her cooler-than-usual mood, or he was misreading it as something he could fix with a proposal, when it was clear at least to Kitty that he couldn't. She had witnessed two proposals already; she considered herself an expert.

'Okay, fine,' Sam appeased the confused diners. 'Esmerelda is like a term of endearment,' he explained. 'Isn't it, darling?'

'No,' she snapped. 'It is not.'

'Okay. Mary-Rose Godfrey,' he said dramatically, smiling. 'My best friend in the whole world.'

'Stop, Sam.'

'No, I can't, I can't stop how I feel for you. I can't stop thinking about you. I can't pretend that we are only friends. Every day when we are together, I feel it inside and I can't tell you.'

Kitty suddenly stiffened beside Steve, feeling uncomfortable with his words. If this was how she was feeling, she couldn't imagine how Mary-Rose was feeling.

'We have known each other since we were six years old. When

you walked into our class on the first day of school with your shoes on your wrong feet I knew that you were someone I had to talk to.'

Suddenly Mary-Rose started laughing. 'That's true,' she said in surprise.

So Sam wasn't reading from his script that evening, but did he mean it?

'And then we started talking, and when we had a fight over whose turn it was to play with the yellow Lego, and you pinched me and got in trouble with the teacher and had to stand in the corner, I thought to myself, that girl has balls. I want to be friends with that girl. Not that I'm into girls with balls or anything,' Sam said, fluffing his lines, and they all laughed. All but Mary-Rose, anyway. She wasn't smiling, not because she was embarrassed but because she was sad, that much was evident. Sam's words were touching, so close to the bone, in fact, that Kitty questioned their authenticity. For a moment, she could tell Mary-Rose did too as she lifted her chin to study his face carefully.

'We were friends all through school, through secondary school even though your mum sent you to that convent school where you had to wear that unflattering knee-length brown skirt and knee-high socks for six years of your life. And I could put up with you being my friend, but it's only the last few months when I've . . .' he looked at her.

'Is this real?' Steve whispered to Kitty, sending a shiver through her body again.

'I honestly don't know,' she whispered back so close that her lip touched his ear lobe. She felt volts of electricity rush through her.

Though distracted by her own feelings, she tried to focus on the drama opposite her.

Sam made his way to Mary-Rose's side; some people had stood to watch, their breaths held. They all believed it was real.

'Mary-Rose Godfrey, you have been my best friend since we were kids but I can't hide it any more. I am desperately in love with you. I know this may seem over the top and terribly dramatic but I know that we're right for each other. Will you . . . will you marry me?'

Mary-Rose's eyes lit up, they were twinkling with tears, she looked absolutely besotted and delighted and happier than Kitty had ever seen her, and even Kitty believed it was completely true, that this was all for real.

Everyone in the beer garden cheered, but while they cheered and looked at one another they missed Sam's wink, and it had the same effect on Kitty as it had on Mary-Rose. It shattered the illusion, brought it home that it all wasn't real. And then came the obligatory hush for silence.

Mary-Rose's smile faded fast.

'No,' she said in the silence.

There was a gasp.

'No?' he asked uncertainly, trying to read her face for signs.

'No,' she repeated firmly, and as she said so, a tear fell down her cheek.

'Is this real?' Steve asked again. Kitty and Steve's heads were so close together that the warmth from his body was keeping her warm in the cool night.

Ambrose's face was one of shock. She instinctively grabbed Eugene's hand, to his utter surprise, but he followed her lead and placed his hand around her shoulders as if to protect her from what she was seeing.

'Please stop doing this, Sam,' Mary-Rose said, choking on her words as more tears fell.

'What?' he asked, genuine now.

Mary-Rose stood and left the table.

There was a stunned silence.

'Hard luck, pal,' Archie said, placing his hand on Sam's back and patting it roughly, though he intended it to be supportive.

Sam looked at Kitty wide-eyed. 'What the . . .?'

'I'll go speak to her,' Kitty said, reluctant to leave the closeness with Steve but knowing it was the right thing to do.

She found her in the snug, with her face in her hands.

'Oh God, what have I done?' she sobbed. 'I just couldn't do it any more, Kitty. I can't listen to that stuff, hoping it's real and knowing it's not.'

Kitty held her close and said nothing but made comforting sounds.

'Now I've made it so obvious,' she sobbed into Kitty's blouse. 'Now he knows and how can I face him?'

'Hey, Mary-Rose, that was the best ever!' they heard Sam's voice as he swung himself into the snug and plonked himself beside them. 'Hey, what's going on? You can stop pretending now; you totally convinced everyone in the place. I've already got two free pints waiting for me on the table. Sympathy pints, I never thought of that one before. Nice twist, by the way. You almost had me fooled. When did you come up with it?' he laughed.

Mary-Rose slowly lifted her head from Kitty's shoulder and looked at him, confused.

'I think I'll leave you two alone,' Kitty said, standing up.

'No, you don't have to do that,' Mary-Rose said nervously.

'Yes I do,' she said, giving her the eyes that said, *tell him*.

As Kitty made her way back outside to the table, her phone rang.

'Sorry to call you so late but I know you guys are still up because I was just talking to Eva,' Gaby shouted down the phone to Kitty. Kitty turned the volume down on her phone.

'Hi, Gaby, no problem, don't worry, everything is going fine.'

'Good, good, but that's not what I'm calling you about. It's the book you gave me. My boss read it today.'

'That was quick,' Kitty smiled, sitting down and waiting for her payback. 'I hope I didn't waste his time too much by sending it in. It was just a favour for a friend, you know?'

'Well, your friend will be delighted because it's good news. My boss loves it. Crime is huge right now and he wants to get in touch with your friend.'

CHAPTER TWENTY-EIGHT

Kitty couldn't speak, she was so shocked. This had not gone the way she had planned it. The plan was for Richie's novel to be rejected, to have a firm letter of rejection written out to him so that she could personally deliver it and thereby deliver the same dagger through his heart that he had stabbed her with. But it was all going terribly wrong. They actually *liked* it – how could this be? He was going to be a published author and that was her revenge?

Kitty needed time to herself to deal with her revenge mess-up so she disappeared to her bedroom to gather herself together. She also needed to think about what they could achieve tomorrow and what the events of today meant for her story. There were twin beds in the small room, with a basin in the corner and a bathroom down the hall to share with the rest of the guests. Instead of trying to sort out her problems all she could think of was Steve, how she and he would be in the same room, how excited she was about that, not that she was expecting something to happen, though she had to admit there was certainly a change between them over the past few days, or was that just her? Was she projecting her feelings for him onto him when in reality nothing about his feelings for her had changed at all? Kitty's track record with men was not good recently. She had dated some nice men who had been good to her in the past, but over the last few weeks, between Richie and Pete, Kitty's neediness and desire to be accepted had sent her into the arms of the wrong men. She didn't feel that she was wrong to have feelings for Steve. He was solid, he had always been there, he wasn't some guy she knew nothing about, somebody who could suddenly surprise her in the morning with a wife and four kids or a penchant for prostitutes. She knew everything about him, *everything*.

There was a knock on the door and she heard Steve call her name. Her heart went into a frenzy and she could barely think, could barely hold a focused thought in her mind.

She opened the door.

'You okay?' he asked, looking at her oddly.

'Yes, why?' Her voice came out a squeak.

'Because you've clearly turned into Tweety Pie.' He picked up on her pitch. He pushed open the door and went inside. 'What's this place like, then?' He surveyed the room and sat down on the bed on the left. He bounced on it lightly and the springs squeaked mightily.

They smiled at each other, and Kitty had to look away, feeling like a schoolgirl with a crush.

'What's up?' he said more gently and she sat down opposite him on the second twin bed.

'I just got a phone call from someone with bad news.'

He looked concerned.

'I sent someone's unedited novel into a publisher to surprise them and, well, it didn't go according to plan.'

'Rejection is the nature of the game. You'll just have to tell your friend to get used to it.'

'It wasn't rejected. And it wasn't a friend,' she said sulkily.

'Whose novel was it?'

'Richie Daly's,' she said glumly. 'Go on, tell me you told me so. That I'm a horrible person, that I shouldn't have done it. I know I shouldn't have, okay? I just found his USB, I knew it was his stupid novel that he was so proud of, assumed it would be a load of crap, just like all his writing is, and thought I'd have a nice fancy rejection letter to send him. So I'm a terrible person, I know!'

The corners of Steve's lips twitched.

'Don't . . . even . . . think . . . of . . .'

He smiled.

'It's not funny.'

'It is kind of funny.'

'Steve, it's not funny,' Kitty protested, but the look on his face made her laugh with frustration. 'Oh God, I can't even do vengeance properly any more. I've lost it, I've lost my mean streak, and it's all your fault.'

'Really?'

She swallowed, not wanting to meet his eye. 'Well, no, yes, well, you were very vocal in telling me exactly who I'd become and I realised I didn't like that very much, so yeah . . . What you say matters to me,' she swallowed hard and decided to go for it, cringing and meaning it in equal amounts, '*you* matter to me.'

He had that look. Oh God, he had that look. Her insides turned to mush again.

There was a knock on the door.

'Ignore it,' Steve said firmly, and Kitty had every intention of obeying him right then. Whatever he wanted, whatever he said.

But the knocking persisted.

Steve shook his head.

She sat there, a grin spreading on her face.

'Hey, guys,' they heard Sam's voice, 'are you in there?'

Kitty had to stand up, but Steve dived for her and pinned her down on the bed.

'I told you not to move,' he whispered, his hair hanging down and tickling her face, as they were practically nose to nose.

'Eh, if you're in there, I'd really appreciate your help.' He sounded anxious. Kitty's eyes looked at the door quickly, then up at Steve.

'I think I preferred it when you were a shit reporter,' he whispered and climbed off her.

She laughed and tidied herself before opening the door.

'Sam, hi,' she said. 'Sorry for the delay.'

Sam looked from Kitty to Steve but was so caught up in his own dilemma he didn't notice anything odd. He walked straight into their room.

'I take it you spoke to Mary-Rose.'

'You knew?'

'Well, she never said anything but I could tell.'

'Tell what?' Steve asked, from where he lay back on his own twin bed.

'That she has feelings for him,' Kitty said.

'Oh, yeah, I could tell that.'

'You could?'

'Of course, it's obvious.'

'Shit.' Sam sat on the bed, still in shock. 'I'm such an idiot. I can't believe I said all of those things. I had no idea . . .'

'What did you say to her?' Kitty asked, concerned now.

'Well, what could I say? I had no idea. I was so surprised, I just said I had to take it all in and think about it.'

Steve sucked in air.

'Think about it?' Kitty asked.

'Well, what was I supposed to say?' He looked from one to the other.

'That you feel the same way too,' Steve said, but he wasn't looking at Sam, he was looking at Kitty.

'But I don't know if I do. I mean, I adore her, she's my best friend, I'd do anything for her, I've just never thought of her in that way.'

'Yeah, well, start thinking about it, buddy,' Steve said.

'But is it possible, for us, after being friends—'

'Yes,' Steve and Kitty said in unison. They caught each other's eyes and smiled.

290

Sam looked at them both again, studied them, glancing from one to the other, and Kitty thought he'd finally got it, that the penny had finally dropped, that he would leave them in peace.

'Do you mind if I sleep in here tonight and you sleep with Mary-Rose? She won't let me in the room and they've no more rooms left,' he said.

Those words Kitty did not want to hear. She wanted to say no, she was so frustrated, thinking of the possibilities of what could have happened that night, in that terribly squeaky bed. She looked at Steve and he was silently smothering himself with a pillow. Kitty laughed.

'Sure, Sam. You can have my bed. Just don't snore or your room mate will take your life.'

After the events of the day were eventually quietening in Kitty's head, she felt herself finally drifting closer to sleep when the sound of music coming from outside brought her to the surface again.

She looked across at Mary-Rose who had finally fallen asleep after shedding buckets of tears, then she got out of bed and padded across the creaking floor to see outside.

'Mary-Rose,' she hissed at her sleeping room-mate. 'You have to see this!'

Mary-Rose groggily raised herself onto her elbows and looked around the room, confused as to where she was.

'Look!' Kitty said, louder now, excited.

Mary-Rose finally registered the music, got out of bed and joined her at the window. It took her a moment, as it did for Kitty to take the scene in. Slowly, a smile crawled onto her face and she looked at Kitty with delight.

'Let's get down there.'

Kitty threw on the clothes she had abandoned before getting into bed and ran downstairs, out of the guesthouse and out onto the road. The night was still, the small town completely shut down, everybody at home and in bed. Above them the clear sky twinkled with a million stars.

St Margaret's bus had been moved from the car park, and was parked in the middle of the road, blocking off most of it, not that there was any traffic to stop. Its headlights were on full and the engine was running with the windows down. The headlights were pointing directly into the old ballroom, the doors had been opened up, the smell of must and damp drifted out from the abandoned barn, which had been the setting for so many of Birdie's dance nights.

Dancing in the shadows was Birdie, her eyes closed, her chin lifted to the sky as she twirled round and round, her arms in the air as if dancing with an invisible dance partner to Ella Fitzgerald and Louis Armstrong's 'Dream a Little Dream of Me'.

Eva was sitting behind the wheel of the bus, holding the bus's microphone to the speaker of the CD player, and standing beside the headlights of the bus were Edward and Molly.

Kitty was entranced by the scene before her. Leaving Mary-Rose, who was equally enchanted, she climbed aboard the bus.

'You did this?' Kitty asked Eva.

'She told me she and Jamie used to break in and dance here at night. This was their favourite song. It's a late birthday present,' she said, her eyes filling as she watched Birdie dancing alone in the old ballroom.

As they were watching Birdie dancing alone, Kitty noticed Molly and Edward in the darkness holding each other close as they slowly circled to the music. Kitty believed she had just witnessed Eva's magic.

CHAPTER TWENTY-NINE

The next morning, the mood was visibly lifted from the night before. Despite Mary-Rose and Sam not sitting near each other at breakfast, Ambrose and Eugene seemed to be cosy, and Ambrose even shared a few words with Regina, though she would barely look at anybody else. Archie and Regina had shared a room too and their closeness and secret looks the next day were obvious for all to see. Kitty felt a little more awkward around Steve than usual, though, and was battling with how to act around him after their conversation had been interrupted last night, though it was easily covered up by the excitement for Achar and Jedrek's big moment.

They made sure to eat a healthy breakfast and got plenty of morale-boosting from Archie, who no doubt was still following his plan to help those whose prayers he heard. Kitty didn't have his 'gift' but she could guess what Achar and Jedrek's prayers were that morning. Steve and Sam were in serious conversation over breakfast, a conversation they continued as soon as they sat beside each other on the bus, and Kitty would have given anything to hear what they were saying. She would have joined in had she not suddenly been at a loss as to how to behave around Steve. Birdie, despite not receiving her money, was in high spirits after her trip down memory lane and her memorable birthday, thanks to Eva, and she was still very much lost in her own mind, falling in and out of conversation as her mind flitted in and out of now and then.

As they were all boarding the bus, the young O'Hara came running out of the bookies with a large envelope in his hand.

'Bridget!' he called. 'Bridget Murphy!'

Birdie paused from stepping onto the bus and turned to him. Edward quickly came to her side and Kitty had no intentions of being anywhere but.

'I'm glad I caught you. I had a lot of convincing to do this morning,' he said, red-faced and panting. 'I'm very sorry about yesterday. My grandmother, she can be . . . well, she can hold on to some things. Her family loyalty is what we love about her but often it's her downfall. But I have loyalty too, to my great-grandfather. I know he was as tight as they come, not the most generous man in the world, but he had a great respect for his business and he was a man of his word. If he placed this bet with you, he would like to see you get the winnings. I hope that you'll accept this money, your winnings, with my greatest respect.'

Birdie looked at him shocked.

'I was very close to my grandfather Jamie. He spoke about you often,' he said.

Touched, Birdie held her hands to her mouth, then to his cheeks. He reddened even further. 'You're so like him, that when I saw you yesterday, for a moment I thought . . .'

'They say there's a great family resemblance,' he said, cheeks still blazing.

'Thank you,' she whispered. 'God be good to you.'

'Thank you,' Edward said.

Kitty helped Birdie on the bus and when they saw the envelope in her hand they all cheered and the celebratory mood was back on again.

'Come on, college boy,' Molly called, though her tone was softer this time, and as Edward looked at her, Kitty could see something between them. She was so happy she could have just leaped for joy.

Regina sidled in beside Kitty on the bus.

'Hello,' she said shyly. 'We haven't had the opportunity to speak yet.'

'Yes, I'm sorry about that.'

'Oh, you've more important people to talk to,' she said kindly, 'For your story. And I won't keep you, I just wanted to thank you.'

'No need to thank me, it was a pleasure for your company.'

'I didn't mean for the trip, though I am thankful of that, and Archie said you paid for our room and that was very nice of you.' She looked down at her fingers, thin delicate fingers that looked like they belonged to a doll. 'But I meant thank you for helping Archie. He said you have done a lot for him. That it was you who told him to talk to me.'

'I don't think he needed much persuading,' Kitty smiled. 'He had his eye on you every time I spoke.'

She blushed at that.

'Well, because of you helping him, he has helped me, so for that I'm truly grateful.'

'He told you about his . . . ability?' Kitty couldn't think of any word for it because in truth she wasn't sure if it was a gift or a curse. If it had helped him meet Regina and if it led to his happiness then she was sure it was a gift but she didn't envy him for it.

'Yes, he did. I heard his entire story and he's a very special man, that much I'm sure of,' she said firmly, implying she wasn't sure if she believed the rest.

'He's been through a lot,' Kitty agreed. 'Can I ask a personal question? You don't have to tell me your personal story but . . . I'm interested to know, was he right about you?'

'About my prayers?'

'Yes. He said that you would sit there saying "please".'

'I wasn't conscious of it.' She looked down at her fingers again. 'But I suppose that is what I was thinking.'

Kitty nodded, dying to hear more but not wanting to push it. Archie was her story, not Regina, but her interest in people was in her blood, at least that's what Constance had always told her.

'I was in a relationship,' Regina said out of the blue when Kitty hadn't been expecting any further explanation. 'For a very long time.' She had that haunted look again that Kitty recognised from seeing her in the café. 'But he no longer wanted to be in the relationship. All of a sudden. Just one day. He didn't give much of a reason. He said it didn't matter but . . .' she shrugged. 'I found it hard to let go. He moved out, changed his number, changed his job. It was like he vanished off the face of the earth. But then I saw him in there one day, at that time in the morning, when I was passing, and I got such a fright that I couldn't go to him. I wasn't ready to say what I wanted to say. I walked on, turned the corner, changed my mind and went back but he was gone. It's the only place I had ever seen him. People we knew had no contact with him. I think he had an episode of some kind; he just dropped his life and made a new one. He wanted to disappear, but I found him in there. I just didn't have the nerve to go inside. I thought that maybe he'd go back, that that was somewhere he went to regularly, so I started going. He never turned up but I couldn't miss a day. I kept thinking: what if today is the day he comes back? And then I couldn't stop going. And the months went by and I still couldn't stop going. Even when I tried to go elsewhere it was as if he was pulling me back. I would always end up there. I know it's odd behaviour.' She looked at Kitty nervously. 'My family, they were worried about me. I know it wasn't normal but I couldn't stop. It was the only new link I had to him. So I kept going, hoping. I always believed in fate. And destiny. And all of those things that I know most people don't believe in. I thought it was a sign, that I saw him there once and I would see him there again. But now I don't really understand the point of it all. I never saw him again. It's been a year,' she said, almost ashamed with herself for keeping up that behaviour.

'You met Archie there,' Kitty said, fascinated with this woman, with this story. 'That was the point. Your old love brought you back there but maybe it wasn't to find him, maybe it was so you could meet Archie. If ever there was a sign or fate or destiny, surely that's it,' Kitty said, truly believing her words just then, despite the fact she didn't believe in any of those things.

It was as though the thought occurred to Regina for the very first time. Her eyes lit up. 'Do you think so?'

'Well, I mean, I don't know for sure, but it sounds like it to me. If you hadn't been brought there by your ex, well then, you never would have met Archie, would you?'

Regina smiled at that and her shoulders relaxed as she accepted the idea. 'You know, this morning was the very first morning in a year that I didn't go to the café,' she admitted quietly.

'And, how do you feel about it?'

She thought about it, looked as if she was going to say something, then backed down.

'Your honest answer,' Kitty warned her, and she smiled.

'Well, honestly, I think that today is the day that he was there. In the café.'

This response took Kitty by surprise.

'What do you think?' she asked Kitty.

Kitty thought about it. Thought about Murphy's Law and the odds in life and she finally couldn't lie. 'I think you're probably right.'

Regina nodded once, then again as she accepted it. She looked across the row to Archie, who was giving Achar and Jedrek tips on breathing. 'But I'm glad I'm here,' she said.

Kitty smiled. 'I'm glad you're here too, Regina.'

*

297

'We're here,' Molly announced, and everybody started stamping their feet on the ground in a big build-up for Achar and Jedrek, who were beginning to look decidedly nervous.

'Don't worry, lads, we have an hour,' Archie said, noticing their panic, speaking as if he was now part of the team. 'Even if the adjudicator doesn't come, we can still do this.'

The plan was for them all to take a walk around Kinsale Harbour on the beautifully sunny May day, as Jedrek and Achar prepared for their record attempt, but then the bride and groom had an alternative idea when they saw Eva.

'Bring your guests in with you,' George's sister, the bride, announced as she greeted Eva and Kitty at the door to the wedding reception. They had finished the meal and the speeches, much to Kitty's relief, and they were sitting down to eat the freshly cut cake. But this didn't allow Eva and Kitty much time to get back to Dublin. They needed to be on the road by 3 p.m.

'Oh, no, I couldn't possibly do that,' Eva said. 'There are so many of them and they're really not expecting to be invited.'

'How many are there?'

'Fourteen people, so we really don't expect—'

'Yoohoo!' she sang to a sweaty member of staff holding three cameras in his hand and taking a group photo of a dozen happy family members. 'Can we set up an extra table in the banquet room, please?' she said breezily as if there wasn't a care in the world.

George Webb's Kinsale home was a stunning waterside house on the Bandon River estuary right on Kinsale Harbour. It had a long lawn, which led to the river at the bottom of the garden where a sizeable yacht was sitting in the water.

Kitty and her unlikely crew stepped off the bus and joined the wedding reception, all feeling underdressed for such an event. All but Eva, that was, who was a vision in her dress and whom everybody had wolf-whistled at when she climbed aboard the bus. As soon as George Webb saw her he left his conversation

298

and went to her. Kitty looked around for a sign of his girlfriend and couldn't see her.

As they dug into the delicious chocolate biscuit cake, Kitty realised why Eva had come with very few bags: the kind of gifts Kitty had so far witnessed Eva give to people weren't the type to be hidden in bags and just as she had this thought, a song began to play from the back of the room. Conversation took a while to end as word spread and finally you could hear a pin drop. The song was 'My Wild Irish Rose' and the singers were two old men, one wearing a red waistcoat with a red and white striped shirt underneath, the other with corresponding yellow and white. They wore white trousers and straw hats with their matching colour ribbon around the rim. Assuming it was part of the wedding musical entertainment everybody stopped eating and turned to watch and listen, but there was one man who knew differently and who slowly rose from his place at the head table, body trembling, eyes shining as he watched the remaining members of his barber shop band, Sweet Harmony, with whom he'd toured the country with fifty years ago. Kitty put their ages at around eighty, like George's grandfather, Seamus, and guessed their fourth member had not been as lucky as they to make it to this stage of his life. As soon as they had everybody's attention, they began weaving their way around the circular tables, eyes bright, big smiles on their faces, entertaining and endearing, voices no doubt more tired than they used to be and missing two crucial harmonies to their song, shoulders hunched and hands arthritic, but they eventually reached the head table where people expected them to address the bride and groom. Instead they went to Seamus, the man standing with his hand on his heart, the affection clearly on his face, his eyes filled with tears. He joined in for the last few lines of the song and as soon as they'd finished, the two men broke into singing 'Happy Birthday to You'.

When the applause had ended everybody's eyes remained fixed

on Seamus, waiting for an explanation, waiting for something more. Seamus was locked in an embrace with the two men, and all were emotional, heads together, showing a bond between them which would make even the kindest of people envious.

Seamus finally looked up to the crowd. 'Ladies and gentlemen, bride and groom,' he addressed his granddaughter, who was wiping a tear from her eye, 'I know we're finished with the speeches but I couldn't let this moment go by without saying a few words, if I may.'

The bride and groom enthusiastically encouraged him to speak.

'I haven't seen these men for fifty years,' he said, grabbing them again, and they stood together, side by side, arm in arm. 'We used to be in a group named Sweet Harmony. We toured the country up and down, left and right, didn't we, boys?'

The two men, far from boys, nodded and reminisced.

'These are the two Bobbys: this is Bobby Owens and this is Robert Malone. Sadly we're missing dear Frankie.' He looked to the other two for confirmation and they nodded sadly. Seamus took a moment at that, mourning the loss of a man he hadn't seen for fifty years, because the friendship now seemed as new and fresh as it had been then. Even more so, because it brought with it the excitement and sentimentality of reunion, of reminiscing, of all things positive and everything dark forgotten and under the bridge. 'There's only one man who could have done this,' he said suddenly, wagging his finger in the air. 'Only one man who takes care of me like this and that's my grandson George. Am I right, George?' he looked to the head table and George looked at Eva. Eva nodded hastily.

'Get up here beside me, George,' Seamus called, emotion in his voice again.

George, embarrassed by both the attention and presumably by the fact he had very little to do with the choice of gift, slowly stood up to polite applause.

'Get over here,' Seamus called again.

'As long as you don't make me sing,' George said, and everyone laughed. He was beautiful – even better turned out than in his office suits – he was charming and dapper, and had old Hollywood star good looks.

'This man is an angel,' Seamus said, his voice breaking again. 'I love all my grandchildren, you know that,' he looked out to the crowd, 'but this man is my angel. We don't see him enough, and he works too hard, but I love him and we appreciate everything he does for us.' He grabbed him then into a tight hug and there was a collective appreciative sound from the crowd.

'Happy birthday, Gramps,' George said.

'Thank you, son, thank you,' Seamus said, battling with his tears again.

Kitty even spotted Nigel, appearing moved among a table of old people and children at the back of the room. Before Kitty had time to pick Eva's brains, the bride and groom, who had been making their rounds of the tables, finally made their way to theirs.

'Eva, thank you so much for our gift,' George's sister, Gemma, said with a catch in her voice. 'It is the most thoughtful gift anyone has ever given us.'

Eva seemed embarrassed. 'I'm so glad you like it, but really, it's not from me. It's George's gift to you.'

'Oh, you can't fool us. I love George with all my heart but I know he didn't have the brains to pull that one off himself.'

'Honestly, Eva, if you're ever in North Carolina, please come and visit us. You are always welcome in our home. It was the kindest, most thoughtful gift we've ever received. No offence, you guys.'

There was none taken, as nobody else at the table had brought a gift, hadn't even known they'd be attending a wedding. A few people mumbled a few incoherent embarrassed responses to that effect but it didn't matter, the groom wasn't listening. Tears had gathered in his eyes.

'And we're so glad Philipa is gone,' Gemma added in a hushed voice.

Eva blushed.

'My father and my grandfather, if they were still alive, would have been so proud,' the groom said in his strong Carolina accent, nostrils flaring and lip quivering to beat the tears.

'Oh, baby,' Gemma said, kissing her husband on the lips.

'Jesus, what did you get them?' Mary-Rose asked as soon as they'd left the table, the groom rubbing his eyes roughly with a handkerchief.

'I designed a new family crest for them. I took things from both sides of the family and also items representing their own life, all stemming from a grapevine because they're a wine region family and live on a vineyard. He was so desperate to find out more about his family name but I couldn't come up with anything so I designed a family crest and had it hand-stitched and printed onto some items: linen, stationery, that kind of thing,' Eva said almost embarrassed. 'I had been trying to find some family members for him but there was no one.'

'That's because there's no such thing as the name O'Logan,' Molly hissed quietly, and for the first time she saw Eva laugh, though she looked a little guilty for it.

'Molly, stop.'

'What? I don't think it's occurred to him that his great-grandfather was a con artist who changed his name as soon as he landed in America, was probably running from the law and just made up some bullshit name to start his new life.'

Edward started laughing loudly.

Kitty thought it was the first time she'd seen his serious face soften so much.

George headed straight for Eva's table, took her by the hand and led her out of the room, Eva's cheeks flushing. Kitty contemplated following them but her phone lit up. It was on silent but it was as though it was screaming at her to be answered: Richie

Daly, the slimeball, whom she'd helped get a publishing deal. She had to take this. She slipped away from the table and out the French doors to the garden, which overlooked the river.

Her heart was thumping in her throat as she answered.

'Kitty,' he said.

'Yes.'

'I didn't think you'd answer.'

'I wasn't going to.'

Silence.

'Well, I called you to say,' he sighed. 'I don't know where to start.'

'Just get to the point, Richie.'

'I want to say thank you, for what you did. For sending my book into the publishers. After what I did to you . . . well, I didn't deserve your help and if you hadn't done it well then I probably never would have. It's been finished for a long time but I just didn't have the confidence, I suppose, to send it to anyone. And, well, so thank you. I don't know why you did it, but thank you.'

If only he knew why she'd really done it . . . She was seething.

'But really why I've called is to apologise for what I did to you. It was despicable. No matter how much I try to dress it up and justify it, I can't. It was really low, you were a college friend and I shouldn't have done that to you. Hand on my heart, I'm truly, truly sorry for any harm I caused you, any upset or—'

'You humiliated me, Richie,' she interrupted.

'I know. Well, I didn't know that, but I can understand how you feel that you were—'

'You humiliated me and used me and made me feel worse than I've ever felt in my whole life.' She felt the emotion in her throat and she stopped before she cried. He would never hear any of her words if she cried.

'I know. I'm so sorry. I want to make things right, really I do. I've spoken to my editor and I want to write a favourable article about you. He's agreed to it, agreed to the whole thing, and I can write what I want. This time it will be anything you want me to say.'

'What makes you think I'd ever want to speak to you again?' she asked, shocked by his proposal. 'I couldn't give a crap what you write about me from now on, I never did, it was the fact you lied to me, slept with me and betrayed something very precious.' Kitty was far from virginal but she did think some things were precious, and sleeping with someone for information was beyond the scummiest thing anyone could ever do. She expected him to snap and defend himself like he did the last time, a coward who couldn't accept responsibility, but in fact the opposite happened.

'I know you're right, I'm sorry. I'll never bother you again. I just wanted you to know that you did the nicest thing for me that anyone has ever done and I can't understand why because I realise what I did to you was the worst and I have to live with that. Anyway, I won't take up too much more of your time, I just wanted you to know that hand on heart, I'm sorry.'

'Well . . . okay,' she replied, not knowing what else to say, wanting to spout more words of hate at him but no longer feeling it was necessary. 'Maybe you could give me a percentage of your royalties or something when the book is published,' she joked.

'Oh, yeah, there won't be a book,' he said.

'What do you mean? I thought they liked it.'

'They did but I had a meeting with the publisher this morning. When he found out who I was he decided not to publish me. I wrote a not-too-favourable article about a colleague of his a few years ago and, well, he definitely didn't forget it.'

Kitty's mouth dropped, she punched the air silently and didn't care who could see her from the wedding reception. No wonder the little rascal was so sorry, his evil ways were coming back to haunt him. When she ended the call she did a little happy dance.

'What's that? A rain dance?' a gentle voice behind her asked.

'I wasn't listening, I just saw you leave the table and wanted to make sure everything was okay.'

She turned round to see Steve a few steps away from her.

'I think today is the happiest day of my life,' she laughed.

'What did you do now, tell me,' he said, and the way he phrased it made Kitty laugh again. 'What?' he asked.

'You make it sound like I'm always getting myself into trouble.'

'That's because you are. And I'm always trying to get you out of it.' He came closer to her and gave her that look that made her feel delightful.

'Um, Steve.'

'Yes.'

'Katja.' One word.

'Ah. Katja is no longer.'

'What did you do to her? Bury her in your allotment?'

He dug his knuckles into her back.

'Oww,' she howled and squirmed, but he still held on to her tight.

'No. We broke up.'

'Why?'

'Why do you think?' He gave her that dark serious look again. Kitty swallowed.

'She felt that I spent more time with you than with her.'

'That's ridiculous. You and I hardly ever see each other,' Kitty spat.

'True. Okay, she felt that I was there for you more than I was for her.'

'Oh. Well. Do you think you are?'

'Kitty, I helped you wipe shit and paint off your door, I gave you my bed and now I'm here in Cork with you pretending to be a photographer. What do you think?'

'I think if I was your girlfriend I'd dump your ass.'

'Would you?'

'Would I what?'

'Be my girlfriend?' he asked. He asked it so shyly, yet so seriously, Kitty felt they were ten years old. She laughed shyly and looked down at her feet.

Steve put his finger under her chin and lifted her head to meet his gaze. 'I promise I've come on leaps and bounds since our last encounter.'

Kitty laughed. 'Hmm, I bet you have. I have too.'

'It wasn't that bad, was it?'

'No,' she smiled. 'It wasn't bad at all.'

Just as he closed his eyes and leaned in to her, the tip of his finger beneath her chin, the water lapping beside them, there came the sound of applause as everyone toasted the bride and groom. As Kitty leaned in to kiss the beautiful, funny, dependable Steve, she happened to look over his shoulder and see someone at the pier, checking his watch, looking rather frustrated and as if he was about to leave at any moment.

'Steve!' she said, just as he reached her lips.

'What?' his eyes opened.

'The adjudicator!' She let go of him quickly. 'We have to get Jedrek. The adjudicator is here.' She let go of Steve's hand and ran up the grassy slope to the party. 'Stall him, I'll get the boys!'

CHAPTER THIRTY

'Yes, my dear, and I love you so much too. I wish you were here but this is my opportunity now to prove to everyone, to prove to you, that I can be something.' Jedrek's voice cracked and he stopped talking to compose himself. Kitty wanted to reach out to him to hurry him on but she couldn't. She was eavesdropping on his phone conversation with his wife, which was beautiful and touching, but they had an impatient judge waiting and an entire wedding congregation lining up along the shore to watch, as Kitty had burst into the reception a little too loudly to announce the adjudicator was there. Much interest had been taken in the table of people quickly escaping the reception and the sight of two men and a pedalo running past them on the grass. So everybody had trickled out of the party to join them on the banks of the river where they were currently waiting for Jedrek to get off the phone to his wife.

Finally he hung up and wiped his eyes, turned to the crowd with pride and confidence in his eyes. 'We can do this, my friend Achar.' He reached out to his compadre and they walked arm in arm down to the water. Everybody cheered as they went.

'Could you do the honours, please?' Jedrek said to Kitty.

'Okay, em . . .' Kitty cleared her throat and Steve circled her and moved around snapping photographs of the entire event. 'Ladies and gentlemen, bride and groom, we're sorry to have taken you from your wedding party.' The bride and groom seemed as excited as everybody else. 'But our friends Jedrek and Achar, who have been in training for almost a year, are about to make a world record attempt for the fastest two men in a pedalo dash. The current record is one-minute fifty-eight point six two and they are attempting to break this record at one minute fifty.'

There was an excited response from the crowd.

'I've seen them do it, but today we are joined by a Guinness World Record adjudicator who will witness this officially for our friends. So please lend your support to our friends Jedrek and Achar!'

Another cheer and James, the adjudicator, immediately perked up at the response of the two-hundred-strong crowd.

'You can do it, Jedrek, Achar.' Birdie gave them each a pink lipsticked kiss on the cheek. Archie slapped their backs and took his place as coach and morale-booster. Steve took photographs, Eva, Mary-Rose, Ambrose and Eugene crowded around them, and suddenly Kitty felt overwhelmingly proud of her little group of random people whom she – whom *Constance* – had brought together.

Everybody neared the water's edge to get a full view of the record attempt.

Jedrek and Achar climbed into the pedalo, cycled slowly out one hundred and fifty metres and prepared themselves. They held hands tightly, said a prayer, looked at one another and passed silent words of support, and then they were ready.

The adjudicator made the official call for them to start, holding the stopwatch in his hands and immediately they were off.

The crowd cheered them on, the bride and groom in pride of place whooping and hollering, delighted to have this entertainment at their wedding. Achar and Jedrek pumped their little legs like they'd never done before, their faces full of concentration, of need, of want, of pure desire to be accepted, to be deemed worthy, to forget about the few years of emptiness and despair they had felt, for this moment to rescue them, to make them feel like men again. The sounds of their encouragement to each other were audible from the water's edge. And finally they reached the one-hundred-metre mark and there was a burst of cheering from the crowd. Jedrek and Achar looked up anxiously to see if they had done it.

'You did it!' Kitty shouted, and the two men stood up and celebrated, hugging each other and jumping up and down so much they eventually fell into the water.

Everyone laughed, and Eugene and Archie helped pull them out.

The adjudicator pulled a rolled-up piece of paper from his bag and gathered a dripping wet Achar and Jedrek beside him.

'Unfortunately I didn't know that I was going to be here today, I was merely accosted by these two men yesterday,' he explained. 'But I had the office fax me some paperwork so that they could have something to see today. It officially declares them as record owners for the fastest pedalo dash by two men in a distance of one hundred metres.'

He presented them with the rolled-up fax, and Jedrek and Achar took it in their wet hands as though it were the Holy Grail. Though it was Jedrek and Achar's win, Kitty felt that all of her little group felt some ownership of it too. They had convinced the judge to come here today and so a small part of it was owed to them. They all hugged each other, congratulating and celebrating at the same time. Finally Kitty found herself embracing Steve.

Their eyes locked.

'Yes,' she said.

'Yes, what?'

'Yes I'll be your girlfriend,' she said softly.

'Oh,' he frowned. 'I don't want to any more. That was so twenty minutes ago.'

She slapped him playfully and he pulled her close. And finally, they kissed.

The cheers increased again, and while Kitty imagined they were for her and Steve, behind them Achar and Jedrek were hoisted up onto Archie and Sam's now very wet shoulders and were being paraded around.

'We'd really better get a move on,' Molly said, looking at her watch, worried. 'I have to get this bus back this evening.'

'Don't worry, we've plenty of time, we can do it,' Edward said, placing a hand protectively on Molly's shoulder, and she softened and smiled.

'Thanks.'

'We'd better make it.' Kitty looked at Steve, worried. 'I have a presentation at the office at six.'

'Can you delay it?'

'I've delayed it a week already. I'm supposed to make a presentation about Constance's story,' Kitty said, sweat breaking out all over her body at the thought.

They were waiting for George and Eva to finish their private conversation, everyone was on the bus celebrating Jedrek and Achar's record attempt, and nobody but Molly and Kitty were starting to get nervous.

'You really know how to leave things last minute, don't you?' Steve smiled. 'So, do you know what it's about yet? The thing that links them all? Because personally I've had a hard time trying to put it all together.' He looked at the gang around him from all walks of life.

Kitty nodded, proudly. 'I sure do.'

'Well then, you've nothing to worry about,' he said encouragingly.

'Apart from our driver,' she said, her voice low.

When Eva finally joined them on the bus, her face was white as though she'd seen a ghost. It didn't go unnoticed by the others but they gave her time to herself as she sat by the window alone in a row.

Shortly after they'd set off Kitty left Steve's side and went over to Eva. 'Mind if I join you?'

'Sure.' Eva gave her a quick smile, but one that didn't reach her eyes.

'Congratulations, you should be really proud about how today went. The gift for Seamus was so beautiful, you even managed to touch an old cynic like me,' Kitty joked.

'Hmm? Oh, yes, that was great. A success,' she smiled.

'Are you okay?'

'Me? Yes, of course, why?' She gave that big pretty smile that did manage to reach her eyes but which Kitty was no longer believing.

'Because you look like you've seen a ghost and you seem . . . down. Did something happen with George?'

'You're ever the romantic, aren't you?' Eva smiled. 'Archie and Regina, Ambrose and Eugene, Mary-Rose and Sam, Molly and Edward – has this just been one big ploy to get everyone together?'

Kitty laughed. 'No, not at all. They all did that by themselves, I assure you, though Sam and Mary-Rose is a work in progress, I think.' They both looked to the two best friends lost in deep serious conversation. 'I think you could give them a gift to help move that along.'

Eva smiled and fingered the bag in her hand. She looked at Kitty and then sighed. 'God, you're impossible.'

Kitty laughed. 'Good.'

'George gave me a gift.'

'Oh? A gift for the giver – I wouldn't be brave enough to pull that one off.'

'This trip has been one of the best, you know,' she said, and Kitty believed her.

'Thank you. What did he give you?'

'A box.' She opened the bag and retrieved a small Chinese lacquered box. Her eyes filled just looking at it.

'I take it that box means something to you.'

311

'Yes.' She wiped her eyes before her tears fell. 'He remembered me telling him about a gift that I'd received, a gift that meant something to me. And he found quite the imitation.'

'Has anyone ever given you something that's moved you so much?'

'Not really,' she said, and the tears fell steadily now. 'Not since I received the original version.'

Aha, she was getting somewhere.

'So you weren't exactly telling the truth about the My Little Pony being the best gift you'd ever received,' Kitty said gently.

Eva laughed and shook her head. 'Sorry. But I think we both knew that.' She sniffed and looked at her intently. 'You can't write all of this, Kitty, because there are other people involved.'

Kitty nodded. 'You have my word.'

'Just write whatever you have to write for it to mean something.'

Kitty completely understood.

'It was Christmas Day and my mother and I were waiting. The food was ready on the table, I can remember the smell, it was so delicious. My mother insisted on traditional Christmas meals. *Her* traditional meals. My father is from Shanghai. He owns a Chinese takeaway in Galway. Wu's Chinese Takeaway. He was two hours late and, well, we were hungry and I remember my mother looking at me and not saying it out loud, but almost asking me what do I think we should do. You have to be a certain way with my mother, or at least I had to be then. I couldn't tell her exactly what I thought because then she would do the opposite. It was like reverse psychology: you had to make her think it was her decision and therefore the right one. So she started to cut into the turkey and it smelled so good, even though it was overcooked and had been sitting there too long. I spooned the vegetables onto my plate and I couldn't wait, I just couldn't wait, I had to eat it. I had taken the first mouthful when I heard the key in the door and I wanted to just die. I couldn't swallow it, I couldn't spit it out. Mother was still carving the turkey for her plate. My dad walked in – I could smell him before I saw him – and he saw us starting dinner without him, which made him angry.

'"Just in time," I remember my mom saying perkily. Too perkily. He knew that we weren't going to wait for him. So he left the dining room. He trampled on all of the presents, smashed a china doll that was for me, pulled down the Christmas tree, pulled down the lights from the ceiling so that they crashed on to the dining table, scratching the beautiful wood. He cleared every surface, the fine china from the display cupboard, everything was in pieces.'

She swallowed.

'Then he went at my mother. Not for the first time either. She still had the carving knife in her hand. It ended up in her arm.'

'Eva,' Kitty breathed, 'I'm so sorry.'

'I'm not telling you this so you'll be sorry.' Eva looked at Kitty. 'You want to understand, I'm trying to help you to understand.'

Kitty nodded.

'I ended up across the road with an old neighbour. We sat in front of her television for four hours before my aunt came to take me home. She only had black-and-white TV and all I remember watching is *I Love Lucy* over and over again. I swear I can't watch that woman to this day, being so stupid and everybody laughing every time she tripped or fell, or did something ridiculous, and all the time my head was rerunning everything that had happened. The old woman, I can't even remember her name, didn't say one word to me for the whole time. She gave me milk and a plate of biscuits and she sat in an armchair beside me and we watched the television in silence. She didn't even laugh, which made the show seem even more pathetic. But before I left, she gave me a gift. It was a small box, a Chinese lacquered box, with a lock and key. She said it was for all my secrets, that every little girl needed a box for all her secrets. I don't know why but it was the most perfect, perfect thing that anybody had ever given me. It was so appropriate. She hadn't said one word about what had happened but she seemed to encompass everything in this one gift.'

'So that's the gift that started you thinking the way you do, that made you want to help people by giving the perfect thing.'

'Yes.' Eva ran her fingers over the box George had given her.

'Did you tell George that story?'

'No, I just told him about the box. I've never told anyone about it. I lost it, though, years ago, when we were moving house.'

'He must have known it was important to you.'

'Yes,' she said curiously.

'Eva, do you mind me asking, how old were you when . . . when you received the box?'

'Five,' she said quietly, and her eyes filled again.

Kitty made a mental note in her mind.

Name Number Three: Eva Wu
Story Title: Pandora's Box

'But anyway,' Eva cleared her throat, her face almost immediately lost the emotion and her beautiful mask was back on, 'I have a present for you.'

'For me? Eva, you didn't have to do that. Don't tell me it's the old men from the wedding,' she joked, looking around.

Eva laughed. 'It's really very small. I wasn't looking for something, I just came across it, and bearing in mind what you've been through lately, it reminded me of you.' She reached into her small bag and retrieved a potted plant. It didn't make any sense to Kitty at all until she read the label at the side.

'Grow your own luck,' Kitty read aloud, and started laughing. It was a pot filled with soil with a small pouch of shamrock seeds attached.

Eva smiled. 'I hope it works.'

'I hope so too.' Kitty swallowed hard, thinking of the road ahead of her. 'Thank you, Eva.'

'I know someone who can help you plant it, anyway,' Eva added, raising her eyebrows, and the two girls laughed.

Raised voices coming from the front of the bus averted everyone's attention. Molly and Edward were at each other's throats again about a turn that Molly should or should not have taken.

'Oh shit,' Molly said loudly, looking in her rearview mirror.

Everyone turned round to see that Molly's comment had been entirely justified. Coming up the hard shoulder of the motorway was a garda car.

'Maybe it's not for me,' Molly said.

'Of course it's for you,' Edward snapped. 'Did you see what you just did?'

'Oh, shut up,' she hissed back.

'Well, slow down, will you?' he said. 'They're getting you to pull in.'

'Fuck, fuck, fuck, fuck,' Molly said to herself, slowing the bus and pulling in.

The garda came round to Molly's side of the bus.

'You trying to kill someone back there?' he asked.

'No of course not,' she said, her voice gentle. 'I just got confused which way to go.'

'Driver's licence, please,' he said, and Molly rooted in her handbag.

Please let her have her driver's licence, Kitty thought to herself, watching the clock. She had to get back to Dublin for her meeting with Pete. She had put it off for long enough, the feature was due to go to print on Monday, which meant she had only the weekend to write it, but not if it couldn't be approved today. Pete would kill her if she didn't make this evening. She couldn't use the guilt he felt against him any longer; it was wearing off.

The garda disappeared to check Molly's licence and Edward

was back to being Mr Nice Guy with an anxious-looking Molly.

The officer returned five minutes later. 'Where's this vehicle from?'

'St Margaret's Nursing Home, in Oldtown, Dublin,' she said, her voice like a child's. 'I work there. We're going back there now.'

'Open up the door, will you?'

She pulled the lever, not seeming so excited by the idea now, and he climbed on board and took a look at everyone. Everybody was silent.

'Doesn't look like the regular nursing home clientele,' he said.

'Ah, yes, well, Birdie here is my patient. I was taking her and her friends on a trip for her birthday. We're going back there now. We have to get the bus back for the Pink Ladies' bridge evening so . . .'

He looked at her long and hard. 'This bus was reported stolen yesterday.'

Molly's face went white.

'Pardon?'

'You heard me. Know anything about that?'

'No, I mean, yes, I mean, no, we borrowed it for a trip for my patient. We didn't steal it. I mean, we're going right back there now.'

The garda stared at her a little longer in a tense silence.

'Could you step out of the vehicle, please, Ms McGrath?'

Molly let out a small squeak before Edward stood up to help her off the bus, whispering in her ear something that Kitty couldn't hear.

'Oh my God.' Kitty looked at Steve wide-eyed.

'What's the problem?' Steve said, unimpressed by the entire thing. 'He's obviously just trying to scare her. *Obviously* she didn't steal the bus. Kitty, why are you looking at me like that? Tell me Molly didn't *steal* this bus?'

All Kitty could do was smile at him weakly. She and he had been doing so well.

316

CHAPTER THIRTY-ONE

Kitty and the rest of the gang, apart from Molly, waited in a café in Mallow town in Cork, while Molly was inside the garda station being questioned.

'I'm not making this up, Pete,' Kitty hissed down the phone. 'Of course, I want to be at the meeting today, but I'm in Cork and there's no way I can get there by six o'clock. What about tomorrow?'

'No, Kitty. I'm not dragging everyone back in here on a Saturday. We've already wasted enough time waiting for your story and we don't even know what that story is! This is ridiculous. Everything revolves around Constance's story, everybody has been working their arses off to meet this deadline, and you are swanning around—'

'Excuse me, I have put every single second I have into this story and you know it. Fine! I'll find a way to get there on time.' She hung up and bit her nails.

Steve looked at her, eyebrows raised.

'Pete's a prick,' she said simply. 'If I don't get there by six o'clock he's pulling my story.' She didn't mean for everybody else to hear but unfortunately that's what happened.

'No, Kitty.' Jedrek stood up. 'We can't let this happen. You must run the story. What can we do to help?'

'Oh, Jedrek, thank you,' she said, touched. 'I appreciate you all caring for me so much but I just don't know how to get to my meeting by six. If Molly doesn't come out of there in the next five minutes there's no way I can make it to the office.'

'No offence, Kitty,' Jedrek said seriously. 'Of course we respect you and your duty to your editor and friend, and we know that your job is important to you, but we have put our lives in your hands. We have told you our private stories and given you the pen to write it. It is not just you who needs this story written, it is us. It is our story.'

Kitty looked at Steve, who was looking back at her as if this was the most obvious thing in the world. The penny finally dropped: this wasn't about her, this wasn't merely about honouring Constance's story and saving her own professional skin. This was their lives, their stories, and she owed these people. Feeling humbled, she snapped into action.

Thirty minutes later, Molly had been freed from custody and they were on the road back to Dublin.

'I don't understand, Kitty, what did you say to them?'

'I just got on the phone to the nursing home, to Bernadette.'

'No, not Bernadette! She'll fire me for sure,' Molly moaned.

'She won't fire you,' Kitty said confidently, 'but she'll probably make your life a living hell for a few months. I just explained the entire thing to her, what we had done and why, and told her to drop the charges and tell the guards to let you go. They're using the local school bus for the Pink Ladies today instead, so we have time so can you please step on it and follow my directions?'

'Why, where are we going?' she asked, startled.

'A little detour,' Kitty said, biting her nails and watching the clock as it got dangerously close to 6 p.m.

At six thirty, they pulled up outside *Etcetera*'s offices in the bus. Pete was close to calling the entire thing off but Kitty had phoned regularly en route and was insistent they could make it.

'Okay, everybody, I promise this will be quick. Follow me, please.'

'Good luck.' Steve winked at her.

Ready for another adventure, the party all climbed off the bus and followed her.

Rebecca, the art director, was standing at the open door looking out anxiously.

'Kitty, thank God,' she said, when Kitty ran up the stairs. 'He's going insane in there. I don't envy you right now.' She pulled Kitty's coat from her shoulders, and then looked at the team of people who followed after her, in shock. 'Who are all these people, Kitty? Kitty . . .?' she followed them all, wide-eyed.

'Can you all just wait here a moment, please?' Kitty said to them, took a deep breath and entered the meeting room. It smelled of coffee, sweat and anger. There was also a lot of frustration and irritation emanating from the pore of every person at the table and it was all directed at her.

'Hi, everyone,' she said, breathless. 'I'm so sorry I'm late. You wouldn't believe what I had to go through to get here.'

They groaned and mumbled something about what they'd been through to get there too but Kitty hurried on, glad to see Bob was in attendance, which meant that Cheryl was no longer in her acting deputy editor role. Kitty looked from Pete to Cheryl and smiled sweetly. 'Hi, guys, nice to see you again.'

Cheryl reddened and looked away.

'Two weeks ago I was given the task of writing Constance's final piece. Something I was hugely honoured to do, and something I thought hard about because as we all know Constance was a true professional, a perfectionist, never accepted anything but the best, and I didn't have a huge amount of faith in myself in delivering. I know many of you in this room felt the same and I understand why.' She swallowed as there were a lot of shared looks to prove she was right. Nobody believed she could pull this off. 'But a lot has changed in two weeks, believe me.

'All I had to go on with Constance's story was one hundred names. That was it. No synopsis, no explanation, no outline, absolutely nothing but a random list of people that nobody had ever heard of. I had no way of contacting them, no way of knowing what the story was about, nothing at all. That's why it has taken me so long to come to this meeting,' she explained. She could see that few people had been let in on this fact. 'It was left up to me to find a common link between these one hundred people and it was believed, *I* believed, that this is where the story lay. So far, I have met with six of those people.'

Pete let out an exasperated sigh.

Kitty turned to him. 'Pete, there was no way in the world I was going to meet and speak with one hundred people within two weeks, people who had no idea that there was an intention for them to even be written about.'

'Constance hadn't contacted them?' Rebecca asked.

'No!' Kitty laughed. 'Constance didn't even know who they were!'

The others looked at each other in confusion.

'It's all so perfectly clear to me now,' Kitty explained. 'The last time I met with Constance she lectured me, as she always did, on the art of writing a good story. She told me that to seek the truth is not necessarily to go on a mission all guns blazing in order to reveal a lie, neither is it to be particularly ground-breaking – it is simply to get to the heart of what is real.

'My job was not to uncover a secret or a lie or find something earth-shattering that one hundred people were hiding from me, it was simply to listen to their truths.

'Constance's idea was this,' she paused. 'It's very simple. If you were to randomly select one hundred people from a phone directory, you would not only find a story, you would find *one hundred* stories, because everybody, *every single person*, has a story to tell. *Every single ordinary person has an extraordinary story.* We might all think that we are unremarkable, that our lives are boring, just because we aren't doing ground-breaking things or making head-lines or winning awards. But the truth is we all do something that is fascinating, that is brave, that is something we should be proud of. Every day people do things that are not celebrated. That is what we should be writing about. The unsung heroes, the people that don't believe they are heroes at all because they are just doing what they believe they have to do in their lives.'

It was completely quiet in the room.

'Everybody has a story to tell,' she said. '*That* is what links us all, *that* is what links all the names on the list. Constance was simply getting back to basics.'

Kitty looked around the room and saw Bob's eyes shining with tears, his chin trembling as he struggled to compose himself as Constance's story finally came to life, as the silenced Constance finally found her voice.

'Constance's story is titled *One Hundred Names* and I'm sorry, Pete, but I don't have one story for you. Right now I have six stories.'

Kitty made her way over to the projector and placed Constance's original list on the surface and flicked the switch. The names were revealed on the wall behind her.

'These are the one hundred names, now, please, meet the people.'

She opened the door and all eyes turned in surprise to see Ambrose Nolan, Eva Wu, Archie Hamilton, Jedrek Vysotski, Bridget Murphy and Mary-Rose Godfrey all enter the room, looking around shyly, proudly, and with confusion all at the same time.

'Everybody please meet name number two, also known as Ambrose Nolan. A fascinating woman who dedicates her life to capturing the essence of beauty.'

Ambrose looked down and her wild red hair covered more of her face than ever before.

'Ambrose dedicates her life to celebrating butterflies; on her

321

conservation site she helps to create new life but in her museum she also celebrates the life of those that have been and gone. I have heard her describe herself as a Small Tortoiseshell species of butterfly, but I liken her more to the Brown Hairstreak.' Ambrose looked up at Kitty in surprise. Kitty smiled. 'Few people have seen this elegant butterfly, but when they do, the female is so striking with its orange band that they never forget its beauty.'

Ambrose's look of surprise slowly transformed to a faint smile of thanks and then she disappeared behind her hair again.

'Please meet name number three, Eva Wu, a woman who was given a Pandora's Box filled with hope at a time in her life when she felt like there was none, and because of that was blessed with the gift of bringing hope into other people's lives.' Eva's eyes filled and she looked down. 'Through her company, "Dedicated", Eva Wu is more than a personal shopper. I liken her to an angel who spends a period of time in people's lives, observing them with the keenest of eyes to make a journalist like me jealous, and gives them the greatest gift of all – not what people *think* that they want, but gifts that people never even know they need at all until they receive them and realise they were incomplete without.'

Birdie, knowing more than anyone in the room that there was truth to this, reached out and held Eva's hand. She rubbed it warmly with her other.

'Meet name number four, Jedrek Vysotski, a husband, father and courageous man, who wanted to prove to the world that he was able to achieve something, that he was worth something, that he could stand out from the crowd even when he felt the world was telling him he couldn't.'

Jedrek proudly lifted his chin higher in the air and focused on the audience before him.

'Jedrek and his friend Achar successfully completed a task that will ensure they are in *Guinness World Records*, where it will be forever in print that they are men of extraordinary dedication and talent. And for Jedrek, proof that he is a man of *worth*.

'Meet name number six, Bridget "Birdie" Murphy, a woman with unfinished business who turned eighty-five years old and collected on a bet she'd made over sixty years ago with a man, with an entire town, who believed she would never live to see this day.' Birdie smiled shyly at the audience before her. 'Birdie is one of the sweetest, gentlest and most inspiring women I've ever met and has shared with me a story of true survival, survival that has been rewarded not just financially but most importantly by being fruitful, by being surrounded by people who she loves and who love her. There is nothing boring about that,' Kitty said to Birdie, remembering Birdie's embarrassment at having to relate her life story. 'At eighteen years old, she took a bet and the bet paid off, and it's a lesson we can all learn from.'

'Meet name number seven, Mary-Rose Godfrey, carer and proposee, a girl who gives so much and for it, receives a proposal at least once a week.' Mary-Rose laughed and a tear trickled down her cheek. 'Mary-Rose's mother sadly suffered a stroke and because of that Mary-Rose was introduced to the world of the sick. She goes to hospitals to do hair, make up and sometimes nails,' Kitty heard Mary-Rose laugh nervously, 'and through these simple acts she is like a beacon of light to the people who ask for her. But what Mary-Rose doesn't know is that it's her and not what she does that lights up the room. It's the conversation she brings, her mere presence, which has the ability to, albeit momentarily, heal people.

'And finally, name number sixty-seven, Archie Hamilton. Archie's beloved daughter, Rebecca, was murdered before her sixteenth birthday. Archie, probably doing what most fathers would do, protected his daughter by seeking out the man who took her life, and took the law into his own hands. For that he spent years in prison but emerged with an entirely new outlook on life. An outlook that is,' she looked at Archie and smiled, 'beyond fascinating and illuminating. Archie believed that God wasn't listening when he needed Him most, he felt forgotten and left behind, and his saviour was to wake up one day to hear the voices of those in need as much as he once was, and have the ability to help answer their prayers.'

Archie's jaw hardened as he tried hard not to let his emotions show.

Kitty turned away from her emotional group of friends and looked back at her colleagues, some who were deeply moved by her words, by their stories.

'What I've told you about them here is merely an introduction to who these people are. There is so much more for me to say about them, and so much more for you to learn about them. Pete, there are so many fascinating, amazing people out there with stories to tell that they don't even know are interesting. The stories are endless; we have an entire telephone directory of inspiration. You've seen the one hundred names, you've seen the people, now I propose that you read their stories in Constance's final piece: one story dedicated to each name on her list, each month, in a feature titled *One Hundred Names*. And when that list runs out we randomly select one hundred more.'

Kitty was finished talking and she held her breath for a reaction. There was complete silence. She looked at the others standing alongside her, not knowing what to say. Mary-Rose's eyes widened, Eva's cheeks pinked, Birdie reached out to a chair to steady herself.

Suddenly Bob stood up, and started clapping, slowly at first, then it built, and Kitty saw the tears in his eyes and gradually the others began to join in, applauding, Rebecca with excitement and the others with appreciation and even admiration. Kitty looked at Pete and he was smiling, a small smile that was gradually building. He looked along the line of people she had brought into the room and then his eyes rested on Kitty. He smiled at her, nodded at her reassuringly so that she knew she'd done it, she knew she'd pulled it off. Then he joined in, clapping along with the others.

Kitty had never in her whole life felt prouder. She put an arm around Mary-Rose, who was beside her, and instinctively they all grouped together in a circle, the little team that they had become, the friends she had made and who she knew she would remain in contact with, and they hugged collectively as they listened to the applause.

The St Margaret's Nursing Home bus pulled up to the famous meeting spot dubbed 'under the clock at Clerys' where they had all met at the start of their journey. Not yet ready to say goodbye, they remained in their seats in a hushed silence. Each took a moment to gather his or her thoughts, to revel in the experience they had just had, most likely the last that they would share together. Archie was the first to stand. He looked around at the others, the quiet still enveloping them all. He nodded to them, and made his way to the front of the bus. Then they all followed.

Despite their promising to meet again – some had swapped phone numbers, some had even already made dates – Kitty knew that realistically it would be a hard task to bring them all together again, to get every single person back in the same room, or on the same bus. But as she watched them from her window seat all go their separate ways, she knew in her heart of hearts that she would do everything in her power to try. She had ninety-four more people to meet and ninety-four more friends to make, but she knew that this bunch would always be extra special to her, for they had helped change her life, had, in a way, saved her. She would reunite them again. One day.

CHAPTER THIRTY-TWO

'This better be good, Archie. I have an article to write, remember?'
Kitty said, as she met him outside the Brick Alley Café on Sunday
morning. He had called her late the previous night after they'd
all eventually got home and had a day to think about all that
they'd seen, done and achieved. Steve had finally left Kitty's flat
to give her time to settle down to write her article, when Archie
had called her and requested they meet urgently. She had no idea
what to expect but she was ready for anything now.

'It's good, trust me,' he said, smiling.

'Where's Regina?'

'It's Sunday morning, where do you think?'

'Ah, church,' she guessed. 'And you don't want to be there?'

He shook his head.

'Changed your mind about helping people?'

'Not really,' he replied. 'I've decided to help some people. Which
is why I called you here.'

'Me? I don't pray,' she laughed nervously.

'I'm not too sure about that, Kitty,' he said softly. 'There was
one thing coming through loud and clear to me.'

Kitty swallowed, completely uncertain as to where this was
going.

'There's someone in there who wants to talk to you,' Archie
said, turning to face the café.

'Who?' Her heart drummed maniacally in her chest.

'Take a look.'

She looked through the glass and there, sitting on the stool facing the wall with the blackboard saying 'Every table has a story to tell', was a man whose back was turned. Instinctively, as if he knew they were looking at him, he looked around and Kitty gasped.

Colin Maguire.

'Archie,' she whispered, suddenly terrified. 'What have you done?'

'All you want is for him to forgive you, am I right?' he asked gently.

She swallowed and nodded.

'I contacted him yesterday. He was happy to hear from me, said he'd wanted to see you too.'

'He did, so he can kill me,' she said, voice shaking.

'No. I think he wants closure too, Kitty. Go on in. You've nothing to lose.'

Kitty looked at Archie, unsure whether to hit him or thank him, but knew that what he'd done had been from the goodness of his heart.

She pushed open the door and stepped into the café. Colin Maguire turned round and stood up from his stool.

And she walked towards him, hoping, and above all, praying, for his forgiveness.

ACKNOWLEDGEMENTS

Thank you . . .
My precious family; David, Robin and Sonny.

Thank you . . .
Bertie, Mimmie, Terry, Georgina, Nicky, Rocco and Jay, Neil
and Breda.
My agent Marianne Gunn O'Connor.
Lynne Drew, Thalia Suzuma, Kate Elton, Belinda Budge,
Victoria Barnsley, Lucy Upton, Louise Swannell, Liz Dawson,
Moira Reilly, Tony Purdue and the huge and wonderful
HarperCollins team worldwide.
Vicki Satlow and Pat Lynch.
All the booksellers who have supported my books and the
readers who have welcomed me into their lives. I'm eternally
grateful for the honour and hope I have succeeded in delivering
something which will move and entertain you.